The Alice Series
Book 1

Alice
of the
Rocks

E. Graziani

Thank you, Nancy and everyone at Fire & Ice for rebranding and publishing this series.

For my family: Nanni, Julia, Alicia, Michaila & Chiara, for your support and patience as I wrote this, my first novel.

And for the women at Morning Rain who gave it its first chance.

Chapter One

Renaissance Florence
Summer, 1512

Distance was all that mattered. For the moment, she feared not what was ahead, only what was behind.

Frenzied and breathless, she paused to catch her breath and looked back at the looming hills behind her. Darkness had befriended her for a time, but her instincts told her that the unforgiving full moon would soon rise, making the likelihood of tracking her down much easier for the Medici guards.

There, amongst a thicket of tender olive trees, she put a hand over her mouth to choke back a cry and glanced skyward to the summer heavens—coal black and heavy with stars.

Inclining her head, she listened, her senses wildly aware. The midnight air was still. So still, it easily gave up the cry of baying dogs in the distance halfway between Fiesole and Florence. The wretched sound was barely audible, but she recognized it all too well.

Relentlessly, they had followed her scent down the steep

slopes of the Fiesole valley from which the town took its name.

The young woman bolted from the grove, her ribs heaving with no benefit as she struggled down the hill to outrun the hounds and soldiers. Suddenly, she came to an abrupt stop. Her blood ran cold, as she doubled back to a clump of overgrown bramble bushes. A shadow moved ahead.

"Blast!" she snapped a hissing whisper at the wild dog and wiped the sweat from her brow on her sleeve. "Away with you!"

In the madness, her drenched muddy skirts caught in the tangled wood and she was faintly aware of stinging on her face as some of the branches scratched her delicate cheeks. There she sat stone still and listened, her heart beating in her ears like thunder.

Dashing out of the shrubs, she continued down the incline, running low to the ground, the dogs yelping far in the distance. At long last, the outline of the city ramparts appeared—the Porta Rossa, the main gate to the city of Florence. Hope was renewed, and she held back a sob.

As the young woman came upon the city walls, she stopped to catch her breath. She looked down at her skirts and brushed off the brambles, then hastily tucked her tangled mane of hair into her bonnet.

As she approached the gates, the cold sound of metal against metal made her start.

"You there, girlie," called down one of the sentinels, in a greasy tone. "What do you mean by being out and about at this hour?"

"If you please, sir, I have been assisting the midwife at one of the outlying homesteads." She disguised her fear with impatience and moved closer to the small door in the massive wrought iron rampart. "I will thank you for letting me enter, sir, lest I should be here all night and be missed by the physician in the morrow."

A pause. "Let her in," mumbled the guard. The gate opened, and she entered Florence proper.

The young woman walked past the ogling sentinels at the ramparts, resisting the urge to look back. *Slow your pace. You have triumphed this far, do not forsake caution now.*

She strolled at first, not wanting to attract attention by running into the dark and deserted streets, but when she was out of their sight, she bolted for the Ponte Vecchio.

Beyond depleted, she crossed the Old Bridge over the murky Arno River and continued her quest, her skirts swishing in the silence. She searched street by street, door by door, determined to find the portico. Her worn and dirty shoes padded softly on the cobblestones on the narrow roads.

Growing discouraged, she looked up in silent panic at the windows above her. They were quiet and dim, haphazardly dotting the frescoed walls of the row houses. She imagined the people inside, sleeping and dreaming—the sleep of the innocent—and ached to be in their place and for Claudio to be safe.

She longed for this because, until just a fortnight ago, the young woman had been a scullery maid—unremarkable, small, and unnoticed—her life filled with uncomplicated daily drudgery in the enormous household of the Duke of Florence, Giuliano de Medici.

She was a kitchen servant, the lowest of the low in the pecking order of the palace: washer of pots and dishes, of kitchen floors. Occasionally, she helped the cooks in cleaning and peeling vegetables, fetching water, plucking fowl, and scaling fish. It was hard work for a young woman of seventeen, but it was the station into which she had been born.

Yet now she found herself running for her life and feeling the most alone she had ever felt in her short existence. "Do not be afraid," she murmured, reassuring herself. "The Master will surely assist us."

As she rounded the corner onto the Via dello Sprone, she peered more intently at the houses, their distinctiveness imperceptible but for the presence of doors every few arms' length out of the corner of her eye, she spotted two tall, marble columns flanking a portico. *There it is! This must be the Master's residence.*

Craning her head from side to side, the girl scrutinized the windows to ensure no one was watching. She approached. It *was* Master Leonardo's portico, exactly how Claudio had described it. She knocked resolutely as she contained her agitation, imagining herself, at any moment captured and dragged off to the Medici dungeons.

Then, far off in the distance, she heard them anew—the dogs. Fear knotted inside her. She knocked again, louder this time. "Please, I beg of you, please answer," she murmured.

Yelps of dogs and voices of men loomed as her fist pounded the wood. Answer, answer, she begged silently.

Finally, heavy footsteps came from inside.

"What the devil! Who is there?" demanded a distant voice from the other side.

Again, she brought her fist to the door. "Open, open... please open," she whispered.

"What in the bloody hell is the meaning of this?" The voice cursed as the steps hastened. "Why am I to be awakened at this uncivilized hour? What in the name of heaven could be so important?"

"Please, sir," she implored. "I beg your forgiveness. My name is Elisa Beatrice de Povri...you must help me, Master Leonardo. I fear the Medici have ordered my arrest, and their guards are close at hand." She paused to gulp a breath. "I have come from Fiesole at great risk this night to plead for your assistance. I beg of you, in the name of Count Claudio Moro, please hear me." Elisa spoke with her hands clasped palm to palm as if the old man on the other side of the door could see her pleading.

And so she waited, her eyes closed in prayer. Would he show mercy or turn her away? She could envision him deliberating. "Mercy, please, sir," she whispered.

There was another pause, then the door creaked open just a sliver. A portly old man in a well-worn calico nightshirt, with long white hair and a beard to match, held a single flickering candle. He blinked at her from the small opening he had allowed between himself and the wild-eyed young girl standing at his doorstep. Master Leonardo da Vinci—this man was Elisa's only hope.

Chapter Two

A lice Ferro awoke slowly to the sound of clattering coffee cups. Her parents were in the kitchen, chattering at top volume in Italian, making last-minute arrangements before their much-anticipated departure.

A chair scraped against the slate floor. She listened and recognized her mother's gait, visualizing her bare feet crossing the kitchen into the hallway and stopping at the bottom of the stairs.

"Ali, wake up," her mother called, a slight lilt in her voice.

Alice half-opened one eye and then the other. She was surprised she'd been able to nod off at all the night before, yet here she was, bleary-eyed and groggy, her flight to Italy just a few hours away.

Smiling, she recalled her friends' goodbyes the night before, particularly Caleb's.

Alice touched her lips, smiling at his last kisses—the kisses that were interrupted by her father sticking his head into the hallway and reminding her that she had "a very busy day tomorrow, so it's time to say goodbye."

"Damn, Papa, really how to rattle me."

Without a doubt, Caleb Fenton was everything a boyfriend should be. He was funny, athletic, sensitive, and bright, all wrapped up in a nice-looking package. And he had made it clear some time ago that he wanted them to be exclusive. She yawned.

Exclusive.

She thought about it as she swung her legs over the side of the bed and planted her feet firmly on her furry-furry rug.

The possibility of a serious relationship someday with Caleb was a definite maybe. She only had one more year of high school and then she would be off to university, maybe the same one as Caleb. Although she didn't like the idea of commitment, she did like the idea of being away from the over-protective eyes of her mom and dad.

Either their relationship would solidify, or they would find that they were totally wrong for each other. Whatever happens, she thought, one thing's for certain, college means freedom at last.

She stretched her arms high over her head, curling her hands into tight fists and rose to go to the bathroom just as her phone softly chimed on the night table. It was Kiana's ring. Ali dove to pick it up and with a sweeping motion, she extended it, and was on 3D chat. "Hey, you."

"Hey," said Kiana. "Nice hair."

Kiana, of course, was her very best friend.

"Okay—did you call me to insult me face to face? Messaging not good enough?" Alice steadied her device, propping it up on her knees.

"Hey, chill, Als." Kiana laughed. "I had to see you one more time before you left. You should be thanking me since I was the one who dragged everyone out early last night so you and Caleb could have a few minutes of face-to-face time alone."

Ali giggled. "Hmm, you're so bad."

"Nuh-uh, you are. The way you two looked at each other—what will you do when you're apart?" Her voice trailed in a cadence.

"Stop," Ali commanded with a grin. "I told you, come September, it's all about me seriously becoming a hermit if I'm going to qualify for admission into the Arts and Sciences program."

"You mean you're going to be an even bigger hermit? How much more can you study before your brain blows up?" A peel of giggles rang out in Ali's room.

"But right now, all I want to think about is boarding that plane, clearing my head and, consuming lots of pizza and gel—"

"Alice," her mom called again. "Are you talking to someone?"

"Come down, Ali. Coffee is ready," her father echoed.

"Okay, I'll be right down," Ali assured. "And good morning, by the way."

"Good morning," answered her father. "Did you even pack yet?"

Alice's eyes meandered over to the closet and bureau, her clothes spilling out of them and her empty suitcase to the side, waiting to be filled.

She looked back into her phone at Kiana. "Ugh, they can be so annoying. I gotta go. I promise we'll talk soon, okay?" Their goodbyes said, she minimized her device, and tucked it into her pajama pocket.

Scratching her back, Alice wandered to the window and looked out at the great maple tree in her manicured backyard. Another hazy summer day in Boston. Yes, she would miss

Kiana and the rest of her friends, but she couldn't help but feel that great things were awaiting her in Italy.

The line-ups at the airport security checkpoints moved at a snail's pace due to the sheer volume of people trying to get through.

Before long, they were seated, briefed on safety procedures, and in the air. Ali's mind drifted as she watched the puffy white clouds drifting by from her airplane window. The last time she had been anywhere near her birthplace was almost eight years earlier. The memories of that trip were a bit faded, but she did recall her aunt and uncle. Leda was a younger, darker version of her mother, elegant and stylish, while Roberto was a young man, fresh out of university. They were very much her family, her only family besides her parents—her adoptive parents.

Nobody was sure exactly where Alice was born. Hers was one of those freaky stories you heard about on the news—an abandoned baby left at a convent door in Florence. News of the child captured national attention in Italy, but no one could offer any clues as to the identity of her mother, or any relatives at all, for that matter.

With no other recourse, the state demanded that the nuns place the tiny infant in the care of an orphanage, and she was finally adopted by Reno and Barbara Ferro. Shortly after, they emigrated to the U.S. on a work sojourn in two top universities, transferring from the University of Siena. This temporary relocation eventually resulted in permanent tenures, Barbara in Linguistics at Harvard and Reno in Physics at MIT. Alice always hoped some of their brains had rubbed off on her, even though they weren't her birth parents.

On the day that they explained to her that she was

adopted, they said that she was special, because she was chosen by them. After that, they didn't talk much about it. She had tried a few times to start a conversation, but it was clear that it made them uncomfortable, so she stopped asking. In spite of this, Alice could never picture being anyone else's. And though sometimes there was friction, all she ever wanted to do was to make them proud that they had picked her.

"*Signorina*, can I get you something to drink?" smiled an attendant, rolling by with his refreshment cart.

"*Sí, grazie, un acqua minerale*," she answered, showcasing her command of the language.

Alice was proud of her fluency in Italian and related it directly to the fact that her parents had insisted on speaking to her in Italian and only Italian until she attended kindergarten.

"So? Excited, Ali?" asked Barbara, unable to conceal her own eagerness.

"Crazy excited. I can't wait to see everything," Ali replied, her eyes flickering with anticipation.

"Don't worry. We'll see everything...only not all in one day," replied her father, looking up from his physics periodical with a smile and wink.

Ali returned his smile as he turned his attention back to his device. His hand swept over it and he resumed the task of devouring his journal.

"I know your Zia Leda and Zio Roberto have a full itinerary for us," Barbara said, as she pulled her device out of her bag and extended it with a flick of her hand. "Now, baby, try to rest...you'll want to be fresh faced when we land." She tucked her buds in her ears and scrolled to select a linguistics periodical.

Alice did manage to doze off and on throughout the flight, but was too excited to actually sleep. Finally, the plane began its steady descent; the familiar 'whirr' of the landing gear releasing below them. Ali looked out, noting the contrast in the countryside from Italy to home. It was dry and parched looking, with the red clay rooftops on the houses dotting the thirsty fields of the Roman suburbs.

The plane skidded on the runway and rumbled down to its taxiing speed as the Cypress trees in the distance swayed in the breeze. Ali remembered the tall, graceful trees and how perfectly 'European' they looked in their elegance. They seemed to be waving 'welcome back' to her. Smiling, she breathed in a quiet sigh as the plane finally reached the terminal. When they were given the all clear, people began unbuckling their seatbelts and reaching to get their stuff.

Grabbing her device, it reminded her she had promised to call Caleb as soon as she landed. She wondered what would be best to communicate with Caleb: voice, text, Face Time...this version of her iPhone Flexi 20S aligned with her internal microchip, too. It could expand into a reading and writing tablet or take and play videos with 3-D holographic options. She could even fold it up and store it in her card holder.

Ali pulled her carry-on from the overhead compartment with one hand, while holding onto her device with the other so she could call Caleb.

"I hope you're not planning on doing this all the time, Ali," cautioned her mother, reaching for her own carry-on. "This is a family vacation, remember?"

"I know, Mamma. I just want to let Caleb know we landed," Ali said, smiling sweetly at her mother.

"Hello," said a familiar voice. Ali flipped her device around in her palm and saw Caleb's face on the panel.

"Hi Caleb, I'm here...in one piece."

"Hey, Ali. Jeez, I miss you already. How was your flight?"

"Long and tiring, and I feel like my legs are rubber." Ali side-stepped as she was jostled in the aisle by a large lady, pulling a bulging knitting bag. "But who's complaining? I'm in Italy."

"Me, that's who."

"Oh, come on now," Ali pretended to scold. "It's only for a month. You'll live. Besides, I'll bring you back something really nice."

"All I want back is you," he smiled. "Against me." His smile broadened.

Ali grinned. "Listen, as you can see, I'm literally still on the plane. I need to get off the phone and get my stuff together. I promise I'll call you when I get to my aunt's, okay?"

"Okay, Ali...I love you, babe. And keep your eyes off those Italian guys. I hear they're relentless over there."

"That'll be my first priority...besides trying out all the gelato I can get my hands on."

Caleb was casually amused. "So, I know your mom's probably already freaking out...call me back soon, or better yet, text me. Love you."

"Promise. Me, too. Bye." With a click, he was gone.

Ali folded the device and slipped it into her pants' pocket, and quickly caught up to her parents. She felt a renewed surge of exhilaration as she realized that she was really in Italy.

Once through customs, they gathered their suitcases into their rented Fiat and wound their way out of the airport labyrinth, past the exotic cypress trees, and onto the Autostrada del Sole, the 'Highway of the Sun.'

As the Fiat nimbly made its way along the oleander lined highway, Alice's enthusiasm gave way to exhaustion as she became ever more aware that she should have slept on the plane.

Chapter Three

Renaissance Florence
1512

"You are Master Leonardo da Vinci, yes?" whispered Elisa, her eyes straining through the tiny opening da Vinci had allowed.

"*Sí*, I am he." He squinted at her as he leaned on the door frame. "But how do you know me?" His eyes fixed on the blood staining her cheek.

"You must forgive me, Master, but I ask that you please allow me to enter," she implored, "or I fear that I shall be arrested and will never be able to answer your queries." She shifted her gaze nervously and peered up and down the street.

Leonardo turned at the sound of barking dogs in the distance, then shifted back to her. "How are you acquainted with my apprentice, Claudio?" His eyes narrowed to slits, giving way to an air of distrust.

"My name is Elisa. I am a servant in the house of Medici, as my parents were before me. I know the Count from the palace." She glanced down at her muddy, torn clothing. "I am certain you must be asking yourself what a waif such as I could be doing, pounding on your door in the dead of night—"

"Surely you know that the Medici name carries influence within the city," Leonardo interrupted, "and that the Duke holds immense power throughout the entire province. You also must know that Duke Giuliano de Medici is my patron. Perhaps you think that this will give me enough reason to open the door to you. You could be a thief for all I know. A bandit."

"Master, I am earnest." Her eyes locked onto his. "And I am in grave danger. You must believe me."

"If you know the Count, then you must know the name of his horse," da Vinci said, his eyes cool.

"Spirit!" Elisa exclaimed. "His mare is called Spirit." Her palms clasped once more.

The old Master squeezed his lips together in silent deliberation. "I dare to think what would happen to me should you be a runaway thief."

"Master, I beg of you, the Medici may be your patrons, but you must know that they are notorious for twisting the truth to suit their own ends." Elisa paused for a moment to allow him to think and let her eyes convey sincerity. "In the Count's name, I beg you."

He inhaled a deep breath and glanced side to side down the narrow street. "Very well, I will assist you—because you are acquainted with Claudio." He pointed his finger at her gravely. "And because I am rather intrigued. But you must listen very carefully. You must do exactly as I say if we are to throw off the dogs and do it quickly—otherwise they will follow you right to my front door."

Elisa nodded fervently.

"You must run to the second cross street, then turn right again. This will leave you very close to the Ponte Vecchio. Repeat this until you have made a complete circle around this quarter. Leave your scent on every door and portico along the way," Leonardo instructed. "The dogs will follow your scent around the loop and be occupied for a while. We will have them running in circles until we determine our next step, yes?" He paused.

"I must go to my workshop...I need to get something. I will close the door, but it will be unlocked. Go now and do as I say. I shall be back well before you return. Come in when you are done...go!" he croaked, causing her to start. He turned on his heel and bustled off into the darkness of the courtyard.

Elisa had no choice but to do as she was told, or her scent would lead the animals to da Vinci's portico. She would never forgive herself if she put the Master in any danger.

She hoisted up her dress and burst into a run, brushing her skirts and shoulders against each entryway in the quarter.

Her breath was aflame again as her ears caught the sounds of guards and dogs getting closer. Trying not to think of the pain in her limbs as she ran, she imagined only the safety that Master Leonardo could offer her once she had finished. She glanced up to the moon, full and round, ready to give her up.

As she reached the corner to run back onto the Master's street, she scanned the laneway down to the Ponte Vecchio. Her heart sank into her stomach. The guards were at the opposite end of the bridge, and the dogs were on her scent.

Elisa burst into a sprint, her energy renewed by the prospect of being mauled to death by hounds. She gasped as she searched for the familiar portico and spotted it again, Master da Vinci waiting at the entrance, waving his arms madly to usher her in.

She dashed across the threshold and held her breath. As she stepped in, she noticed a strange mechanism on the back of the heavy door. It looked like a series of small gears, levers, and bolts.

"Step aside, my dear, whilst I attempt to conceal your scent," the old man whispered.

She pulled her attention away from the strange devices and observed him as he held a small pouch in his hand. He untied it cautiously and with a nimble motion sprinkled the powdery contents on the cobblestones leading up to his doorsill and inside his courtyard. Elisa had to hold her hand to her nose. The smell was overpowering—like rotten eggs.

"Sulfur," cackled the old man. "A very versatile substance. Now listen carefully." He pointed a crooked finger across the courtyard, beyond a leaky fountain to an ancient batten-board door. "Proceed straight through the *piazza* and into the study, through that door. Once you are in, try to conceal yourself. Stay there until I say it is safe, yes? I will cover up your scent if they suspect you are here." His head cocked toward the noise in the street.

Sounds of door-pounding, dogs baying and people shouting obscenities were everywhere in da Vinci's quarter now, as the hounds followed her false trail from door to door. The entire neighborhood was thrown into upheaval by the searches.

"Go now child," he urged her.

"Master Leonardo, I am forever in your debt," Elisa said disarmingly. She smiled, inclined her head and kissed his hand in gratitude, then set off to hide in the darkness.

Da Vinci covered her steps with the remaining sulfur and waited, hoping that the powder would confuse the dogs. The guards may be a bit less thick, though not by much.

"Do not be too quick to obligate yourself to this old man, child," she heard him murmur as she set off. "You are not saved yet."

As she huddled, trembling in the Master's study, Elisa noted that the guards and the hounds, sounded like they had passed the house. Could it be that his plan had worked beyond his expectation? This simple solution to the problem had made it appear that da Vinci's house and only his, out of every house in the quarter was not suspect of harboring her. Perhaps she had been mistaken and the guards were that thick.

∼

While Elisa hid quivering with fear in Leonardo's study, the Master waited until the commotion outside was over and then slowly opened the door to the street. The guards were still nearby, questioning one of his unwitting neighbors.

"I tell you I know nothing of this girl," shouted an old woman across the laneway. "I was asleep until your dogs from hell awoke me."

"Did you find anything?" shouted the commander to a guard inside.

"Nothing, sir."

"Very well. Next house then."

"What? That is it?" said the woman. "No explanation? No apologies? Why...you people are a scourge, I tell you! You think that you can do as you—"

"Silence," the commander sputtered, a hard edge in his voice. "I am here on orders from Duke Giuliano de Medici, and you shall speak to me with respect."

Upon hearing the Medici name, fear welled up in the old woman's eyes, and she held her tongue.

It was a common reaction to the mere mention of that family name. They were as intimidating as they were wealthy, and firmly in control of virtually every affair, business or otherwise, in Florence. A ruthless group they are, albeit with an eye for the fine arts, thought Leonardo.

The commander glanced across to where da Vinci stood peering into the street. He bowed. "We regret disturbing you Master da Vinci. We had not intended to wake you. Our dogs did not approach your portico. Have you by chance heard or seen a young girl, in servants' garb. She is perhaps fifteen or sixteen years of age. She is wanted by the Duke for high treason."

Leonardo's heart jumped. He took a breath to steady himself. *I have a traitor in my house? If the Duke learned this, he would be very unwilling to continue his patronage.* Leonardo had several projects commissioned on behalf of Giuliano de Medici. His hand wiped the emerging beads of sweat from his brow.

Da Vinci returned the bow. "I thank you, Commander for your consideration, however as you can see your attempts at silently searching my neighborhood were unsuccessful. The barking of your dogs, pounding of doors, and shouting from my neighbors are enough to wake the dead!"

The commander bowed again, perfunctorily, as he bristled at da Vinci's comments. "I would ask, sir," as he sniffed the air with a notable scowl, "what is that foul smell? It seems to envelop this entire area."

"Ah, yes, Commander," said Leonardo. "Quite perceptive of you. I was engaged in a somewhat risky experiment, and I did not realize the potency of the concoction. Suffice it to say that the ingredients resulted in quite a nasty reaction, and I have a colossal mess to contend with. Would you care to investigate?" The old man grinned coyly, as he motioned to the courtyard inside.

"That is not necessary, Master da Vinci," replied the commander, his fingers clamped on his nose and looking anxious to leave. "We have quite a long night ahead of us."

"Of course, I understand," said Leonardo, a smile dancing around the corners of his mouth. "I shall keep my eyes sharply open for this girl. Good night, Commander."

"Good night, sir."

The old man swiftly closed the door, engaged its intricate series of locks, and crossed the courtyard to the study. Despite his unease at having an alleged escaped criminal in his study, he remained highly fascinated by the mystery shrouding her visit. He would not turn her in—not just yet.

He opened the study door and scanned the vast, jumbled room for the young maiden.

The room was not a traditional study at all. It did contain hundreds of books and other bound materials, as well as countless stacks of parchments, diagrams and manuscripts, but it also held numerous shelves containing a curious assortment of machines, odd devises, and mechanisms in various states of construction. A large table off to one side was flanked by smaller ones full of containers of fluids holding various animal and human organs and tissues. In the middle of the room were several half-finished sculptures, hammers and chisels, as well as easels, large and small. The sketches, paintings, and diagrams were far from completion.

Leonardo distinguished a form in the far corner of the study. There sat a trembling lump of blankets on the floor, which he quickly determined was Elisa. He grabbed a flask of water from a nearby table, imagining that she must be parched through and through after what he surmised must have been a lengthy trek across the countryside. The old man spoke calmly so as not to frighten her.

"Come out, child," he said reassuringly. "The guards have gone. You are safe, for now."

Elisa cautiously removed the blankets covering her head. "Am I to assume that I am out of danger?" she asked, incredulous.

Da Vinci nodded, somewhat warily. She shuddered and tearfully clamped a hand to her mouth. The Master looked about awkwardly. "There, there, Elisa," he said, trying to comfort her. She looked up at da Vinci, and brushed her tears away with the hem of her skirt, then gratefully accepted the flask. With giant gulps, she drank down the refreshing water.

"Master Leonardo, it is true that I will be forever in your debt," she said, wiping her mouth. "You have saved my life, I am quite certain of that. I cannot bring myself to think of what could have happened to me had I not found Count Claudio's mentor."

"Now, now...stop crying and tell me of your business here," said the old man in a soothing voice. "You say that your parents were servants in the house of Medici? That is very interesting. The great Lorenzo de Medici was once my patron, as was Cesare Borgia and as now is Giuliano de Medici. Might I have known your parents, my dear?"

"You may have. Before the Borgia took power in Florence, my mother was a cook in the palace, and my father was a blacksmith."

"I see. Then perhaps you should tell me why you are fleeing from the Duke. And for that matter, how is the Count involved in this?"

Elisa's eyes locked onto the old man's gaze for what seemed an endless moment, then she closed them tight. Taking in a deep breath, the girl found her voice once more, and began to speak.

Chapter Four

Italy
2029

Alice was startled awake by her mother's gushing over the familiar sights of Siena. They had made it in just in time to see the city basked in glorious lavender and pink twilight.

The little Fiat swiftly wove its way down a circular via, which opened up to a breathtaking piazza. It was shaped like a fan and surrounded by noisy cafés in front of the most remarkably ornate antique buildings. This was the *Piazza del Campo*, the main city square and the venue for the famous *Palio* horse race. In the open-air restaurants and bars, an eclectic collection of locals, tourists, and backpackers sat, all taking in the lights and beauty of the city on this muggy Tuscan evening. At the center of the piazza was the town hall tower, the *Torre del Mangia,* and topping off the medieval skyline were the bell tower and the dome of the cathedral.

Reno drove with expertise and familiarity down a street not too far from the center of town. Ali read the street sign on the side of a building; this was her aunt's street, the *Via Condotta*.

She remembered the artisan bakery on the corner, its doors open, and the heavenly aroma of freshly baked bread wafting out into the neighborhood. She closed her eyes and breathed in deeply...that incredible smell was just as she remembered it.

"Here we are," declared Reno, pulling up beside the centuries-old building. Just as they stepped out of the car, a delighted squeal had them look up in unison to the uppermost balcony.

"Barbara...Reno...up here!" It was Alice's aunt and uncle. In an instant, they were down in the street embracing them with tight hugs, tears, and laughter.

"Oh...I simply cannot let go!" cried Leda. "But we must, otherwise we will be run down by these Vespa scooters." The five of them burst into laughter.

"What is your secret, Leda? You do not age at all," Barbara said to her younger sister as they climbed up to their flat.

"Time passes for everyone, my darling. I feel it every time I scale these stairs." Leda wrapped her arm around Barbara's shoulder, a suitcase in the other hand.

Ali smiled at the conversation. Leda and Roberto were full of plans. They would visit Pisa, Lucca, and Florence, and some of the surrounding villages. There was even talk of a few days on Lake Como and Venice.

But first, they would see Siena.

The weeks flew by in an endless whirlwind of touring. They visited bustling, modern cities and quaint villages where time stood still. Museums, cathedrals, and art galleries were Alice's new dwellings in the daytime. Piazzas, trattorias and cafés were her hangouts at night. Ali saw the sunset on the Canal

Grande in Venice from the Rialto Bridge as well as the sunrise over the majestic Matterhorn in the Valle d'Aosta. And in-between she indulged in her gelato eating goals, much to her delight. But what she looked forward to the most was the promised trip to Florence.

In between, of course, she found opportunities to post some incredible 3D's on her WrapAround account. She spoke with Caleb, Kiana and her other friends, filling them in on the sweet life she was living.

"I miss you, Als," said Caleb during one particularly long conversation. "Can't wait for you to come home. Seeing you on WrapAround just isn't enough. You belong here—with me."

"It's just for a couple more weeks, Caleb," she pointed out reassuringly. "You'll survive without me."

She sensed in his voice that he was pining for her and even though the thought was thoroughly evil, it gave her the tiniest feeling of satisfaction. Ali thought about their first meeting, how they became friends and then how their friendship progressed to another level. It was all very logical that they dated—they shared the same school, goals, and friends. But for all the reasons that she had for being with Caleb, there was a tiny part of her that felt something was missing. It was hard to pin down what.

"So, family, where are we off to tomorrow?" Ali asked, stuffing what remained of a veal scaloppini in her mouth after a long day of shopping at the local marketplace. "You know, Mamma," she added, "I think I could get used to this lifestyle if I stay here much longer." She grinned and shot a mischievous side glance at her parents.

"Alice, we would love it. My darling, you don't even have to ask to stay here. It does get lonely, just the two of us some-times, doesn't it, Roberto?" Leda said, passing her more bread.

"Since you ask, we do have something special planned,"

Leda gushed. "We are going to visit Florence...by way of an exquisite little villa in the Tuscan hillside!"

"No way," said Alice. "A villa near Florence? Mamma, Papa, did you hear?"

"I did," said Barbara, beaming at her sister. "A villa in the Tuscan hills—whatever inspired you to do such a thing?"

"The owners are friends of ours," replied Leda as she stood and began to clear the dishes. "A very nice couple. We were chatting some weeks ago about your visit, and shortly after, they insisted that we stay at their villa."

"How nice of them. It will be a vacation to remember, Ali, that is for certain," laughed Reno. "And did we thank you yet for insisting we visit?"

"Please, shall I give you a countdown?" Leda smiled and continued to work.

No sooner had they finished their conversation, when Reno's phone signaled, and he stepped out to take the call. The rest continued to chatter while the table was cleared, however, when he returned, Ali could tell by the look on his face that it wasn't good news.

Chapter Five

The drive back from the Pisa airport was disheartening for both Ali and her aunt, despite Roberto's best efforts to cheer them up.

I'm here on my own. Just when we were starting to reconnect. Damn. Ali stared out the window at the blurry countryside passing them by at an insane speed. *Jeez, the only thing slower than 70 MPH around here is a house,* her father had said on their way up to Siena. The thought brought a smile to her face.

Reno had been called back to Boston. The head of the Physics department at MIT had suffered a near-fatal heart attack, and Reno had to step into his shoes.

"I don't want to leave you here by yourself, baby," Barbara declared to Ali, torn between staying with Alice and leaving with Reno. "There's a very important project that they are working on and it's at a critical stage right now—they need your Papa to step in for Doctor Shinehoft."

"Mom, it's okay. Really," she had assured her mother. Ali knew Reno was a scatterbrain when he was working. He barely ate when he became preoccupied. "You go with Papa. I'll be fine. It's only a couple more weeks." With her parent's permission, she decided to stay behind. Her aunt and uncle appeared shattered to see the rest of their family vacation plans evaporate with a single call.

It was a tearful goodbye for the sisters at the airport. "Be good. We'll see you soon," said Ali's mom as she gave her a last hug.

"Come on, sweetheart," cajoled her aunt, as they sped toward Siena. "I will miss your Mamma and Papa terribly, and I do wish that they could have stayed, but let's try and make the most of this situation, yes? We will go to the villa tomorrow and you will forget all about missing them. I promise, you will fall in love with it."

"I know. I'm just disappointed because we were just starting to reconnect and…this was supposed to be a family vacation." Alice sighed, frustrated that her parents were called away just when they were beginning to loosen up a little. She glanced up at her aunt who looked positively hurt. *Think positive. What's wrong with you? You're in Italy for God's sake!*

"What I mean to say is," Ali forced herself to sound more upbeat. "I'm very lucky to be able to stay with you now that they had to go." She smiled wanly, trying her best to sound eager. "Really, I'll be fine."

~

The next morning Alice repacked her bag, and they left right after breakfast. The mountain scenery driving north was picturesque, but Ali was preoccupied. *Just make the most of it. This may be a good chance to practice being a bit more independent.* Positivity, she chanted silently, positivity.

"So," Ali said, perched on the tiny back seat of the sports car, "exactly where is this villa?"

"It is in a pretty little town called San Miniato," answered Leda, "which is only about twenty minutes from the center of

Florence. It's surrounded by trees and vineyards. The town is a favorite with many of our friends. People whose names you would probably recognize have stayed there. I am sure you will love it."

Leda wasn't kidding. When Roberto turned the sleek black Citroen onto the elegant cobblestone driveway of the estate, the vista that opened before her was enough to take Ali's breath away.

The curvy driveway was lined to the villa with rows of graceful, swaying cypress trees. Roberto steered up the private drive to reveal a four-storey, stuccoed country villa surrounded by rolling meadows of neatly manicured vineyards and ancient olive trees. The sprawling estate sat on a hilltop just outside the village, and the front grounds were generously peppered with oleanders and fig trees.

Roberto pulled the car up to the front of the old-world wooden door, which was flanked by two antique sconces. Alice slowly opened the car door and stepped out, inhaling deeply, taking in the pastoral, fragrant setting around her.

"Oh, my gosh," was all she could manage to whisper. "This place is beautiful."

"Come, Alice," her uncle waved her over with a mile-long grin. "Let's go meet Anna and Dario, our hosts. One of the attendants will get our bags. Do you know that this is a working winery? It—"

No sooner had her uncle spoken, when a young man strode out from behind the building on the opposite side of the house. Alice glanced at the figure walking toward them and was immediately taken aback by his appearance. His tall frame made his body look lanky, but as he got closer, it was plain that he was anything but. His pace was dutiful, his eyes were fixed on the pavement in front of him, and his dark hair, looked carelessly left to its own ends.

The boy was simply dressed in dark jeans and a crisp, white

shirt, sleeves rolled to the elbow, revealing strong sinewy arms against the thin cotton fabric. He was a stunning young man with physical qualities that conveyed effortless beauty, triggering her mouth to curve into an unconscious smile as he walked toward their car.

She exhaled. The world fell silent and everything slowed as if someone had hit a pause button.

When the boy looked up, his eyes, dark as the night, found Ali's, and he froze, too. He stood immobile for a long moment, the emotion in his gaze so intense, it was palpable.

Then he moved toward her, slowly at first, then faster.

Chapter Six

Renaissance Florence
Summer 1512

Elisa Beatrice de Povri began her story for Leonardo from the beginning, a beginning that Elisa hoped the great Master could recall: her parents' history with the Medici, as told to her by her friend, Caterina.

"My parents, Monica and Enrico de Povri were from Fiesole, but resettled in Florence when they became servants for the Medici family—under Lorenzo the Magnificent's rule."

"Yes, I recall that time," said Leonardo. "Florence was quickly becoming a haven for promising young artists and savvy bankers. It was the home of a new age for aristocratic society, and the Medici family was one of a few influential houses greatly responsible for this new 're-birth,' as they were calling it. They dominated the city's government for decades and patronized some of the greatest artists in Florence, me among them."

Elisa's eyes glazed over as she listened to Leonardo go on about his patron. When he finished, she spoke. "This is true,

Master Leonardo, but it is also true that because of their power and influence, many of the other great families were in the habit of conspiring against them, the Forloni family being one of them. It was not surprising that even servants were caught up in the unfortunate events, my parents among them."

"As I understand it, the conspirators were gathered up and questioned by the Medici prison guard, each prisoner succumbing to the excruciating pain, giving names of others involved until there was no one but innocents left to name. My parents were two of many who died for a conspiracy, about which they knew nothing. I was an infant and was left an orphan. Out of the Medici family's so-called pity and goodwill I was allowed to stay in the palace, to be raised by the servants. I grew up in the busy palace kitchens and eventually became the charge of a young scullery maid."

Elisa's eyes took on a lively quality. "Caterina was also alone. She looked after me, much like an older sister would. I truly consider Caterina to be my only family, and she, in turn, loves me as if I were her own blood."

"She taught me the necessary lessons of surviving life as a servant in the Medici palace. Do your chores religiously, be loyal to the family, and blend into the background. After all, a servant's drudgework in a palace is better than life outside in the unknown as a peasant."

"However, soon afterward, the Medici were ousted from power by the merciless Cesare Borgia, if I recall correctly," Leonardo interjected. "The Borgia invaded Italy under the command of the French king, Charles the Eighth, and Florence hired the military leader to manage its affairs—all of the courtiers were banished, too. And still you remained in the palace?"

"Yes, sir," Elisa agreed. "Caterina and I worked there under the House of Borgia. In fact, I would see the King, from time to time, in the palace. But there were rumors of treachery and other horrible things, and the servants do not dare hazard to comment on such speculation. No one would question the disappearance of a scullery maid. So, through the years, I grew to be an obedient girl, a hard worker, and dutiful in my chores. Caterina always reminded me to look down and not look in their eyes," she continued. "Not out of respect, but so that my face remains unnoticed."

"And then the Medici regained control." She breathed unsteadily and cast her gaze to the floor. "Nevertheless, my friend knew that one day a courtier would notice me. This attention could either be a great blessing or a curse, depending on the man who took note. Unfortunately, that day could not be put off indefinitely."

"Do not be afraid, my dear," Master da Vinci spoke in a soothing, calm voice. "You may trust in the fact that Claudio has sent you to me. I will do what I can to protect you. But to keep you from harm, you must tell me what you have done, and what this has to do with the Count."

"Master Leonardo, I swear on the souls of my mother and father, I have done nothing wrong, but alas I fear that I am destined for the same end." Again, tears clouded her vision. "I swear to you, sir, that Claudio is guilty only of speaking his mind and protecting my honor. He is unaware that I am here. He believes that I am far from Florence, far from the danger that awaits me here—a danger from which he could not save himself because he chose to save me and my friend instead."

Her voice was even, but her eyes told a different story. "If I could somehow take back the events that have transpired in the past few days, I would—even if that meant never having felt the truest love. I would never in my most horrible nightmares have imagined that one moment could be responsible for both the happiest and the most desperate days of my life."

"And my pupil, the Count?" asked Leonardo, narrowing his eyes. "What has he to do with your love?"

"It is he—my lord Claudio," Elisa held her hands over her face in shame. "He is the one. He is the one I love, and it is he who will die because of me." She wiped her tears with the palms of her hands. "Claudio has also been accused of treason and murder, but his only offense was defending my honor and my dignity against the Duke's horrible, lecherous nephew, Bruno."

Leonardo shook his head. Claudio's family was one of the aristocracies in Florence, the son of Count Giacomo and Countess Maria Moro, both well-respected and loyal courtiers who had fled with the Medici when they were banished from Florence. Their devotion to the family was unblemished. So how could this news be true?

"Tell me what has happened, girl," Master da Vinci said, bringing his hand to his mouth.

Elisa collected herself. She thought back to the incident that had begun all this. To the moment when she had met her beautiful Count Claudio. Had she known that night that their lives would be placed in such danger, she would have chosen an alternate route to the kitchen. Her eyes glazed over. How simple it would have been, she thought, to just not have known him.

The Master tapped her hand, rousing her from her thoughts. "Go on, child," he said quietly.

"My apologies, Master Leonardo. It has been many hours since I have slept." She rubbed her eyes and continued. "The first time I met the Count was a happenstance. Of course, I had seen him about the palace, but I made certain that he did not see me. At the time, I had no idea who he was. Caterina had always warned me to stay clear of the noblemen in the court as she was certain that their position in society had taken their souls and that the women servants were often at their mercy. For some of us, it might be an honor to...have been with a noble, but Caterina and I did not want this type of attention, if you understand my meaning, Master Leonardo."

The old man nodded. "Yes, my dear, I understand perfectly...go on, now."

Elisa methodically recounted the details that had led up to that night. Leonardo listened carefully.

When she had finished, the old man sat back, holding his fist to his lips. Elisa, with eyes locked onto his, waited for a response. After moments of agonizing silence, he spoke.

"With whatever means I possess to assist my young pupil and you, Elisa de Povri, I will do it. But we must act quickly." He took in a deep breath and shook his head. "I cannot bear to think what should happen otherwise."

Chapter Seven

Florence
July 1512...A Few Weeks Earlier

The day presented itself cloudy, cool, and damp, which was an uncharacteristically drab day for a Tuscan summer. Claudio had saddled up his mare, Spirit, and swiftly rode to Leonardo's secondary studio in Galluzzo. As he wound his way up the slippery hillside to the Master's workshop at the monastery, he dodged tree limbs and other debris that littered the landscape—the results of a wild thunderstorm the night before.

Claudio recalled the conversation he'd had with his mother, between the thunderclaps, about his studies with da Vinci. Countess Maria had fallen into the habit of looking over his shoulder and scrutinizing his work, though she had not a clue what he was doing. He loved his mother dearly, but at times she could be incomprehensibly annoying.

"Claudio, you know that you are now the heir to your father's fortune," began Countess Maria in her usual authoritarian tone. "And you have been guaranteed a place in one of the Medici banks. Why do you insist on continuing to waste your time with that madman?" She shifted forward on the settee, emphasizing her state of increased annoyance. Dropping her voice to a whisper, she leaned in. "In fact, Clarice recently advised me that he persists in writing with his left hand. Can you imagine? And he writes backward. What in the devil's name for?"

She resumed her flawless posture. "He has been admonished by the Church on many occasions, Claudio. Honestly, you are a man of nineteen years of age. You should think seriously about your future and not waste time on frivolities." She gave him an exasperated look that was all too familiar.

"Oh, but I am serious, Mother." Claudio grinned, looking up from his worktable. "I plan on becoming a very rich count, with an abundance of land that I lease to peasants. Oh, yes, and in addition, I plan to marry a very rich woman whose social status is either equal to, or surpasses my own. And I also plan to work day and night in one of the many Medici banks to generate even more money for Duke Giuliano. Would that make you content, Mother?" His voice dripped sarcasm. To his infinite delight, he detected a flash of irritation on her face that she could not manage to hide.

The Countess's voice took on a cold quality. "You can make all the fun you want, my son, but you should be aware that your security in this world depends on the willingness of those in power to protect you. Do not make light of the Duke, or any of his family for that matter, for you do not wish to feel his wrath." She paused for a moment, then her voice relaxed. "The House of Medici has been very good to our family."

Sighing, she walked to his worktable and brushed a tuft of hair from her son's eyes. "My dearest Claudio, I only wish the best for you, but you must think seriously. And since you mention it, I have begun to look for a suitable wife for you."

Claudio grimaced. "A what? Mother, I insist that you stop

this search at once. I have no intention of marrying anyone now. Although, there are a few young ladies in Florence that come to mind who would undeniably be delighted to be my wife—"

"That is quite enough, thank you very much," interrupted the countess. "Really, Claudio...you are quite incorrigible." She huffed out a breath and then allowed herself to soften. "Mark my words, my dear, you had best be thinking about your future. Trust me. I will find you the best match. In the meantime, you must practice discretion and restraint. You are only as good as your reputation, after all."

As Claudio guided Spirit up the rise to the monastery, he smiled to himself, thinking of his mother, laughing at the ridiculous conversations he shared with her. The Countess was narrow-minded at times, but she did have the best intentions for him, of that he was certain. Claudio also knew that an arranged marriage was inevitable.

Yet, he could not help thinking that every young maiden in the court was unabashedly self-absorbed, and he did not relish being married off to someone he hardly knew, let alone did not like.

At last, with a final saunter, Spirit crested the ridge, bringing Claudio to the outer grand entry of the monastery. He secured his mare to a nearby post and stroked her nose. Then he made his way to the door, knocked, and waited. Impatient, he knocked again.

Finally, someone on the other side unbolted the locks. A monk, slight of build and stature, opened the massive door in what seemed like a Herculean effort. The young friar smiled a toothless grin.

"Good morning, brother." Claudio stepped inside, as he thought of how they could not possibly have found anyone smaller to do the job. He thanked the little novice monk and hurried through the familiar courtyard to Master Leonardo's living quarters on the north side of the complex.

Upon arriving, he rapped sharply on the door, as at times the Master was so engrossed in his work that he did not hear.

"Who is there?" called a gruff voice from the other side. Claudio recognized it as his teacher's.

"It is I, Master—Claudio."

He heard da Vinci as he worked the locks. The old man yanked the door open, wild eyed and disheveled, and pulled Claudio in by his collar before slamming the door shut. "Master, what is it—are you quite well?" he asked, straightening his shirt.

"Ha, ha!" Leonardo cackled. "My boy, I have encountered something incredible. It is a momentous discovery, Claudio." His hands gestured madly in the air, his face beamed. "Yes, my boy, though I am not quite sure what it is. But...it is colossal. Hoh, hoh!"

Claudio was at a loss as he watched his usually composed teacher howling with laughter. "Quickly, come into the study," da Vinci croaked, pulling Claudio by the hand.

"What is it that you—"

"Silence!" shouted Leonardo and clapped a hand over his mouth once he realized how loud he was being. He led Claudio to the inner room.

Leonardo had demanded the utmost privacy while he worked on this time-consuming project, not even allowing his most trusted student to enter his cluttered workshop on the days he focused on this, 'fascinating, yet very dangerous experiment'.

"You must be aware that Francesco knows nothing of this," he confided. "You are the only one that I can trust with this brilliant discovery." Francesco was one of Leonardo's other pupils, one of his most brilliant.

"Last evening, I was continuing my work on the experiment...you know the one, the secret one." He drew in a breath. "I had a theory, wherein I believed that if one could harness the power of a lightning strike, one should be able to use that power to his advantage."

Claudio gulped. How could anyone think that they could possibly control something as mighty as a bolt of lightning? But then again, it was Leonardo he was speaking with. His teacher looked like he had not slept for days.

"With all due respect, Master," Claudio said. "I find it difficult to imagine that something so formidable and potent could be 'caught', so to speak."

"Aha, my boy, but that is the essence of the study of Nature, the very root of the discipline—to imagine. Now, take heed. In my observations, I noticed that these bolts of intense light are naturally attracted to metal objects, like the bell in the monastery tower. These bolts clearly possess immense power, but how does one hold onto it? How does one control this energy, this immeasurable force?" He gushed on his theories, as he scurried to his inner studio. "Well, I decided to try. My curiosity got the better of me, I am afraid. First, I staked metal rods in the ground, hoping the metal would somehow hold on to the power, but the bolts just seemed to dissipate into the earth."

"After several other fruitless attempts, I decided I needed a chamber, a metal chamber to which the power could be brought and where it could be held—to house it. I found some discarded copper...that came in quite useful." He chortled proudly. "Needless to say, I was successful in that—and more. The storm last night proved to be very beneficial."

Master da Vinci smiled broadly as he unbolted the door to his laboratory, and with a sweeping motion of his arm, directed Claudio to look inside. "And now..., behold!"

The action by Leonardo proved unnecessary, as the vision before his student was at the very least resplendent. Its brilliance engulfed Claudio with a light so radiant, so beautiful, and so strange that he could not look away.

"What the devil is it?" exclaimed Claudio, his mouth dropping open.

"Indeed, I do not know, my boy," whispered da Vinci, grasping Claudio's arm to keep him back. "I am not quite sure what I have created. I can only tell you how this happened... I did seem to trap the lightning bolt."

"Yes, sir... it appears you did." Unable to tear his gaze from it, Claudio moved toward the spiraling phenomena, though he did not know whether it would harm or heal. "How...how did you..."

"Come and sit down." Leonardo moved Claudio away from the hypnotic effects of the chamber and pushed his bewildered student into a chair. "In constructing the metal chamber, I had to make certain that all other elements were removed—air, for example. The chamber had to be devoid of all things to make space for the energy of the lightning bolt. I constructed this air suctioning machine to do that." He pointed to a contraption that looked like a large backward bellows.

"Then I placed copper plates in the chamber to further enhance the attraction, after which I positioned a large copper rod outside of my apartments, on the rooftop of the monastery, and fed it into the chamber, sealing it so that nothing else could penetrate it save for the energy of the lightning bolt."

"Master, what exactly is in there?"

"Well, that..." Leonardo's voice dropped to a mesmerized whisper. "That is the question."

Claudio arose and stepped warily toward the copper structure. It was large enough to hold four grown men on the inside, with room for movement.

"Sir...the copper—from the new church?" Claudio asked,

with a sideways glance. The question was moot as he knew where the copper sheeting came from. A newly commissioned church was being built near the Master's Florence residence. The builders used copper sheets for the *cupola* or dome of the church.

"Well...yes," Leonardo responded, a hint of guilt in his eyes. "At times, a man must do what a man must do to further the cause of his work. And it only cost me a portrait of the master builder's wife. Ugh. Not a handsome woman." He shuddered. "As I was saying..."

But da Vinci's rationalizations for his tactics in acquiring building materials were lost on Claudio. The fascination of exploring what was only a few paces from him rendered him oblivious to anything but the stunning spectacle before him.

As da Vinci continued his revelations regarding the experiment, Claudio stepped closer to the chamber doors, and braced himself for the brilliance. He held a hand to his eyes and peered with his peripheral vision into the center of it. The two metallic plates, about the height of a man, which stood at opposite sides on the inside of the cube were aglow with a brilliant white light, and there was a low hum in the air. They were vibrating with energy. Claudio felt like a thousand needles were grazing his skin.

That sight, however, could not compare to the strange vista Claudio saw in the center of the chamber.

In between the metal plates was a swirling array of dazzling, multi-colored beams of light. It was almost too beautiful for words. At the center of the spiraling strings was a black hole with a white light in its center. The entire array extended far beyond the limits of the metal assembly. Its formation reminded Claudio of a cone, rising and falling.

Moreover, rays of light attached to the edges of the black opening, altered and transformed the boundaries, combining themselves and then separating again, in an endless prism of undulating, narrow beams of brilliant rainbows. The effect was hypnotic, and Claudio had to shake himself back, so he could focus on Leonardo's explanation.

"So, this is why I believe it is more than a captured lightning bolt," finished the teacher quite matter-of-factly.

"I would certainly agree," said Claudio, more calmly than he thought the words would leave his lips. "But what is it?"

"Yes. That is the other question. And there is more, my boy. That is not the most intriguing piece of the puzzle." Leonardo's tone took a serious note. "Observe this."

Da Vinci pulled up one of the sleeves on his cloak. Steadily, he put his arm up to his elbow inside the chamber and it disappeared. Claudio stood, open-mouthed and speechless, staring at the wonder before him.

Chapter Eight

Tuscany, Italy
August 2029

Ordinarily, alarm bells would be going off in Alice's head if any other stranger had been rushing toward her like that, but there was nothing ordinary about this young man. She stood, mesmerized by his eyes, and couldn't tear her gaze from his.

The boy strode faster toward her, crossing the driveway, not breaking eye contact. His expression held a mix of disbelief and utter relief. Raising his hand as if he were about to touch her, Ali thought the gesture felt like a natural reaction to seeing an old friend or loved one. He had almost reached her when her uncle intervened.

"Hey! What do you think you're doing?" snarled Roberto, stepping between the two. "You need to step back." He held up his hand to halt the newcomer. "Who are you?"

The young man stopped short of walking right into Roberto head-on but he kept his eyes on Alice.

"I—I work here, sir. I am the attendant." Although he was

speaking to Roberto, the attendant's eyes were giant zeroes locked onto Ali's.

"Hey," said Roberto, snapping his fingers. "I'm over here."

"I must ask your forgiveness, sir." After glancing briefly at Roberto, he promptly directed his eager attention back to Ali. "And you, too, *signorina*. I'm sorry but, you remind me of someone I knew." He swallowed and then began again. "I will get your bags immediately. Excuse my rudeness." Despite what he said, he stood rooted to the spot.

"No trouble at all," Ali replied. She stared at him, unable to move.

"Hello!" shouted Roberto. "The bags. Get the bags—in the car." There was an awkward silence as the four of them exchanged looks. Roberto finally ended it by throwing the boy his keys.

"Yes...thank you, sir." Distracted, he stumbled away to Roberto's Citroen to unload their luggage, while he simultaneously kept his eyes on Ali. His preoccupied struggle with hauling the suitcases to the villa was even more comical. The absurdity of the scene gave rise to a peel of giggles so unexpected, Ali clapped a hand over her mouth to hide it. But instead of being offended by her laughter, the young man looked back at her from the villa entrance and chuckled, nodding his acknowledgment with a bewitchingly crooked smile.

Wow! Those eyes, Ali thought, and let out a heavy sigh. She had never seen eyes like that...she stopped as she considered that last thought. *So dark, so intense, like...black fire. Oh my god, did I actually think that? black fire?*

"Alice?" her aunt called out to her. "Do you know that boy?"

She reflected, then turned to her aunt. "No, Zia Leda, I'm sure that I haven't met him...I mean, I've never been here, so how could I?" Something skittered in the pit of her stomach.

"I thought I was going to have to slap him out of that trance he was in," sneered Roberto.

Leda chuckled. "Well, for someone you don't know, you two certainly looked like you shared a moment." Her eyes narrowed. "Alice, believe me, these local boys can spot a tourist instantly."

Leda took Ali by the shoulders and looked her straight in the eye. "Listen carefully and take my advice, sweetheart. Be cautious. The boys here are not like the boys in America. Their words are like honey. They tell you what you want to hear, but in the end, they know you will be going home."

"I got it. Don't worry," Ali said, as casually as she could manage. "I'll steer clear."

Leda reached into the car, grabbed her purse, and turned toward the villa. "And more times than not, they will break your heart."

"Listen to your aunt. She's right," added Roberto, following Leda to the house.

Alice was left at the entrance, stupefied. This was the most powerful déjà vu she had ever experienced. It left her mysteriously exhilarated, yet anxious. She paused, trying to gather her thoughts, but everything around her felt surreal.

As she was about to turn to follow her aunt and uncle into the villa, Ali saw the young man emerge from the side entrance, his face, flushed. He stepped onto the cobblestone drive and their gazes met again. This time, he slowed his pace, as if to keep Ali from thinking he was charging at her. Slowly and carefully, he moved closer. Alice could feel the chemistry connecting them, an intense physical awareness like energy flowing between their skins.

"Excuse me...I need to move the car, *signorina*." He gestured to the Citroen. "Pardon me, please."

Alice realized she was still standing in front of the car door. "Oh. Yes." Shaking herself into reality, Ali moved aside so the boy could park the car. As she moved, her hand brushed ever so slightly against his, resting on the door handle. "Sorry." She smiled up at him, as he was considerably taller.

His touch, though inadvertent, made her skin tingle. It was only when he shook his head and found his voice to say, "It was my fault," did the connection break. Ali's heart raced laps around her chest as the thought, *who is this guy?* echoed in her mind.

Chapter Nine

Renaissance Florence
1512

Leonardo cackled his triumph as he watched a bewildered Claudio. The young man could not believe what he was seeing. His teacher's arm had disappeared into the chamber array and then just as easily, he had pulled it back out.

"What is this magic? Master, this is beyond comprehension, beyond...I do not know what." Claudio's eyes were wide as saucers. He shared da Vinci's passion for the advancement of the study of Nature, and oftentimes his mentor would comment that he saw himself as a young man in Claudio, but this was bizarre, even for a lad who was always full of questions and an open mind.

"This is not magic, boy," snapped da Vinci, his tone serious. "What you are seeing is Nature at its most powerful. It is knowledge—*scientia*—if I dare to call it that." He paused and considered further. "Then again, perhaps it is a passage to Hades...at this moment, I cannot be sure."

Leonardo and Claudio stood silently and stared at the light, lost in thought.

"What does it feel like, sir?" Claudio asked.

The old Master reflected. "I should say it feels as though millions of tiny insects are crawling on my skin. The sensation is not painful yet at the same time, not the most pleasant."

"Have you tried to see inside the chamber?"

"How do you mean?"

"Have you tried to see where your arm is going? Reason would tell us that if it is not visible in the chamber, then it should be visible elsewhere."

"The thought had occurred to me, however, I preferred to wait for an assistant in the event something should go wrong. I am an adventurous old fool, yes, but a good student of Nature has a healthy respect for the likelihood that if something can go wrong, it will."

"Master, please...may I?" asked Claudio, nodding toward the array.

"Indeed," da Vinci gestured toward it.

Claudio slipped off his jacket and roughly rolled up his tailored sleeve. Little by little, he slid his hand into the glowing spiral and observed as his arm gradually disappeared into the strands of light. He and the old man exchanged glances. The strange phenomena had uncharacteristically quieted them both.

Claudio felt a million tiny pinpricks on his skin. It was breathtaking. Something pulled on his arm as if he had submerged it into a vat of thick syrup, but there was no pain. Claudio tried to move his hand around to see what effect that would have. As he hypothesized, he could feel his hand moving, although he could see nothing.

Finally, the young student had to propose the inevitable. "Master, we ought to try to see what is on the other side."

"Yes, young Claudio, you are most correct," conceded da

Vinci, scratching the top of his head pensively. "But how to go about it?" he pondered. Then finally, "I must simply look inside. But you shall hold onto this frail old man, for I fear I have not the strength to pull myself out again."

"Agreed," replied Claudio. "How long shall I let you observe before I pull you back?"

"I do not know...count to ten?"

Claudio had no idea if this was akin to a death sentence for his mentor, but it was the logical way to proceed. How extraordinary this whole thing was. But he must maintain a level head, even if he felt like jumping out of his skin with anticipation.

"Very well, sir. Give me your arm."

Da Vinci extended his arm to Claudio while he drew in a deep breath. The youth could feel his teacher's hand shaking.

"Wait, sir," cautioned Claudio. "Perhaps if you are anxious, you should let me go first."

"Ah, no, my young friend. If the need should arise, I will require your strong grasp to pull me back. I fear I may not have the strength to do the same for you."

Claudio nodded, agreeing with his teacher. Besides, it was his Master's discovery. He should have the pleasure of exploring it first. "Good luck, then, sir. I will not let go." Holding Leonardo's arm tightly, Claudio watched as the old man advanced slowly to peer into the array, carefully positioning his head inside its strands. Da Vinci's face gradually disappeared into the colors of the chamber, the pinwheels swirling around his wispy grey hair. The slightest hint of white light emanated from the outer edges of his silhouette, reminding Claudio of the halos the Master painted around his angel's faces.

Moments into the array, Leonardo's grasp tightened around Claudio's forearm, prompting the immediate release of the old man from the chamber with a sharp yank, nearly causing them to fall to the floor. The Master was visibly shaken, his breathing shallow.

"Are you well, sir?" Claudio asked, trying to steady his teacher.

But Leonardo remained silent and distracted as he furiously rubbed the unseen pinpricks from his face.

Claudio allowed da Vinci some time to collect himself before asking the thousand questions chasing each other in his mind. "What did you see in there, sir?"

His old eyes were glazed over, and he appeared confused. "Indeed, what did I see?" responded Leonardo.

"Master da Vinci! What did you see?"

"I saw..." he paused and drew in a breath. "I saw a great light as bright as the sun. And within it I saw..."

The young student found it increasingly difficult to control his impatience. "Please, sir, this is very important. Perhaps, the most important discovery of our age."

"You have a curious knack for understatement, my young friend," said the Master.

Even in a daze, the old dog still has a capacity for sarcasm, thought Claudio.

"I saw faces and people and places," Leonardo whispered. "They seemed to be underwater...unclear. They were swirling, like the lights." He turned to look at the array and then back at Claudio. "That was what I saw." He exhaled. "Then you drew me out."

Claudio's mind reeled. He had seen and heard many strange things living a privileged life as a courtier in the House of Medici, but this was exotic and untried. He darted to look at the side and the back of the solid, copper chamber. There was no aperture, no opening or window.

People in the chamber, swirling like lights underwater? What did this mean? Was the Master seeing spirits? The questions flowed overwhelmingly into his mind like a river brimming its banks. Was this witchcraft? *Think logically, Claudio! Think as the Master taught you.*

"Master," Claudio began, trying hard to keep his voice even. "Suppose I were to investigate? Would it be possible for me to witness what you saw?"

Leonardo turned and stared for a moment beyond his student, deliberating. "I think that may be an excellent idea. You may have a greater capacity for the uneasy feeling it gave me upon entering."

Claudio felt both anticipation and fear after hearing the Master's last comment. He was about to experience something from which others would run. Anyone else would have deemed the chamber an instrument of the devil and believed that they were witches. Was he in his right mind to risk going in? He swallowed his fear and prepared himself for his foray into the unknown.

"Now, my young friend, not too long," said the Master. "I will try to hold fast."

He walked to the edge of the chamber threshold with his dazed teacher in tow. Da Vinci took Claudio's arm, and the younger man inhaled. Then he mustered his courage and moved forward.

When he plunged his face into the array, he felt as though his skin was being pulled by a thick liquid. He could breathe as usual, but his senses were so heightened that his breathing was abnormally accelerated. The tingling on his skin was uncomfortable, but it was nothing he could not tolerate.

There was a bright light, and then the swirling began. A few moments into the aperture, he had managed to adjust his vision so that he could properly see his surroundings. Faces of strangers and images of strange places collapsed into each other in endless currents of color. Unknown things, clearly visible, yet translucent, swirled in an eddy and then disintegrated before his eyes. He likened it to having a giant, overly diluted palette of watercolors twisting and turning, the colors running into one another, creating new ones, and then disappearing only to begin all over again. The vision before him was fearsome, yet compelling.

Claudio felt a tug on his arm. Though he hesitated, he knew that it was time to exit the chamber. Da Vinci pulled harder, and Claudio conceded.

Somehow, in his heart, the young man already knew that this thing..., that this event would lead to things as of yet, unimaginable.

Chapter Ten

As the weeks went by, the two scientists continued to observe, test, and evaluate the powers of the array, sketching and recording each event. Claudio would steal away from the palace at the first hint of the rising sun and not return from the abbey until the moon was high in the heavens.

A particularly startling discovery was that the further one ventured into the brightest light, the clearer the swirling pictures became. This discovery itself was fantastic enough, yet the visions that it yielded were even more overwhelming.

Leonardo and Claudio could tell by the visions that the people in the eddies were odd.

"Make certain you note how they dress." Da Vinci wagged a finger at Claudio's journal one afternoon after a round of observations. "Men sporting odd long pantaloons, women with skirts above the knee...and their hair is strangely short. The surroundings—no cobblestone in the street, the architecture is puzzling. Everything is different and each surge bears images, unlike the other ripples in the strings." Leonardo wanted every unknown detail recorded, but some of the places they saw, they recognized.

"Master, would you like me to note the familiarity of Florence that was visible in one of the eddies?" asked Claudio. "And the carriage moving without a horse, sir?"

"Oh, yes that—blast, if I find the scoundrel who stole my plans!" bellowed Leonardo, waving a fist in the air.

Claudio listened to his teacher as he paced, his hands folded behind his back, thinking aloud as he conjectured. "The people who appear and disappear in the chamber's swirls— they bear no swords and have no horses. If I were to hazard an educated guess at what this all means, my boy, I would say that the swirling points are shadowy glimpses into another epoch. Of different times, different places, if you will—the surging filaments may be moments in time. What time, though, is a mystery," Da Vinci mused as Claudio recorded.

In time, the visions, which only lasted moments, became clearer and sufficiently stable so that what appeared to be another world or age was playing out before their eyes, oblivious to their observers. Although they could not rationalize these visions, da Vinci and his student believed that they were, in fact, taking place. They were not spirits. These were people going about their business, playing out before them in an endless cycle of churning events. The lightning experiment's results were there, before their eyes.

But what would they do with this discovery? And, more importantly, how would the phenomenon be received by Leonardo's patrons? He would not be surprised if they were tried as witches. This discovery might be mistaken for the work of the devil—dark forces on the brink of being unleashed into the population of Florence and ultimately the world. It would not help that da Vinci was already looked upon unfavorably by most of the Church because of his research.

In the end, they decided that perhaps it would be best if they kept the entire affair a secret for a time. At least until they could conduct more experiments. Why, for example, did they not see their hands or arms in the chamber when they entered the strings?

And perhaps more importantly, what would happen to them if they stepped through?

~

Sitting at his workspace in Leonardo's abbey workshop, the young Count revised the copious notes in his journal. By the time he had finished his last entry, he had decided that once Leonardo returned from his audience with the Duke, he would present his teacher with a possible answer to their quandary. No sooner had he finished the thought when da Vinci came barreling in and he was not in good spirits. Cussing and sputtering his anger, it was apparent that he had had words with Duke Giuliano de Medici.

"Of all the short-sighted, narrow-minded, obtuse, and controlling—" he stopped when his eyes found Claudio at his desk.

"Oh, good evening my boy," da Vinci muttered with a side glance. "The Duke is displeased that I have not finished his latest commission—the portrait of his niece, Clarice. What a complete waste of time. To be forced to paint the portrait of a spoiled, insolent, adolescent brat when I should be unravelling the mysteries of Time." His voice thundered in the cavernous room as he worked himself into a fury.

Claudio knew exactly what da Vinci meant. Clarice, the Duke's niece, was a tiresome sort and completely absorbed in herself. *Now. Ask him now while he is already angry...his reaction cannot be much worse than this.*

"Speaking of your latest discovery, sir, I wonder if I could make a request." Claudio fumbled for words as Leonardo listened, out of breath from his rant.

After a moment's consideration, da Vinci halted. "Yes...yes, go on."

Claudio cleared his throat. "I believe firmly that it would be a prudent time to explore the array completely."

The old man blinked, found a chair, and sat, intrigued.

"That is...I would respectfully suggest that I, or we, if you prefer, fully enter the chamber and investigate the moving portraits. Would you not agree, sir?"

Leonardo was silent. He drew his hand to his mouth and looked beyond his young apprentice. Claudio knew that the old man was thinking. His mind was racing, mulling over the multitude of unknowns, variables, and contingencies associated with this new and unknown science.

"My boy," he said finally. "You may find this hard to believe, but yes, I have thought about entering the chamber. I have also thought about the danger that would be associated with such an action. This is not a model or a sculpture. It is real and capricious and, in my opinion, ominous. I wonder, my young apprentice, if you have considered all the facts before proposing to enter it."

He folded his hands over his rather large belly and looked at the floor of his workshop, as though he could find the answer there. Claudio thought about how wise he looked at that moment. The young Count trusted his Master, and he knew that whatever Leonardo decided that it would be the correct choice.

"I cannot say that I know what will transpire, for I am not a seer, however I do know that nothing is gained without some form of risk. That, my boy, is true, not only for this, but for most things worth gaining in life." The old man shifted his weight on the stool and stroked his beard. "I say, yes, my young friend. We proceed. However, I will go first...alone."

"Of course, sir, as you wish." Claudio was thrilled to the core with anticipation. "But if you please, Master, upon your return, may I have the opportunity to enter as well?"

"Certainly...if I come back, that is." Leonardo was almost hesitant.

Claudio did not know what to make of da Vinci's apprehensive tone. If Leonardo was uneasy about entering the chamber, then perhaps it was best if Claudio insisted on going first. He could not bear to think that something could happen to his teacher. If he should be harmed—or worse, perish in the chamber—then, the world would lose a great man.

"Master, begging your pardon," he said, "but would it not be best if I went in first?"

Da Vinci shook his head. "No, no. I will not hear of it. I am old, and you have your whole life ahead of you. A bright young mind such as yours is needed, for our future's sake. And besides," he added gruffly, "I could not forgive myself if you were harmed on my account. No, Claudio. I will go first."

Once the two scientists had discussed the time limit allowed in the array, and were prepared, they proceeded to the inner laboratory where the chamber was located. Without speaking, Claudio and da Vinci strode to the structure. Though anxiety was abundant, their trust in each other was stronger and did not require words. Teacher and student turned to each other, simultaneously grasped the door, and swung it wide open.

~

Before them, the strings danced in an endless spiral of color. The swirls twisted continuously in and out of focus. Shadows of people, places, and things melted and swam into each other like a turbid lake of unceasing experiences. The bright circle of light in the middle was as intense as the sun, though its intensity had decreased in the weeks since its inception.

Claudio observed Leonardo as they stood at the chamber threshold. He looked wise, yes, learned, yes, but also old and vulnerable. Would the Master be able to withstand whatever might occur? There really was no question as to who should venture into the unknown first—it would be Claudio. It had to be. All of these thoughts reeled through Claudio's mind in mere seconds.

He had made up his mind. Impulsively, he pushed Leonardo aside. With a deep breath and a sprint, he stepped into the chamber. The last thing he heard before the spirals took him was da Vinci crying, "No!"

Thousands of unseen needles pricked his skin. So brilliant and blinding was the light at the center that he had to cover his eyes. The sensation of dull pins was not painful, but uncomfortable and intense. With a hand shielding his eyes, he started to move to the center, and the spirals decreased as well as the light. But what? There was an opening directly in front, another door. As he moved further into the chamber, he could feel the pull on his body increase, the pins and needles sensation became stronger, washing over him.

He tried to steady himself, holding his hand up to his eyes to check for burns. His skin was unharmed, but the burning sensation intensified. It was painful, but he could tolerate it. He turned his head to look behind him and decided that the chamber opening looked intact. Once more, he turned to walk to the other side, his movements slow.

The opposite side was pulling him, the force attracting him by means of some unseen power. Claudio looked around and wondered what happened to all the people in the spirals. How could they be there and then not there? Had they been banished by some hidden force? He felt the energy tearing at him, as though his skin was being pulled from his bones. His heart raced, and his breath was shallow. It was time to abandon this quest and go back.

Not daring to venture to the other side of the white light, he could only imagine the fate he would suffer. Feeling defeated, the young pupil braced himself for the uncomfortable sensation of stepping back. Claudio covered his eyes and turned, aiming for the bright light in the middle.

When Claudio stepped back into the room, his teacher was still bellowing for him not to go in, still shouting, *no!* and still trying to recover his balance. Leonardo's eyes were like saucers when Claudio sprinted back into the room, trying to steady himself as his eyesight adjusted to the evening light.

"Claudio, are you quite well? Are you harmed?" cried the old man, rushing to him, clutching his arms. He roughly felt Claudio's limbs to make certain he was intact.

Claudio checked his skin for burns, but there were none. "No, sir, I am not harmed." But his head pounded. He fell to one knee to regain equilibrium, and his whole body ached as though he had been in a sword fight with three men.

"Well, in that case, what in the name of Hades did you think you were doing?" Leonardo roared, nearly, lifting himself off the floor in anger. "I told you that I would enter the chamber, and you directly disobeyed me. You are a very fortunate, young man, that you came back alive. And then, no sooner do you enter, but you hastily reappear. How did you turn round so quickly?"

Claudio furrowed his brow and rubbed his forehead. "Begging your pardon, sir, but I was in the chamber for a while."

"But no, you came right back again." Leonardo crinkled his forehead, his fury forgotten. "Why, I...I barely had a chance to steady myself after you almost knocked me over, and then you were here."

Once Claudio had regained his bearings, he told his teacher everything—each minute detail and sensation. Leonardo recorded the experience, writing feverishly. But still, they were stumped by the inconsistencies in the passage of time. Could Claudio have imagined that so much time had passed? And the pulling sensation—was that a by-product of the great amount of power held in the chamber? The two men delved into the possibilities, but with no relevant knowledge to draw on, they finally postponed their studies.

After agreeing that adjustments needed to be made to the array before they could investigate further, they decided speculation needed to wait for another day.

Claudio rode Spirit back to Florence late that evening, preferring a gentle stride to his usual gallop, deep in thought about the day's events at the abbey. He and Leonardo would have to continue to explore the power of the chamber, but for now, he needed rest.

Exhaustion was overtaking him, yet his mind still raced from his experiences in da Vinci's studio. The investigation of the chamber, and their experiments—it all added up to a whirlwind of thoughts rattling about in his mind. The closer he got to the palace, the more his thoughts shifted from the frenzy of the past weeks to his mother. He did not look forward to running into her.

Claudio was born a privileged child, the only child of the Count and Countess Moro. His parents, Giacomo and Maria, were closely allied with one of the most powerful and wealthy families in Italy, the Medici of Florence. Lorenzo de Medici or "Lorenzo the Magnificent," as he was referred to by his court, prided himself on being a great patron of the arts and wished for artists such as Botticelli, Raphael, and Michelangelo to flourish, but his business and position kept him constantly occupied. Instead, Claudio's father was entrusted with endowing healthy patronages to promising artists in and around Florence on Lorenzo's behalf.

Young Claudio had forged an instant friendship with the artist commissioned by his father, and Leonardo became Claudio's teacher and mentor. When Count Giacomo passed away, Leonardo became as close to a second father as any man could be to a grieving youth, sometimes to the chagrin of the Countess. Countess Maria had become particularly unbearable lately, because of Claudio's constant absence and his association with 'that insane old man.' He recalled their most recent conversation and braced himself for more of the same.

Upon arriving at the stables, Claudio handed Spirit off to a stable boy and darted for the palace, entering through the courtyard. It was very late. As he passed courtiers in the corridors, he nodded politely or bowed, depending on their title. Most of the courtiers were tolerable with the exception of a few. Unfortunately, the handful that were intolerable were the closest to the Duke. Namely, his niece, Clarice, his nephew, Bruno, and that pompous sycophant, Enzo, who was usually riding in Bruno's wake. They had all been friends at one time. Claudio was still associated with them, but the two had become so superficial in their thinking that they had become boring, even irritating.

Since he had begun studying with da Vinci, his indulgent days in the palace—hunting, studying languages and noble sport such as perfecting his skills with the foil—had all become shallow and without substance. He had discovered an entirely new world of thought and knowledge that he had never known. His mother saw otherwise, though, and seized every opportunity possible to tell him that he was wasting his time.

The young Count rushed up the winding marble stairs, passed the walls covered in frescoes and tapestries, to the courtiers' private apartments. Upon approaching the ornately decorated doors, he forced himself to be cheerful. He entered and heard the gentle sound of the harpsichord.

"Good evening, Mother," he said pleasantly, peering into the music room.

The Countess sat poker-straight at the instrument. It was one of her sources of solace, besides her son, since the death of her beloved husband, Giacomo. She paused for an instant, then continued to play.

"Good evening, Claudio...and where have you been since breakfast?" Claudio knew she was feigning ignorance.

"I have been at Master Leonardo's study at Galluzzo. You knew that, Mother."

She paused her piece and turned to him with a glare. "At dinner, the Duke asked me where my son was. Would you like to speculate what I responded?"

"Not really," he answered, his tone flat. He yawned as he removed his jacket.

"First, I apologized on your behalf and conveyed your regrets at not being able to attend...once more. And then I told him the truth. That you were with da Vinci." Her tone indicated increasing irritation.

"Good for you. And what did His Grace say?" asked Claudio. He strode calmly to the decanter and poured himself a glass of wine.

"The Duke wishes for you to begin your apprenticeship in the Banker's Guild." Her voice increased in volume.

He gulped down a mouthful of wine and shook his head. "I cannot do that."

"For heaven's sake, Claudio—the position is guaranteed."

Countess Maria stood up from the harpsichord and walked over to her son. "It was bought and paid for by our family's loyalty to the Medici. Stop wasting your time and think about your responsibilities and your father's wishes." She softened her tone, her expression taking on a gentler appearance. "My dear, it is also time for you to think seriously about taking a wife."

"Mother, you have not an inkling about my work with da Vinci. It is new and greatly promising...and I have no intention of taking a wife at the moment." Claudio rubbed his eyes, which ached for sleep, then drew in an impatient breath. "You recall, Mother, we agreed, I would study with Master da Vinci for a year or two and then I would take my place with the Medici."

"It has been well over two years, my son and really, Claudio, people are beginning to talk. Duchess Filiberta has confided in me. You are a Count—you must start acting like one."

"Yes, I know. You never let it slip my mind for long." He set his empty glass on the side table and waited on the settee for her to continue.

The Countess observed her son. He clearly took after his father, dark and strong with all the fire of his Sicilian Moorish heritage. But as generous and loving as he was, Claudio could also be stubborn, with an unwavering mind of his own.

"You know, my dear," she said, "I hear from the other ladies at the court that Clarice de Medici is positively smitten with you. She would be a good match for you. And she is a lovely girl."

"Mother, please...I am too tired to continue to spar with you in this matter. Can we please postpone the issue until tomorrow?" Claudio sighed, rubbing his temples.

"As you wish my dear," she agreed, hesitantly. "But at least indulge me in this one request. Why do you and Bruno not go and have a little fun tomorrow night? There is to be a banquet in the Great Hall. The heads of all the major Medici banks are invited. Please attend. I want you to enjoy the company of your friends and fellow courtiers." Her voice held genuine concern. "Master da Vinci has been keeping you laboring at that workshop until all hours, and I dare say you are looking positively ragged. You do need to enjoy yourself from time to time, am I not right?"

Claudio allowed his head to drop onto the back of the sofa and let out a defeated sigh. He was beginning to soften.

"Please, do this for me," Maria pouted. "And for your father."

He looked intently at his mother, hands folded across his chest. He should let his mother win this one, otherwise, there would be no living with her. Perhaps he could satisfy her wishes. There would be no harm in enduring an hour or two with friends, and he could always go back to the abbey after dining.

His brows set in a straight line as he answered in a deceptively ominous tone. "Very well, Mother. I will agree to attend dinner at court with Bruno tomorrow, if you will please stop vexing me." His demeanor softened at his mother's beaming, and he leaned over to give her a kiss on the cheek.

A broad smile crept across his chiseled face, as his eyes took on a boyish quality. He gave her a narrow side glance, which prompted a rich laugh from the Countess, a full laugh that Claudio could not resist.

Perhaps, he thought, *I may even enjoy myself.*

Chapter Eleven

T he next day, in the palace kitchens, the cooks and maids were hard at work preparing for the evening's banquet dinner. When the Medici threw a banquet, not a florin was spared. Giuliano de Medici's guest list rarely varied. A handful of trusted courtiers made up his inner circle, but also present would be the Duke's business associates, guild leaders, and a variety of assorted parasites, who, were it not for their fawning flattery, would starve. The immediate family of the Duke was always present. Occasionally, they were joined by artists and entertainers such as Raphael and that rather strange old man, da Vinci.

Elisa avoided the gathering after the wine began to flow. In fact, her only interest in these banquets was to catch a glimpse of one beautiful young nobleman named Claudio.

She had literally run into him a few weeks earlier in one of the palace corridors while she was carrying dirty crockery to the scullery. He had turned a corner at full speed and collided straight into her. His resulting graciousness had almost made her cry. The young maid was not accustomed to being spoken to so kindly by a noble.

With her bonnet tightly wrapped around her chin, and strictly avoiding eye contact, she was certain he had barely noticed her beyond helping her to pick up the dishes she had dropped. Surely, he had forgotten about the entire incident as soon as he bid her 'good evening' and went on to wherever he was going. But her heart still fluttered when she thought about it—*he said, 'good evening'*.

She sighed and dreamed of the beautiful Count while she scrubbed the cooking pots. *Count Claudio is so different from the rest of them*, she mused. He apologized to a scullery maid. She had never heard of such a thing, and when she told Caterina of the incident, she, too, was taken aback by his cordiality.

It was a far cry from that horrible Bruno. Bruno thought himself to be quite the ladies' man, and all the servants knew that he never overlooked an opportunity to demonstrate his power over women. He made it abundantly clear that he did not take kindly to refusals once he had made up his mind.

Occasionally, as she cleaned or cleared a table, she would steal a glance at her Count from a distance. He was often with Bruno and another minor courtier, Enzo. Bruno and Enzo were handsome youths, too, but their hearts were cold and their words harsh, to anyone not of their social standing. Their interactions with the servants were aloof and condescending. Not like Claudio.

Yet, she had no business even daydreaming such foolishness, that he might speak to her again one day. It was out of the question to speak to him unless she was spoken to first.

Elisa knew she was in an impossible position and hated to admit it to herself, but she secretly wished for another such encounter. Perhaps, this time, she would muster up the courage to break Caterina's rule and speak to him. However, despite her wishes, deep down the young maid knew that what she was thinking was ludicrous—the chance to truly converse with him would never happen.

"Elisa!" shouted Caterina impatiently, as she picked up her tray to return downstairs. "Elisa, really. Are you dreaming with your eyes open?"

"Oh, Caterina," Elisa snapped back to reality as she watched Caterina bustle away. "My apologies."

She resigned herself to her chores and focused on preparing the table for the meal.

In the great hall, she had set the last place at the head table, when a familiar laugh resounded from the grand staircase. The laughter was followed by the robust voice of the young courtier, her exquisite Count Claudio. He was in the company of his friends, Bruno and Enzo, as all three swiftly descended from the upstairs apartments and engaged in a raucous conversation.

Elisa had carelessly discarded her bonnet upon her shoulders while she worked, revealing her hair and face. She turned to look at him and, without thinking, she flashed a magical smile to her young Count.

This spontaneous, innocent, and innocuous act would change her life forever.

Claudio was the first to catch sight of the girl. He halted on the landing and intuitively smiled back with a polite nod. He remembered her. She was the one he had almost knocked over as he was rushing through the palace on his way to the abbey. He recalled how immensely shy she was, so much so that she avoided his gaze completely while he helped her clean up the mess.

The young Count had noted her fine-looking features at the time, but now he realized the full measure of her beauty. This girl was as naturally lovely as she was unpretentious. Honey-brown hair and the face of an angel—but her smile was the thing, the delicate smile that graced her fair face...it was absorbing and enigmatic.

The conversation behind him stopped abruptly as the other two men turned to see what became of their companion. Enzo craned his neck around the pillar to see what had riveted Claudio's attention, with Bruno not far behind.

When the girl grasped that all eyes were on her, she snapped out of her reverie and quickly adjusted her bonnet. She tucked her hair back underneath it, and tied the bands tightly around her chin. Rushing back to her chores, she shifted the dishes about in her tray and quickly scooped them up to leave.

But like hyenas hunting their prey, both Enzo and Bruno intercepted her before she could take a second step back toward the kitchens. Anxious and trembling, with her eyes downcast, she tried to bypass the two men, but each time she moved right or left, they matched her steps, and stood in front to prevent her flight. Her face was red with shame. She finally spoke. "Begging your pardon, my lords," she stammered. "I...I must get back to the kitchens."

"The kitchens, my pet," cooed Bruno, drawing a deep breath. "But what does a lovely flower such as yourself have to do in the kitchens? Stay with us. Better yet, you should join us for food and drink later tonight. I am sure you have not tasted wine as sweet as that which flows from the Duke's cellars." He smiled, but his grey eyes were cold and watery.

The two courtiers howled with laughter, but Claudio saw nothing humorous in this folly.

"Truly, you belong not in a kitchen, my pet, but on the arm of a nobleman," said Enzo, taunting her with an exaggerated bow. "You are new here, I believe, and quite exquisite. I have never seen you before." His aquiline nose reminded her of a hawk's beak, preparing to tear into her flesh.

They circled her as a pair of wolves would surround a

wounded deer. The girl stood as still as the palace statues and tried desperately to maintain her composure. Her downcast eyes welled up with tears.

"If you please, my lords, I must return to my duties. I am... begging you, my lords..." Her voice quivered. Obviously mortified to the core, she could not bring herself to look at the two noblemen who were ogling her as if she were a piece of meat.

"Not so fast, my delicious young maid! I implore you." Bruno let his gaze wander up and down her body lazily before sliding it up to her face. "Stay. I have never had the good fortune of making your acquaintance." He slowly untied her bonnet and slipped it off her head. Her lovely hair spilled out of the cap and framed her delicate face. "Well, well, what have we here, Enzo?" Bruno whispered hungrily as he wound a lock of her hair around his finger and sniffed it. The girl stiffened and closed her eyes as if it would make it all go away. He gathered the tendrils that lay on her shoulders and gripped them in his hand, pulling her face toward his. "You are simply too delicious to ignore."

"Yes, she is quite lovely, do you not agree, Claudio?" Enzo grinned, his eyes washing over the maid.

Claudio knew where this was going. Watching this girl suffer made his stomach turn. She was obviously innocent, and there was nothing Bruno enjoyed more than increasing his number of conquests. If someone did not act soon, Bruno would humiliate her.

"Hands off my woman, you bloody rogues," Claudio said, half-smiling. With determination, he stepped between the girl and Bruno. As he threw his hands up in an exaggerated motion, he was not exactly certain what his next words would be. "The girl is mine. I...I claimed her some time ago. Now, be off with you both, fools!" He casually waved them off and feigned laughter as he grabbed her bonnet from Bruno's hands. Claudio turned to the girl so only she could see. He gave her a quick wink and handed her back her bonnet. Then he took hold of her wrist and gently squeezed it.

Claudio was not surprised when Bruno was taken aback at the news of his latest conquest. He could imagine what the Duke's nephew was thinking. This innocent-looking creature, one of Claudio's women? He was usually interested in the more earthy types. The sort of woman usually kept by the kinds of company Claudio preferred—guild members and artists—they were not from the nobility, but neither were they scullery maids.

"My sincerest apologies, my friend. I was not aware that she was yours," drawled Enzo, leering at the maid.

Bruno added, "I thought you too busy assisting that old man to have time for such frivolous activities." As Bruno whispered his bane, he drew closer to her and took in another deep breath.

Claudio saw her swaying unsteadily and, without thinking, he drew closer to her and balanced her trembling body against his. Her breathing was shallow, and though she was deeply afraid, Claudio knew that she dared not walk away from her tormentors. If she did, she would unquestionably be accused of disobedience and would suffer the consequences. "Very well then, Claudio," said Bruno, roughly grabbing her other hand. "If she is your woman, what is her name?"

At this, Claudio stood dumbfounded. Silence hung thickly in the air.

"Begging your pardon, my lord," the young beauty meekly interjected, as she turned to Claudio and curtsied deeply. "Your servant, Elisa, must return to work. I fear that I am quite behind in my chores. I remain his until later."

Claudio smiled. "Yes, of course, Elisa." He nodded to her with authority, hoping that he sounded convincing. "I shall see you hence at the usual place."

Claudio turned to Bruno. "Release her," he ordered.

Elisa turned to Bruno who still had a firm grasp on her other wrist. She nodded toward her hand, and reluctantly he let go. Claudio knew Bruno was accustomed to having what he wanted. And it was obvious he wanted this girl. Even after their little act, it was unlikely Claudio had convinced him that he had any claims on Elisa.

The maid gathered up her dishes and with a quick parting glance at Claudio, she hurried out of the great hall. Claudio watched her leave. How graciously this young woman had handled the entire distasteful incident. He vowed that he would seek her out in the morning and ask forgiveness on behalf of his friends.

Bruno and Enzo watched her leave, too, but Claudio was confident his friends' thoughts were much less valiant.

Chapter Twelve

All through dinner, Claudio was preoccupied with catching a glimpse of the servant girl. Craning his neck to survey the expanse of the great dining hall, he searched, but to no avail. She was nowhere. Instead, he was forced to listen to the giddy ramblings of the silly girl sitting to his right.

Claudio had been strategically seated beside Clarice de Medici. He was sure this was his mother's handiwork; to spur a connection between them—to encourage them to engage in inane conversation about other pretentious aristocrats in Lucca, Venice, or Milan, who were probably, at that very moment, having the same irritating gossipy conversation.

"But now, my lord, enough about me," Clarice finally breathed. "I have heard so much about you from your dear mother." She casually placed her hand over his and squeezed it ever so slightly. As always, she was impeccably dressed. Her deep burgundy bonnet was held securely in place by a decoratively beaded ribbon intertwined through her braids. The rich crimson of the headpiece further accentuated the pale, waxy complexion on her pointed face. Directly across from them,

Bruno and Enzo were already on their way to drunken rowdiness.

So, it *was* mother's work, Claudio thought, fuming. He turned to make eye contact with her, hoping she could see his irritation, but Countess Maria was deeply engaged in conversation with Duke Giuliano and his wife.

Claudio surveyed the hall. Lively discussion was all around him. The men exchanged views on the Medici enterprises and the audacity of the French invasions of 1494, while the women were more concerned with the latest fashions and the newest trends in fabric. There were quite a few nobles in attendance this evening at the opulent table, decked out with sumptuous dishes for them to enjoy.

It would be fitting to pay a visit to the Duke and his wife before I depart, which, cannot be too soon, Claudio thought. It may also give me a chance to speak to Mother about taking liberties with the seating arrangements.

"If my lady Clarice will excuse me, I should like to make my salutations to Duke Giuliano and to Duchess Filiberta before the meal is done." Claudio began to rise.

"Who are you looking for, Count?" Bruno shouted. "Are you looking for the maid?" He and Enzo collapsed with laughter.

"Quiet, Bruno," hissed Clarice. "Really, brother, at times you are most difficult to indulge." She turned her attention back to Claudio, squeezing his arm. "Do not be gone long, my dear."

Claudio almost cringed as he nodded his assurances to Clarice, to which she offered a satisfied smile through her thin lips. He bowed, pulled himself away, and circumvented the court musicians to make his way through the crowded hall to the head table.

As Claudio traversed the magnificently appointed room, he felt Bruno's eyes follow him. He bowed deeply to Giuliano and

Filiberta, both in regal splendor—but not before he glanced sideways to his mother with narrowed eyes.

"If it pleases Your Grace," Claudio said, holding his bow, "may I take this opportunity to bid Your Grace Giuliano and Duchess Filiberta a good evening?"

"Good evening, young Claudio," said Giuliano.

Claudio winced at the frostiness in his voice and eyes.

"You wait until the middle of the meal to acknowledge us?"

Rising, Claudio inclined his head as an admission of guilt. "My sincere apologies, Your Grace. You see, I was captivated in conversation by a certain, Clarice." He turned his head toward the young lady who immediately presented a toothy smile whilst fanning herself. "And I simply could not tear myself away."

The Duke followed Claudio's gaze. "I understand perfectly," he grimaced. "Tell me, young man, where have you been these last weeks?" He arched a brow. "Your mother tells me you are anxious to apprentice with one of my master accountants. She claims you are brilliant in whatever task you set your mind to. Is she correct?"

Claudio shot a glance at his mother who, in response, turned her attention to the intricacies of the stitching in her gown. "My mother gives me too much credit in terms of cleverness, Your Grace. But I am an apprentice, of sorts, already... with Master Leonardo da Vinci. I am involved with him in the study of Art and Nature."

Claudio's mother let out an almost imperceptible groan.

The Duke nodded. "Ah yes, Master Leonardo. We have commissioned his work from time to time. He is very skilled... but rather odd." Giuliano paused. "Nevertheless, you must begin thinking seriously of your future. Pursuing the Arts is all well and good for a time, but our business is wealth." He leaned forward in his chair. "If Clarice is to marry, she will marry a man loyal to the Medici empire. We require loyalty and attention to the business at hand. Do you understand, young Claudio?" His final words were more of a command than a question.

Filiberta, silent until now, spoke up. "My lord, must you take such a harsh tone with the boy? Certainly, he will come around to assisting you in administering your empire. Will you not, Claudio?"

Claudio glanced at his mother. He was fully prepared to let the Duke know what he thought of his business and of Clarice, but his concern for his mother's welfare was more powerful than his urge to rebel.

He bowed to Filiberta. "My lady is very kind and most indulgent." He turned back to Giuliano. "I understand perfectly, Your Grace. Rest assured that I shall seek out the guidance of the master accountant as soon as my work with Master da Vinci is complete. It shall not be long, now." He bowed perfunctorily. "If Your Graces will excuse me, I bid you a good night. I must return to the lovely Clarice."

He backed away to a respectable distance, then turned on his heel and returned to his table. *Why can I not control my own destiny?* Breathing deeply to check his anger, he sat down once more next to Clarice...at least he would not need to speak as much.

"The Countess tells me that you are studying the art of painting with that strange old man. Tell me, is Leonardo da Vinci as eccentric as they say he is?" She squeezed Claudio's arm, leaned in close and whispered in his ear. "Does he really have cadavers hanging in his workshop?" A silly giggle escaped her.

"My dear Clarice, whatever you may have heard, I am sure it has been greatly exaggerated." He gingerly removed his arm from her grasp. "Master Leonardo is a brilliant man. He is not only a gifted painter but an accomplished scholar of Nature.

He envisions things in his mind that neither you nor I could even imagine."

Her ridiculous comments were now more irritating than usual.

"Claudio, you take that old man, da Vinci, too seriously... and yourself, for that matter." Annoyance and disapproval were evident in her tone, as she feigned an exaggerated pout. "Why...have a look at my brother, for instance. He does not take anything seriously. Yet, nothing is taken from him...he is not punished...he is still a courtier, still of high lineage." She sighed and looked back at Claudio, batting her eyes. "And you, my dear Count, shall take your place in a Medici bank. I will see to that for you, if you so desire."

"Many thanks to you, my lady." Claudio bowed his head. "I am certain that you and the Duke are most generous. Perhaps, in the near future, when I finish my studies with da Vinci."

"You cannot be serious." Bruno interjected. "My sister has just offered to secure a place for you in the Medici empire and you throw it back in her face? I thought you an intelligent man, Moro. How many men would take your place at this moment?"

"Believe me, Bruno, I intended no such offense toward your charming and generous sister." Claudio noticed the people nearby falling silent. "Clarice's, and indeed, your family's kindness toward mine is never taken for granted."

"Ah, but indeed you seem to be preoccupied of late, my friend," said Bruno, his face a sneer. "Very busy with some task or other, that is, quite frankly, taking up much of your time. Is it your little 'friend' or something else? Come now, Claudio, do tell us. We will keep your secret." He picked the meat out of his teeth and sat back in his chair.

"No, Bruno...I cannot. It is something...that I am unable to discuss," replied Claudio somewhat frustrated, taking another sip of his wine.

Bruno turned an exaggeratedly surprised face to Enzo and they burst out laughing, their guffaws drawing more stares from the surrounding court. "What? You cannot discuss it?" cried Enzo. "What could be so secretive that you are not able to speak of it over dinner with your friends?"

"Master Leonardo wishes me not to, and I must respect his wishes."

"I shall remind you that I am the Duke's nephew." Bruno leaned into Claudio's face. "If I wish you to tell me, then you shall."

"Bruno—stop!" cried Clarice, looking around at the staring guests. "Be quiet and stop maligning Claudio. What do you care about it, anyway?"

"There should be no secrets in the court," he replied, pouring himself another glass of wine. "If there are secrets, there is something hidden. Anything that is hidden is a threat."

"I assure you there is no threat to anyone," upheld Claudio, teeth clenched. The two men stood up, chairs clattering, their fists curled tight. The great hall fell quiet in anticipation.

Clarice took Claudio's arm and Enzo grasped Bruno's. "Claudio...please," whispered Clarice. "Please sit."

Claudio looked at his mother, at the Duke, and then back at Bruno. "It is a work of art...for the Duke. It is nothing more." He hated lying, but under the circumstances, he could either lie or come under suspicion for treason.

"See that it is not, my friend," Bruno replied, sitting down. "For the Medici family has many tentacles. We are far-reaching and our blood binds us together. We will all have our fun, but in the end, we have our obligations...to our families as well as ourselves."

"Well said, my brother." Clarice raised her glass. "To His Grace, the Duke of Florence."

At the head table, Countess Maria chimed in. "To His Grace." She glared at Claudio.

Claudio reluctantly raised his glass as well. "To the Duke." The hall joined in while Claudio remained preoccupied with thoughts of his own.

Chapter Thirteen

Distracted and anxious for the remainder of the evening, Elisa was thankful that the rest of her tasks were relegated to the kitchens. The challenge of maintaining her composure after what happened in the great hall was overwhelming, especially when pretending that all was well in front of Caterina.

The moments dragged on as she completed her drudgery until finally, the time came for her to return to her chambers in the cellars of the palace. With candle in hand, she made her way down the spiral basement steps. The little nook that she shared with Caterina was sparse but clean. The few meager sticks of furniture and straw cots occupying the small space were orderly and kept with pride—the walls whitewashed and scrubbed. Elisa placed the candle on the table beside her bed and loosened her bodice. As she scanned her four walls, she came to the horrible realization that it would always be like this. This was her life; she had no hope of anything more.

Because of whom she was, she would never be able to protect herself. There would always be someone who would take advantage of a girl, a poor servant, and she would always be defined, not by the person she was inside, but by who she served. She would forever be at the mercy of others.

How could life be so unfair as to allow everything to so few and give the many, so little? Everything that she had feared would happen to her had taken shape that evening, in the form of Bruno de Medici. *It will always be like this,* she thought as she hung her head to cry.

Though she was weary, sleep was still eluding Elisa when Caterina entered the tiny room. The degradation she had suffered at the hands of the noblemen troubled her. With the events of the night playing over and over again in her mind, she remained silent, not wanting to speak of it. Instead, she feigned sleep. She knew that if she allowed herself to tell Caterina what happened, that her friend would surely become ill with worry. Elisa loved her too much to burden her, so she would keep it to herself and steer clear of the nobles.

"Sleep sound, my friend," Caterina whispered pulling the thin covers over Elisa, and quickly got herself to bed, oblivious to the evening's events.

Elisa's thoughts drifted back to her previous musings. For the young men that had so mercilessly taunted her, she had only feelings of disgust. Surely two more foul human beings had never drawn breath. But to Claudio, for defending her, she was grateful. Despite her profound embarrassment over the Count witnessing her being degraded in such a way, she was not surprised that he had stepped in to liberate her from what could have been a horribly inescapable experience. Truly, had he not been there, she would have feared for her honor. Bruno and Enzo would have done what they pleased with her, and there was nothing that she could have done about it.

But how could a servant possibly repay such a debt of gratitude?

As she lay in bed, she relived experiencing the touch of Claudio's hand firmly clutching her slender wrist as he pulled her away from Bruno and the instant that she looked into his face, those beautiful features unaware of their power. Even in her worst moment, she had felt a bewitching exhilaration when he touched her.

In the few short moments that she was close to him, despite her fear, she had memorized all that he was. But his most distinctive feature was his eyes, so dark and intense, his pupils almost indistinguishable. He was exquisite to look at, and she felt herself moved by his memory.

Yet better than that, Claudio had defended her when her station in life kept her from defending herself. Though she was nothing to him, he had intervened before Bruno's hand slid to the fasteners on her dress.

Of course, she was a silly girl for even contemplating that anything could come of the Count's act of kindness. It meant only that he took pity on her. Nonetheless, if she saw him again, she would discreetly thank the young Count for his abundant mercy. Elisa resolved to remember forever that, for a very brief moment in time, they had stood together, he swathing her hand with his own.

Chapter Fourteen

Following the dinner, Claudio left the dining hall as stealthily as possible. He was hoping that his absence would go unnoticed. Undoubtedly, Clarice would bore some other poor soul with her incessant chatter.

He hoped to see Elisa about the palace on his way to his apartments to ensure that she was well and had not suffered any injury. How could he have called Bruno and Enzo his friends? How could they even call themselves human, taking advantage of the poor girl, taunting and ridiculing her? It was unexplainable how some men were never able to progress beyond selfish indulgences.

With his thoughts constantly pulling back to Elisa, Claudio entered his apartments and prepared for bed.

"Bruno? Bruno, Enzo? Where in the devil are you?" hissed Clarice. Though the palace garden was one of the last places that her brother could be found, Clarice could not find him elsewhere. Shortly after the Duke had made his exit, Bruno had left the dining hall as well, most likely on the search for one of his women. She desperately needed to speak to him in private regarding Claudio. In a sense, she was pleased that her beautiful Count had departed the dinner early as this gave her the opportunity to pursue a quest of her own.

"Bruno." She paused. She was about to turn around and abandon her quest when she heard a grunt.

"What? What do you want?" gurgled a voice from beyond the shrubbery.

She darted in the direction of her brother's voice and found him behind a tall shrub, slumped over on a bench, obviously drunk. "There you are? Where have you been? I have been looking for you all night."

"Clarice, did it ever occur to you that perhaps I did not want to be found?"

"Oh, rubbish! Stop indulging yourself and listen." She sat down beside him, not even bothering to look at him. "You and Claudio have been friends for some time, have you not?"

"Hmph!" Bruno sneered. "We have. Although, I cannot say we have spent much time together of late...he has been...busy." He snickered from the side of his mouth. "I am willing to wager that he is involved in some clandestine behavior."

"That is entirely ridiculous." Clarice brushed the whole notion aside with a dainty sweep of her hand. "Did you see us sitting together tonight? Would he not make a positively beautiful husband?" She giggled. "Did you know, Bruno, that his mother related to me that she believes we are an impeccable match? And I whole-heartedly agree. Do you not?"

"Clarice, did you not see what happened between that idiot Moro and me this evening? We almost came to blows, for God's sake...are you blind?"

"Silence, Bruno! I will not hear of this nonsense any longer. The Count is an honorable gentleman."

His only answer was a splutter. "Hmph!"

"You both had too much to drink, that is all," she contin-ued. "You will be fast friends again in the morning—I am certain of it." And with that resolve in her mind, she returned to her probing. "Now, when he talks to you of me, what does he say?"

Bruno took a soberer expression. "Clarice, let him be. Why do you not find someone worthy of you?"

"What do you mean 'worthy of me'? He is a count and a courtier. He and his family have been loyal to the Medici since before our uncle was crowned Duke. Since before the exile."

"Yes, yes, I know...but of recent, he has changed and rather drastically. He is constantly preoccupied, and he has developed an arrogant and disapproving air about him. Ever since he began studying with that pathetic excuse for a painter, he will have very little to do with anyone at court. He has also become rather boring," Bruno drawled dryly, putting his hand to his heart, as if pretending to be deeply hurt. "So boring, in fact, that I have no interest in inviting him along on my hunt tomorrow. Enzo and I leave in the morning."

"You are fools, you and Enzo," said Clarice with a disgusted glare. "And you must curtail your wine and ale consumption, my brother, you are beginning to imagine things."

"I am not imagining things, sister," he retorted indignantly. "For good measure, I will tell you that besides being busy with da Vinci, he has also been very busy within the palace."

"What are you going on about?" Clarice rolled her eyes impatiently. "Stop talking in riddles and be out with it."

"Your Claudio has taken up with a scullery maid from our own palace—a lowly servant girl, the lowest of the low."

The words stunned Clarice. She glared at Bruno with profound fury in her eyes as her fists tightly clutched the sides of the bench. Could this be true? She thought a moment. Claudio had barely exchanged two words with her at dinner tonight. And he did appear completely preoccupied, not once commenting on her beauty. *I am Clarice de Medici—how dare he ridicule me in such a manner? And with a scullery maid!* Her mind reeled as she tried to stop herself from screaming with rage.

"Are you certain of this? Because if you are lying to me, Bruno, I will certainly—"

"You will certainly what?" he interrupted. "And I am not lying. Even I could not make up such a bizarre story as this."

She should have known that his aloofness had not been her fault. After all, she was the pride of the palace. In her mind, she knew that she was exquisite and sought after by any number of men in the court, yet Claudio would not even pretend to enjoy their conversation at dinner. She was of impeccable lineage and the niece of the Duke, skilled in playing a variety of musical instruments, educated in Latin literature and had studied the Church fathers among other things. Why was he having such difficulty falling in love with her? It was quite unacceptable.

Quivering with rage, Clarice's mouth worked for several seconds before she managed to speak. "Bruno, you must show me this...girl, who has caught his fancy," she hissed, distractedly squeezing at the pendant about her throat.

Then, a perfectly horrible thought came to her. A plan that would surely solidify the union between herself and the Count and banish all others from him. A plot that, if played right, would dispose of the servant and would place Claudio in her, Clarice de Medici's, debt forever. "Never mind, brother. I have another plan."

Chapter Fifteen

The next morning, Elisa awoke as usual to the sounds of bustling in the servant's quarters in the bowels of the palace. Caterina gently jostled her awake. Elisa pulled herself off of her tiny cot and quickly washed in her basin, still unable to rid herself of the troubling visions from the night before. Absentmindedly, she prepared her work area for her duties—another day of washing floors, collecting dishes from the Duke's servers and washing them, plucking fowl, and preparing breakfast, lunch, and dinner.

She climbed the stairs as she had thousands of times before to the exit adjacent to the main palace, to get to the well for fresh water. Once outside, it took a moment for her eyes to adjust to the morning sunlight, and when they did, she was doubtful if what she saw was real.

Count Claudio was not ten paces in front of her, sitting on the side of the water tub. He stood up and calmly waved. She noted that he was wearing riding pants and boots. He was most likely on his way to the stables to fetch a horse. She stared wordlessly across at him, her heart pounding.

"Good morning." He smiled and inclined his head in acknowledgment.

She spun around, wondering to whom he was speaking, but there was no one behind her. Suddenly realizing that he was there for her, she could not decide between sheer panic or unbridled joy—the two canceled each other out.

"My lord," was all Elisa could manage. This was no illusion. She bowed her head and curtsied deeply. "My lord, I..." she stammered, feeling her cheeks flush. "My lord will please allow me to express my gratitude to him for last evening." The words tumbled out of her mouth. "His mercy is plentiful and undeserved," she said, trying to hide her surprise.

The Count strode to her and took her hand, raising her up from her curtsy. Her hands felt like ice in his. "I shall not hear of it, Elisa," he said. "I should beg forgiveness on behalf of the company I was keeping last evening. Unfortunately, lord Bruno is not in the habit of being denied what he feels should be his. I would avoid him for a while if I were you...until you slip his mind and he goes on to his next object of desire."

She felt safer just listening to him.

"Very wise words, my lord." Elisa was finally able to breathe. She lifted her gaze up to his. "My thanks once again, my lord. Good day." She forced her gaze from his and gently pulled her hand away. Though his grasp was firm, he let go of her without hesitation. Reluctantly, she backed away to a respectful distance before turning to the well, after curtsying her final farewell.

"Wait," he called out to her. "Uh...do you live here? In the palace?"

Elisa stopped mid-step and turned to face him. "I do, my lord."

The courtyard was filling up with other servants and Elisa became increasingly aware that they were witnessing her talking with a courtier. Even amid the other servants, scullery maids were considered humble. She should not be seen speaking with him, though she was desperate to stay. If someone were to deem it unacceptable, she could be punished.

"Well then, perhaps I shall see you again?" Claudio walked toward her.

She took a step back. "As my lord wishes." Elisa could not stop her voice from betraying her unease.

"I assure you that I mean you no harm," said Claudio, matching her steps. "I understand that trusting me after last evening is difficult, but I rather think of myself as different from them." He smiled warmly, which allowed her to feel more at ease.

"Begging my lord's pardon, but I do trust him, it is just that when his—"

He shook his head and put his finger to her lips. "Please stop speaking to me as if I am not here. You may use 'you' when you speak to me. I promise it is all right."

Elisa paused, and then took a leap of faith. "Begging your pardon, my lord, but I do trust you. It is the others I mistrust, and frankly, fear as well." She hoped that she had not been too inappropriately direct.

"If Bruno or Enzo bother you again, I am certain that someone will assist you...or you may come directly to me."

Elisa could contain the truth no longer. Her voice was barely above a whisper. "My lord, my duties here in the palace must be carried out as I am told, notwithstanding the unwelcome advances of certain courtiers. Regrettably, I am quite powerless to defend myself against lord Bruno's attention. And with respect, you cannot be in all places at once."

Claudio's expression became serious. "Has this happened to you before, Elisa? Is that why you are so frightened?"

"No, my lord, quite the contrary, in fact." She looked up from the dusty courtyard and into Claudio's eyes. "My friend has taught me that pretty girls are very much at risk in the palace, by all manner of the men contained within. But we must suffer the consequences if we offend someone of your status."

Elisa shuddered at the thought of what would happen if she rejected Bruno. "If I refuse the advances of someone like my lord Bruno, he would be able to depict me in any light he wishes, no matter how outrageous. And of course, he is the Duke's nephew—no one will question his motives or his truthfulness. If I raise his ire, I could be in grave danger. I may be expelled from the palace and left to fend for myself, or worse... and what of Caterina? I cannot bear to think of her alone. It is in her character that she would come with me. And if that is so then who would take us in? We are not skilled, we have no guild—we have nothing."

She paused to collect herself. The words she spoke were bleak in their candor. "So, you see, my lord, I am at the mercy of the Duke and those around him. I fear there is no desirable outcome for me now that lord Bruno has caught a glimpse of me. It is only a matter of time and opportunity before I am once again at his mercy, and I am forced to yield to his wishes."

The Count listened absorbedly. Elisa tore her gaze from Claudio and looked around. All the servants in the courtyard were watching her and the young courtier. She must end the exchange or risk even further attention.

"Begging your pardon, my lord, I do not intend to be rude, but I must get back to filling the buckets." She held up the pails in her hands and gestured toward the well. "The dishes await me." She let the tiniest hint of a smile cross her lips as she glanced at Claudio.

"What is your family name?"

"I am called Elisa Beatrice de Povri, my lord—"

"Here," he said, holding out his hands. "Give me the buckets, and I shall fill them for you Elisa Beatrice de Povri." He took the heavy wooden pails, strode to the well wall, and put them under the water spout, pumping so enthusiastically that water sprayed over both of them.

"No!" she shouted, mortified at the attention he was drawing. "Begging your pardon, my lord." She pulled back, at once surprised by his persistence and recalling whom she was addressing. "I mean to say, sir, please do not disturb yourself—"

"Nonsense, Elisa. This is no bother at all." He slowed his pumping and adeptly filled the buckets with water. Once finished, he held up the containers with a broad smile on his face. "Ready," he announced and began walking toward the main house, easily hoisting them up in his strong hands.

She stepped in front of him, head bowed, and firmly took hold of the pails. "Please, my lord. This is not work for a noble." She tried to take the buckets from his hands. "I know my place, my lord. I thank you for your kind concern, but you need not worry about me. I will weather this somehow. I thank you again for helping me...your servant."

"Very well, but I am still your lord, as you say. You must do as I ask."

Elisa let go of the water vessels and peered at the ground as she was certain she had angered him. "Yes, my lord."

He set one down and lifted her chin, so their eyes met. A sly smile was playing on his lips.

At that moment, she felt time stand still. She could hear no birds singing, no water lapping against the well walls, no murmuring from the people around them going about their business.

"In that case, Elisa, you must allow me to carry these down to the kitchen for you. In addition, you must agree to see me again...wherever and whenever you please, of course...as long as it is soon."

Elisa bit her lower lip to ensure she was not dreaming. "My

lord, are you certain? With me...a scullery maid? And you, my lord...a count?"

Claudio raised an eyebrow, his eyes humorous and tender as he feigned offense. "Are you questioning the good judgment of a courtier, my lady?"

Elisa could not hold back a beaming smile. She felt her face flush with color. "My lord, I fear I must do your bidding, or I shall never leave this courtyard."

They burst into laughter, and in what felt like an instant, Elisa's quiet desperation became delight. He was gracious, and he was unbearably beautiful. In barely a moment, she felt a renewed hope at happiness—the weight of all her sadness had been lifted from her shoulders. His mere presence made her heart race, and now that he wanted to meet with her again—she could barely breathe.

"Come to the entrance of the palace gardens after the midday meal." He titled his head questioningly. "You should have a rest period then, yes?"

"I have, my lord."

"Good. Promise me that I will see you then, my lady. But I shall help you with these, now."

"You have my word," she promised, her feet barely making contact with the ground as she floated dreamily back to the palace. She was in awe. He addressed her not as a servant, but as a woman.

Minutes stretched into hours the rest of the morning, as Elisa went about her duties. When she had finished, she tore off her apron, adjusted her bonnet, and dashed to the garden, a paradise of shrubbery and florals usually enjoyed by the upper crust of Florentine society. She could not be gone long, as

Caterina would wonder where she was. The last thing she wanted was to worry her.

Elisa dashed from the palace and rounded the courtyard wall in a run. The cobblestones eventually gave way to white pebbles the closer she got to the garden entrance. That was when she caught a glimpse of him, leaning against the ancient wall surrounding the oasis in the city. He saw her and immediately stood straight awaiting her approach.

The Count had changed into a summer brocade vest with a simple white linen shirt underneath and wore his riding boots with his rapier sword sheathed in its scabbard. The summer heat intensified the pungent scent of the flowers: roses and oleander. She smelled their aroma, like exotic spice, all the way out to the pathway.

Once she was within an appropriate distance, she curtsied and bowed her head out of respect. "Good afternoon, my lord."

"Good afternoon to you, Elisa." He smiled charmingly as he took her elbow, raised her back to a standing position, and returned the bow. "You are particularly lovely this afternoon. Even more beautiful than this morning."

Her natural blush deepened to a crimson at the compliment. She paused for a moment, not knowing how to respond to such praise. "My lord is too kind and generous with his words."

"I speak only the truth," he said as he placed his hand once again, very gently, on her elbow to guide her into the garden. "I have a gift for you...I hope you like figs."

He took a handkerchief from his breeches' pocket and from it handed her three ripe figs. "I picked them myself on my way back from Master Leonardo's studio in Galluzzo."

Elisa's eyes lit up at the sweet treat, but she hesitated. How should she react to such attention? Why was he being so kind to her?

"You do not like figs?" Claudio asked, as she made no motion to take them.

"Begging my lord's pardon, but it is not every day that a count brings gifts to a kitchen servant," she said, surprising herself at her own honesty.

"I promise that this is not a trick. Truly, they are for you... as a treat."

"I will accept my lord's gift, but I only ask that he share them with me."

"And I will agree to share with you on one provision."

"Yes, my lord?"

"That you stop referring to me as 'my lord.'"

"But...what shall I call you, my lord...I mean...what does my lord, require...or I should say..." This, she thought, is a terribly awkward moment.

"There now, no need to panic, Elisa, simply call me by my name...Claudio. All my friends do."

A courtier calling a commoner friend? She was taken aback.

"I am your friend?" Elisa asked, bewildered.

"Yes, you are. Now, say my name," he ordered with a most endearing, crooked smile.

Her mind raced. Could this truly be happening, or was she imagining the entire day? Was she still asleep, dreaming about the Count coming to her defense from the night before?

"Elisa...please," he coaxed.

"Claudio." She laughed nervously and covered her face with her hands.

He threw his head back and let out a huge laugh. "Now, that was not so difficult, was it?"

"No...Claudio, it was not," she said, finally exhaling.

They walked to a marble bench under a clump of cypress trees, away from the hot Tuscan sun, and shared the figs while engaging in simple conversation. Claudio politely inquired about her day's events in the palace, and she, his, at times enduring awkward silences, but both knowing that silences did not matter much between new friends.

"...and then, to our utter surprise, we found Paolina in the laundry tub, singing loudly with a tankard of ale in her hand." She brought her hand up to stifle the giggles as she related the story. However, it was not long before Elisa rose to excuse herself. "I must reluctantly take my leave, Claudio...I need to return to my chores. There are many before the evening meal."

"May I walk you back to the palace?" he asked politely.

"I would like nothing more, but I must decline. I do not want to draw further attention to myself."

"Do you know, Elisa, I am willing to wager that any other servant would revel in such an opportunity, to be seen with a count?"

"Perhaps, I am not like any other servant," she replied, half-smiling.

His mouth twitched with amusement. "My lady speaks the truth, no doubt," he acknowledged. "You must promise me that you will grace me with your presence again soon."

She paused and shyly looked at this sweet young man. "It would be my honor, Claudio."

"Tomorrow evening, then. Here in the garden?"

"If it pleases my lord, after my evening duties." But her generous smile suddenly disappeared, as the images of yesterday's events pushed into her thoughts.

"What is wrong, Elisa?" Claudio asked, in a soothing tone.

"My lord, though I am honored to be in your company, I am afraid that the other courtiers will not look agreeably on our friendship." She stepped toward the trellis, wondering to herself what she was doing there. Instinctively, her arms crossed over her heart as she had caught a sudden chill, though the sun was straight overhead.

Claudio drew closer to her. "If you are concerned about

Bruno and Enzo, you need not be," he spoke gently and soothingly. "They departed on a hunting excursion for wild boar in the Apennines, so you need not worry for a few days, at least. In any event, I will assure you anew that Bruno's interests are fleeting, and granted you are deserving of any man's attention, however, his thoughts are probably preoccupied with another potential paramour by now."

She turned to face him, and he was very close. He leaned toward her and the two stood for an instant, only a breath apart. Years of subservience made Elisa take a hasty step back, nearly stumbling, but Claudio grasped her hands and steadied her.

"Careful, now," he said gently and released her. "Elisa, you need not worry, as long as I am here." His reassuring gaze held hers and her misgivings gave way to trust as a new and unexpected warmth surged through her.

Chapter Sixteen

There was no doubt in Claudio's mind—this girl was special. He was spellbound by Elisa, by her every word. He could not recall meeting a girl of her honesty. Her directness, her cleverness and openness were intensely refreshing. Only her delicate beauty could approach the quality of her character.

Having grown accustomed to being fawned over and flattered or having to do the same to his superiors, he could not remember the last conversation he had in which he felt both parties were being sincere.

The hours dragged by until finally the evening came. He tore to the garden especially early so that she would not need to wait for him alone. Claudio looked up when he heard her approach, her subtle steps crunching on the white marble pebbles, and he walked to meet her.

With what he was certain was the silliest of grins, he beamed at her as she reciprocated, out of breath from her rush to the garden. Claudio stood rooted to the spot as he marveled at how lovely she looked after what he was sure was a harsh day in the kitchens, which made him appreciate her natural exquisiteness even more. Then he remembered his manners and began a polite conversation.

"Good evening, Elisa." He bowed.

"Good evening, my lord." She curtsied.

"Please, call me by name." He raised his hand, inviting another attempt.

"My apologies." Red-faced, she attempted once more. "Good evening, Claudio."

"There, it was not so difficult as last time?"

"No, it was not. You are quite effortless to speak to...for a courtier, that is." She weighed him with amused wonder, peering up from a bowed head.

"Oh, am I, now? Well, I am glad that I please you, my lady." Claudio inclined his head as he would to any noble lady.

Elisa laughed and played along. "Arise, noble count, and walk with me." The two strolled side by side through the aromatic summer garden, scented heavily by the white roses, jasmine, and citrus generously planted in amongst the abundant greenery. Ivy grew wild and plentiful on the ground and crept its way up around the many sculptures of water nymphs and goddesses.

The waxing moon was at a half crescent but shone brightly amongst the stars in the sky, lending its light to create a glistening quality to the white pebbles on the garden path. The park was paradise on earth, but all that was wasted on Claudio —he could not tear his eyes away from the lovely young woman at his side.

As they walked through the winding paths among the shrubs and oleanders, admiring the splendor of the garden, Claudio was entirely focused on Elisa. Hers was an angelic face, with soft features that did not command attention, but enticed one to appreciate effortless beauty.

He was drawn to Elisa, to her exquisiteness, her poise, and her grace, partly because she was not tutored in the fine arts of proper etiquette and social graces. She had not had the benefit of being taught the refined art of conversation and how to display one's social status through the ostentatiousness of dress. This girl was real. She appealed to Claudio because of what she was not—a replica of all the pretentious noblewomen in the court.

"You look very lovely this evening," he blurted out.

"And you are too kind," she said appreciatively, keeping her gaze downcast. "I am afraid that in my haste I did not have much time to prepare. It was busy in the kitchen, and I was concerned that I would be late." She peered up at Claudio and smiled.

A tingling feeling arose in the pit of his stomach, tempered by the reminder of the harsh reality of what Elisa had to do every day in order to live.

"I am very sorry, Elisa," was all he could think of to say.

Her head tilted toward him. "For what?"

"For everything...for all that you must do—probably without anyone giving you so much as a 'thank you' for completing your work with dedication and dignity, and not one soul noting that you do so. And for the humiliation you suffered the other night at the hands of Bruno and Enzo."

He took her hands in his and felt their roughness and then looked at his, smooth and soft. "For this, too. Look at your hands." Tenderly, he kissed her palms. "Excuse my forwardness." He was genuinely at a loss at how he could have been so liberal with his emotions to someone he barely knew. He gently let go.

"You must not apologize, Claudio." She gathered his hands in hers. "It is the way things are. You did not create this for me —it is the way I am accustomed to living my life. It is the only life I have known. You are affected strongly now because you have just learned of it."

The strength of her words was too much for Claudio to

bear. "There must be something that can be done to alleviate your situation. Is there not? Must you live like this forever?" Just thinking that she had no alternative, no one to turn to for help, angered him.

"Please, can we not speak of this anymore?" implored Elisa. "Let us enjoy our time together. Tell me of what you do—that is much more interesting than dwelling on my daily drudgery. What occupies your day?"

"Very well, as you wish," agreed Claudio, motioning to a bench under a large cypress. "Perhaps I shall begin with what interests me the most—have you heard of a man called Leonardo da Vinci?"

Elisa listened attentively while Claudio related his experiences involving his mentor and teacher. They sat at length, talking about his interest in Art and the study of Nature, about da Vinci's genius and outrageous experiments.

"My mentor is a lover of art, invention, and creativity. His unceasing thirst for the pursuit of knowledge and his keen eye for innovation is unparalleled," Claudio said sincerely, with obvious respect for the old teacher. "I am blessed that I was granted the opportunity to work with a man of such superior intellect, despite the fact that there are people in this very city who believe that Master da Vinci is a madman. People do not understand his genius as Leonardo is truly a man ahead of his time—one day, Leonardo will be known throughout the land and perhaps even beyond."

Elisa listened and was completely absorbed in his funny, and sometimes shocking, anecdotes. "How very interesting. Tell me about where he lives."

"The Master divides his time between two workshops," explained Claudio. "The first is within the city, which also happens to be where he lives, near the Ponte Vecchio, and the second is at the Carthusian Monastery up near Galluzzo. His first studio is also his home, in fact, you may have seen it. On the Via dello Sprone? Ornately carved black marble columns?"

Elisa shook her head. "I believe I know the street, but I never took notice of any dwelling in particular. The next time I am in the city center I will look for it. It sounds terribly exciting."

"Perhaps I will take you there one day...if you permit me to. There is another apprentice who studies there with me. He is called Francesco. He is older than me—and very loyal to the Master." He went on, encouraged by her interest. "The second workshop was necessary due to the nature of his recent experiments and the rather significant size of his latest project..." Claudio trailed off, thinking that he should stop there otherwise he may inadvertently reveal too much about the chamber. He had complete trust in Elisa, but the less she knew about this particular experiment, the better for her. There was no sense tempting fate.

Elisa waited patiently for him to continue. "Yes...please, go on."

"Enough about me, now," deflected Claudio. "You say you have a sister. Does she resemble you much?"

"I am afraid not...she is *like* a sister to me. We are both alone, so we are really the only people we can call family. My father and mother, originally from Fiesole, were servants in the House of Medici, but they were killed many years ago. Caterina took care of me after my parents were executed by Lorenzo the Magnificent for treason. Father and Mother did no such thing of course. They were falsely accused, but they had not the slightest chance of proving their innocence." She bit her lip and took in a deep breath, furrowing her brow. "That was during the time just before the Medici were overthrown. They were grasping at anything to stay in power, torturing and murdering anyone under even the slightest suspicion."

Claudio was speechless. How could he have been so utterly preoccupied with himself that he was oblivious to the wickedness inflicted on other human beings right under his nose? "Executed by the Medici? I am so very sorry, Elisa...I had no idea. I do not know what to say." He knew that the Medici treated their enemies harshly, but killing innocents was an entirely different matter. Were his parents not aware of such travesties? And if so, how could his mother continue to associate herself with these people—and insist that he do so as well?

"Well, it was a long time ago, and I only have the vaguest shadows of memories of my parents. Mostly from what other people have told me."

"And I thought my family had suffered because we were exiled for a few years. This pales in comparison," mused Claudio, quite troubled.

Elisa took his hand. "What has happened, has happened." She looked up at the moon that had almost crested over the horizon. "Oh, my goodness—I must be on my way back to the palace. I see that the moon does not make exceptions for me. It has traveled far in the sky and warns me of my tardiness." She reluctantly stood up to leave.

Claudio arose as well. "It seems you are constantly leaving me. Must you go?" he asked, not letting go of her hand. He was beguiled by her candor and innocence. He could not let her go.

"I must. Caterina will wonder where I have gone."

"Well, I would not want Caterina to worry." Half-heartedly, he surrendered her with a smile. "I will let you go...but you must agree to meet me again."

Elisa blushed beautiful roses on her pale cheeks and laughed nervously. "How could I refuse such a command?" She squeezed his hand gently and pulled away, walking slowly toward the trellis archway. "Until next time, then."

"Wait...Elisa," Claudio blurted. The words...he could not find the words. "I..." Had her beauty, her smile, and her sweet nature captured his heart?

He moved to her and tenderly grasped her hands, gazing into her eyes. With a whisper, he asked her permission, "May I show my affection for you, my dear lady? May I kiss you?"

For an instant, Elisa could not meet his eyes. When she felt her heart would jump out of her chest if she did not soon decide, she answered him in a whisper. "You may, my lord."

Without reservation, with the purest of tenderness, he gently grasped her shoulders, drew her closer, and kissed her, softly, like suede on velvet. She hesitated, but just for a moment, then returned the sweet touch of his lips with equal fervor—one kiss. When it was over, Claudio raised his mouth from hers and opened his eyes. There was no need for words—he knew. Claudio had fallen in love.

He spoke first, his voice a husky whisper, his strong hands still holding her slender shoulders. "May I see you tomorrow, my darling?"

Elisa caught her breath and answered dreamily. "I am afraid that I have no choice." She reached up and kissed him again, wrapping her arms around him. This love was all-encompassing, mind, body, and soul. They held each other and began swaying to the song of the crickets in the garden.

"Now," as her emotions whirled and skidded inside her, she forced herself to say, "I really must go."

"May I walk you back to the palace, my lady?" asked Claudio, brushing his lips over the top of her hand.

"Of course, my lord," Elisa agreed. Her consciousness ebbed and flowed, and temporarily permitted her to throw caution to the wind. Reluctantly, they released their embrace. She slipped her arm through his and walked under the aromatic trellis back to reality.

Chapter Seventeen

Master da Vinci was grappling with a particularly stubborn complication that threatened the ability to further investigate the chamber. Sitting pensively at his work table in the monastery workshop, he stirred his mutton stew and wondered why his most brilliant pupil, Claudio, had not attended his studio in the last few days. Nonetheless, with or without an assistant, his work had to continue, so he decided to ask Francesco for support in the meantime.

Leonardo's problem was that he did not understand why the eddies in the array were so unstable; it irritated him to no end when he could not understand something. The spirals would ebb in and out, flash an image and then fade away. The visions were unstable and varied too wildly for him to learn anything meaningful from them. His studies of this magnificent new discovery had hit a stone wall.

"Perhaps," he mumbled to himself earlier that evening whilst he shuffled back from the refectory with his dinner, "I am approaching this problem from the wrong direction."

In his studio, the old man puzzled intensely, mulling over

the problem, repeating the process which led to the creation of the miracle in the chamber in the first place. Leonardo replayed it in his mind...*copper chamber walls, reverse bellows, copper rod, lightning. Think about the simplest solution. How does one make any substance more stable? How does one make something move less? I need to find a way to stabilize the images so that they can be examined more closely, but how? But how can I stabilize a substance I know nothing about?*

Leonardo stirred his stew. It was nice and thick, just the way he liked it. He scratched his head and looked deeply into his supper, searching for the answers to his queries in the mixture of broth, potatoes, and meat.

There must be an answer, he thought. "To thicken a stew, one adds more ingredients to the broth...the less liquid, the thicker the stew, the less it sloshes in the bowl. Could this be said for nearly any substance? Could it be true of the eddies in the array?" The old man was stumped, but he persevered.

The array was created quite by accident—the intentional harnessing of the power in a bolt of lightning created this strange phenomenon. If he could duplicate the result, add more of what makes the lightning powerful, would that increase the density of the power in the array and possibly stabilize the eddies? He could not predict this. What if he was wrong and, more importantly, what would be the result if he failed?

"No matter," he thought out loud. "We cannot enter the array again if it is not stable...it is too dangerous, and I refuse to risk anyone's life for it." He scratched his head and peered around his workshop. "I must prepare the chamber again in the event of another storm. Once the materials are ready outside, all we need to do is wait. Then, I either succeed or fail. If we do not attempt to advance in the study of Nature, then we stand still and might as well retreat to the dark days."

With a new resolve and a plan, Leonardo prepared his

things. He would set out the next morning for his studio in the city; he required additional materials if he was going to replicate the experiment. After he was successful in obtaining the things he needed, all he had to do was wait for a thunderstorm.

The old Master set about gathering his plans, florins, and all things necessary for his journey. Da Vinci frowned as he recognized he would have to wake Francesco to assist him in his journey. Perhaps they would run into Claudio in the city.

At the same instant da Vinci rose to gather his things for Florence, Clarice strode like a soldier on a mission to Countess Maria's apartments in the Medici palace. She wanted to learn exactly why Claudio was not present at dinner this evening. Bruno and Enzo had departed for a hunting trip that very morning, and she was absolutely certain that Claudio had not joined them. He should have been at dinner in the great hall, but he was conspicuously absent.

Might it be possible that he was upset with her about the other evening and all the drivel that her brother was spouting at dinner? Bruno, in his drunken state, had fallen asleep in the garden, the fool. And he wondered why Claudio always cuts a better figure than he.

It was clear to Clarice that her brother was jealous of the Count in every way that he could be: Claudio's intelligence, his appearance, the way he did not need to try with the ladies... and even the respect that the Duke had for his desire to learn. For all of these reasons, Clarice believed Bruno felt more and more threatened by Claudio as they got older.

But Clarice had troubles of her own. She loved Count Moro, yet he did not appear to share her affections. She was terribly witty and indulged him in stimulating conversation, but he seemed bored with her; cordial, yes, but that was all.

There were many men who would be pleased to have her. She was a prize—she knew it. She needed to act fast, because soon her uncle could very well marry her off to another noble to improve relations with another region, and then she would have no chance with Claudio at all.

Was it possible that he was with that maid girl now? That strumpet of a servant, instead of with her, Clarice de Medici? "No! It cannot be!" she declared out loud.

She continued with resolve to her destination, her gown swishing down the opulent hallway. Claudio would not disgrace himself in such a manner...he would not choose a scullery maid over a Royal.

She wondered if this dire state she was in was due only to the drunken ramblings of her sulky, spoiled brother. She hated Bruno. "How could we have come from the same womb?" she cried completely aghast. "How could he do this to me, lie about the man I love? I will set him straight. Claudio is working, that is all. He is working with that madman again." She would speak with Claudio herself and clear things up once and for all.

By the time she rounded the corner to Countess Maria's apartments, Clarice had convinced herself that there was nothing to be concerned about and was almost calm again. She had managed to talk herself down from her fury just as she knocked at the Countess's door. Rather annoyed at having to wait, she knocked again, this time more sharply. She heard footsteps on the other side, and soon enough, the door opened. It was one of Maria's maids. She curtsied deeply, and offered a greeting, but Clarice ignored her, sidled by her and entered right away in search of the Countess.

"Where is she?" demanded Clarice. Within seconds, Countess Maria appeared, clearly not expecting a visit. She bowed her head respectfully. "Good evening, my lady. Please, make yourself comfortable. May I offer you something, a refreshment perhaps?"

"No, nothing," replied Clarice impatiently. "I am here to speak with Claudio, if I may."

"It would be my pleasure, my lady, but regrettably," Countess Maria swallowed, "he is not here."

Clarice squeezed her lips together until they were a thin white line and turned a deep crimson.

"But if my lady would like to sit and attend a moment," Maria added, "I am certain that he will—"

"I will wait for no one!" Clarice cried out, with an unmistakable emphasis on each word. She sniffed and tried to compose herself. "Excuse me, madam, but he and I had quite a lovely time at dinner last evening, and I was looking forward to his presence at table once again, tonight. I would like to know where he is, if you do not mind, Countess Maria."

"My lady," she said, the tone in her voice begged indulgence, "I am certain that he is at the studio of that painter Leonardo da Vinci. My son is quite interested in the 'study of Nature' as he calls it. Claudio is an inquisitive soul." Maria was growing slightly red-faced herself. "He always has been, and enjoys the old man's curiosities, but deep down he is a very wise man of business, and I am quite sure that—"

"I cannot tell you how happy I am to hear of it," Clarice cut her off before she could finish the sentence. She felt immense relief at the news. "Not that he is da Vinci's student...heaven help us," she drawled, rolling her eyes and waving away the mere thought of such a folly. "No, da Vinci is not the one who concerns me, but that he is with a...oh, never mind." She shook her head and arose to leave, straightening her gown. Pausing, she thought for a moment. If Maria did not know, then she should be informed of such a scandal. If she was aware of it, then she should be ashamed that she could not have put a stop to it. And if it is a lie, then she needs to quash it. "Is it possible that Claudio is involved with...a servant...here —in the palace?"

The Countess blinked, her expression blank. "My lady, I am certain that it would not be possible. He does not even hunt anymore. Alas, he is kept very busy assisting his teacher."

"Oh," Clarice sniffed, utterly satisfied with herself. "Just a rumor, then...a silly rumor. Spread by my silly, envious brother. No matter." Her demeanor changed completely. "Please tell Claudio when he returns that I look forward to seeing him tomorrow." Her skirts swished briskly toward the door, and the young maid rushed to open it for her, curtsying deeply to the noblewoman.

"Without a doubt, my lady, he shall enjoy your company at dinner tomorrow evening. I shall see to it myself," said Maria, her voice tense.

"Oh, wonderful, Countess Maria," gushed Clarice. "Have a glorious evening." With a conclusive rustle of her silken gown, she sauntered out.

"Likewise, my lady...'til the morrow." Maria smiled, rising from her curtsy.

But on her way out, Clarice could not help but notice that the Countess's smile did not reach her eyes.

Chapter Eighteen

Tuscany, Italy
2029

It was nearly dusk in Tuscany, but Ali figured that Caleb would still be awake even though it was six hours ahead in Boston. He had left two messages that afternoon. "Hi, Caleb, it's me," Alice said cheerfully. She was on the balcony of her villa room, overlooking the lush rolling hills.

"Hey, Ali, how are you? I tried to Facetime you earlier, but I couldn't get through."

"Sorry. I had my phone in my wallet. What's up?"

"Just thinking about you. Wanted to hear your voice, see your face. And...looking forward to you coming back." He spoke in earnest until he ran out of reasons.

"It's only two more weeks. Wait, you want to see something amazing?" Ali smiled broadly and aimed her screen to the hills behind her, catching herself in the 3D image. The sun was cresting over the western ridge, setting off a dazzling display of color.

"That's amazing, Als. Like heaven. I wish I was there with you."

Unexpectedly, she felt a twinge in her stomach. She caught herself thinking of the luggage guy from the driveway.

"Me, too." She tried to change the subject. "So, have you been to your residence at Syracuse, yet? You must be dying to move in."

"Well, yeah, I guess so, but it's mid-August. Still too early."

"Oh...right," she said, her mind a million miles away.

"Well...tell me what you've done," he said. "What unbelievably awesome things have you seen?"

"You know," Ali smiled at his feeble attempt at sarcasm, "the usual touristy things: sightseeing, restaurants, ancient ruins—all that stuff."

"Yeah, sure," he sighed. "Are you trying to make it sound trivial on purpose? 'Cuz, you don't sound like yourself."

Ali's stomach did a somersault. "No, of course not. That's what we did."

"Okay, relax. I just meant that you don't have to worry."

"Well, why would I worry?" Ali tried to stop herself from responding to him defensively, but she couldn't help it. There was only silence from Caleb. "Uhm—I'm sorry. I think I'm just tired." She was starting to perspire.

"That's okay," he shrugged, oblivious to her anxiety. "But seriously, I'm counting the days. I gotta get ready for my shift at Walgreens...love you."

"Me too."

"I'll call you next, okay? Be good."

"I always am. I'll text later." Alice contracted her device and looked intently at the neat rows of grapevines rising and falling on the hills. She thought of the conversation with Caleb —she was definitely short with him. But why so suddenly? *Maybe it's because of that weird anxious feeling I've been getting since*

I got here. Come on, shake yourself out of it and live in the moment—it's your favorite time of day, twilight.

Listening, she noted the turtle doves in the nearby trees, chirping and cooing to their young, settling them in for the night. Alice took in the last bit of pink sun peeking out from behind the horizon in the west, slowly sinking down to a tiny brilliant sliver. The rolling hills were the most incredible shade of green against the lavender sky. Off in the distance, her eyes feasted on multiple tiers of grape vineyards, sculpted into the faces of the gently sloping mountains with olive trees tucked in between. Everything was so calm, so serene, so peaceful.

Yet, in this magnificent tranquility, Alice sensed that nonsensical, uneasy feeling creeping back. "What is that? Why do I feel this way? Maybe I miss Mama and Papa more than I thought I would."

No, this was something else. This was a kind of agitation... something disquieting. Something to do with that over-whelming feeling of déjà vu she had when she saw that boy coming toward her. That had been unbelievably weird. Apart from the fact that he was absolutely the most beautiful person that she had ever laid eyes on, there was something so familiar about him. She couldn't get him out of her head.

What is wrong with me? Obsessing over a stranger is totally unlike me. "Stop it," she blurted out. "I am strong, in control, and I am my own person. I make the decisions...I am in control. Breathe in deep...and out."

"I am Alice Ferro. I am in control. I love Caleb Fenton, and he loves me. Just breathe and relax..." she whispered over and over, needing to convince herself.

"*Buona sera,*" a deep voice from below called her out of her thoughts, familiar and smooth as velvet.

Startled, Alice jumped back from the railing. She scanned around and then down from her balcony to the courtyard. It took a moment for her eyes to adjust, but a figure came into focus below her. It was the boy from the driveway looking up at her, with two deck chairs in his hands. He set one down and waved up at her, almost shyly. Her heart skipped a beat.

"*B-buona sera.*" Her words stumbled out. She tried her best to keep her voice steady. "Nice night, isn't it?" She winced as she heard her own words. *How lame can you be?*

He cleared his throat nervously and flashed a smile at her, so irresistible that her stomach turned to a slushy mess.

"I hope I am not interrupting you," he said. "But there does not seem to be anyone returning your conversation, so I thought you might like someone to talk to, if that is not too presumptuous of me."

Alice felt her face flush. He must have heard her murmuring to herself. How cocky can you get? "Well, maybe it is presumptuous of you. I don't even know who you are. I mean I know that you work here, but that's all I know." Her tone bordered on positively frosty.

Ugh. Overcompensating.

"Oh. Excuse me." He bowed deeply, his hand to his chest, exaggerating his regret. "I beg your forgiveness. I am but a lowly employee, here only to serve you."

A stab of regret mixed with surprise poked her chest. "Th-that's not what I meant," she stammered nervously, wondering how she could salvage this. "That's ridiculous, it has nothing to do with it. It's just that...well...I, uh, my parents are very protective, and they wouldn't like me talking to people they don't know, that's all."

"But you are all the way up there, and I am down here. I will not harm you, I promise. My arms are not that long." He smiled charmingly, holding up his arms up to prove it. "We are just having a friendly conversation between servant and hotel guest."

"Of course, I'm sorry," she said, unsure of what to say next. "So, what do you do here, besides carry luggage?" Ali winced. She had meant to sound clever, but feared she came off like a snob.

"A little of everything. I carry these, too." He gestured to the chairs, now sitting idle. "I live here, with my aunt and uncle, and I help out whenever I can. This place has been in the family for generations." He crossed his arms over his chest and looked down at the cobblestones, shifting his weight.

"That's nice. Do you work here in the summer or something?"

"Yes and no. I live here, yes, and work here, yes, but I also attend university. My relatives were kind enough to take me in. You might say that I am like their son."

"Oh—I'm so sorry. I didn't mean to be insensitive."

"There is no need to apologize. It happened a while ago...it feels like forever," he added quietly.

"What would we do without aunts and uncles?" Alice rested her chin on her crossed arms as she leaned on the balcony's edge.

"This is true," he said and glanced at his watch. "Well, I had best be going. The morning comes quickly. Perhaps we will see each other again tomorrow. *Buona notte.*"

"*Buona notte,*" echoed Alice, beginning to regret her flippant behavior. She felt like kicking herself. Could she have sounded any more condescending?

This poor guy was just walking by and decided to make polite conversation with a nut talking to herself on a balcony, and what does he get for it? An insensitive exchange with a spoiled brat. I wouldn't like to be spoken to like that.

The only thing I can do to correct the situation is to apologize. Properly. Face to face. I mean you have to be courteous to your hosts, and he is my host, since he's practically the villa owner's son.

Alice rattled off a few more reasons for seeking out the young man the next day, and slowly she convinced herself that her need to see him again was totally necessary and purely altruistic.

Chapter Nineteen

The warm water was soothing, and the soap smelled of freesia. Ali allowed the calming spray from the shower to flow over her. The night had, in spite of 'balcony boy's' prediction, passed slowly and restlessly. She woke up every twenty minutes or so, checking the time on her phone.

Strange dreams infused her mind when she did sleep. They made no sense, but they were vivid—and oddly familiar. In one, she saw herself running down a dimly lit marble staircase, desperately trying to get away from something, but she couldn't. The more she tried to run from the shadowy figures, the slower she ran, like the stairs were telescoping in front of her. She roused herself awake, as anxiety closed in. Later, she dreamed of the boy in the white shirt, but something was different; she was in awe of him. She tried to get to him, but she was pulled into a bright, white light which made her to cry out in her sleep, and wrench upright in bed.

She was thinking of him again. Damn it!

Alice squeezed her eyes closed and whispered to herself like it was a mantra. "Okay—dry off, blow-dry hair, apply some make-up, and then go downstairs to breakfast or Leda and Roberto will wonder where you are."

Soon enough, she was ready to descend to the dining area for the buffet breakfast. Ali slipped on her low-heeled slides, grabbed her bag, and fished her room key out of the side pocket. As she pulled open the door and locked it behind her, she wondered where her aunt and uncle would be taking her today. They must be planning on Florence—maybe the San Lorenzo market or the Palazzo Pitti. The Boboli Gardens would be nice.

Striding briskly down the hall to the elevator, she made a mental note to keep an eye out for the boy in the white shirt. A purely cordial and brief but sincere apology would be appropriate in making amends for her impulsive remarks last night. The entire scene played out in her mind—she knew exactly what she would do.

He would be outside somewhere, working on the landscaping, or something. Naturally, her approach would be casual as she walked over to him and bid him *buon giorno*. Then she'd offer him a heartfelt, *I'm sorry that I was so rude last night*. She would follow that up with a, *please accept my apology, I wasn't quite myself*.

Preoccupied with practicing her admission of guilt, in addition to fretting that she was late for breakfast, her pace quickened as she moved down the corridor. She turned a corner to get to the lift and ran face to face, or face to chest in her case, straight into balcony boy.

"Whoa!" exclaimed Ali, screeching to a halt so suddenly that her sunglasses flew off her head and into a corner of the hallway.

"That was close," he exclaimed at the same time, struggling madly to maintain control of the bags in his arms. The reflex from both was a nervous laugh.

"Excuse me, miss, it was entirely my fault." With a quick

motion, he set down the bags and scooped up Ali's glasses, placing them back on her head.

"No, not at all." She blushed. "In fact, I was hoping to see you again today...I wanted to apologize to you...for my comments last night. They were totally insensitive."

He tilted his head. "I do not understand." An elfish grin crept across his lips.

Alice paused. He was so easy on the eyes. She roused herself and looked down at the tips of her shoes, feeling the color rising in her cheeks. "I–I was trying to figure out how to apologize for last night."

"Why? Did you do something to me?"

They looked at each other quizzically and exchanged grins.

"What I mean is, I just thought that maybe I sounded thoroughly snobby and incredibly arrogant, and I–I didn't want you thinking that I was like that." She brushed a wisp of hair out of her eyes. "I'm actually a genuinely nice person, and I don't think I showed you that side of me last night, so...I'm sorry."

Unexpectedly, he took her fingers in his. His eyes held hers as he gently brought her hand to his mouth and brushed his lips against it, barely touching it.

Ali tried to remember to exhale. Did men like this still exist?

"If it will make you feel better." He released her hand slowly, and added, "I will accept your apology, but there is no need for one. I very much enjoyed our talk. Perhaps, I can come by again tonight, if it is permissible? You are here with your parents?"

"Yes, it is permissible," Ali allowed, struggling to keep her balance, as she suddenly felt unsteady. She inhaled. *Why does this keep happening? Don't pass out, don't pass out.* "But the couple I'm with are my aunt and uncle. I came here with my parents, but they had to go back home to Boston. Urgent matter."

His face broke off to a look of utter surprise. "So, you live in America?"

"Yes, Massachusetts—you've heard of it?" she asked.

The color drained from his face. He swallowed hard.

"Are you okay?" she asked.

"Yes," he said softly. "I assumed you lived closer...you speak Italian with almost no accent. How long will you be here?"

"I have only two weeks left." Suddenly, it hit her. Only two weeks. Somehow, that suddenly became very important.

"Well then, we do not have much time—" He hesitated, took a deep breath and started again. "I-I mean, if you will permit me to, I would be honored to show you around. This part of Tuscany is more beautiful if you see it from the perspective of a local and not that of a tourist. There is great beauty in the undiscovered villages, away from the roads usually traveled."

Ali was intrigued. His speech sounded more like poetry than conversation. His gaze confident yet polite, made him even more fascinating.

"Uh," she stammered, "Uh, my aunt and uncle are taking me to Florence today, but...maybe tomorrow we can..." she trailed off, suddenly remembering that Roberto and Leda were still waiting for her in the breakfast nook. "Oh, my gosh...I have to go. They're waiting for me downstairs, and I am sooooo late."

"Then you must go and not keep them waiting, miss." He grinned and bowed slightly, making a sweeping motion with his arm toward the elevator. "Perhaps, later, we can make arrangements for a drive in the country. Trust me, you have not seen Tuscany until you have seen it from the back of a Vespa."

Alice's face lit up with a huge smile, freckles and all. "Sounds amazing," she replied, biting her lip and suppressing an overwhelming urge to gush.

"I look forward to it." He tipped his chin, gathered up the suitcases and walked away, not taking his eyes off her until he turned the corner.

Alice stood rooted to the spot, until the pinging of the elevator doors broke her reverie.

Oh, my gosh! she thought. "Wait! Hey, wait...what's your name?" she ran after him, stopping in front of the staircase as he was descending. "I'm Alice."

"Alice. How exquisite." He graced her with a final dazzling smile. "My name is Claudio." Both paused as if there were a million words between them yet unspoken. Then, with an incline of his head, he turned the spiral on the landing and he was gone.

Ali heard the lift doors down the hall slip close with an abrupt swish. She turned and watched the little red lights on the control panel signaling its ascent to the third floor.

Claudio, she mused. What a pleasing name. But no sooner had she finished her thought, when a powerful wave of déjà vu hit her. It was unbelievably strong, so strong that she had to lean against the wall for support.

Claudio. Could she know someone with that name? Pondering, she remained leaning until the hazy feeling cleared. She shook herself out of the fog, turned and with her hand pressed firmly on the wall for support, stepped into the lift and pressed the down button.

Chapter Twenty

Glancing across to the breakfast nook, Ali spotted Roberto and Leda, their hands intertwined over three steaming cups of espresso, obviously in love. If she and Caleb were to stay together, would they look like that twenty years from now? She strode over.

"*Buon giorno,*" she said, pulling up a chair. "Sorry I'm so late, I was talking to a friend."

"Buon giorno, Ali," said Leda.

"Good morning to you, too. Did you sleep well?" Roberto asked, pushing the chair in for Alice. Leda smiled and slid the small but powerful cup of espresso towards her niece.

"Ah, yeah...maybe I could get a cappuccino instead." Ali grimaced, raising an eyebrow. She hadn't yet developed a taste for the thick brew.

"So, you've already made a friend here." Roberto raised a hand to the waitress and ordered a cap.

"Well, he's not exactly a friend. He's the guy from the parking lot. You know, from yesterday," she said, grabbing a brioche.

"Ali," Leda said with an apprehensive tone in her voice.

"Please be careful. You know how your parents are...and we are responsible for you."

Alice shifted uncomfortably in her seat. "I know Zia... really, it's okay. He's a nice guy, very polite."

"My darling Alice," smiled Roberto, patting her hand. "He could be the King of France, but he is still a young man. Just be wise is all we are saying. Agreed?"

"Agreed, but really, it's nothing," insisted Alice. "What's on the agenda for today?"

"Well, we thought that we would let you decide our day. You tell us."

"Let's see." Ali grinned, stroking her chin as she weighed the options. "How about Piazza Michelangelo, above Florence, and then a maybe a walk on the Ponte Vecchio, or to the marketplace? I promised someone back home that I would bring him back a little something."

As the waitress set a steaming cup of foamy cappuccino in front of her, Ali thought about how it felt being dutiful to Caleb. But that word, 'dutiful' nagged at her. How could she be thinking about being 'dutiful' already? Shouldn't she be feeling that 'crazy-in-love, missing-him-in-the-pit-of-her-stomach-until-the-day-she-would-be-in-his-arms-again' type of feeling? Not dutiful. Ali smiled wanly at her aunt and uncle, hoping for some encouragement.

"Yes, of course, for your young man?" asked Leda.

Alice nodded. "That's the one."

"Brilliant," exclaimed Roberto. "That is our day, then. When we have had enough of Florence, we will come back here for dinner...bene?"

Benissimo! Having finished their coffee and pastries, they rose to leave the serene country villa for their day in the city.

But behind the front desk, which was situated in the lobby across from the dining area, Claudio had been busy placing billing notes into the mailboxes. He had overheard Ali's conversation with her aunt and uncle, as he kept his back toward the lobby.

When Ali's voice trailed away, and he was certain that she wouldn't notice his presence, he slowly turned around. Certain that she was out of the villa, he slid down to the floor behind the desk in a crouch, his stomach churning with a sick feeling.

"After all this time," he murmured. "Waiting for her to come back to me, after all the countless hours yearning for her, trying to find her, she is in love with another."

The ground had been pulled right out from under him. How could he not have foreseen this? He had never for a moment considered the possibility that she may be involved with someone else. After all, she was breathtaking. Just being around her, experiencing her presence was enough to make any man fall for her. It was entirely not her fault, and under the circumstances he should have expected this.

Indeed, this was a cruel turn of events. Could he allow himself the indulgence of believing that he may hold her again? And could she ever love him in return? He took a deep breath and closed his eyes. What would he do now? He had to think, and fast.

Chapter Twenty-One

The next morning, Alice awoke to the song of cooing pigeons on her balcony. Her feet still hurt from the day before...all that walking had taken a toll. That would be the last time she wore new sandals on a walking tour. But Florence was worth it. Every piazza, every gallery, every statue, and antique building façade screamed history and culture. And the gelato...the gelato alone was worth every step.

But as glorious as the day had been, she would not be spared another restless night. The strange images haunted her sleep. She realized that, at times, dreams could be odd and make utterly no sense, but to have them repeat themselves was something that she had never experienced.

She found herself on a bumpy road holding a tangled ball of yarn. Caleb approached her from one side of the road and calmly offered to untangle the yarn for her, while on the other side of the road, a lion roared in anger. The kicker was that the ball of yarn was ablaze, and her hands were burning—it was a bright white light. But all the while she stood there, very serene, very calm. Then the road in front of her turned into a raging ocean. She began to cross it, and that was when she woke up shuddering in a cold sweat. How weird that she should dream the same dream two nights in a row.

The sun barely had a chance to make its appearance, when she heard muffled voices coming from the other side of the terrace shutters—one of them sounded familiar. She wrapped her robe around her, brushed the sleep out of her eyes, and half stumbled to the windows. She popped open the shutters and peeked out, conscious of the fact that she had just rolled out of bed and not wanting anyone to see her with her hair bushed up to the ceiling.

As she swung open the window shutters, one of the hinges let out a loud squeak. The two young men below turned their heads up in her direction. In the new orange light of the morning, she saw that one of them was Claudio. She stared tongue-tied, surprised at her own feelings of delight in seeing him.

"Buon giorno, Alice." He nodded at her with an incredible smile. "Excuse us. Did my cousin and I wake you?"

"Buon giorno, Claudio." She worked very hard to maintain her composure as she raked a hand through her hair. "And no, not at all."

"Did you sleep well?"

"Very well, thank you," she lied.

"Oh, excuse me...Alice, this is Luca. Luca, Alice."

Oh, my God. I haven't even washed my face. "Nice to meet you, Luca."

"The pleasure is mine," the young man said. "Claudio was right, you are a beauty. Now I know why he is so smitten with you."

Claudio nodded in agreement, gesturing in Alice's direction. "You see now that I never had a chance, Luca."

Alice laughed out loud.

"I was telling my cousin that I will be taking you for a tour of some of the less often visited Tuscan villages. Some of them dating back to the Etruscans. I hope you are looking forward to it as much as I am. Once I am finished with a few errands, I will pack us a picnic and pick you up at the front of the villa, say about ten o'clock?"

"Excellent...I—" She stopped, licked her lips, and reined back her enthusiasm. "I mean, yes, tennish is good. Should I bring something?"

"Just you. And we have a full day ahead of us...in case you need to let your aunt and uncle know."

Damn. Forgot about them. Well, I'm old enough to make up my own mind about a tour guide. And they'll probably appreciate the time alone together, anyway.

"I'll let them know. See you then. Nice to have met you, Luca." She drew the shutters closed and then sprinted for the bathroom, unabashedly giddy at her spontaneous abandon, which was about as uncharacteristically 'Ali' as you could get.

After messaging Caleb that she was going on a guided tour of Etruscan villages with a boy who worked at the Villa, she began the task of persuading Leda and Roberto that Claudio was just a friend.

"I'll be fine, believe me," Ali reassured them. "I'm an excellent judge of character—just like Papa. Besides, you know where he lives and works. What could possibly happen? He's taking me to the local sights, that's all...nothing suspicious or sneaky. Besides, don't you two want some time to yourselves to enjoy your holiday at the villa?"

At first, they hesitated, but in the end, Alice was able to convince them that they had nothing to worry about. Caleb eventually messaged back:

<Getting my stuff organized for residence. You
know how to take care of yourself, but it's

the guy I don't trust. I guess it's okay with
me if you go.>

Alice read the message on her device, and she was irked. She was not asking Caleb's permission, she was just giving him the courtesy of letting him know what she was doing. How could he think that she was asking for his permission to go on this innocent little sightseeing outing with a friend?

<Thanx for your approval...good luck moving.>

The text back read,

<Whoa, you're the one out with someone else...
I should be the one who is pissed—take it
easy>

∾

Alice chose an aqua blue crop top and white walking shorts, a comfortable combination for a day under the heat of the Tuscan sun. Her hair was carelessly tied up in a loose ponytail on top of her head to keep it all off her neck. She grabbed her satchel, iPhone, and shades and dashed off to meet Claudio.

As she stepped outside of the villa's double doors, she spotted him tying a picnic basket onto the back of a little motorcycle, a Vespa. Alice smiled to herself. What could be better than to trek Tuscany on a Vespa?

"Ciao, Claudio."

"Ciao, bella." The words were like music. Claudio stopped grappling with the bungee cord and stood up to look at her, his eyes giving way to a look of appreciation. Shaking his head, he flashed an irresistible smile and gestured for her to take his hand. "If you are ready, my lady, your chariot awaits." He motioned for her to mount the bike and held out her helmet. "I hope you like figs...I packed some for lunch today."

"Yum, I love figs. Are they from the trees in the back?" She took her helmet.

Claudio swung a leg over the seat of the Vespa and twisted around to watch as Ali settled herself behind him. "They are... I also packed some fresh bread, cheese, and mineral water," he said, adjusting his visor.

"Sounds fabulous, but I wish you would have let me help you with it. I should have contributed something." Her skin tingled as she snapped her chinstrap on snuggly, secretly anticipating his closeness during the ride.

"Think nothing of it. It is nothing fancy, just a *spuntino*. Besides, you are my guest, so I will take care of it this time. Next time, you will make the picnic. Agreed?"

She nodded in accordance. "Sounds fair to me. So, where to first?"

He turned his face slightly to her as he powered up the Vespa and reached around to gently take her hand. "Hold tight around my waist. These roads can get bumpy."

"Absolutely. And watch the curves—they can be dangerous, too." Alice grinned playfully.

Claudio laughed softly. "Of that, I am entirely certain. And in answer to your question...where the road takes us."

With that, he applied the gas and sped off down the cobblestone driveway. Alice held on tight, moving from side to side in unison with Claudio and the bike as they wound their way through villages and multi-tiered farmland. The Vespa zoomed nimbly by scenic olive groves, chestnut trees, and the occasional holiday villa perched on a hillside.

"So seriously, where are we going?" Alice half-shouted at Claudio so he could hear her over the engine.

"First, we are off to Greve, a beautiful village in the Chianti region. It has an incredible view and even better wine. We shop there and afterward, we can have lunch in Fiesole. There is an ancient Roman amphitheater there and Etruscan temple ruins, all in a quaint hillside village. The last stop is a surprise... you will have to wait for that one."

"That sounds amazing," cooed Alice. "Will it take long to get there?"

"Not long at all. The great thing about Tuscany is that everything is close together. In fact, we are about to take the cut-off on the next round-about to get to our first stop."

The road brought them to a traffic circle, which had several exits to various locations. Claudio took the exit marked Greve in Chianti. He skillfully guided the Vespa up the moderate incline and circumnavigated the narrow turns. The warm summer sun poked through the abundant oak and chestnut trees lining the road, offering dappled shade to the couple on the *motorino*, the leaves like sieves to the sunlight.

Claudio maneuvered the bike into the narrow streets of the old village. Ancient ivy covered the whitewashed stucco walls of the houses. Cascading fuchsia and red geraniums tumbled out of the flower boxes adorning the weathered windows, while pristine shirts and tablecloths hung fluttering in the breeze from the clotheslines. The young couple drove by local neighborhood bars where old men sat, playing cards, and sipping espresso. To Alice, the whole scene felt like she had stepped into a postcard, like a snapshot in time.

Claudio steered the Vespa toward an artisanal bakery, tucked in the main piazza, where the aroma of freshly baked panini and ciabatta bread would wear the resolve of even the most avid carb counter. The next stop was at an ancient delicatessen, for fresh prosciutto and cheese.

With the picnic basket filled to the brim, it was time for them to head to Fiesole for lunch in the Etruscan ruins. It was a pleasant ride, and the picturesque country roads were lined with charming villages from another time.

She glowed as she held on tight to Claudio, looping their way up to Fiesole. Alice breathed in the clean country air when the town appeared over the crest of a hill. Then, without warning, an overwhelming sense of doom enshrouded her. Her throat tightened, and a cold sweat began to take hold. The closer they drew to Fiesole, the more crushing the anxiety became.

"Claudio!" Ali shouted in his ear. "I need to stop...stop now." The blood drained from her face, and her hands were like ice.

"What is it?" he asked.

"I...I don't feel right. You need to pull over."

He found a shady green space by the side of the road, with a little sanctuary to Saint Francis, and scrambled to pull into it.

"Alice, what is wrong?" He helped her off the bike and onto a moss-covered retaining wall.

She couldn't find her voice to answer.

"How about some water?" He reached into the basket and produced a cool bottle of San Pellegrino, twisted off the top, and held it to Ali's lips. She sipped slowly at first and then gulped a mouthful.

"Now, take a deep breath. Try closing your eyes for a minute," he said, breathing along with her.

Ali felt the blood returning to her face. The water and the deep breathing kept the looming unconsciousness at bay. "Wow—I'm so sorry." Wiping the sweat off her forehead with the back of her hand. "I don't know why this keeps happening to me."

"Perhaps you are hungry. Do you want to stop here to eat?"

"No...no, I'm okay...really. Let's just go to the ruins and have our picnic."

He watched her with a worried look.

"Claudio, I'm good...maybe just a little shaky, but...good. Come on, let's go."

He helped her to get onto the Vespa, and she held on tight, aware of her unsteadiness but stubborn in her resolve not to let it ruin their day.

"Look, up ahead!" she exclaimed, perking up as she pointing to the crumbling columns in the distance. "There it is...the amphitheater!" The ancient Etruscan ruins stood ahead in all their splendor. Standing steady as sentinels of an age past, they bore witness to an untold number of stories of the people who had taken refuge in their inviting space. But today, they were there only for Ali and Claudio.

The couple chose a spot under an enormous chestnut tree, directly overlooking the amphitheater. They sat among an ancient crumbling cluster of marble columns that looked like they had been lying there for centuries, abandoned and forgotten, while wildflowers and grasses flourished up around them. They reminded Ali of frail, old soldiers, who had long ago fallen asleep at their post, too aged and tired to continue their sentry.

Feasting on sharp pecorino cheese, warm ciabatta bread, and freshly picked figs, they washed it down with sparkling mineral water blushed with a hint of Chianti red. The day was as perfect as it could be, clear and sunny with the occasional cloud in the azure blue sky, offering Ali and Claudio a breathtaking view of the entire city of Florence.

"This was the most incredible picnic, Claudio," Ali declared, raising her glass. "Not only because of the food... which was delicious. I mean who would have thought that figs on bread would taste so good? But I mean, this place...I can't describe it—it's a scene from a painting, a work of art." She searched for the right words, but they eluded her. "It's like we have Florence at our feet."

Claudio nodded. "Are you feeling better now?"

"Yes. And I feel good here," she said. "I've heard my parents talk about places like this all the time...it's almost like I'm home, you know? Like, I belong. I probably remember the scenery or something from when I was little." She took another nibble of pecorino cheese soaked in wine, loving the combination of tastes. "I've been here before, did I tell you? When I was younger, my parents brought me back here."

"And that fainting spell you almost had back there, did that happen before, too?" he asked.

"Once or twice since I got here," she replied, downplaying it. She thought about it, trying to understand. "I almost feel like I'm missing something significant when I get that feeling, like it's just beyond my grasp...I get uneasy...and then just as quickly, the feeling is gone." She massaged her temples as she spoke. "I remember it happening was when I was here, in Italy, years ago. Sometimes it got really bad."

"So, you do remember this place," Claudio said, swallowing a mouthful of bread and figs. "You have been here before?" His gaze intensified.

"No, not here specifically, but I feel as though it's very familiar, like I've seen it in a dream or something." She shook her head. "I guess it's what we call déjà vu in America—a feeling that you've experienced the same thing before. Do you know what I mean?"

"Yes, I do." Claudio sipped his mineral water and glanced sideways at Ali. "You said you have been to Italy before—do you visit often with your parents? Were you born here?"

"Actually, my story is a little...how can I put it...unusual." Ali sighed deeply and took off her sunglasses. "I was abandoned when I was a baby, here in Florence," Ali continued, "and adopted by my parents. Eventually they immigrated to America—they're both professors, my dad at MIT, my mom at

Harvard." She looked up at the clouds. "We came back for a visit when I was younger, but...I haven't been here since."

"Do you go to school?"

"Last year of high school, hopefully university next year. You?"

Claudio grinned and leaned back on one of the columns. "This past year, I have been studying astrophysics at the University of Milan, with my cousin, Luca. This summer I needed to come back to...help out."

"Impressive," she said, shifting her weight to look directly at him. "What about your family?"

"My father passed away some time ago. My mother is gone, too. I am staying with my relatives at the villa for the summer, to work."

"I'm so sorry about your parents."

"Yes, me too." Claudio cleared his throat. "He was a very good man, my father...loyal and trustworthy. He taught me the value of pursuing one's dreams instead of just following the easiest path, the path laid out for you."

"Your father sounds like he was a very wise man." She threw a crust of bread to a few pigeons waiting patiently nearby. "And your mother?"

"My mother had an entirely different type of thinking... with the best of intentions for her son, of course."

"Don't they all have the best of intentions?" Alice said wryly. She raised her glass again. "To parents."

He clinked Ali's glass and then took a sip of his water. "Is there someone special in America? I mean...do you have someone in your life right now?" Claudio asked, looking away.

She stiffened and shifted her weight. "I guess you could say that."

"How long?" he managed to choke out.

"About a year, now," she answered. Ali watched as Claudio's expression changed. "Hey...you okay?"

"Yes, perfectly fine." He cleared his throat and continued. "Are you engaged?"

"Engaged?" Ali grimaced, surprised that he would make such an assumption. "I'm still in high school!" She laughed without humor. "I don't even know what program to take in university, never mind engaged. That's way off in the future. Besides, Caleb is a nice guy, but...I don't know." She lost her thought. "Anyway, there's lots of time for that. What about you?"

"No one," he replied.

Ali watched the color return to his cheeks. "Really? No one? I would have thought that someone like you would have his pick of anyone he wanted." A hint of a smile danced on her lips.

"And why is that?" Claudio leaned in.

"Well, you're attractive, obviously." She laughed and felt the tiniest suggestion of a blush creep across her cheeks.

"I am? Obviously?"

"Well, yes. But beware, I've been warned about guys like you." Ali's eyes narrowed as she faked mistrust. "People have told me not to trust you because I'm easy prey for the local boys." She put her hand up. "So be warned...I'm onto you!"

He threw up his hands. "You got me. I admit defeat. You figured out the master plan."

Ali giggled. "Hey, I just thought of something." She jumped up, dashed to the bike, grabbed her satchel, and plucked out her phone. "Ah—this will be perfect." She strode to waist-high crumbling column at the edge of the picnic spot and placed her device on it.

"I got a new phone, and it can take 3D shots of everything around it...voice and everything."

Gracefully, she backed away from the device, and sat back down beside Claudio. "Smile," ordered Ali, as she placed her cheek against his to pose for the video. "It plays back in high-res 3D—it's awesome," she added proudly. Claudio, a broad smile on his face, grabbed her slender wrist and stood, pulling her to her feet.

"Well, we cannot just sit here, then. Come on, dance with me."

He took her hands in his and improvised a loud song, singing uninhibitedly off-key as he stepped forward, left and right, guiding her in his spontaneous dance. Alice laughed without reservation. His silly steps were totally out of character, which pleasantly surprised her.

"Right now, big finale—" He scooped her up with a final swaying motion and dipped her gracefully, guiding her arms and holding her tightly at the waist his lips only inches from her own. Lifting her back up with no effort, he kissed her hand, his eyes never leaving hers. Ali's world stopped for an instant. She allowed herself the pleasure of gazing into his eyes, but only for a moment. She broke contact, and walked briskly to retrieve the device.

As suddenly as it began, Alice made it stop. "Um, I think I'll have another fig." Ali picked one up from the basket and turned to glance at some far off point in the distance.

Claudio sighed, with a fleeting look of disappointment in his eyes. "One more and then off we go."

"Are we going into Fiesole next?" she asked, with a little too much inflection in her voice.

"Are you sure you are up to it today?" An impish grin stole across his lips. "You know, if you faint, I just might have to revive you."

"Really." She shot him a side glance, and fake punched him in the arm. "And how will you do that?"

"Never mind," he smirked. "Let us go into Fiesole, my lady."

Chapter Twenty-Two

Leaving the ancient Roman ruins behind, Claudio navigated through the tiny streets of Fiesole and into the piazza. As they entered the square in the medieval town, he pulled up to a little café for an espresso. They chose a seat outside, *al fresco* under a canopy of tangled honeysuckle vines. Fragrant, sweet flowers hung over the lattices, enticing hummingbirds to sip at the nectar. Alice and Claudio's picnic had stretched into most of the afternoon, and the sun was beginning to sink its way lower and lower in the sky. The heat began to ease up, and the cool breeze from the higher elevation offered them respite.

Coffee was brought to them, rich and dark, with a foamy top, accompanied by a glass of ice water to quench their thirst. Claudio dumped three spoonsful of sugar into his little cup and drank his shot of espresso down in one motion. "Ah, delicious," he said and smacked his lips. "Nothing revives one like a good, strong espresso."

Ali was still trying to drink the first sip of it without grimacing. "You know...I really need to develop a taste for this...next time, cappuccino," she said and pushed her cup away.

Snickering, he flashed a smile her way. "Be strong and drink it down. I guarantee you will feel better after you drink it."

She tried hard to be annoyed with him, but it was impossible. Determined to show him she could handle it, she pulled the cup back toward her. "Okay, big shot...watch this." She lifted the tiny cup to her lips and then hesitated. "No sugar." Wincing, she drank the dark brew down in one gulp. "Ah, delicious," she said with a shudder.

"All right, I give in...you are a formidable espresso drinker." He sat back, laughing, his arms raised in defeat. "Some gelato now?"

"A gelato sounds like heaven...I need to get that taste out of my mouth." She shivered in mild disgust. "*Cioccolato*, please."

With a few words to the waitress, the espresso cups were whisked away and replaced with little plastic cups, one filled with chocolate gelato for Ali and the other brimming with a lemon *granita* for Claudio.

"Come on," he motioned, rising with his ice cream cup. "Walk with me. This town is too beautiful to just sit in a bar letting it go to waste."

"Good idea," agreed Alice, grabbing her stuff. "I must have put on five pounds in these past weeks. I need to walk it off."

"I doubt that," he said, helping her with her chair.

"No really," she laughed. "My pants are actually getting tight."

Claudio exhaled as they turned onto a quaint little street, lined with flower baskets carefully preserved on the balconies. "You know, I really must say something," he said, removing his sunglasses and focusing on her eyes. "You are a beautiful woman. Why are women so ready to criticize themselves because they have indulged in good food and drink?" He stopped walking, becoming more impassioned as he spoke. "You should worry only about pleasing yourself."

Ali arched a brow in surprise at his distinct opinion. She stopped alongside him. "I am happy with myself...but I also believe in being healthy."

He nodded in agreement. "If it is for you, then okay, but not to please others—men in particular or others' ideals of beauty." He collected his thoughts, his tone softening. "It is a shame that women have not been able to advance beyond that, when there has been so much progress otherwise."

"Well, I think I understand what you're trying to say, but sometimes women can't help falling into traps like that...what with so many things around us, media, peers..."

"Look, Ali...believe me, women have come very far since the days when they had to rely on men for their survival. I feel that women today should learn lessons from the past. Maybe... fight to hold on to the power and dignity women of the past fought so hard to attain."

Alice was floored. "All I said was that my pants are getting tight...relax. Besides, things aren't all *that* much better. There are still pricks in positions of power who think it's okay to take advantage of a woman, pressure them to have sex, there's still date rape, there's..." her voice trailed off. "Maybe we can talk about a lighter topic."

"Pricks is right," he murmured, then studied the ground as he walked. "Sorry, Alice. I did not mean to get so serious, but... I just feel very strongly about certain things."

"I can see that." She looked at him quizzically, paused, glanced at her gelato, and then looked back at him. "Would you feel better if I finished my ice cream?"

"That would make me very happy." His voice took on a less surly tone. He peered at her again, this time with a half-smile.

Ali couldn't resist the temptation to hip-check him out of

his seriousness. She moved her hips to the side for momentum and—*thump*—their hips connected.

"*Whoa!*" She howled with laughter at the expression on his face, then ran off into one of the little side streets. "That'll teach you to get too intense."

"Hey!" He tried to check her back, but she was too fast for him. "Come back! You cannot do that and get away with it!"

"Watch me!" she cried, running ahead of him, looking back and egging him on.

"You had better run!" Claudio ran after her, laughing, almost dropping his granita.

Heads were beginning to turn in the little street. Like two children playing tag, they dodged the ever-present motor bikes whizzing by them like dragonflies in the narrow laneways. Claudio was fast, but Ali was more agile. She ran like a gazelle, laughing all the while, disappearing from Claudio's sight around corners and then coming into view again.

"Alice, wait for me!" he shouted.

Then, as he turned a sharp corner, he almost slammed up against her tiny figure. Ali's hair had at some point fallen out of the hair tie and was blowing freely in the breeze, her chocolate gelato lay spilled over on the ground. She stood still as a statue, staring up at a double doorway with an elaborately decorated arch.

"Alice," he said as he halted. "What?"

Her face had turned a waxy white, her breathing was shallow, and she was trembling. Ali's gaze was fixed on the door as if she expected it to come alive.

"Ali, tell me what you are feeling."

"I've been here before." She felt the sweat beads forming around her hairline, though her hands were ice. "That door." Her head began to spin, and there was a loud buzzing in her ears.

"Claudio," she whispered.

He moved closer, just in time to catch her as she collapsed.

～

Darkness surrounded her. Sometimes grey spots would fade in and out of sight. And then, darkness again. There was conscious of a buzzing sound, her limbs heavy, unresponsive.

Arm, why can't you move? Leg, move.

She had no energy to open her eyes, much less hold up her head. The buzzing in her ears sounded like a cicada, ebbing and then surging—it was almost painful.

Wawi...wawi.

Someone touched her forehead very gently, with something cool and soothing...*wawi...wawi.*

She felt tapping on her face and her hand.

"Ali! Wake up!"

Her eyes opened to the fading sun. Claudio was holding her, his arms around her, a sopping cloth in his hand, and there was an elderly woman beside him, holding her hand. A bag with baguettes and other grocery items spilled on the ground beside her. Behind her stood a bewildered and worried-looking little boy. He stared suspiciously at Alice as she lay helpless on the cobblestones.

Ali was relatively conscious, but she couldn't speak. *Where am I? Oh, yeah...I'm with Claudio...in...Italy...a town in Italy. Should I know this lady? No...don't recognize her. And who is the little boy?* The old woman released her hand.

"Thank God, Alice, you are awake!" Claudio breathed a huge sigh and held her close. "What happened? You just crumpled like a rag doll."

She licked her lips. Her mouth was parched, and her tongue felt like sandpaper. It was beginning to feel like someone was pounding on the side of her temples with a jackhammer.

"I'm fine," she croaked, her voice sounding as dry as her mouth felt. "Can I have some water?" She could barely lift her head.

Claudio turned to the old woman. "*Acqua, per favore.*" She handed him an opened bottle and he managed to get it to Ali's lips.

She sipped the water down gratefully and soon felt human again. Ali looked at the little boy and smiled. He returned the gesture with a tentative grin, front tooth missing, now appearing less anxious.

Although she still felt unsteady, she got up, depending heavily on Claudio for support. "This is really getting silly—this fainting stuff." She held onto the wall for additional support. "I'm so embarrassed," she said to Claudio, unable to look at him.

The old woman and little boy hesitated to leave, but Ali assured them that she felt much better and that she had taken up enough of their time. She thanked them for their water and for their care. They said *arrivederci* walked across the tiny street, straight through to the door opened it, entered, and closed it behind them—the one that had made Ali faint.

Ali and Claudio looked at each other. He tightened his grasp on her, as though he were anticipating another fall into unconsciousness. "Claudio," she said, "I remember now...the door. Her throat tightening, *No! Not again! Breathe!*

"Alice, we should go." He guided her to turn around. "Come on. This is not a good place for you."

"Wait!" She pulled away. "Let me breathe...let go!"

Ali took in a deep breath, exhaled, and looked intently at the entry, focusing only on the calmness, the early crickets squeaking their evening trills, and the breeze in her hair. She closed her eyes and opened them again. The pounding in her head had dulled.

"I'm okay now...I'm fine." She stooped and picked up her

satchel, beating Claudio to it. Beside it was her hair tie. "Wow, you know, I just...I just don't know what happened to me, but...when I saw that door..." She chose her words carefully as she put her hair in a fresh pony tail. "It felt like...overwhelming claustrophobia...like someone was squeezing my head in a vise." She gasped and came to a realization. "I think I just had an anxiety attack." She massaged her temples with the tips of her fingers, looking up at Claudio. "Do you think that might be it, some kind of really severe anxiety attack?"

"Maybe." He glanced at his watch. "Look, Ali, it is getting late anyway. It is almost seven...we should be getting back." He took her hand and lead her to the piazza.

She hesitated at first, but then conceded. Maybe he was right.

"Okay, you win." She nodded and matched her stride with his. "But promise me we'll come back?"

"We will see." They walked quietly through the twilight, back to the busy Fiesole town square.

"Just out of curiosity," she asked, "where else were you going to take me today? You said you were going to surprise me."

He squeezed her hand. "You have had enough excitement for one day, yes?" He gestured to the Vespa parked in front of the cafe. "If you feel well, we will go tomorrow. I promise."

She agreed.

A freshening breeze passed them, which helped to clear her head. It would be a nice night for a walk. She bit her lip and worked up the courage to ask. "So, what are you doing later tonight? Are you working?"

He replied with hopefulness in his tone. "No, not working. Spending it with you, if you like."

"Yeah, I would like."

"Meet me at the front doors of the villa, about nine—I will show you something amazing."

Chapter Twenty-Three

After a day of picnicking and gelatos, the furthest thing on Ali's mind was food, but Roberto and Leda had insisted on dinner at a trattoria in town, and considering she had spent the day away, she felt it was the right thing to do to spend time with her family.

"Ali, you're not eating your dinner," Leda noted, reaching for the balsamic.

"I had a big lunch," replied Alice, picking at her farfalle Bolognese. Nine o'clock already, she thought impatiently. She was late and worried that Claudio would think she had stood him up.

Her uncle drove back at a leisurely pace, pointing out the twinkling lights in the distant towns, commenting on how enchanting they were. It took all the strength Ali had to keep from screaming, "Hurry Up!"

The Citroen found its way up the cobblestone driveway, just as it had on the first day. She marveled at the fact that she could not have known the significance of the decision to take an Italian holiday—the decision that brought them to this villa at this particular time. Who knew that she would meet someone like Claudio, so unlike anyone else she had ever known? So appealing and so...enigmatic. Like he was put there to make her question the path she was on.

Really, she thought, you make your own destiny. But sometimes you may be placed in a situation where there was only one possible outcome, no matter how much you thought you were in control of your own life. Could this be one of those times?

Pulling up to the grand entrance, Ali saw Claudio sitting patiently on the ancient stone retaining wall along the garden adjacent to the villa. When he saw the car, he stood and walked over to meet her.

"Is that the boy from today, Ali? Are you going out again tonight?"

Roberto meant well, but his concern was unfounded.

"I promise we won't be out long. We're just going for a walk."

"Not too late, Ali. I'll come and check on you at eleven?" cautioned Leda.

"Thanks, Zia," she replied, darting out of the car.

Her uncle stepped out, turned to Claudio. "One hour, then home."

"Yes, sir." Claudio grasped Ali's hand, and they walked toward the village.

"I missed you," he said sincerely.

"How can that be, we were just together," she teased.

"I still missed you. How are you feeling tonight? No more fainting?"

"No, I'm fine."

They strolled without a care, by the castle of San Miniato, on the same cobblestones where countless other couples had promenaded for centuries.

"Look over there, in the meadow," Claudio whispered and pointed to something so ethereal, it took her breath away. Ali thought she was watching tiny fairies in a field. She marveled at the dancing fireflies in the pasture, listened to the frogs croaking their nightly warbles in the distant ponds, and wondered at the crickets chattering endlessly in the tall grasses by the road.

Ali pointed to the moon, adorned with a cloak of a million stars. "Look up there. It's a full moon tonight."

Claudio turned to look at her instead.

"Soon, I will take you to the Uffizzi. There is something there I want you to see," he said. "There is a collection of sketches and paintings from Leonardo da Vinci on display from London. It is a perfect opportunity to see some of his later work."

"All right," she agreed. "Sounds incredible."

"But for now, let us just listen." He guided her to a wrought-iron bench overlooking the meadow and motioned for her to sit. "Close your eyes and just listen."

Ali complied and took in the music of nature at night. The concert was peaceful and calm. Both enjoyed it without the necessity of words.

As they listened, Claudio cupped her cheek that was turning a rosy red, and slowly leaned into her. Ali's hand was shaking, her mind repeating the same sentence over and over. *Don't do this...don't do this.*

When their lips met, the kiss they shared stole the words they didn't need to say. A kiss like this was a beginning, a promise of so much more to come. When they broke apart, Ali rested her forehead against his and sunk into his hold.

They didn't dare talk about what each was thinking or let themselves reflect on the inevitable, that they must soon part. The present was all that mattered, right now, this moment. They wouldn't spoil it with the future.

Chapter Twenty-Four

The next morning, the weather matched Ali's mood. A dreary misty rain had started overnight and seemed like it was going to hang on for the day. *No matter*, thought Ali, *Claudio is working this afternoon, anyway*. As much as she hated to admit it, she found herself quite miserable, wanting to be with him every minute.

She had checked her messages, too, something that she hadn't done since the day before. She had five—one from her parents, one from Kiana, and three from Caleb. She had returned Kiana and her parents' call but couldn't bring herself to message, let alone call, Caleb back. She felt guilty, yet she couldn't help herself...she had to see Claudio again. She was drawn to him. She had heard that phrase a thousand times, but now she really understood what it meant.

Roberto and Leda knocked lightly on her door. "Looks like a good day to go to the Uffizi—it's raining," said Leda.

"Thanks so much for the invite, but I think I'm just going to make some calls home. You know—to my friends." She held up her phone. "And Claudio had mentioned that he wanted to take me to the gallery. He said that there is a collection of sketches and paintings from Leonardo da Vinci on display from London. Apparently, it's a rare opportunity."

Leda sighed. "Darling—"

Ali knew what was coming.

"Do you know how difficult it will be for you to leave if you became too attached to your new 'friend'?"

"But we are just friends. That's all. We just talk." Ali thought about what she just said to her aunt. Did she believe herself?

Leda pursed her lips. "You know that we are only trying to protect you, *tesoro*, not spoil your vacation. We don't want you to get hurt and neither do your parents. Just remember that. It may be a good idea to limit the time you spend with him, if you allow yourself any time at all. Again, it is your decision."

Leda set off from Ali's room to join Roberto, but before leaving, she ensured that she left her niece with some cautionary words to mull over. "Think about it, Ali. About hurting over a little summer romance that will not last beyond a few days."

With her aunt's parting remarks in mind, Ali thought about who was going to get hurt. To say herself would be stating the obvious, but there was Claudio too, if she was reading him right. And that reminded her of Caleb. She prepared herself for the call. It was about one o'clock, so it would be just past dinner in Boston.

Maybe I should call Kiana, again instead. She perked up. *No, she'd know instantly that something was up. I'll call Caleb. Come on, woman up and call him!* She spoke his name into her phone. Hopefully, he wouldn't answer.

Her thoughts raced while the phone rang. *What am I going to say to him?* Two rings, three rings, four...voice mail...*Thank God!* she sighed. This, she could handle. "Hi Caleb, it's me... sorry I missed you. I'll call back later. Bye."

She lay down on the bed with a flop, her head over the

edge. "Oh, my gosh. I'm going to mess everything up. Maybe I should tell Claudio I can't see him anymore. That would be the right thing to do." She got up and paced. *Crap—why isn't my heart listening to my head?*

"Stop this whole thing now, Alice. Think straight and be rational. You are on vacation for another week and a half and then you go home. Be sensible and stop complicating things."

She stopped pacing and thought ahead to that evening, when she would see him again. Claudio had mentioned that a certain spot on the very road that they were walking on, just past the castle, had an incredible view of the evening sun as it set. The vista was supposed to be legendary.

Her emotions were a tumble of confused thoughts and feelings. "You have to tell him tonight. You can't see him anymore." With a roll of her eyes, she conceded to her common sense.

But what will I tell him if he asks why not?

"Why not? I'll tell you why not, Claudio, because I'm falling for you. Oh, my God, I need to end it now."

As if by divine intervention, the clouds lifted just before the dinner hour, which allowed the lingering afternoon sun to make a welcome appearance on an otherwise bleak day. Roberto and Leda had returned from Florence with a bag of freshly baked bread, thinly sliced prosciutto ham, and a salad of fresh tomatoes and mozzarella cheese.

Ali joined them in their room, and the three ate quietly on their balcony overlooking the Chianti vineyards. Ali nibbled, but had no appetite. Roberto sat silently, observing the two women, his chin resting on his folded hands. "Would anyone care to tell me why we are so gloomy this evening?"

"Not now, darling," Leda put a finger to her lips.

After staying for what she thought was a cordially appropriate amount of time, Ali stood to leave. "I'm going out for a little while, and I promise I won't be long."

Leda tagged along as Ali went back to her room to grab her bag. "Does it have anything to do with what we talked about today, Alice?"

"Yes, Zia, it has everything to do with what we talked about today," she said, returning her aunt's serious gaze. "I'll be back soon." She turned silently and left the room, purposely leaving her phone behind.

Ali walked somberly to the lift and stood staring at the down button. Pressing it would be so final, like setting off an irreversible chain of events that would bring her to leave Claudio behind. So, there she remained, putting off the inevitable.

I can't just stand here blinking at these things forever.

Her finger reached for the orange LED, but she couldn't do it.

Maybe I'll just use the stairs.

She took her time down the marble staircase, through the lobby, and walked through the front double doors, meandering to their meeting place by the garden. This time she waited for him, sitting on the retaining wall.

Before long he appeared, hurrying from the side door of the villa. Upon seeing her, a dazzling smile split his face. "Ciao, bella."

"Ciao, Claudio." She smiled back and reached for his hand, but then pulled it away, reminding herself of the reason for her being there. "Let's just walk awhile."

"Of course. What is the matter?"

"Let's walk to the spot—the one you want to show me."

She turned her head, pretending to admire the scenery, but secretly hid her eyes, which were becoming misty.

Claudio took his cue from Ali and walked silently beside her, not asking any more questions.

"Right here." Claudio gestured and guided her to the look-out. He put an arm around her waist, but she pulled away. The confusion on his face made Ali want to cry. Still, he said nothing.

The sun was sinking slowly in the sky.

Ali focused on the miracle taking place in front of her. They stood side by side, leaning on an ancient hillside abut-ment just past the castle of San Miniato, quietly taking in the spectacular scenery, the rolling hills dotted with whitewashed villages, tufts of cypress trees, and shrubbery that accented the meadows of grape vineyards and olive trees. It was like feasting on a gigantic Renaissance painting.

The sun put on its farewell performance for the day and finished its last dance in the sky with brilliant reds, oranges, lavenders, and some otherworldly colors for which Alice knew there were no names. This, thought Alice, is truly paradise on earth. There was no other way to describe it. And with a clarity so real and so true, she knew that there was no one on earth that she wanted to share it with other than Claudio.

There it is again—I admit it. Now, what the hell am I going to do?

"Oh God, Claudio," she said aloud. "How can anything be so beautiful? It makes me want to cry just looking at it."

Ali gazed at the pastoral landscape, but what really made her want to cry was the fact that she didn't have much time left before she had to board the flight back to reality. The short time spent with Claudio had been dreamlike. It was as though she was living out someone else's life, seeing through another person's eyes. She was another person around him, playful and adventurous, carefree.

She didn't even care that her aunt and uncle didn't trust

him—that they believed the only thing he was interested in was taking advantage of her. She knew they couldn't have been more wrong. Ali trusted Claudio completely, yet, she couldn't forget that her days in Italy were numbered.

When Ali thought about going back to Boston and seeing Caleb again, she felt a stab of guilt. Caleb was in love with her, and she had let herself fall for Claudio. How could she have let this happen? She wanted to please her parents, to live up to their expectations and make them happy—after all, as an adopted child, *they* had chosen *her*. As these thoughts of surrender and uncertainty raced through her head, she could hear her father's voice asking her why she would set herself up to be hurt.

Though she craved more time with Claudio, her moment of rational thinking had brought her back to the here and now. She could let it play out and regret it or leave him and save them both significant heartache.

Ali summoned up every drop of self-sacrifice she possessed and decided that, for everyone's sake, she could not let this progress. She had to let him go.

"Claudio, I need to say something," Ali began. "You know that I care for you and that the short time we've spent together has been...like a fairy tale, but I feel like maybe this is moving too quickly. I have to leave soon and—"

"This is no fairy tale, Ali. Believe me this is real...this is real for both of us." Claudio's tone was strained.

"Claudio," she said, unable to look him in the eye, "the last thing I want to do is hurt you, but you need to understand that I have someone in Boston who cares about me very much. I have a lot of time invested in that relationship. I'll only be here a few more days. And I've only known you for a couple of days."

"Alice, are you hearing yourself?" He threw his hands up,

exasperated. "You are talking about someone you say you love like you are talking about a bank account."

She shook her head and thought about rephrasing. "What I meant was that I have to respect the time I've spent with him. I don't want to demean it by having a holiday fling over here that I might regret. It wouldn't be fair to him. And my parents...they expect more from me—like being responsible." Her voice cracked.

"There is nothing cheap about what we feel for each other," he asserted, searching her eyes for a reaction. "I know what you are trying to do, Alice. You are guilty because you feel a sense of obligation to him. But falling in love has no timetable or schedule...you just know that it is good and right. It does not matter how much time you have spent with him. You are here with me—now. And I know, time notwithstanding, I know you love me as I love you. There is nothing cheap about what I feel for you, my Alice." His voice was firm, unhesitating. As he stepped closer, he let his hands slide up her arms to her shoulders, then back down to her slender wrists. He took her hands and kissed her palms.

"Oh my God, this is crazy." Ali's eyes welled up as she tried to look away. "Claudio, why are you doing this to me? Why are you torturing me? You must know that whatever is going on between us cannot go on. I live on the other side of the world for God's sake!" Wiping her tears away with the back of her hand, she tried to keep her voice from shaking. "Can't you see that this is hard for me, too? That it's tearing me apart inside? I'm trying to be strong and do the right thing...before someone gets hurt. Before you get hurt. I couldn't bear that." The intensity of her tone surprised her. She was trying to do this gently, but emotions just spilled out of her.

"Hurt. Alice, you do not know about hurt. And neither does your Caleb." Claudio spit out the name. "And if you truly had feelings for him like you say you do, then you would not be here with me." He paused as a haunted look took over his eyes. "Listen—you are here because you feel something that you cannot explain. You feel drawn to me like I am drawn to you. There is an affinity between us, Alice, a bond that is beyond time and space. It cannot be measured in days, weeks, or even years. You are for me, and I am for you. We are soul mates—can you not feel it?" He clutched her arms and made her look at him. "I know you can."

Ali knew he was right. She did feel it. She had felt it the moment she first saw him. If only she had time to think logically. She couldn't think straight when she was with Claudio. She needed to sort through her feelings and reflect on what would happen if she let this go on.

Plus, she knew practically nothing about Claudio. All she knew was that his parents had passed away and he was living with his aunt and uncle in the family villa. Still, even though she had only met him a few days ago, she felt she had known him much longer. Could he be right? What was this connection she couldn't explain? She gazed up at him, and his eyes were pleading with her.

"Listen to me, Ali, please," he begged. "No one is saying you must make a decision now. You still have time here with me...why do we not just be together? Enjoy each other. Do not worry about me...I can cope with my feelings. I know what I want. All I ask is that you not go home with the regret of not knowing what you could have experienced here, with me."

She couldn't bear to hear him imploring her like that. Her resolve was getting weaker as she thought over what he said, with what could only be described as a combination of empathy and desire.

If she wasn't strong enough to let him go now, what would she face when she had to board the plane home? Then again, things could change dramatically in just days. If she let the relationship run its course, she might find out that she wasn't in love with him and there would be nothing to pine about.

Ali tried to free her hands from his, but he wouldn't let her go. Looking into his eyes, she appealed to him one last time in a whisper, "Please."

He looked straight back into hers and whispered, "Stay with me."

She gently pulled her hands from his and Claudio looked like he had been dealt a blow to the stomach.

"Please, Alice. Stay with me. A few days with you are worth a lifetime to me. I will be happy with that, if that is all you will give me."

Ali's heart melted. If this was a fleeting summer fling and nothing more, then it could never last. This passion was akin to fireworks bursting in the sky—beautiful fire, but short-lived. Of course, it must be like that. If it wasn't, her whole life was about to be turned upside down. She didn't have the strength or desire to make a case against his wishes. Her heart would claim victory over her common sense for this struggle.

She breathed in deeply and turned the corner, and her life would never be the same.

With tenderness that surprised even herself, she slowly took the palm of his hand and placed it on her cheek. She looked up into his dark eyes and unsealed her heart to him. "Claudio, I don't know if I'll regret this, but...I can't help it. I don't know anything anymore—what I do know is that I can't live with 'what ifs' forever."

A flash of hope sparked in his eyes.

"What if I had just let things move forward? What if I could have found a life with someone I've only known for a few days? What if I would have let myself fall in love...what if...." her voice trailed.

She sniffed and closed her eyes a moment, gathering the strength to say what she had been thinking but not admitting to herself since she saw him walking from the rear of the villa the first day they got there. "For once in my life I'm going to live in the moment and follow my heart. I don't want to play it safe. I don't want to worry about what other people want from me. I just want to enjoy being with you. I don't even want to think about what can happen or what will happen or who is going to think what. I don't care. Right now, right here, I want to be with you."

The tears finally came, and Alice hid her face in his chest. He held her tightly, his strong arms around her minute frame. She felt a surprising sense of relief as she let her emotions wash over her. She could just live for now, with no burden or apprehension about tomorrow.

He let go of her to be able to see her face, to wipe her tears away with his gentle fingers, to hold her face in his hands and draw it closer. "Alice...you said it is so beautiful here, that it makes you want to weep...I know something about crying for the love of beauty," he confided. He held her gently, speaking softly and sincerely. "But I do not mean for the scenery...I mean for you. You cannot begin to imagine what you would do to me if you left me. You would take my soul—my very heart—if you leave."

His gaze traveled over her face and searched her eyes as he tucked a honey-brown tendril of hair behind her ear. Slowly lowering his mouth to hers, he kissed her, a soft, tender, lingering kiss. Then, with eyes closed, he murmured, "I love you," against her mouth.

His words coated her like velvet, soft and warm. She let herself relax and allowed every emotion inside her to swim to the surface. She couldn't have felt more right, more at home in his arms. Standing on tiptoe, Ali wrapped her arms around his neck and returned his kisses, as both slipped blissfully out of reality.

~

Alice didn't care about the cost of their declaration of love. Nothing was important right now except each other and the truths the two had shared.

They strolled back to the villa in an aura of newborn love, oblivious to any consequences that might be awaiting them. Everything in nature had taken on a new wonder, with a multitude of reasons to admire the complexity of its existence, its very form and composition. But good sense still had to prevail.

"I really need to get back," said Ali, grudgingly. "My aunt is probably ready to send out the troops."

"I can speak to your aunt," replied Claudio, gallantly. "Tell her it was my fault, that I kept you too long."

"No, I don't think so," Ali said with a grimace. "It'll be better if I talk to her—alone. I'll just tell her we want to be together."

"Whatever you think is best. But if you need me, I will be outside your balcony window for a while...just in case."

Alice giggled. "You're too much."

"Too much what?" he asked sincerely.

"Just a figure of speech. It means sometimes I don't know how to take you, the way you do things...it's unusual."

"I see. Well, I will try to be more 'usual.'"

"Don't you dare...you're perfect the way you are."

The villa loomed before them, illuminated as they rounded the corner onto the cobblestone from the road. Claudio reminded her. "So tomorrow then, Florence—you and I."

"Agreed...if Leda ever lets me step foot out of the villa again. Speaking of which..." Ali spotted Roberto grabbing something from the Citroen—his wallet. When he saw them walking up the driveway, he closed the door and slowly approached them, his hands in his pockets, eyes to the ground.

"Alice," he nodded to her. "And you are Claudio, I presume."

"Yes, sir. It is a pleasure to meet you." Claudio held out his hand to shake.

Roberto did likewise. "The pleasure is mine."

Ali looked at her uncle quizzically.

"Alice, your aunt and I were talking and…if you wish to see this young man, it is your choice." He nodded to Claudio. "But don't be too long. It's getting late." He turned and walked back to the villa.

Alice stood rooted to the spot. "Well, that was easy," she said. "A couple of hours ago you were a teenage Casanova, now it's not a problem? Goodnight and thank you very much. Weird."

"My family probably just reasoned with them, that is all. They most likely convinced them that forbidden fruit is more powerful than common sense."

"What does that even mean, 'forbidden fruit'?" asked Ali with a grimace.

"It means that maybe they decided it was better for them to let whatever is happening between us run its course." His gaze shifted to the villa. "You know—reverse psychology. They probably think we are not aware of that concept."

"No, it's weird—welcome, but—weird," she said, walking past him to a look-out point, thinking about what could have softened her aunt and uncle.

"Can you not just trust them…believe that perhaps they know what they are doing?" His gaze followed her as she moved by him. "Stop analyzing so much and just enjoy living."

She stood at the retaining wall and looked out onto the darkened valleys surrounding the villa. It was almost midnight and there was a chill in the air. The moon climbed in the clear, cloudless sky, surrounded by millions of tiny points of light, like tiny diamonds on an inky quilt.

Claudio followed her. "Please, Alice, trust me," he implored. "Trust what you are feeling." Gently, he turned her around and held the backs of her arms, pulling her closer. "Trust me with the time we have left." He craned his head so that she could not avoid his gaze.

She brushed her nose against his cheek. "Of course, I trust you."

Chapter Twenty-Five

The night passed. Again, for Alice sleep was hard to find, with events from the past few days being perfect fodder for a whirlwind of thoughts in her head. When she did manage to drift off, fleeting images of Claudio, Caleb, and herself at the edge of a lake of fire, calmly discussing the ruins at Fiesole haunted her.

But the strangest thing was the door. In her dream it stood on its own, by the lake of fire, and she knew that behind it was cool clear water, waiting for her. She recognized the door, too. It was the one that old woman and little boy had entered in the little Tuscan village they had visited, the one that had triggered her black-out.

When she awoke, Alice wondered what her dream meant. Was it a message or a memory? *I should invest in one of those dream interpretation books next time I'm in a bookstore.*

But the dreams would have to wait. More important things were top of mind that morning. Alice hurriedly prepared herself for her day with Claudio. But before she left, she took a moment to check the messages on her phone. Caleb had called her again while she was sleeping, but she would have to call him back later as Leda and Roberto were waiting at breakfast, and it was already past nine.

Fumbling with her satchel, she wondered what could have been behind the change of heart, so unexpected, yet so refreshing, on the part of her aunt and uncle. On her way out of the elevator, she looked over to the breakfast alcove and stopped in mid-step. There, at a table littered with coffee cups and half-eaten pastries, were her aunt and uncle, their friends, Anna and Dario—and Claudio.

Alice strode over, unsure of what to say.

Claudio spotted her first and stood, a broad smile on his face. He went to her and took her hand.

Leaning into him, she whispered, "What's going on?"

"Are you ever on time for breakfast?" he asked his voice jovial. Then quietly, "Do not worry, everything is fine. Come on. There are two people I want you to meet." Ali followed his lead.

"Buon giorno," said Alice as they approached the table. She stepped forward to give her aunt and uncle a peck on the cheek.

"Alice," said Claudio. "I would like you to meet Anna and Dario."

Anna smiled cordially, and Alice offered her hand.

"Buon giorno." Anna's hand was smooth and warm.

"*Salve*, Alice." Dario kindly shook her hand.

Ali turned to Claudio. "I had the pleasure of meeting them a few days ago—they are my aunt and uncle's friends."

"I know. Anna and Dario are my aunt and uncle," Claudio announced.

Alice turned to Claudio with a smile. "Wow, small world."

"Yes, it is," agreed Roberto. "We had no idea that Claudio was Anna and Dario's nephew," he explained. "We had never met. I was on my way to look for you last night, and I happened to run into Dario at the front desk. We began to talk and eventually the subject got around to visiting nieces and nephews, and...well, you can figure out the rest."

Dario nodded. "You may as well take advantage of our resident tour guide, Alice. He seems to be enjoying it."

"*Sí, cara*," Anna grinned. "We hear that you are going into Florence today. Have fun. But before you go, a nice cappuccino."

"Sure, thanks so much." Ali nodded.

Then Leda leaned in closer, almost to her ear. "But please be careful." She exchanged a glance with Roberto.

Ali nodded.

"Ready to go?" asked Claudio casually.

"Ready." She stood without a second thought to her cappuccino. "Strange morning," she whispered to herself. Alice turned to Claudio's aunt and uncle. "Nice to meet you."

Ali and Claudio walked side by side to the Vespa.

Despite everyone's casualness, she felt something had changed—and not casually. She couldn't put her finger on why she knew things were different, but she felt it in her bones. "Are you sure you're telling me everything, Claudio?" she asked.

"I want to show you something special in Florence, Alice," he answered. "I hope that then, things will begin to make more sense."

She surrendered and accepted his hand. "Whatever. Let's go."

Ali held Claudio tight, as the *Vespa* sped in and out of traffic into the historical Florentine city center. His heartbeat throbbed against her ear at her touch.

Today was the day, he thought. His mind was a jumble of

overly practiced phrases and imagined reactions at his impending revelation. But through all this, whatever happened, one thing he knew for certain—never would he become too accustomed to appreciating the silken touch of her skin, the inviting curve of her face, or the intoxicating sound of her voice.

Claudio tried to clear his head as he looked momentarily up to the sky at the unrelenting sun and reached under his helmet to wipe the sweat from his brow. He welcomed the wind on his face as a relief from the stifling Mediterranean humidity. Claudio navigated the *Vespa* through tiny side streets, covered in ancient cobblestones which had been worn down to a shiny finish by centuries of pedestrian hustle and bustle.

"We're almost there aren't we?" Ali shouted to him over the noise of the tourists and street vendors at the Porcellino market. A left turn just before the Ponte Vecchio brought them to a busy cross street from the Lungarno Acciaiuoli, and then to Via de Girolami.

Looming in front of them in all its antique grandeur was the Galleria degli Uffizi, one of the grand dames of all art galleries.

"The Uffizi," gasped Alice. "I've heard so much about this place. About the art. I can't imagine being in the same room with works by Michelangelo and Leonardo da Vinci." Her eyes swept over the architectural details of the old building.

Statues stood in the arches running all the way across the front of the gallery. It was like a who's who of great historical figures...Machiavelli, Raffaello, Petrarch, and da Vinci.

Claudio pulled the bike into an empty spot, parked and halted the engine. His nerves were jumping.

"Well, here we are." He removed his helmet and turned to Ali. She had her helmet resting on her knee and her eyes were glazed over. Had the anxiety hit her again?

"My darling," said Claudio, waving a hand in front of her face. He hated what this was doing to her. "Alice? You look like you are in another world, again." He dismounted and held his hand out to help her off.

"Sorry. I'm just a little overwhelmed. I mean, I've heard about the masters, but to see their work up close, that's an entirely different thing." Her sea green eyes looked apprecia-tively at him as she handed him her helmet.

Claudio kissed her on the forehead and squeezed her hand tight, then kissed it gently, trying not to give away that he was incredibly nervous.

With their arms linked, they walked through the gallery entrance to the security point. Claudio had to marvel at how much he loved her—at how easy it was to love her. He had never felt so close to her as he had in the past couple of days. If possible, he loved her even more now than he had before. She was articulate, confident and self-assured, almost buoyant, with a touch of the unpredictable, yet she still possessed a glimmer of the shyness that he found so irresistible and endearing. A more perfect woman could not have been created.

Was it right of him to set her entire life upside down? To shatter everything she knew to be the truth? And to what end...to honor an old promise made so long ago?

It had to be Ali who made the ultimate decision to stay or go.

Claudio was pensive as she chattered about this painting and that one, commenting on the colors and textures or the fact that she remembered this Donatello from an art class or that Caravaggio from a coffee-table book she had at home.

They wound their way through endless pathways, rooms covered with Botticelli's and Raffaello's masterpieces.

And then they reached the gallery which held the special exhibition. It was a collection by the old Master, da Vinci.

Claudio had heard that one particular painting would be on exposition, the 'Madonna of the Rocks' from London.

Yes, this is a good place to start. Time is running out. The painting will be the catalyst for the conversation. I will wait for her reaction and after that, I will have to improvise.

He saw the top of the painting's arched frame just up ahead; a crowd of people were gathered around it. Gently, he guided Alice to the image. Its colors were almost as intense and vibrant as he remembered from so long ago...da Vinci's unmistakable left-handed stroke of the brush, his texture and *sfumato* technique, the perfection of his detail, all reminded him of the Master.

"Alice, come with me. I want to show you a painting that is very special to me. It is by da Vinci. He called it The Madonna of the Rocks."

They stopped arm in arm, in front of the painting. The canvas was framed with an imposing, thick, arched support, adorned with gold leaf. The painting itself was a rather dark representation of the Virgin in an open-air cave with her arm around a child. Another child sat at her feet, and beside that child was an angel. The most breathtaking angel there ever was, with an indescribably delicate and gentle quality, calm and tranquil.

"Alice, do you see?" Claudio whispered, watching her intensely. "Look closely." Claudio sensed Alice's breathing change as she scanned the painting. The angel, with sea green eyes and a mane of wavy honey-brown curls, was so familiar, the fair skin and the curve of the angel's face.

"Yes, Claudio, I see it," she whispered, not taking her eyes off the image. "The angel looks a lot like me. It's a beautiful painting. What a thoughtful thing to do—to remember such detail about a work of art. You wanted to show me how much I look like the angel...the angel of the rocks."

Gently, he reached for her chin and turned her face so that

their eyes met. There was no easy way to say this. He could not make it any less disturbing or bizarre. In the end, she may not believe him at all. She might just think he was crazy.

"Alice, please understand that I love you more than you will ever know and that I would never do anything to harm you." He glanced at the painting and then looked back at her. Her eyes searched his for the truth. "My love, I must risk telling you this. You will probably think that I have lost my mind, but I do not have much time. I ask one thing of you, and you must promise this before I tell you."

"I promise." She shifted her gaze from him to the painting again, mesmerized by it.

Claudio hesitated. "Elis—I mean, Alice..." he caught himself.

"Yes?" She reached for his hand, focusing on him now. "I'm listening. What's wrong—your hands are like ice—and you're positively grey."

"I...I ask you to trust me," he stammered out. "I ask you to just hear me out and to trust me, because what I am going to tell you sounds impossible..." He trailed off, looking at all the people around him. Then again, maybe it was best that she was surrounded by others; she might feel safer and not run screaming from the madman in front of her.

"Claudio, whatever it is, as long as what you're trying to tell me about isn't against the law, we'll work it out. How bad can it be?" Her eyes were drawn to the canvas again. She took a small step toward it. "It's amazing. She looks so much like me." Ali was spellbound by the image.

"Okay," he swallowed and then spoke. "You are leaving in a little over a week and...well...Alice, there is no other way to do this but to just tell you. The angel in the painting looks like you because it is you. Master Leonardo painted this canvas with your face, after you disappeared many, many years ago."

To his surprise, Alice showed no reaction. She stood still, her flecked green eyes like polished jade, only blinking at him.

Chapter Twenty-Six

Renaissance Florence
1512

Claudio kissed Elisa good night under the nearly full moon, neither wanting to part, neither wanting to wait until the next day to hold each other. Their souls were already as one, smitten in the space of no more than a few hours.

"I cannot bear to say good night, my lady," murmured Claudio kissing the back of Elisa's hand, "as time will rob me of yet more moments that I should be spending with you. I do not wish to sleep. I wish to be with you."

"My lord, retire quickly and time will pass unbeknownst to you." She gently brushed the hair out of his eyes. "Time is the one thing that is for certain...there will always be a tomorrow. And my tomorrows are yours, Claudio."

"I will see you in the courtyard in the morning, then?"

"I will be there." Elisa leaned forward and placed her cheek against his chest, listening to his beating heart. "You have made me so happy, my lord." Claudio put his arms around her and pressed his face against her hair. She paused and closed her eyes, treasuring the moment. But all moments must end. The kitchen maid looked up and allowed the Count a dazzling smile. After that, she reluctantly turned, and he watched as she disappeared through the servants' entrance.

As though in a trance, he shook himself back to corporeality. Claudio's mind reeled with happiness and raced at the events that had taken place that night.

His heart was on fire with love for her, his Elisa.

Contentment and true fulfillment could not be obtained this easily, he mused. What had he done to deserve such happiness, with a woman like her? A woman, devoid of malice and vanity, and filled with wonder and curiosity. A beautiful woman who accepted herself and her life without bitterness and resentment, though she would have been well justified to feel both.

Despite all these glorious thoughts of love, he had to go home and try to sleep. How he would manage that would be anybody's wager, he was so euphoric he would probably never be able to sleep again.

Somewhere in this maelstrom of thought, he realized that he had not been to see da Vinci for a few days. In his new excitement about Elisa, the chamber experiment had escaped his attention entirely. There could possibly be new developments of which he would not have knowledge. Deciding to make use of his energies, he hastily made his way to the palace stables to find Spirit.

"Let us be off, old girl." He patted his horse's nose and nodded his thanks to the bleary-eyed stable hand. "Might as well visit the Master as long as I am up—I know he will be awake—he hardly sleeps at all." He murmured to himself, a hopeless grin on his face.

At an easy gallop, Claudio rode through the warm night air to Master Leonardo's studio in the Galluzzo monastery, the fireflies guided him to his destination as they danced in the meadows.

Claudio moved leisurely, with Spirit snorting her complaints every so often at being awoken late in the evening for a long ride. The moon was on the cusp of being full, which to Claudio's advantage, provided him with enough light to navigate safely up the steep hill.

Coming closer to the abbey, he realized that the sentry was probably asleep and that knocking loudly to awaken him would upset the entire brethren. Claudio decided to go around to the rear, where the outermost quarters of da Vinci's studio was located. He wondered if he climbed onto Spirit's back, whether he could reach the lower window and knock so that the old Master would let him in.

He circled around, staying close to the wall as there was a steep drop from that angle. Wild blackberries and thorny bushes grew untamed, and Spirit had to step carefully to avoid them.

Finally, the mare and her horseman reached the small window with its medieval stain-glass depiction of Baby Jesus in the Manger. The bright colors of the glass were lit up from behind by a flickering candle—a sign that the Master was still awake. The window was too far up to knock. Claudio dismounted, reached down to the ground, and scooped up a handful of pebbles, tossing them one by one up to the window. The light inside the room moved and eventually a shadowy figure, candle in hand, appeared on the other side. He wrenched the handle and swung it open.

"What is that!" shouted da Vinci's other student.

"Francesco, down here," whispered Claudio. "Look down here. It is Claudio."

"What are you doing here so late?" demanded Francesco, perturbed. "It is well after midnight and you are out roaming the countryside?"

"Where is the Master, Francesco?"

"He is preparing to depart for Florence in the morning. He requires some materials for the experiment you and he were working on..." The words came out while he tried unsuccessfully to hold back a yawn. "I believe he called it the chamber?"

Claudio's heart jumped. "What is wrong with the chamber?"

"I have no idea, and at this hour, I do not—"

"Never mind," Claudio hissed at him. "Come around and open the door, you—"

As he was about to finish the sentence in a curse, he saw da Vinci's white head peek through the window behind Francesco. "Why...is that Claudio down there?" he asked, delight in his voice, as if it was a visitor coming for an afternoon visit, not someone throwing rocks at his window in the middle of the night.

"Yes, Master da Vinci, it is Claudio. Will you please ask Francesco to come down and allow me entry?"

"Of course, he will. Off you go." He waved his student away to open the door as requested.

In a flash, Claudio was back on the mare, awaiting entry to the abbey. He heard the opening of locks as he secured Spirit, and after what seemed an eternity, the door opened, allowing him access inside.

"The old man has been wondering where you were," said Francesco. "You have been busy, I presume." He yawned again as they walked to Master Leonardo's quarters.

"My dear Francesco, I have been very busy. Very busy falling in love with the most beautiful, kind-hearted, gentlest woman in the world."

Francesco shot him a sideways glance. "Should I have asked?"

"Without a doubt, you should be so fortunate!"

"And who is this beautiful, kind-hearted, and gentle woman who has captured your heart, my friend?"

"Her name is Elisa, and she is a scullery maid in the Medici palace," Claudio replied proudly, not thinking anything unusual of the match.

Francesco halted mid-step. "I beg your pardon, but..." He laughed out loud, tapping his ears. "I thought for a moment you said she is a scullery maid."

"Indeed, I did," replied Claudio, who continued walking.

"Are you mad?" asked Francesco, scrambling to catch up to him. "Falling for a servant? A scullery servant, nonetheless, not even a lady-in-waiting."

"It does not matter, Francesco. I do not care what she has come from, nor what anyone may think about it."

"Well, my friend, perhaps you should start thinking about it—how long have you known this girl?" asked Francesco incredulous as they turned into the hallway to da Vinci's studio.

"Forever," said Claudio, dreamily. At least in his heart it felt like forever. When he noted Francesco's skeptical look, he amended his answer. "Three days."

"You are mad." Francesco shook his head and held the door open.

"Mad in love," Claudio corrected him, and he stepped determinedly into the studio.

Da Vinci came out from the chamber room to greet him. He could not wait to tell Claudio of his new idea. "Claudio! At last. Where have you been? You have not attended for a few days, now. Is all well?" His tone was a mix of relief and annoyance.

"You have no idea how well everything is, Master da Vinci," interjected Francesco with a smirk.

Claudio elbowed him in the side. "My apologies, sir. I will

explain later. But first, what of the chamber? Is everything satisfactory?"

"Oh yes," his eyes glinted with excitement. "All is well. In fact, I have speculated on how we may study the swirling elements in the chamber array more closely." Da Vinci beamed with anticipation. "Or at the very least, I may be able to make them more stable, to diminish their fading and resurgence. By doing so, we may be able to enter the chamber and explore its images with a greater measure of time."

Francesco and Claudio listened closely as the Master explained, taking in his new theory.

"In conclusion," he finished, secure in his own reasoning, "all we do after we prepare the copper pole, is to wait for a storm...and pray that we will seize yet another of the celestial phenomenon."

His students exchanged wary glances. They were mortals playing with the fire of the gods. "If you believe that this will work, Master," Claudio responded, "then, of course, we will assist you." Their teacher was not in the habit of being questioned once he got something into his mind.

"Wonderful, lads! Then you must both stay here this night and accompany me into Florence in the morning." He could barely contain his eagerness. "We will depart as soon as we wake." He peered at Claudio. "Claudio, are you in agreement?"

But the young Count was preoccupied thinking of Elisa. If he was not at the palace, she would wonder where he was. He did not wish to cause her any undue concern or have her worry that harm had befallen him. Perhaps, if they departed early enough, if they made haste in the morning, he would be on time to meet her.

"I am Master Leonardo," Claudio replied.

"Good. Francesco will carry what we need on his mount, and you and I shall depart on Spirit in the morning. Early."

Chapter Twenty-Seven

The sun was about to make its first appearance of the day over the eastern horizon, yet the three men were already approaching the city ramparts. They entered Florence, with Claudio gesturing his acknowledgment to the guard on the watchtower.

At the studio, da Vinci dismounted and swiftly pulled out a key, which when inserted into the lock, prompted a series of whirring and clicking sounds.

Once inside, the pupils unloaded da Vinci's belongings from the horses and made certain that everything was in order before they took their leave. "Will there be anything else, Master?" asked Francesco.

"No, lad. I need to rest now. You, gentlemen, return home. I will procure what is required for the chamber later." Leonardo yawned and arched his back, trying to shake off the aches and pains of the ride. "I will have need of you here by tomorrow evening. We must transport the goods back to the abbey as soon as possible...and pray for a storm as you have never prayed before."

"Of course, Master Leonardo," responded Francesco.

"Until tomorrow, sir," agreed Claudio. "Good day."

~

The sun broke over the treetops, as Claudio rode to the palace and Francesco returned to his parent's homestead below Fiesole. It was just past dawn.

After handing off Spirit to the stable boy to be fed and watered, the bleary-eyed young count walked from there to the back entrance of the palace, by the little courtyard where he had first spoken to Elisa.

There were tell-tale signs that the palace was beginning to stir itself awake. He was tired, but all he could think of was her, the girl he had fallen in love with. He decided that he would come back later or perhaps find her in the palace kitchens.

Climbing up the stairs to his apartments, he wondered what she was doing. Was she asleep, or just waking up to confront her daily chores? Was she thinking of him as he was of her, or was her mind occupied by some task she was about to undertake?

He hoped that she was tranquil, and nothing had upset her. He could not bear that. He needed to be with her, to watch over her, to protect her. Still deeply absorbed in his thoughts, he walked down the sumptuously decorated hallway leading to the Moro apartments, its corridors carpeted with woolen rugs, and its walls adorned with portraits of the Medici family, both present and past. The candles in the wall sconces glowed warmly as he strode by.

Claudio was beginning to feel the fatigue from the restless night before. Leonardo's guest accommodations were not exactly the most comfortable, as he and Francesco had to manage with a few blankets and a couple of hay beds in the corner of one of the studio rooms. And though the journey from the abbey to Florence had never seemed that long, Claudio was anxious to see Elisa again.

Had it only been a few hours since they had last been together? It felt as though time was standing still. He resolved that he would refresh himself and be gone forthwith to the kitchens to find her.

Claudio gripped the ivory door handle and stepped into the rose-colored marble foyer. To his surprise, straight across from the entrance, lay his mother, dozing on the red velvet settee.

"Mother?"

She was fully clothed in evening dress, and when he spoke, she awoke with a start. "Mother, why are you not in bed?"

Countess Maria's face quickly fluctuated from relief to anger. "Oh, Claudio, thank the blessed Lord, there you are!" She rushed to him with open arms, hugged him tightly, then stepped back and sharply slapped his arm.

Claudio yelped in surprise. She had not smacked him since he was a child. "What the devil was that for?"

"That was for worrying me half to death. Where have you been all night?" She turned to the window and threw open the drapes. "Look outside." She pointed toward the sun. "It is well into morning. Where were you and with whom?"

"I was with Master da Vinci and Francesco last night, at the abbey," he replied calmly. "What is all this about, Mother? It is not as though this has not happened before. And please do not strike me again." He rubbed his shoulder, almost amused at the fact that she thought she had given him a proper thrashing.

Relief once again flowed over her face. "Thank goodness you were with him." She sat back down on the settee, closed her eyes, and set her head against the cushy upholstery, chuckling.

Claudio did not know what to make of this or her concern.

She was well acquainted with the fact that he would occasionally spend the night out of the palace. It had never bothered her like this before.

"Are you feeling ill, Mother?" he asked softly, as he sat down beside her.

"Oh no, very well, thank you."

"Good. Then perhaps you can explain why you saw fit to beat me?"

"Oh, stop exaggerating." With a handkerchief, she wiped the perspiration from her temples. "Late last night, Clarice came here, very agitated. She had missed you at dinner and was curious as to your whereabouts." Maria paused, then began again with a snicker. "Apparently, there is a rumor about the palace that you have been carrying on with one of the servants —a scullery maid." She closed her eyes and laughed heartily.

The Countess appeared to ponder this for a while, her hand draped on her forehead, then opened her eyes with a pinch of renewed energy. Turning to look at her son, she reached over to caress his hand. "Is that not the most outrageous supposition? Imagine...you with a scullery maid."

Claudio fiercely pulled his hand away, though this time it was he who had shades of fury on his face. He felt violated for Elisa.

"And what of it—if it is so, about the maid?" Claudio seethed with anger as he rose from the settee without breaking eye contact with his mother. She searched his eyes and once the reality of the situation sunk in, her face changed completely.

The Countess' demeanor took on a calm, cool, dispassionate appearance, stiffening straight up on the settee as she adjusted the crumpled folds in her gown. "Well, then. I can assume from your response that the ridiculous rumor is not so far off the mark, after all." Her lips curled in anger, though her voice was calm and steady.

Despite the fact that he was furious that someone had run to tell his mother about his personal business, Claudio responded in an equally composed manner. "I was planning on telling you myself, Mother. I will have you know, I am not ashamed of my relationship with Elisa. It all happened rather quickly, and last night after meeting with her in the garden, I decided to ride to Master da Vinci's studio in Galluzzo." He paused a moment and waited for his mother's reaction.

"Go on." Maria stared out blankly.

"By happenstance, he needed me to stay the night to assist him in travelling back to the city in the morrow. So, Mother, I have not kept anything from you—I simply have not had the opportunity to inform you of Elisa."

Countess Maria winced at the maid's name. "If that is so, that you have had a relationship with her but for a day, then how did Clarice know of it as long as she did?"

"Clarice, again," hissed Claudio. "She was no doubt egged on by her drunken brother."

"Nevertheless, she was speaking the truth." The Countess sighed deeply and snapped her gaze away from her son. "Yet, it has only been a day or two in which she has had occasion to spread the rumor throughout the entire court." She stood, tucked a stray tuft of hair back under her headpiece, and peered angrily at Claudio. "We shall arrange to have the maid removed. Before long, the entire sordid affair will be forgotten, and you shall take your place with the Medici, with Clarice at your side." She started for the door.

Claudio's hand moved fast to take hold of his mother's arm, intercepting her before she could grasp the doorknob. "Mother, listen to me." His eyes burned into hers. "You shall not, under any circumstances, give orders either harming Elisa or removing her from the palace. She will not be maltreated or injured, or I shall hold you responsible."

"And what if I do?" Her gaze did not flinch; her voice held no emotion.

"Then I shall leave, and you will never see me again. You will be alone, Mother. Alone." He paused to emphasize his point. "Will it be worth it?"

The Countess stood silent for a moment, her fingers on the bridge of her nose, eyes closed. When she opened them again, her expression was weary and wistful. "Claudio, you know that all of these riches, my title, my vestment in the court of nobles —all of these things and more would mean nothing to me without my son. You are all that I can say is my very own."

She approached him and extended her hand, adjusting his untidy collar. "You are as your father was, always immersed in art and curiosities, ceaselessly working to bring another artist or sculptor to the attention of the Medici. However, unlike you, Count Giacomo of Elba was soft-spoken and wise. You are headstrong and impassioned."

Claudio allowed himself a crooked smile. "Perhaps I have inherited those qualities from my mother." Claudio took the Countess' hand. "Mother, you must know that I love you and ordinarily I would, without question, respect your wishes, but this girl..." he paused to find the words. "This girl is in my heart. I could no more leave her than I could live without drawing breath." His eyes searched his mother's, desperately wanting her to understand.

After a heavy sigh, she spoke. "Very well," she conceded, half-heartedly. "I will not have you miserable on my account. Your will be done, my son. I shall hold onto the hope that this is merely a fling."

"Thank you, Mother," breathed Claudio, offering a weak smile. "If Elisa is banished from the palace, she will have nowhere to turn."

"Is that so?" The sarcasm in the Countess's voice was obvious.

"Really, Mother, you should be well acquainted with the Medici traditions in treachery and ruthlessness."

"Nonetheless, my son," Maria softened her tone, "I beg of you to exercise the greatest of care in this...situation. I had the distinct impression that Clarice was relying on your accompaniment this evening."

"I have no intention of accompanying Clarice to dinner tonight, or any other night, for that matter." He rolled his eyes at the prospect of such an event. "I plan to meet Elisa shortly, and if she is able to, then I intend to be with her as much as possible throughout the day."

Anger and frustration broke from the Countess like water from a dam. "Oh, Bacchus, help us all. I have lost my son to a scullery wench." Tears burst from her eyes. Slowly, she walked toward her private quarters.

Claudio hesitated and then in two strides he was at her side. "Please, Mother...Elisa is a good, honest girl. Her strength of character and kind disposition, despite her lot in life, have truly endeared her to me."

Through her tears, Maria looked wearily at her idealistic son. "My darling son, have you considered that she might want you only because of what you are?"

"Never. That is how certain I am of the quality of her character."

"Then have you never thought of what will happen to you?"

"I have, Mother." He reached to comfort her. "I am prepared to leave here if that is what the Duke wishes. If Clarice poisons his mind against me. And that is the only reason he would banish me, for he has no quarrel with me, nor has he ever cared with whom I keep company. Lord knows, he himself has known a courtesan or two in his time."

"And what of your mother, Claudio?" She sniffled and wiped her tears with a lace handkerchief. "What would happen to me should you refuse the Duke's wishes?"

"You can come with me. I will always take care of you. Though I doubt that anyone would dare touch you because of something that I have done."

"Do not even say it." Maria held her son at arm's length and looked imploringly into his eyes. "You are my son, my only son...I will always take your side, but I tell you I do not like it. I beg of you, please tread softly, at least until you are certain of your association with this girl. Promise me that much. Do not tempt fate. Please."

Claudio weighed his options and considered his mother's warnings. He did not care about what anyone thought of him. He could always work with Master Leonardo as his apprentice, and then make a good living in the artists' guild. It was his mother that concerned him. She was afraid, he knew, of another exile from the palace, another long uncertainty, of having to find other wealthy landowners with whom to live. Her title was all she had. "Very well, Mother. I pledge to be careful, and I shall return to Master Leonardo's studies as usual. And I shall continue to seek Elisa's company. Is that clear?"

"It is. But do not forget that I am your mother," she reminded him sternly.

He kissed her cheek and responded with a trace of laughter in his voice, "That would be quite impossible."

Once he was in his apartment, he splashed water on his face from the basin and changed into fresh clothing. If he was to meet Elisa in the courtyard by the fountain, he would have to make haste.

~

"And what if it is so...about the maid?" shouted the voice on the other side of the door.

Now this voice, she thought, *is certainly the young Count's.*

Then there was a muffled woman's voice. *Perhaps the countess Maria?*

"...the rumor is not so far off the mark."

Yes, Gabriela thought, *that is she.*

As lady-in-waiting to Lady Clarice de Medici, Gabriela knew very well that Lady Clarice was not the kind of person who easily trusted others. In fact, she was suspicious of everyone. She would not leave anything to chance, especially when it concerned something or someone that she desperately wanted. So, she had sent Gabriela to observe, eavesdrop, and scrutinize the Moro's private apartments in the palace, whenever the opportunity presented itself.

The lady-in-waiting passed those apartments most days and usually, there were not many voices or unusual activities from the suite of rooms. But this morning was different. The voices were loud, and they sounded angry.

Gabriela had pressed her ear right up against the door and could plainly hear everything that the Count and his mother said.

The conversation was indeed interesting. Her mistress would appreciate knowing the facts, though the information would undoubtedly anger her. Lady Clarice was frightening when angered.

She continued to listen attentively.

"You are my son...my only son."

How sweet was the love between a mother and son? thought Gabriela. It was a pity that she had to report to Lady Clarice with the news of that son's infidelity to her mistress.

Chapter Twenty-Eight

T he evening that Claudio went to the stables to take Spirit to Master Leonardo's, Elisa returned to the palace, drifting on wings of happiness. She was free of any worries or concerns; they were cast to the wind, like dandelion seed heads meandering in the breeze.

Elisa entered the palace without a sound, but inside she thought she would burst with joy. Her happiness was indescribable, her emotions spinning. When she finally reached her little cranny of a bedchamber, she saw that Caterina was sound asleep, with her threadbare covers tucked around her. The dampness of the lower levels of the palace made the conditions clammy and cool, even in the throes of summer.

The young maiden recited a silent prayer of thanks. Was she so blessed as to have the love of such a man? Surely, she must be dreaming. Even if he had not been a count, she would love him just the same, if not more.

As she slipped out of her day dress and into her thinly worn nightgown, Caterina stirred and turned over. The candle was still burning on the rickety table in the corner, now flickering wildly as Caterina created a breeze with her flimsy covers.

"Elisa," Caterina mumbled groggily. "Elisa?"

"It is I, Caterina," replied Elisa in a whisper. "I am here…go back to sleep."

"It is late. Where have you been?" Caterina questioned, as she lifted herself up on her elbow.

"I went for a walk in the gardens. It is such a beautiful night."

"The gardens? At this hour of the night…by yourself? Elisa, that is unwise." Caterina shook her head in disapproval. "Next time ask me to go with you." She set her head back down on the hay bed and rolled over, adjusting her blanket over her shoulders.

"Oh, of course, I am quite distracted of late." Her thoughts turned to the morning when she would see Claudio again. She let the happiness soak right into her bones and the idea was so exciting that if she did not tell someone she was sure that her emotions would certainly bubble over and engulf everyone in the palace.

"Caterina." She drew a deep breath, not knowing how Caterina would react. "Do you recall that handsome young man…the noble…Count Claudio? Dark eyes and hair?"

Caterina rolled back over to face Elisa, rubbing her eyes. "Who?"

"Count Claudio," she repeated, pressing on, "Countess Maria's son…he is one of the young courtiers."

Caterina shook her head, then her bleary eyes suddenly became clearer. She sat up, her head askew as if she was putting two and two together.

"Wait one moment," she said slowly, looking intently at Elisa. "Would this young Count Claudio be the young man you were speaking to in the courtyard by the well?"

"Yes!" exclaimed Elisa enthusiastically. Observing her

friend's disapproving glance, she pulled back her eagerness and let her shoulders slump down.

"You have caused quite a stir, Elisa," Caterina said sternly. "A few of the women approached me in the morning about you. It seems you and the Count were friendly enough to start tongues wagging. Remember what I have always told you?"

"I know, Caterina," she replied, eyes firmly fixed on her shoes. "But sometimes things happen and...well...you do not expect to...what I mean is..."

"What are you trying to tell me?" asked Caterina calmly.

Elisa grew nervous. Caterina would not approve of her feelings concerning the Count, but she had no choice but to be honest with her friend...Caterina was all that she had.

Caterina remained silent through the entire recount, only letting out a horrified gasp at the encounter with Bruno and Enzo.

"So, that is where I was this evening...with the Count." Elisa sat quietly and waited for Caterina's reaction.

Caterina nodded and sighed deeply. "What would you have me say?"

Elisa shrugged while Caterina remained silent. "I would like to hear you say that you are happy for me."

A corner of Caterina's mouth twisted upward, still silent.

"Say something...anything," appealed Elisa.

"Count Claudio may have protected you from what would have been a dreadful ordeal with those detestable men." The hatred stirred in Caterina's eyes. "But he is a highborn." She looked imploringly at Elisa.

"Do you not think I am aware of that?" Elisa replied, emphatic. "Caterina, you do not understand...he is different. He is kind and gentle and he speaks to me like I am a person of worth."

"How can you be sure of what he is thinking? Who knows what his intentions are? You say you have spoken to him only a few times, yet you believe that he loves you? Do you really think that is possible? Think, Elisa...he is a courtier."

"I know. And I am telling you that it does not matter to him. I am certain of this, as I am certain that the sun rises every morning," Elisa declared.

"Why did you not heed me and stay clear of them?" questioned Caterina.

"I did stay clear!" she cried in defense of herself. "I did everything you told me to do, but they found me just the same —they took off my bonnet and Bruno pressed his body against me." She looked away. "Claudio intervened, otherwise I do not know what end I may have come to."

Caterina walked to where Elisa sat. She took her young friend in her arms and rocked her. "There, there. Do not fret. I am only trying to protect you."

Elisa nodded and wiped her eyes. "Yes, I know." The two were quiet for a long time.

"Very well, then, Elisa. If you say that you love him, then I believe that you do." Caterina sighed and raised her palms in surrender. "I ask only three things, and then all I can hope for is good fortune for you. Be discreet: you never know who may be watching you. Be sensible: he may change his mind if one of his friends or another noble discovers the situation. And for heaven's sake, remain chaste, I beg of you."

Elisa blushed. "I...uh...of that, you can be certain."

Caterina yawned and gave Elisa a peck on the cheek. "Now Elisa, I am very tired. And you should be, too. Go to bed. We can talk more of this in the morning." She pulled the covers up to her neck. "Dawn will be here soon, and the masters and mistresses will want their breakfasts. Not that they have done anything to stir hunger. Good night, now." Before long, poor, overworked Caterina was fast asleep.

Elisa sat awhile, thinking of how hard she and Caterina worked. She thought of her family and Claudio's. They were as opposite as opposites could be, as far as breeding was concerned, but in their hearts, there were no barriers.

"My dear friend, I know what you are thinking...they are not all lazy and selfish," she said wearily. Elisa bid Caterina a silent good night, snuffed out the candle, and advanced to bed herself.

As she slipped into her little cot, she discovered the extent of her fatigue. Setting her head down on the straw-filled pillow, she drifted off to sleep, her dreams filled with images of her beautiful young man.

The next morning, Elisa awoke to the sounds of the bustling corridor outside of her tiny quarters, with the other servants exchanging good mornings amongst themselves, preparing for another day.

She washed and made herself presentable, dragging a comb through her untamed hair, and nearly running for the water containers.

"Why such a rush to fill the vessels, Elisa?" Caterina asked, her eyes narrowing as she prepared the plates for the morning meals to be brought to the masters' and mistresses' rooms.

"We will require water for the morning, will we not, Caterina?" Elisa said shyly.

"Of course," she responded with a suspicious tone.

I must try to appear less eager to get to the courtyard, Elisa thought. She let out a nervous giggle and proceeded up the narrow stairwell, with the water pails in hand.

Breathless with anticipation, she stepped into the court-yard and quickly glanced over it, searching for Claudio.

He was not there.

Elisa scanned again.

She was exceedingly disappointed. Had she missed him?

Had he been called away? She hesitated to fill the jugs too quickly and slowed down the pace of her work.

Hoping that he would appear, Elisa sat for a moment or two by the ledge of the water well, but her hopes were dashed. She rose reluctantly from the little ledge, disappointedly filled the pails and started back down to the kitchens, much slower than she had ascended them.

In the working area of the refectory, Caterina and a few of the other women servants had set out breakfast for the kitchen staff. Cook had put out barley bread in a bit of goat's milk sweetened with honey, but Elisa was not hungry; she was still troubled that Claudio had not been in the courtyard.

Noticing her distraction, Caterina prompted her, "Step to it, Elisa, come and eat. We must prepare the breakfast trays soon."

Paolina snorted. The toothless old woman had been a laundry maid in the palace since anyone could remember. "I think she is daydreaming about her young man. She is looking smitten, if you ask me."

"Ooh!" said another old maid. "She and the young Count were making very good conversation yesterday morning."

"Stop it, you old crows," cried Cook, a very large woman with a booming voice and a personality to match. "If you put such enthusiasm into your chores as you do gossip, you may actually accomplish a good day's work."

Caterina shifted her gaze to Elisa with an 'I told you so' look. "Sit down and eat your breakfast," she whispered.

Elisa bowed her head, blushed with embarrassment, and pulled her bonnet tighter around her face. She sat silently and nibbled at her bread, while the other servants ate their morning meal, gossiping and cackling.

While dipping the bread in her milk and honey, Elisa heard a faint knocking at the refectory door. She turned and gasped when she saw Claudio framed in the doorway, his brocades and linens a contrast to the modest surroundings.

"Good morning, ladies. My apologies for interrupting your meal," he said, tipping his head.

The servants sitting around the table, let out a surprised, "Ooh!" and scrambled to rise. A resounding "Good morning, my lord," was recited almost in unison by all.

"My lord," Cook said surprised, stepping into the little servants' refectory from the cavernous Medici kitchen. She curtsied and then managed to sputter, "How may I assist your lordship so early this morning?"

"Please, be seated," he said. "It was not my intention to disturb your breakfast." His attention was focused on Elisa who was standing quietly with her head bowed. "I came only to pay a visit to a certain young lady." He pointed to Elisa who was trying very hard to be unassuming. "That young lady, there," he continued. "The one with her bonnet wrapped very tightly around her face. I believe her name is Elisa." A grand, crooked smile crept across his face.

Elisa was attempting to suppress a huge smile of her own. Every fiber in her body tingled at his presence in the servants' refectory. She felt a slight nudge come from behind. It was Caterina, her face a mix of astonishment and concern. Elisa sensed Caterina's apprehension, and though she felt encouraged by her nudge to do the Count's bidding, she also felt an obligation to her friend's unspoken trepidation.

Elisa thought for a moment before speaking. "My lord, nothing would please your servant more than to visit with him, but I cannot yet leave my fellow servants. There is much to be done before the household rises for the day." She could not help but feel deep regret even as she chose to do the right thing.

The Count bowed respectfully and then responded, "Well, perhaps if I help, you will all be finished your tasks sooner, and you will be free to leave with me for a short time."

The entire staff gasped in a breath. Cook spoke first. "Begging the Count's pardon, but that will not be necessary. With respect to my lord and his kind intentions, it is not his place to assist the maids." She motioned to Elisa. "If it pleases Elisa, she may attend a visit with his lordship."

Elisa looked longingly at Claudio, then at Caterina.

Caterina grasped Elisa by the hand and turned her, so she could see her eyes. "Do you wish it, Elisa?"

Elisa nodded enthusiastically. "Very much so, Caterina."

Caterina paused for a long moment and then let go of her hand. "Then you shall go with his lordship." Glaring boldly at the Count, she continued, "I trust that my lord has only the most honorable intentions towards my very dear friend."

Claudio bowed his head to the woman. "I have only the deepest respect and affection for Elisa."

Elisa looked at her imploringly for her blessing.

"Do not worry then, Elisa," said Caterina her smile warming. "We will complete your portion of the morning chores." She glanced at the other domestics for approval and after acquiring it, she directed her attention at the Cook.

After a brief pause, Cook responded, "With respect, my lord," she said with a raised brow. "I ask only that she be back soon."

"You have my word, Cook." And with that, he grasped Elisa's hand, and they headed up the stairs to the servants' courtyard.

Elisa untied her bonnet and let her honey-brown curls fly free as they ran up the narrow stairs hand in hand. "Where are we going?" she asked, her voice ringing with contentment.

"It is time you met Spirit," he replied, echoing her delight.

Both were at their happiest, unaware of what was yet to come.

Chapter Twenty-Nine

S pirit was fast as any horse could be. She was an Andalusian: black as the night and nimble as the wind. When Claudio rode her, she was an extension of his own body, responding to the slightest degree of leg pressure or pull of the reins.

To Elisa, riding Spirit was an entirely new experience. First, she had never been on a horse, and second, being so close to Claudio was extremely pleasant. She rode like a lady, side saddle, just as he showed her. Her arms holding tight around his waist, and her cheek resting on his back was a perfect fit.

They began with a steady stride through the city streets, but once outside of the ramparts, Spirit could stretch her legs. Claudio rode her only up to a gallop with Elisa on her back, but when Elisa dismounted, he showed her the speed of which his mare was capable. Elisa watched her Count, as regal as could be on his black mare, racing free—no boundaries, no limits. Claudio pulled on Spirit's reins, smoothly bringing the mare from a hearty gallop to an effortless halt.

"Oh, Claudio, she is beautiful," Elisa exclaimed, patting

Spirit on the nose. The black horse whinnied proudly, as if seeking approval for her performance.

"She is," said Claudio as he descended, extracting a bit of carrot from his pocket. "Would you like to feed her?"

He showed Elisa how to feed her, hand flat. "Ah, she is so gentle...like her master." Elisa smiled shyly, brushing her shoulder against Claudio's chest. His hand reached for hers and kissed it tenderly, then held her warm, slender fingers against his face.

Spontaneously, with the utmost tenderness, she reached for his lips, touching them with her fingertips.

"My lord," she murmured, her lips a breath away from his. "My lord, Claudio, you have captured my heart." Her love for him filled her.

"And you have conquered mine," he whispered back. "Utterly and completely. I am yours as long as you will have me."

She buried her face in his chest as he held her close.

The night before, his image had inhabited her dreams, and all she thought of was the next moment that she would be with him, when she would be by his side. But now she was curious. She needed to ask him a question that had also been haunting her.

"I am here, unreservedly devoted to you..." She looked up at him intently, almost afraid to ask what he saw in her that she could not see in herself. "But why? Why me, my lord? What is there for you to love?"

He pulled away from her tight embrace and held her tenderly at arms lengthy, locking onto her gaze, his own, astonished. "You really do not see what an exceptional young woman you are, do you?" he asked, taking her face in his hands. "My love, the way you view the world around you inspires me. You force me to be a better man. Your kindness and wit, your strength of character—I see you, so patient, and so gentle. You see beyond my title and wealth and love me for the person I am...not for what I represent. You, whose parents were murdered at the hands of a man obsessed with preserving his sovereignty. You should hate me." He ran a hand over her hair. "I cannot help but love you—you are everything to me."

Elisa's heart jumped when she heard his words. "How could I hate you, my darling Claudio? When I am not with you, I imagine us arm in arm, walking together, in the garden." She reached to caress his face.

"You make me so happy, my love." Claudio kissed her forehead, then his hands slipped around her back to bring her closer. "You are more a noble than any noble I know. I love you because you are the first woman who has made me feel alive. You have awakened something in me that I have never experienced before: caring for someone else more than I care for myself. That is, you, Elisa."

There was no need to speak. Her eyes declared her every emotion.

He brushed her lips with his and tenderly kissed her. "I have revealed my true feelings to you, my darling, and I do so without any reservation—but I must tell you that certain people may...may disapprove of our relationship."

Elisa frowned and stepped back. "You have told the other courtiers?"

Claudio was silent, which to Elisa spoke volumes. Her face clouded with uneasiness. "Your mother?"

Claudio nodded and reached for her hand, letting out a long, audible breath. "Yes, and no. I would have informed her nonetheless, however my mother was informed of our association by someone else in the palace. We had words regarding a visit from Clarice last night."

As he spoke of the exchange between his mother and Lady Clarice, Elisa became more and more fearful—worried not for herself, but for him. She could not bear it if he was harmed because of her carelessness.

"No. No, this cannot be!" Elisa cried. She felt as though she had fallen from the highest precipice. "Quickly, take me back to the palace. Do you not see that you may be ostracized because of me? Or worse...you may be harmed."

"Do not worry about me," he replied calmly. "And I promise that Clarice will not hurt you. I will not let harm befall you."

She bit her lip. "From what you have told me, her ladyship is in love with you," said Elisa. "She will discover our...association and will act on it. I have been told that her ladyship can be ruthless if she is angry. I do not care what happens to me. It is for you that I am deeply concerned." She squeezed his hand. "Please, my lord, take me back."

"Very well, my love, I will take you back to the palace, but you shall come to realize that—what is this?" His voice trailed off, as his gaze fixed on the horizon opposite Florence. Five men on horses were coming their way, the sound of multiple hoofs arising in the distance.

Claudio boosted Elisa onto Spirit, then scrambled on himself and pulled the reins around so that Spirit was facing the horsemen. The Duke's personal guards rode toward them with Bruno heading the contingent, Enzo by his side.

"Claudio...what do you think they want?" Elisa tried to maintain evenness in her voice but was failing.

"Stay calm," he replied confidently. "They are most probably on their way home from the hunt. Let me speak to them...that is, if they even decide to stop."

As the riders came closer, Elisa's unease increased. When they were upon them, the horsemen presented a threatening sight against the pastoral scenery of the Tuscan hills.

"Good day, Moro," drawled Bruno. "I see you are with the servant again." He turned his attention to Elisa. "However, did you manage to escape the bowels of the palace? Do you not have floors to scrub or dishes to wash? Or food to scrape off plates to bring to the pigs in the palace barns?"

The Duke's guards found this remark so humorous that Elisa fully expected one of them to fall off his horse. She grasped Claudio's hand and squeezed it again, looking down to avoid their piercing gazes.

Bruno made her feel worthless. Against the backdrop of Claudio's love, the feeling was intensified. He opened the world to her, making her feel like she could offer more than just a life of servitude. Bruno threw all that back in her face. She was just a scullery maid, and she would always be just a scullery maid.

Claudio's face was an angry red, his jaw tight, and Elisa could clearly hear him gnashing his teeth. She could only imagine what he was thinking.

"Please do not," she whispered. Humiliation and temper waged a war inside her.

"If that is so, then you had best be getting back to the palace, Bruno. Your breakfast is waiting for you...in the palace barn."

The guards thought that Claudio's remark was even funnier than Bruno's.

"You dare speak to me in that fashion!" thundered Bruno, the veins in his forehead about to burst. "You have been keeping company with the lower orders too much and too often. First da Vinci, and now this little trollop—you have been influenced by your time with commoners and are becoming as insolent as they are."

Claudio's hand was inching closer to the rapier at his side; his teeth clenched in anger. This was not lost on Elisa, and she began to fear that the young Count was about to lose control.

Instead, he said, "The vulgarity of your words, my lord, can only be as a result of your drunken tirades. You force your venom upon people who could not possibly protect themselves against you." Claudio's words were like deep cuts on Bruno's character—ones which few people would hazard to inflict. "You, sir, are a coward of the highest order."

"I should run you and your woman through, right where you stand," Bruno spat, enraged. He reached to pull the sword from its sheath, but the guards quickly intervened, recognizing that this would give rise to an explosive situation.

"My lord," said the captain of the guard to Bruno, strategically steering his horse between Bruno and Claudio. "Perhaps it is best to proceed to Florence. We are here to protect you, but this protection does extend to others considered nobility in the Duke's court," he said, nodding to Claudio. "Let us go from here. We were expected back yesterday."

There was a long silence as Bruno debated his next move.

"We will meet another day then, Moro," said Enzo, breaking the silence with a chill in his voice. "We shall leave you to your...business." He turned toward Florence with the smuggest of looks. The guards took their cue from Enzo and followed, galloping toward the city. Bruno lagged behind long enough to offer one last threat.

"You must believe that I am an imbecile, Count." Bruno's words were almost a whisper. "I know what you are planning... your mother is constantly at my aunt and uncle's sides, peddling your virtues. And you, romancing my sister, while you slither up to my uncle like a snake at every opportunity. Yes, I know what you are playing at. But as God is my witness, you shall never rule Florence. The throne is mine, and I will die before I see you on it."

"Are you completely mad?" Claudio hurled the question at Bruno with a disbelieving grimace. "Is this the poison that you have concocted in your twisted mind—that I want your crown...and your sister?"

"You have made it clear in your actions, especially in recent weeks...and I hear my uncle speak of—"

"First of all," Claudio interrupted, "whatever your uncle may be saying—you have twisted it around to suit your latest bone of contention—myself. My mother wishes only to secure me a place of business in the Medici banks. And Clarice has obviously mistaken mere civility and polite conversation for love. I assure you, I have no interest in—"

Bruno held his hand up to silence Claudio. "I do not expect you to admit your deception and lies when directly faced with your accuser...and this harlot you are stringing along for your pleasure..." Bruno's angry gaze swept over her. "It stands to reason that you must maintain your façade, the self-righteous façade of the Moro line, when in reality, you are a liar and a traitor."

"I do not wish the crown," Claudio said calmly, his hand moving closer to the hilt of his sword. "If there is reason for your uncle to doubt your ability to rule the Medici banks as well as the Duchy, if there was a snippet of such conversation that you became privy to, then, quite frankly, you should be pondering the reason why he doubts you. Look to yourself for the reasons why...not to others. Lastly, if you in any way disrespect the woman that I love by such references again, I shall have to teach you a lesson in common courtesy." Claudio's hand twitched as he kept it close to his sword.

"You dare to threaten the heir to the throne of Florence? This shall not go unpunished. Know your place, Moro, know your place," he snarled through gritted teeth. Then he turned to Elisa. "And you, sweet thing, one day—in one way or other —you will be mine." He turned quickly and rode off to join the others.

Elisa and Claudio stood still, watching and waiting for Bruno, Enzo and their entourage to be out of earshot. When they were far enough away, Elisa finally exhaled and spoke. "I am to blame for this." She felt ice spreading through her body. "Take me back to the palace and I shall ask Bruno, for his forgiveness. He will spare you if I make my apologies, of this I am certain!"

"You will do no such thing, Elisa," hissed Claudio.

"Did you hear what he said to you? Bruno called you a traitor. He will harm you. He will have you arrested and only God knows what else. Please, I beg of you, do not go back to the palace."

"Listen to me," Claudio said steadily as he grasped her hand. "I am more afraid of what he will do to you to get to me. We must return to the palace to gather your belongings, and when it is dark, I will meet you outside in the servants' courtyard. We must leave for a while. It is not safe for you there anymore, that has been made clear. I will take you to Fiesole and find lodging for you. You will be safe there until we decide what to do next."

"But what of Caterina? She will make herself ill with worry," said Elisa, wringing her hands. "I must tell her."

"It is best that she knows as little as possible. Do not be afraid...we will not be gone long...a day or two at the most, just so you are out of harm's way. When I speak to the Duke of the situation, I am sure he will understand and show clemency. Bruno will not harm you if he knows his uncle is suspicious of his actions. He is the only male heir to the throne. He will not put that in jeopardy."

Chapter Thirty

Upon reaching the palace, Claudio and Elisa separated at the courtyard; he headed for his apartments and she to the servants' quarters. Elisa crept down the entrance stairs and peered into the kitchen—all was quiet. It was late afternoon, and there was a lull in activity between meals. She stole into the hallway and managed to reach the kitchen without being seen. Caterina was at the table with one other kitchen maid preparing rolls of pastry for the evening banquet.

Elisa crept to the doorway. "Caterina," she whispered.

It drew no response from her friend.

"Caterina," persisted Elisa, her cheek color was that of ashes of roses.

"Wha...what? Elisa. You are back."

"Shh," whispered Elisa, her finger to her lips. She motioned for her to follow, then disappeared into the shadows.

Caterina looked around, then to the other kitchen maid. "Keep kneading until it is well blended, then put it in the pot." She wiped her hands on her apron as she walked to the hall. "I shall return shortly."

Elisa waited for Caterina to join her in the hall and then both stole silently down the hall into their little room.

"What is it?" asked Caterina. "You look as though you have seen the walking dead."

"I-I came to tell you that I must leave the palace for a while," Elisa stuttered. "It is not safe for me here."

Caterina's eyes became giant saucers. "What!" she cried. "Whatever for? What has happened?"

Elisa explained the foul incident which occurred earlier that afternoon between her, Claudio, and Bruno. "I should have stayed away, as you said." Elisa stopped talking as she noticed Caterina becoming increasingly distracted, angling her head to one side to look behind and beyond her friend. Elisa turned to check their door, which was slightly ajar. The shadow was plain to see—against the opposite wall across from their room was the figure of a woman, hunched close to their alcove.

Caterina crept to the door and motioned silently for Elisa to follow her. When she was close to it, she sprinted around and lunged forward into the hall, grasping the old washer woman by the shoulders. Though she struggled, she had no chance of escaping. Elisa was surprised at Caterina's reaction.

"Caterina, have you gone mad?" scolded Elisa.

"The stench of a rat hangs in the air, Elisa," grimaced Caterina. "The stench of a much larger rat than the usual rodents we are accustomed to. What is your business here, old woman?"

Paolina, still struggling, cackled harshly, "Yeah, Caterina, you should be listening to Elisa."

"Caterina, release her," cried Elisa.

"Why were you listening at the door, Paolina?" demanded Caterina, ignoring her friend. "Tell me, or I shall slap that last tooth out of your mouth!"

"Mercy, please Elisa—Caterina is possessed by a demon, she is—"

"Silence, you crow. Do not speak to her," Caterina said, scowling at the old maid. "I have a notion that there may be an old bird willing to give insight to others regarding business that does not concern them."

Elisa put her hand to her mouth and gasped. "No. Paolina, is this true?"

"No...not I, dearie," Paolina said sweetly. "Who would listen to me? I am an old woman. Please, Caterina, I beg of you —let me go."

Elisa was about to respond when she heard the clicking of heels descending the stairs leading to the kitchen. Elisa put a hand over Paolina's mouth, but it was too late—the steps came closer, and before they could act, a lady dressed in silks and lace turned the corner and was upon them. She stopped and looked at the scene in the alcove with daggers in her eyes aimed at Paolina, who was still thrashing about, struggling to free herself from Caterina's firm grip.

Paolina screeched under Elisa's grasp, "Miss, miss, help me, miss!" she begged, holding out a trembling hand to Gabriela. In response, the lady conveyed an air of impatience and irritation. In a huff, she turned on her heel and hurried up the stairs, Paolina's supplications ignored entirely.

Elisa recoiled her hand. She recognized Clarice's lady-in-waiting. Had she come down here for information regarding Elisa? And now, what of Caterina?

"Caterina, release her. You cannot risk staying here. You must come with us, now."

Paolina was reduced to a hollering mess. "They gave me money for it...I am an old woman. They gave me money for it..."

"Let us go! Now," implored Elisa. She grasped her friend's hand and ran up the stairs to the courtyard.

~

Simultaneously, Claudio entered the palace, stealthily moving to his apartments, hoping that his mother was elsewhere. It would be necessary to obtain a supply of florins if he was to arrange for lodging for a few days, until he could explain the situation to Duke Giuliano.

He entered unnoticed, strode to the armoire, and swiftly threw a few gold coins into his satchel. Upon gathering up what he thought was a sufficient amount, he turned to see his mother, leaning on the doorframe with her arms crossed.

"Where are you going with all those florins, Claudio?" the Countess asked coolly.

"I need them, Mother...for a friend." He did not meet her eyes when he spoke.

"Which of your friends is benefiting from your father's wealth?"

"Mother, please, I cannot speak now!" he bellowed impatiently.

"You are not leaving this palace. As long as I am alive and standing, you are not leaving with that...maid!"

"I will," he hissed. "If you choose, you may come as well. She will be harmed if she stays here, that swine Bruno has made that plain enough."

"Go with you? Are you mad? You have known this girl for a few days, and you will throw your life away for her?" She clasped her hands tightly. "I beg of you, please, listen to me. We will speak to my lady Filiberta. She is merciful...she will—"

"I cannot take that chance. I must be sure that she will not be har—"

"And what will you do?" Maria spoke through heavy tears. "Think, Claudio, think. You do not know the hardship of being in this world without a title to your name. Will you live as a servant all your life? A commoner?"

"If the woman I love can do it, why cannot I?" he replied, throwing up his hands. "I am taking Elisa and going to Fiesole. Someone there must remember her or her parents. I cannot bear to allow her to live here as she does another moment."

The Countess crossed the room and found her settee, her shoulders slumped in desperation. Claudio's gaze held pity, as she wept into her hands. As he slung his satchel over his shoulder, his heart broke for her. He could not leave her like this.

He strode to her side and spoke in a calmer tone. "Mother, I will return soon, when Bruno has had the opportunity to forget his anger. I promise you."

"What of Master da Vinci?" she asked.

It was not lost to Claudio that she was grasping at anything to keep him there. "Francesco is perfectly capable of assisting the Master in my absence," Claudio responded. "Elisa is in much greater need of me than da Vinci. Her life is in peril."

"Do you not see, my son that yours may be as well?"

"I have made my decision, Mother. You can help me—or not."

"Oh, my dear son," she said with resignation, dabbing at her eyes. "Bruno is crafty and shrewd. I will do what I can to protect you, but I beg of you, please, do not be gone long." She grasped him in a loving embrace, and then, just as quickly, released him and turned away.

"Thank you." He was at the door in two steps and out of the palace before anyone spotted him.

Upon reaching the stable, he soundlessly set to work preparing for the journey to the small hillside town, a quarter-day's ride away. The stable hand darted to gather up Spirit, when Claudio had a thought—he glanced down at his clothing —brocade vest and breeches. "You, there," he said to the stable hand, tugging at his vest. "Would you like to trade— mine for yours?" The man grinned appreciatively.

Claudio changed into the rough, brown linen tunic, handkerchief and pantaloons. This change in appearance would help him and Elisa blend with the people on the street. Alternatively, Claudio's vest and breeches looked quite nice on the stable hand. As Claudio finished saddling Spirit, the two women dashed into the stable. He was surprised that a visibly upset Caterina accompanied Elisa and listened carefully as the situation was explained to him in the short form.

"I see you have changed," Elisa noted.

"We must blend in. And we must go now," Claudio directed, as he rushed to assist the stable hand prepare the other horse. "It is very late in the day and we must move fast if we are to arrive at Fiesole before nightfall."

Caterina wrung her hands. "My lord, I must confess, though I trust his lordship, I have heard rumors about Duke Giuliano's nephew and niece. Their rivals have a nasty habit of disappearing. I would not want any harm to befall my lord or Elisa. She is innocent."

"And that is precisely why we are departing." Claudio waved them over. "Quickly, come here. We must proceed to Fiesole directly while we still have light."

Claudio assisted Caterina and Elisa to mount a gelding. Caterina had never ridden before, so Elisa had to take the reins. "Here," he said, handing her the ropes. "Hold them securely but pull gently. This way for left, and like this for right. Pull on both to stop. Follow my lead and stay calm."

He turned at the sound of footsteps outside, heavy boots and many of them, advancing toward the stable.

Claudio leapt onto Spirit. They moved out from the back of the stable, briskly but not so fast as to arouse suspicion, then out of the palace courtyard, and onto the busy Florentine streets. Once they were over the Ponte Vecchio, and through the city ramparts, they sped to a gallop, and headed toward Fiesole over the rolling Tuscan hills.

∼

As Gabriela approached Lady Clarice's apartments, her door burst open and Bruno stormed out. Gabriela stepped back, slamming against the wall to let him by. His eyes were red with rage. The lady's maid stepped into Clarice's quarters to find her pacing like a caged animal in her velveteen day dress. She wondered if she should hazard telling her ladyship the latest news.

"If it pleases my lady," said Gabriela, curtsying and breathless from her run from the kitchens. "I must inform her that I overheard the two maids pressing the old woman, Paolina, about information. They must suspect something. There could be a risk that Claudio's servant girl will run away if she fears she has been discovered." Gabriela stepped back as Clarice clenched her teeth and curled up her fists like little white hammers. Obviously, Bruno's visit had upset her, but now the noble woman was enraged. A guttural scream escaped with incredible force from her elfin frame. Then, just as suddenly, the most devious expression overtook her face.

"That scullery maid dares to leave the employ of the Duke without permission from the overseer." Like a whirlwind in motion, she turned to Gabriela. "Do not just stand there, you fool! Help me to change."

Chapter Thirty-One

The travelers reached the little hamlet of Fiesole after nightfall, guided by the distant candle lights in the village windows. Weary from their journey, they found a small lodging house. The young boy who appeared from the living quarters to take their horses rubbed his eyes as if he had just been jostled out of bed.

"One room, please. Three beds," requested Claudio to the man in the inn. They had nothing but the clothes on their backs, and the innkeeper looked them over rather curiously as he brought them to their tiny room. Two rudimentary beds, a small cot in a corner, and an oil lamp sitting precariously on a crooked table were all that occupied the room. It was clean, and it had a window, which had been opened to let in the cooling night air.

"Begging my lord's pardon," said Caterina as she peered tentatively around the room. "I ask that he forgives my forwardness, but how long will we be here...Elisa and me?"

Claudio looked over at Elisa, and she nodded her approval as she turned down one of the beds. She could not bear to tell her friend that she was the cause of all this.

"First of all, Caterina, you take the bed here, I will sleep on the cot." He motioned his permission for her to sleep on the more comfortable bed, and she obliged. "I am willing to wager that all this business will be dismissed in a day or two, as soon as Bruno has forgotten about the incident from this morning." His voice was soothing and calm. "You already know that Clarice is terribly jealous of Elisa. Bruno mistakenly believes that I am a threat to his rightful claim to the Medici Empire. Together they would spin any lie to cast doubt upon my character and to be rid of Elisa." He reached for Elisa's hand. "I will attempt to ride into Florence, perhaps in a day or two, to speak with the Duke myself."

"I hope my lord is right," said Caterina. "Master Bruno is not often forgiving, I have heard." She moved over to the bed and sat down, her shoulders slumped, clearly surrendering to the fatigue.

"Rest, Caterina," Elisa assured her friend. "You must trust the Count. He knows what is best for us both. Now go to sleep. We will talk more about this in the morning. Good night." Elisa turned down the lamp, so it cast a dim glow.

"Good night, my dear," Caterina replied, laying down and resting her head on the pillow. "You had best be getting to bed, too, my lord. Good night." She barely set her head down before she was asleep.

"Sleep well, Caterina," Claudio said quietly. He turned to Elisa and saw that despite her stoic face, there were tears on her cheeks.

"My love, please do not cry. All will be well, I promise." He outstretched his arms, but she stepped back.

"No...no please. The Duke will heed his niece and nephew, my lord. They will poison his heart against you, and he will have no choice but to punish you."

"Shh," he whispered, a finger over her lips. "You will wake Caterina. Come with me."

Claudio took the lamp and grasped Elisa's hand, which was cold to his touch despite the summer heat. Quietly, they stepped down the dim stairs to a back courtyard, slipping out of the moonlight and into the shadows of the chestnut trees. It was late, and the space was deserted.

They stopped just outside the door, so they would not be heard. "Listen to reason, Claudio," she entreated as soon as she was certain to be out of earshot from anyone in the inn. "I do not want to be the cause of this madness. Return to your rightful place at the palace, with your mother and the rest of the court. You need not be concerned about my safety. Caterina and I will fend for ourselves...we always have."

"No, Elisa," he replied with gentle authority. "My rightful place, as you call it, is here with you." He stroked her cheek with his hand, and she pressed into it, closing her eyes. "None of that means anything to me, if I must have it without you. What good will it do me to return to the court, when my heart is a slave to you?"

"Why are you tormenting me so?" Her voice was mournful. "I am trying to spare you, to send you back where you belong. Away from me and the misfortune I have brought upon you—"

"Enough, Elisa. You are not responsible for Bruno's behavior. He is. And one day he will pay for this." She shivered at the sound of his name. Claudio draped his arm around her shoulders. "He will pay, I swear it."

They stood silently against an ancient tree for a while, and held each other, neither having the energy to speak any further on this business. Finally, they turned and without so much as a word to each other, slipped through the door back inside to ascend to their room. Drained, there was nothing else to do but go back upstairs and attempt to sleep.

~

Elisa slept little. Haunting images pervaded her sleep: horses running in the night without riders, empty saddles eerily bobbing toward nowhere, tiny lights in the distance atop a city rampart, dancing and floating like fairies in the night air. Closer and closer to the lights, the dark horses galloped mindlessly up the hill.

Could the horses be afraid of the dogs behind them, yelping and barking, so close to their prey? The dogs were too far away yet. Faster, run faster!

"Run! Run to me!" she heard herself shout from the ramparts. The dogs had almost reached the horses. The poor animals could not outrun them...closer and closer.

"Run!" was all Elisa could manage to say because someone was shaking her—shaking her whole body. She tried to turn her head to see who was jostling her, but she could not take her eyes off the dark animals running toward her.

"Elisa, wake up!"

Slowly the sleep drained from her body, and her sluggish mind reluctantly regained awareness.

"Wake up. Something is wrong." It was Claudio. He had insisted on staying up to keep watch.

Elisa bolted upright in her bed, her head jerking toward the window. She could hear them. "What? No! You do not think —" She could not speak the words.

Very faintly, through the open window, she heard the distant barking of dogs and the sound of galloping hoofs. The silent stillness of the night afforded great clarity to the faraway thunder of the equine team, as the little inn was not far from the city wall's edge.

Fear froze Elisa. She could not think; she could barely breathe.

Claudio grasped her arm. "Elisa, you and Caterina must move quickly. Caterina!"

Caterina awoke with a start. "What is it? Elisa? Where are you!" she cried.

"If they are on the hunt, the dogs will lead them to us," Claudio explained. "We must get you out of here, now." He seized his rapier and ushered them swiftly out of the room, leaving the lamp behind should it give them away to their pursuers.

~

The trio scrambled down the back stairs to the little courtyard as the horses and dogs grew louder in the distance. They knew that the clearer they became, the closer they were to the ancient walls. Claudio reckoned that they would be at the inn within moments.

"To the horses," he whispered. "Our best hope is to try to outrun them."

With their backs against the courtyard wall, they held their breaths. It was utter darkness, but they found the stable, connected by a doorway which led to the barn on the opposite side. Claudio motioned for the women to stop and listened carefully.

The heavy thuds of the horses' hooves resounded on the dirt road beyond the enclosure, led by the yelping dogs. Voices shouted out the occasional command to the animals.

Elisa peered at Claudio in the darkness. He held up four fingers. "Four horses, four riders," he mouthed, his voice barely perceptible.

A heavy knock fell on the door; the rattle of metal made gave away that it was delivered with the hilt of a sword.

Claudio motioned to Elisa to look up beyond the wall of the courtyard. Candles were lit in the windows of the modest houses around the inn. The occupants were being awakened by the noise.

"Aye sir, what is your business here?" came the voice of the innkeeper.

"We are the cavalrymen of His Grace, Giuliano de Medici," one of them declared. Clattering swords and footsteps indicated that they were dismounting. "We have reason to believe that there is an enemy of the Duke within these walls."

"Here? Why we have not—" The bewildered man's line of questioning was cut short.

"Who have you accepted for lodging this night?" asked a familiar voice.

Turning to Elisa, Claudio leaned in to her ear. "That is Enzo's voice—the snake."

Claudio took Elisa's hand. She, in turn, grasped Caterina's and all headed to the stables. Their worst fears realized, there was only one thing to do—run.

Furtively, close to the shadowed walls, they made it to the stable door unseen. The Count hastily untied the horses from their stalls, thankful that their saddles were still on securely. The horses stomped and snorted in protest, and Claudio grasped the reins to settle them.

"A young man and two young women," replied the innkeeper, on the other side of the stable doors. "But what have they done to—"

"Where are their horses?" Enzo demanded.

"In the stables, but you cannot enter from—"

"Silence!" bellowed the commander. "Stand aside!"

Claudio held out his hands to form a step and helped the women mount the gelding, then he threw them Spirit's reins. They tried to hold the horses steady as he listened, ear to the door for the next order.

"You two lads, into the inn!" barked the commander. "My lord, you come with me. We shall head around the back to the stables."

The three in the stables heard men run and swords scrape as they were drawn from their scabbards.

Footsteps echoed in the street, and the stable doors on that side rattled. The iron latch held fast. Claudio looked at the women and put his finger to his lips.

"Blast! The doors are locked," cursed Enzo from the other side. "There must be a way in from the house. Get inside and open them. I will stay in the event they try to escape this way —and get the damned horses and dogs. Hurry!"

This was it.

Claudio turned to Elisa in the dimness of the stable. Securing her escape was all that mattered.

He clambered upon Spirit and pulled the other horse closer. Claudio found Elisa's face, still strong and hopeful, the shadowy curves lit by the dim glow of the neighbor's lanterns as they streamed soft beams of light through the spaces in the barn door. Though he tried to appear strong, uncertainty and fear were rioting inside him. Yet, all those feelings faded against his love for the woman by his side.

Clasping Elisa's small hand, he ran his fingers through her hair and stroked her face tenderly, then pulled her close. "Elisa, my love," he whispered in her ear. "When I give you the signal, you and Caterina must bolt and ride out of Fiesole. Get as far away from Florence as possible. Do not look back. You—"

"No, Claudio, no." She shook her head vehemently, and her voice broke. "I will not say goodbye." She clasped his hand tighter.

"You must...you must save yourselves. Do not fear for me... I know how to defend myself." He tried to sound confident.

"But there are four of them...you will never be able to..." her voice faltered.

"Please, my love," he begged, doing his utmost to remain calm. "There is not much time. This horse is swift. Ride like the wind, as fast as he will take you. As far away as you can."

Claudio removed his satchel filled with gold florins and handed it to Elisa. "Here. Take this—and take on new names when you reach another village. Never come back. Do you understand?"

Elisa held fast to his hand and shook her head.

"Caterina," he said with authority, grasping at anything to convince her. "I am a count in the royal court of Florence, and you and Elisa shall do as I say."

There was a pause and Caterina glanced nervously at her friend. "Elisa," Caterina finally uttered. "He is a count. It is your duty to obey."

Elisa clenched her jaw.

"Elisa, go," Claudio hissed, his voice urgent.

She paused and considered it, as all the while the sounds of capture surrounded them. For an instant she looked over at Caterina, then her eyes held Claudio's once more. "Very well— I will go, not because it is my duty, but because I love you too much to put you in harm's way any longer."

Claudio breathed a sigh of relief.

They shared a quick kiss and a last look in the shadows of the stable. Then, with a swift fluid motion, Claudio reached down with the tip of his sword and flipped the iron latch open.

Chapter Thirty-Two

"Well?" da Vinci was listening intently to every word of Elisa's extraordinary account. "What happened next?"

Elisa took another mouthful of water from the flask and continued. "Claudio unlatched the doors. They swung open, surprising Enzo...confusing him...of course, with two massive horses making a dash for it." She paused, thinking of Claudio's bravery.

"Go on," the old man urged.

"Claudio kept Enzo busy while Caterina and I veered to the right, up the winding road until we felt it was a safe distance. I heard Claudio warn Enzo to hold his sword. We turned back for an instant to see what was happening..." She stopped and stared at the space in front of her.

"Yes, and then?" da Vinci's eyes were wide and spoke fear.

"I saw everything," she breathed shallowly. "Enzo came at Spirit with a sword, trying to get at Claudio. Claudio told him to back away, but he was relentless. His sword grazed the horse, and then Spirit whinnied and reared up at Enzo. Claudio tried to control her, but he was barely able to stay on.

The next I saw, Enzo was on the ground, lifeless. Spirit had kicked him in the chest and pushed him against the wall of the inn. I screamed for Claudio, but he shouted at me to go."

Elisa swallowed back tears. "In the moment that the entire incident happened, another guard came out. He saw everything, how Enzo had provoked Spirit and how the horse acted out of instinct—protecting itself." She sniffed. "But he shouted 'murderer!' He accused Claudio of murdering one of the Duke's courtiers. Of setting the horse on him and not fighting honorably. Then the other two appeared on horseback, with the dogs at their sides."

She turned to look directly into the old Master's eyes. "Claudio tried his best to fight them off. He kept them at bay for a while, but they were three on one." Elisa sipped from the flask. The fresh water felt good flowing down her throat.

"The last I heard the guards say was that Claudio would be taken away on charges of treason against the Duke and for killing a noble. One of the men shouted that once he found me, I would be brought to the palace to face my fate as well." Elisa shook her head, eyes wide. "Master Leonardo, they will try him for murdering Enzo, but it was not his doing, and I know that despite what he asked me to do, I cannot leave him to answer for this lie. I saw the truth. The guards are liars, as is Bruno, and Bruno will not rest until Claudio is tried for treason."

"And what of Caterina?" asked Leonardo. "Where is she?"

"The guards set the dogs after us. We rode as fast as we could into the center of Fiesole. In the piazza there was a fountain—dogs cannot smell their prey in water—and they cannot outrun a swift horse. There was no need for Caterina to sacrifice herself for my own indiscretions. I forced her to take the florins, convinced her to leave me at the fountain and take the horse, which would be much faster without me. In any event, they have no interest in her. I jumped into the water and hid in the fountain until I was sure that the dogs had passed me by. Only one of the guards was following us." Elisa shuddered and wrapped one of the old blankets around her shoulders. "Claudio must have been taken back to Florence by the others. As for Caterina, my supposition is that they followed her until they lost her scent."

The Master pieced the remainder of the story together. "And upon losing her scent," he said, nodding, "they returned to Fiesole to retrieve Enzo, at which time the dogs picked up your scent again and—"

"And they have been following me all night. I ran from Fiesole to Florence to find you. The only thing I could think of was to come to you. Master da Vinci, he loves you like a father. You know that he is not guilty. It was an accident...they are lying. There must be something that you can do!"

"This is Bruno and Clarice's doing, I can feel it. And in his zeal to please Bruno and the Duke, Enzo paid for it with his life." He stood and paced, wringing his hands. "As sure as I know Claudio, he is loyal to Giuliano de Medici. Of this, I am certain."

A sharp rap at the door interrupted his pacing. Leonardo and Elisa looked at one another, fearing the worst.

Leonardo motioned to Elisa to get back under the mountain of rags and to stay down. "Shh, do not worry, my dear. I will send them away."

The old man hurried back through the courtyard. He cleared his throat as he approached the door and tried his hardest to act unaffectedly. "Who is it?" he asked.

"Master," returned a low voice on the other side. "It is I, Francesco. I have a very urgent message from Claudio. He is in danger. I must speak with you."

Da Vinci let the man enter, then swiftly closed the door behind him lest he be discovered.

Francesco entered, short on breath, and looking flushed.

"Where is he?" da Vinci questioned as they walked briskly to the study.

"He is waiting for you at the Certosa Monastery," Francesco answered.

"At the monastery?" asked Leonardo, puzzled. Then remembered the girl under the pile of rags. "You may come out, Elisa," the old man called out, then closed the study door behind Francesco. "It is safe."

The girl removed the covers and stood up, which took Francesco by surprise. "You are Elisa, I presume." She nodded, with an apprehensive smile on her face.

He turned to da Vinci. "Will this night's surprises never end?" Da Vinci chuckled.

"Claudio is waiting for the Master at the Certosa Monastery," relayed Francesco. "And I am entirely certain that he would be pleased to see you, as well."

Elisa jumped up, a look of renewed hope in her eyes. "Oh, thank God. Is he well? Do you know if he is well?"

"How did he manage to escape to the abbey?" questioned Leonardo.

"Claudio overpowered the guards. It was easy when there were only two of them. He rode Spirit to my home just outside of Fiesole, so that I could relay the message to you, Master. Finding Elisa here was a fortunate happenstance." He looked at the young woman with a smile. "He thought you halfway to Prato by now."

"We must go then, quickly. Let us go to the monastery, Master da Vinci." Elisa was already standing and prepared to rush out.

The two men peered at her, blinking. "It would be much too dangerous," declared Leonardo.

"It is almost morning, and the guards are still searching," added Francesco. "Perhaps we should wait until tomorrow. The guards will have suspended their search and—"

"We cannot wait until it is convenient," the maiden asserted. "We shall depart now. Perhaps, if I were to dress as one of your pupils, sir. Like a boy. The guards do not know me, and they will listen to you if you say that I am one of your apprentices." Her voice was growing in pitch with anticipation.

Leonardo and Francesco exchanged glances, then reluctantly gave in. "Who would want to deal with her wrath?" whispered Francesco to his teacher.

"Come on, let us go!" she shouted to the men.

"You did hear the lady, did you not?" said Leonardo firmly to his pupil. Then to Elisa, "We will think of something on the way there to assist you and Claudio, my dear. I promise you."

Leonardo touched her cheek affectionately and began to pack the items he had acquired for the chamber modifications. The old man glanced back at Elisa as he and Francesco packed up. "You will see, child, all will be well." Da Vinci's words reassured her.

There was hope now that Claudio was safe. Elisa felt an unexpected surge of energy. She had told her story, and now she would see her love again. Someone must be listening to her prayers. She also prayed that soon she would be reunited with Caterina. When all this was over and done with, she and Claudio would find her. All these comforting thoughts gave her the strength to go on.

Chapter Thirty-Three

I t was nearly dawn when Elisa, Francesco, and the Master arrived at the abbey. Though guards had been posted at the city gates, Leonardo had talked his way through with only the briefest exchange.

"I assure you that I know nothing of this, Commander." Leonardo sniffed coolly. "Incidentally, I am in a terrible rush to return to my studio with my apprentices and my supplies to get started on a project for the Duke, thank you very much. May I proceed?"

A knot tightened in Elisa's stomach as she listened, in her boy's garb, her face covered by a collar and floppy cap. She passed very credibly as a boy. This would help when they reached the abbey, too, as women were not allowed.

Once through the gates, Elisa mounted Francesco's old horse with Leonardo while Francesco walked. Clouds had begun to gather in the Florentine skies in the early morning. Another day of stifling weather was brewing, with the clouds in the heavens twisting and churning like grey blankets on the horizon.

When approaching the monastery from the pastures

below, Leonardo spied several brothers strategically placed on the top of the tall walls surrounding the abbey. He hoped Claudio had informed the Abbot about the situation at hand.

He knocked on the imposing doors, as Elisa dismounted and with a signal from one of the monks above, they opened. A little monk led them in. Beyond him were dozens of brothers, all going about their business, tending the grounds and gardens and drawing water.

"Good day, Brother Antonuccio," Leonardo offered as the three entered the abbey with their horse and supplies. Beside him, Elisa furtively scanned the courtyard.

"G-good day to you, Master da Vinci." Antonuccio, a very slight man, examined Elisa, who still had her collar and hat in place. "You have an anxious visitor waiting for you in your apartments, sir. And the Abbot F-federico wishes to see you," added the little monk, ominously before he went on his way.

"Yes, I thought that he might. Thank you, Brother." Da Vinci sighed. "I must attend to a few things and then I will make haste and see the Abbot. Come now, lads." He motioned for Elisa and Francesco to follow.

As they reached Leonardo's private quarters, the Master put his finger to his lips, urging Elisa to be silent—one can never be too cautious.

The old man reached for the door handle; it was bolted from the inside.

"This is Master da Vinci," he relayed in a low voice, "and I have Francesco and another, very worried, young lad with me, anxious to enter." He winked at Elisa with a sly smile.

They heard footsteps and bolts being drawn. The door flew open and there stood Claudio, bloody and slightly beaten, but otherwise looking well. His face brightened as he hugged the old man and clapped Francesco on the back. "You are all a welcome sight—"

He stopped and gazed down at the boy in the floppy hat

and pulled up collar, and his smile turned to amazement. Leonardo had anticipated the young Count's reaction with amusement, and he was not disappointed.

Claudio removed Elisa's cap, and with one motion, scooped her up in his arms as if she were a rag doll. The two relished the moment, oblivious to anyone or anything around them. Francesco and da Vinci, fumbled with supplies and bolted the door, their gazes awkwardly avoiding the outpouring of affection between the two young people.

"My love." Claudio took Elisa's face in his hands, kissing her eyes and forehead. "I thought you lost forever—God be praised...but, Elisa, why did you come back?" He shook his head. "I asked you to run."

Elisa returned his kisses. "I could never leave you, my lord. My heart and my soul would be easier to leave behind." She buried her face in his chest.

"How did you and the Master...how did you find your way to him? And Caterina?" Claudio asked.

"You mentioned where he lived, and I remembered your description of his portico," said Elisa. "I believe Caterina managed to get away. The guard followed her horse while I went back to Fiesole without her. I escaped on foot to Florence, hoping to find the Master, all the while being followed by the guards and those horrid dogs. I knew that from everything you told me about Master da Vinci that if anyone could help us, he could." She sighed with relief. "And what of you?"

"You do not have faith in me, my love. Did I not assure you that the Medici guards were no match for me?" He smiled. "I needed to distract them from you somehow. Two of them escorted me out of the village, leaving only one behind with the dogs to track you."

She became serious once more. "But the guards accuse you

of murdering a noble...in addition to the charges of treason, now you shall have murder to answer for."

"Nay, that is not true," he shook his head. "Inasmuch as I regret Enzo's demise, I warned him to stay clear—he knew very well Spirit does not take kindly to having a stranger come her way with a sword. She reacted as any horse would in such confusion. The poor devil got in her way, and he paid for his zealousness with his life."

"I know, Claudio...I saw everything. You had no fault in that. But they are planning differently—I know it."

"You must stop worrying, child," said da Vinci, struggling with a roll of fresh rope. "We are safe at present. We shall eat and drink and then think on it. For now, though, I must ask my apprentice to help bring in the materials required to perfect the chamber."

Claudio glanced at da Vinci and Francesco, both busily bringing in the items to refine the chamber. Claudio started toward Leonardo, then stopped. There was a rumbling of thunder, faint but distinct.

Da Vinci perked up his ears at the sound of distant thunder rolling into the Tuscan valley. For the farmers in the field, it meant welcome relief from the many days of hot, dry weather. For the Master, it meant opportunity; the opportunity to again harness the power of a lightning bolt.

Chapter Thirty-Four

A timid knock produced Antonuccio. "Begging your pardon, sirs," he spoke softly, his eyes to the floor. "B-breakfast."

Elisa scrambled to put her hat back into place, while hearty trays of bread, broth, meat, fresh water, and ale were brought in by the young brother and a few other novices from the abbey's refectory. They placed the trays on any empty surface they could find in the jumbled clutter of Leonardo's study and left. The meal was a welcome respite, as Claudio and Elisa could not remember the last time they had eaten. Sitting all together, comfortably gathered around a makeshift table, the group enjoyed their meal in relative calm, while the grumbling thunder crept closer to the abbey.

Once they had finished their breakfast, the old man spoke. "I am very pleased that you have found each other once again, however, there remains the imminent danger of the Medici's wrath. You can be certain that charges of treason and murder are not taken lightly. I have seen my share of travesties of justice through the years, and so have you, my dear," he gestured to Elisa, a tankard in his hand. The Master's gaze went from Elisa to Claudio. "If I were you, my two young friends, I would leave this place. Perhaps journey to Milan. I know many influential people there and could write a letter introducing you. You both could find employment there and live relatively good lives."

Claudio considered the option that the old man presented to him, but he knew he could not carry it out.

"But what of the Countess and my family's name?" asked Claudio of his mentor. "Will my mother have to live her life in the shadow of my shame? Because of an accusation that was created out of a spoiled heiress's jealousy and a drunken man's envy? And what of Elisa's reputation?" Claudio's agitation grew. He felt he had lost all control over his fate. "I think not, sir. I refuse to run and hide like a criminal. I will have my say and my vengeance. My name will be cleared, and Elisa shall no more be at the mercy of the likes of Bruno."

"Your ideals are admirable, my young friend," chuckled Leonardo, "and I admit that I respect that you would choose not to run, but to face your accusers." He glanced at Elisa who was concealing a yawn. "However, now is not the time to fight that battle. You are both exhausted. Try to close your eyes for a while. Things may be different after you have had some rest. It is better that you stay in my apartments—for safety."

The two agreed that rest would be a wise course of action, considering that they had not slept the night before. They fashioned some makeshift bedding out of straw cots, old clothes, drop cloths and sacks, and made themselves comfortable. Meanwhile, the rumblings of thunder came louder, with strength and intensity growing as the storm drew closer.

Da Vinci angled his head and listened, growing equally excited with each thunderclap. He turned his attention to Francesco. "My boy, if it is not too much trouble...if you are finished your meal, would you assist me outside? With the copper...before the storm is on top of us?"

Francesco obediently complied and gathered the tools and supplies required for the adjustments to the pole. The thunderclouds on the horizon were menacing, and Claudio knew Leonardo could not have been happier at the prospect of a good, strong lightning bolt for his new copper extension.

Claudio and Elisa watched as da Vinci drew an ornate key from his robe and inserted it into a contrarily unremarkable keyhole to an adjacent room. A series of whirrs and clicks sounded, and the door opened. Upon entering, Francesco stopped for a moment, open mouthed to gaze at the chamber, but only briefly as Leonardo urged him to make haste.

A ladder stood in the center of the space. They clambered up, and opened the access to the rooftop. The rain had already begun and was coming down in droves, spattering the old Master and Francesco with huge raindrops even before they were outside. The skies had darkened immensely, giving the impression that it was evening instead of mid-morning.

As the door remained open, Elisa craned her head to look inside the room. The chamber, in all its strange and curious presence was clearly visible.

"What is that?" asked Elisa, her gaze still focused on the metal structure, with its low humming sound and brilliant light emanating from within.

Claudio smiled and moved closer to Elisa. "That," he paused, thinking of how to explain it and whether he had the energy at this point to do so. "That is one of the Master's experiments. I will explain it in the morning, my love. Now, we both need to sleep." He yawned so intensely, his entire body shook.

"My love, what a predicament you find yourself in because of me," she said as he wrapped his arm over her shoulders. She tucked her shoulder under his, laying her head on his chest, forgetting about the chamber.

Claudio leaned back on the pile of old clothes and sacks

and turned his body so that Elisa's ear was right over his heart. "Do you hear that, my lady?" He put his hand to his chest. "That is my very heart speaking to you."

"Really?" Elisa smiled playfully. "And what is it saying, my lord?"

"It is telling you that I prefer being in this 'predicament,' as you call it, with you by my side, rather than spending a lifetime apart from you with all the courtiers and nobles in Florence."

Elisa laughed softly. "You are mad," she said, and turned to kiss his cheek.

He cupped her chin in his hand and drew her near to him, tenderly kissing her. Surrounded by a newly formed tranquility, they closed their eyes.

"I love you, my dearest heart," whispered the young Count. "I shall never leave you."

"And I love you," whispered the scullery maid. "I will be yours, always."

As the words left Elisa's lips, an enormous thunderclap shook the abbey to its foundations, but its intensity was not loud enough to drown out the sudden pounding on the door.

Claudio and Elisa sprang to their feet. There would be no sleep this day.

A voice from the other side of the door bellowed, "In the name of Duke Giuliano de Medici, I command you to open the door. We know you are in there, Count Moro."

"Claudio, they found us," Elisa whispered, her eyes wild.

"Blast those devils. Do they never give up?" Claudio murmured.

The commander's voice was all too recognizable. Alongside it were other stern voices, but they did not resemble the shouts of the guards.

"These are papal lands. You may not enter here," one said patiently.

"I repeat, sir, there is no count here—only Master da Vinci and his apprentices," said another.

"There is no count here..." said a third.

"The Duke is a supporter and patron of the Master. Does he know you are here?" asked the first voice.

The pounding resumed, followed by more orders to surrender.

"Halt there, sir," came a new authoritative voice. "I am Abbot Federico of the Carthusian Monastery, belonging to His Holiness Pope Julius II. You are on papal lands, Commander, and I must ask you to leave immediately."

"I shall do no such thing, Abbot," replied the commander defiantly. "The Count shall be arrested. Are you in the habit of allowing traitors and murderers into the monastery?"

Claudio rushed to the entry leading to the chamber room. He motioned for Elisa to join him, locking the door behind her. "Wait here," he whispered, and scrambled up the ladder to open the door to the roof. The rain came sideways on the high winds of the rooftop, with bolts of light and deafening thunder all around. He had to shout out to the two men, making the final adjustments to the extension, to be heard. "We have company downstairs—the Duke's men are at the door!"

The men hurriedly finished securing the extension and rushed inside, taking the ladder down behind them, in case the guards decided to invade the apartments from the rooftop. It looked as though they had fallen into the Arno as they were soaked to the bone.

Claudio clambered back to Elisa and grasped her shoulders. "Listen to me, Elisa. We must assist the brothers in fighting off these men. There is no telling how long they can keep them back. The guards do not know that you are here. You must stay here, in the inner room. Lock the door and hide and stay hidden, no matter what happens." He took her hand and led her to the locks. "Lock like this—you see?" He showed her how to work the device. "If they capture us...if we do not return, when it is safe to do so, get to Spirit and escape."

Elisa's eyes were wide and darted from the lock to her young man. "How can cloistered monks take on the Medici army?" she asked. "It is a battle lost before it has begun."

"Do not be deceived by their gentle demeanor and white robes, my love—the Abbot made them ready for this. Many of the novices are mercenaries who abandoned the French army in the last battle for Florence from the Borgia's. Scores of them are more experienced in battle than the guards."

Lightning flashes and claps of thunder succeeded each other relentlessly. "Promise me you will stay out of sight," he begged, unsheathing his rapier.

"I–I will." She watched him draw his sword. "I will stay here. I will be here when you come back."

Claudio paused to look into Elisa's eyes, gentle and pleading.

"Claudio," Francesco urged, "the time is now." He and Leonardo grabbed their swords and were out the door. The storm raged inside and out, the lightning unyielding.

"Wait!" Elisa exclaimed, holding Claudio back. "You must make a promise to me, now. Promise me that you will come back. You must come back to me."

"I promise you that I will. I will always come for you."

"Please, be careful, my love," she said through tears, finally releasing her grasp.

He kissed her on the forehead, turned, and charged out toward the fight against the Medici guards.

⁓

Elisa shut and locked the door, then put her ear to the wood and listened.

"Enough of this," the commander bellowed. On his orders, the pounding resumed, this time mixed with the scuffling of feet and the clashing of swords.

"Ready, lads?" shouted da Vinci.

"Onward, sir. Ready!" Claudio and Francesco declared.

She heard the apartment door open, the three men shout and rush into the fight. The thunder, lightning and torrential rain persisted outside, while another storm played out right inside the Certosa Monastery.

"There he is! The Count!" shouted a guard.

"He is the one we want, we have no quarrel with the rest of you," cried the commander.

"He is a child of the church!" declared the Abbot. "While he is in our monastery, you shall not harm him."

Clashing metal and shouts and cries of pain echoed throughout. It was all too much for Elisa to bear. It sounded like every man in the entire abbey was outside the door. Covering her ears, she scanned the room, searching for a place to hide.

The sword fight raged, spilling into da Vinci's apartments. Through the door, she heard tables turning over, liquids splashing to the ground, and glass crashing to the floor, breaking into pieces. The cries of battle all but drowned out the boots and sandaled feet, scuffling and struggling for better positions.

The minutes became hours for Elisa, as she listened to the sufferings in the melee, not knowing what was happening, not knowing if it was Claudio who was hurt. She knew that though Claudio, Francesco, and da Vinci were talented sword fighters, they could not keep the entire detachment at bay.

"Ahh! Blast! You wretched—"

Elisa's worst thoughts were realized—Claudio cried out in pain.

Blinded by instinct, she impulsively tore open the door to see. When she did, one of the guards saw her. She scarcely registered his stare—she was filled with terror at the prospect of Claudio being injured.

"Claudio!" cried Elisa, desperate to find him in the melee. "Claudio, speak out! Where are you?"

At that instant, a blinding bolt of lightning illuminated the room with a brilliant light, accompanied by an enormous deafening thunderclap. Elisa shouted out, startled to the core.

The fighting stopped at the ear-splitting blast that resounded from the rooftop of the inner room and shook the entire abbey. Her skin tingled more than burned, as though she was grazed by a thousand pins and needles, and the air all around smelled of scorched metal.

"Claudio!" cried Elisa, still shuddering from the enormous thunderclap, and the strange sensation it left behind, but undeterred in her search for Claudio. Some of the guards were withdrawing from da Vinci's apartments, as the monks continued to fight, valiantly pushing the soldiers out of the living quarters in the north wing of the abbey.

One of the guards pointed to her. "There is the girl!" he shouted. Her cries for Claudio had given away her presence.

"Elisa, get back in that room!" shouted out Claudio, breathless and struggling. He had a large wound on his forehead, and a cut through his shirt, which revealed a bloody gash across his right shoulder. He was at a disadvantage as he held his sword with his left hand, favoring his right arm, holding it close to his side.

Elisa saw him struggling, the blood trickling in his eyes. "My God, you are hurt terribly!"

"Save yourself, go now!" shouted Claudio.

A few of the monks gasped and stared, and that was when two of the guards closest to the inner room ran for her.

Terrified, Elisa turned and darted back, securing the ornate locking device on the door behind her. Why had she not listened to Claudio and stayed inside? Now he had to worry about her being captured, too.

Fists pounded at the door; shouts and scuffles came from the other side, trying to break it down. Scanning the room, she looked for somewhere to hide. Elisa headed for the ladder to go to the roof, but then she remembered the copper box, the large one resembling a chest. She ran for it.

There was a brilliant light coming from inside it, more powerful than before.

Elisa scrutinized it, unsure if she should go in. The light could burn her, but she had to try. There was nowhere else. She reached out to grab the levered handle and pushed down...*drop, clunk*.

She unbolted the latch, shielded her eyes, and moved quickly inside. There was no heat, only a sharp tingling feeling on her skin. In two quick steps, she was in. The air was thick, like obscure honey. It drew her in and with no effort at all, she disappeared into the new brilliant pull of the chamber.

Chapter Thirty-Five

In the apartments, the men tried to keep the guards back. The brothers fought a good fight, even though many had not used their skills in swordsmanship for years. There were too many men of the Medici empire, whose abilities in warfare and battle were far greater than that of the brothers. Many monks became frightened and retreated, leaving other, stronger monks to fight.

Claudio and Francesco grappled hard with the men attempting to arrest them. The guards retreated out of the north side of the abbey. Leonardo and his brave students continued to fight alongside the brothers until the last of the guards were driven outside the monastery. Even Antonuccio proved himself brave in battle, his mallet a formidable weapon.

When it was safe, a breathless and bleeding, Claudio turned to his teacher. "I must go back to your apartments for Elisa."

Leonardo sat on an alcove window ledge, breathless. "Go..." he said, gasping. "Francesco and I shall join you shortly." The old Master waved for Claudio to be off.

Francesco nodded to Claudio. "I will help him back."

Though he was so exhausted his muscles throbbed, Claudio raced to Leonardo's quarters, praying that Elisa was unhurt.

Wincing from the wounds, Claudio grasped the door handle and called out, the weariness in his voice evident. "Elisa? It is I," he gasped for breath, holding his shoulder. "Open the door, my darling."

Brother Antonuccio came to him with a wet cloth to wipe down his wound. His shirt was red with blood. Patiently, he waited, but there was no answer.

"Elisa!" He waved away the monk, and then spoke back at the soundless door. "The guards have retreated. It is only me."

Antonuccio cleared his throat.

"And Antonuccio," he added obligingly. No answer. Why would she not open to him? Could they have gotten in through the roof, even in this raging storm?

Da Vinci and Francesco finally joined him. He turned to Leonardo who leaned against a wall, his eyes closed in fatigue, yet smiling in satisfaction, no doubt savoring the taste of victory not tried since much younger days.

"Master, praise Bacchus. Will you open the door, please?"

"Of course," the old man said, opening his eyes. He produced the key from his breast pocket, but before giving it to Claudio he turned to the little monk. "It would be best if you waited outside, Brother."

Once Antonuccio had obliged, Claudio fumbled, fitting the ornate key into the opening. The door opened with a clank.

The sight that befell Claudio was too much for him to bear. A perfectly formed spiraling cone revealed itself from the open chamber door. No eddies, no multi-colored strings or crystals.

Just a black cone-shaped chasm with a point of white light in the middle and sweeping arms of light emanating from the center. It looked as though it extended into infinity, reaching far beyond the material earthly confines of the chamber. The hum was gone.

Cautiously, Claudio entered the room. The other men followed closely behind.

"Elisa?" Claudio uttered, as he walked toward the chamber. He felt a surge of energy as he drew near it, tingling on his skin. With a sense of foreboding, he peered inside. There was nothing. No sign of her.

"Do you think that she may have...in there?" Francesco edged closer to the chamber.

"No, she would not have," da Vinci reassured.

"I do not know," said Claudio, quietly. "What would a person do when they have been hunted like an animal for two days?" The tears began to sting his eyes. "Elisa!" he shouted, then looked toward the opening in the rooftop.

The men watched him, puzzled expressions on their faces as he put the ladder back to the opening to the rooftop and clambered up. In the driving rain, he saw no sign of her. Could they have taken her? If so, the ladder would not have been where it was placed before the fight. He scrambled back down, drenched, his shoulder scorching with pain.

Lightning struck again, followed by another thunderclap, this time further from the abbey. The storm was moving on. The three men looked up to the copper rod attached to the chamber. The copper was intact, but the supports holding it to the structure were blackened and charred.

"Look at the ropes," Leonardo motioned to the inner extension of the rod. "Lightning has made contact. You see?" He indicated the inside of the chamber. Da Vinci was right; the copper rod had worked again, and the unspeakable power of the lightning bolt had been harnessed.

"No more eddies." He walked to the chamber door and stood beside Claudio. "It should be stable now."

"What do you mean, 'stable'?" asked Francesco.

"He means that the currents are not merging and blending into each other," explained Claudio. "The moving portraits were to be more constant so that we may investigate them... but now there are no eddies at all. And Elisa? She could very well have tried to hide in here." He felt as hollow as his voice sounded. How could he rescue her from something so elusive, so puzzling? "Master?" Claudio turned to da Vinci. "If she did enter the chamber, I must try to find her."

"The poor girl," said Leonardo, shaking his head. "I understand that you love her, but do you know what you might be risking? We know nothing of this. It is a puzzle even to me. I cannot direct you one way or the other." He looked at Claudio's defeated and broken expression. "But I can try to help you."

A knock announced one of the brothers, come to speak to the Master. "Sir," said the monk, through the wood. "Abbot Federico wishes to speak with you, now that the Medici army is safely contained outside of the abbey."

"Not now," said Leonardo, impatiently waving him away.

"Sir," the monk insisted, "Abbot wishes to know why they were after the Count, and who is the young lady?"

Leonardo sighed. "Yes, of course. Inform the Abbot that I shall be there shortly to explain." The brother left. Da Vinci turned his attention to Claudio who was standing so close to the structure he was practically inside.

"Not so close, lad," said the old man.

"I think that...I think I hear something," murmured Claudio, ignoring the Master's warning. "It is a child, or...listen, come here and listen."

Leonardo moved in closer. The cries could barely be heard —faint cries, far into the chamber, beyond it if that could be.

"Is that Elisa crying?" asked Claudio, tilting his head toward the sound.

"Why...that is a child's cry...an infant," said da Vinci.

"I must go in." Claudio stepped forward to enter the chamber. "She might be hurt or in danger."

Francesco grabbed his arm. "What do you think you are doing? We know nothing of this strange magic...of what may be in there."

"I cannot leave her," Claudio snapped, his voice desperate. "She is alone in the unknown. Do you expect me to leave her in there?" He pulled his arm away from Francesco's grasp.

Leonardo surveyed him for a long moment. Finally, he spoke. "Go then, lad. Go and seek her out." He put his hand consolingly on Claudio's shoulder and nodded his approval. "Though we do not know how this will affect you—neither your body nor your mind. This is strange Nature to say the least."

"I promise I shall not stay long, sir," replied his student.

"Wait!" Francesco grabbed hold of a long rope and threw it to Claudio. "So, we do not lose you."

Claudio accepted the rope gratefully and tied it around his waist. With an expression that was tight with strain, he nodded to da Vinci and Francesco, and without another word, he entered the chamber.

~

Claudio stepped forward.

His skin stung, and darkness surrounded him. Stepping into the portal was like walking into a wall of heavy syrup. He sensed his body falling backward while he pressed forward. Simultaneously, he felt the sensation of being pushed ahead by something unseen while fighting something else that pulled him back. Claudio checked his body; he was unscathed, the rope still tight around his waist—he gave it a tug for good measure. His eyes looked back, following it into the chamber, where it disappeared into the spiraling black hole. The cone faded, giving way to darkness, and then he was on the other side.

Claudio warily tested the floor before putting his full weight into his next step. The surface appeared to be solid—solid cobblestone. Examining the walls and ceiling, he let his eyes take in the details. The shape and dimensions of the room looked familiar. If he did not know better, this space looked exactly like Leonardo's studio, though entirely stripped of all its contents, down to the bare walls and floor. There was only an odd little lamp in the corner on a spartan wooden table. It gave light, but no fire.

"Hello?" he whispered, stepping back a pace or two. The word hung in the air like a wisp of smoke.

This prompted a gasp from somewhere. Claudio's eyes came to rest on the ancient door. There was a sound of fumbling with what might have been a succession of locks and chains, and then the doorknob slowly turned. Little by little, the door opened, just enough for two faces to poke through. They were monks, discernible by their robes, however they were different. These brothers wore ivory-colored habits with black scapulars over top.

"Hello. Am I in the Certosa Monastery?" asked Claudio with some trepidation.

"You are," said one.

"Is Master da Vinci here?"

Still outside, the monks exchanged incredulous glances and looked back over their shoulders. They opened the door wide enough for them to enter the room, quickly closing it behind them. One brother was very tall and thin, the other short and rather portly. The shorter of the two was holding a baby.

"You're Count Claudio Moro...of the Medici?" he enquired, inspecting him.

Claudio looked down at himself. He did rather look like he had been through a war, bloody shoulder and all.

"Yes, brother, I am," Claudio answered. "And who are you? You do not look familiar." These monks were odd in their demeanor and seemed very tense.

The short one holding the baby spoke up. "I'm Brother Sardo, and this is Brother Matteo. We were sent to collect the baby."

"If you please, brother, may I ask if you have seen a girl come through this chamber?" Claudio asked, motioning to the structure behind him. "Her name is Elisa. Golden brown hair, green eyes?" Claudio thought to himself how absurd he must sound, as if it were every day a girl stepped through a strange gateway into another realm.

The two exchanged glances, then Brother Matteo replied gently, "The girl is all right, sir. She's not hurt."

"Oh, thank the Blessed Lord," Claudio breathed a sigh of relief and bowed to them as a gesture of gratitude. "You must bring me to her." He glanced briefly at the infant.

What in heaven's name are two monks doing with a baby in a monastery?

"You knew Leonardo da Vinci?" asked Brother Sardo, with awe in his voice. He held the baby very carefully as it wriggled about, making cooing sounds.

"Well, of course, I know him. What do you mean knew? Has something happened to the Master?"

"Uh...Not at all sir, everything is fine." The words were strange to Claudio as they resounded in the empty room. The monk looked sheepishly at his companion.

Claudio felt panic rising in his throat. Had his stepping into the chamber somehow affected his teacher?

As the monks conferred in whispers, it became apparent to

Claudio that they were discussing something of great impor-
tance. The two paused for an instant, and then the tall pinch-
faced one folded his hands together into his cloak sleeves and
stood even taller as he spoke. "You must excuse Sardo. He's
rather awestruck at your being here, as am I."

"Awestruck?" Claudio did not understand. "Please, brothers, please direct me to the young lady." He looked again at the
baby. Its swaddles looked familiar.

"Count Moro, with all due respect," the monk replied, "you
must listen now...stay calm and listen carefully. We've been
instructed by Master da Vinci to explain things to you. And
then we must send you back."

"If I am at the Certosa Monastery, then the Master should
be here! Where is Elisa?"

The smaller monk cleared his throat. "Count Moro, we're
of the Cistercian order in this monastery, and yes, you're in the
very same monastery, in the very same room where you and a
brilliant man named Leonardo da Vinci created, though inadvertently...a time portal—a rift in time, as we call it," advised
Sardo calmly.

"A what? A ri...how can this be? Where are the Master's
belongings? The door is not even the same!"

Brother Matteo slipped his hand into his habit and
produced an ancient-looking piece of parchment from his
sleeve. It was an envelope with lettering on it. He extended it
to Claudio. "See for yourself, if you don't believe us. This letter
is from your teacher."

The young Count did not know what to think. Was this all
strange magic from the chamber? Or had he become ill
because of it and was imagining things? He craned his neck to
see the parchment. It was an envelope with writing in da
Vinci's hand. He took it and looked more closely at the script.
It was, unmistakably, the backward writing that Leonardo
insisted on using, his characteristic loops and spikes. It read:

To my pupil, Count Claudio Moro, from his teacher, Leonardo da Vinci.

"Enough of this. What are you playing at?" growled Claudio. He grabbed the tall monk by his robes with his fists and shoved him against the wall. "I see his note, but where is he? And where is Elisa? Take me to her now!"

Brother Matteo put his hands to his face to protect it. "Please, sir," the short one said soothingly, taking a step back. "You'll upset the child."

Claudio let go and looked from one to the other. He took a shallow breath and tried to settle down.

"There's no easy way to say this, sir." The tall one nervously licked his lips and spoke. "Da Vinci has been dead for a long time. And this child—this child is your Elisa. This note was written five hundred years ago, on that very day in your time. That—" he reached over and tapped the letter, "is the year that you have come from, 1512. We are in the year 2012."

Claudio was speechless. His senses were in a fog; he could neither hear nor see, as his vision swam unsteadily in front of him.

"Read the note," urged the short one. The baby gurgled and cooed softly, comfortably wrapped in the monk's arms.

The Count did as he was asked. He held up the worn parchment note and read the front, flipped it open, and began to read his Master's familiar writing:

For Count Claudio Moro.

Take heed as what you are about to read will be disconcerting. You have stepped forward in time to the future. You are in the year 2012 on precisely the same day as it was in our time, on the other side. I will ask that you trust me, your teacher, and believe that this letter has been held in a safe place in the Certosa Monastery in the care of people whom I know full well I could trust with my life. I have written this letter in anticipation, many years ago, that you would try to find Elisa this very day. My good friend, Abbot Federico, has assured me that this message will be carefully preserved, on his instruction, for generations to come, until Elisa and you find yourselves on the other side on this fateful day. I cannot explain what unforeseen circumstance caused Elisa to emerge as an infant, but you must trust that she will be safe with the brothers on the other side and return to your own time immediately. I believe that I may have a method to return her to us, but first I require your assistance. You must trust me and return through the Chamber at once.

Your teacher,
Master Leonardo

Claudio could not tear his gaze from the letter. Master da Vinci must have written this letter to him from the past knowing that he would step through this very day...and he was warning him to return to his time without delay.

With his brows drawn together in an agonized expression, he looked up at the two monks who were patiently waiting. The baby—Elisa—had fallen asleep in Brother Sardo's arms. With a heavy heart and eyes brimming with tears, he gave the letter back to the brother. Claudio reached to touch the baby's hand and instinctively she wrapped her tiny fingers around his thumb. Defeated, he could bear this no longer, as he was close to sobbing.

Gently, he kissed the baby's forehead, unwrapped the tiny fingers from his thumb, and placed Elisa's hand under the blanket. With incredible effort, he forced himself to turn toward the chamber to go back.

But before he disappeared into the darkness Claudio managed to say to the monks, "Please...take care of her. Ensure that she is loved and looked after. I promised her, I would be back for her. Somehow...I will find a way."

Chapter Thirty-Six

Florence, Italy
2029

Alice stood blinking at Claudio. They were still in front of the painting in the Uffizzi. *All that build-up for a dumb practical joke?*

"That's very funny," she chuckled, shaking her head. "You almost had me believing something was up. Looking all worried and everything...nice acting job." She began walking away.

"Alice, this is no joke," he said seriously, taking her arm.

"Didn't know you had that kind of humor in you," she managed a small tentative smirk. "That was good, though. Okay, can we go on now?" She needed to leave.

"We must talk about this." He was keeping his voice low, but people were beginning to look.

Ali's eyes scanned the room. "Is this one of those prank shows or something?" she said, her voice louder to the people around her. Then she turned her head and spoke directly at Claudio. "Because I'm telling you, the joke's over."

"Alice, please. Come with me outside." Claudio placed his hand on her elbow and gently guided her to the exit.

"Where are we going?"

"Outside."

"Where?"

"I need to explain this further." His hand on her elbow became a firm grasp, leading her through the exit and into the square in front of the gallery where artists sold their treasures and talents to the tourists in the piazza.

"Explain what?" she asked, walking briskly beside him. "You can't be serious." Her vision swirled as the foreboding and anxiety came tumbling back.

Claudio easily sensed her unsteadiness. "Relax, I have you."

"No, you do not!" She pulled her arm away, expecting Claudio to resist. When he didn't, she almost knocked over an easel.

"Hey, watch what you're doing!" the painter yelled out at her.

"I'm so sorry," she apologized, steadying his easel. Then she turned her attention back to Claudio. "Do not touch me in that way. I am a person, not a thing for you to push around."

Claudio backed off, putting his hands in the air.

The painter stood up. "Is everything all right, signorina? Is he bothering you?"

"No, I'm good, thanks." She looked at Claudio with a grimace. "Can we get out of here, please, and can you tell me what the hell you're talking about?"

"Good idea. We will go to the Boboli. It is just over the Ponte Vecchio and down the street to the Palazzo Pitti." He held out his hand for her to take it. She opted to accept it as she was still a wobbly.

They found the Vespa and were across the bridge in no time, zipping through the heart of the old center. Claudio parked across the street from the incline up to the front gate of the Palazzo Pitti.

"I can't shake this feeling that something is wrong." Ali rubbed her forehead, which was beaded with sweat. "This time it's really powerful."

"All that has to do with what I tried to explain to you in the Uffizi. Try to hold on, we are almost there." Claudio's hand moved from her arm to her waist, supporting her as they walked to the entrance.

Admission was paid and through the portico they went. Heads turned as the young man led the young lady, rather green in the face, through the palace. They avoided the galleries and went directly outside to the adjacent Boboli Gardens.

A fair walk to the sumptuous green space was ahead of them, but the sunshine had a calming effect on Alice. Her mind was whirling between thoughts of running from the man who was supporting her and intense curiosity about what he meant in the gallery. Ali walked for a while, silently, not even noticing the park's delights.

They ventured under an avenue of trellises made of ancient trees, bent to resemble an arbor tunnel. Neatly landscaped pebbled pathways wound their way amid citrus trees, with sculptures and statues abounding.

Alice found herself regaining some steadiness as she sat on a marble bench, directly across from a statue of Neptune spouting water.

"Okay. I feel better," she said, brushing strands of hair from her eyes with the back of her hand. "Thanks for your help." She took a gulp of water from her bottle, then she eyed him with a cynical expression. "Now explain to me what you meant back there...in the gallery...about Leonardo da Vinci."

"Look, I do not blame you for thinking I am insane." He

shook his head and looked to the sky. "Sometimes I wonder if I am going crazy."

Alice ignored him and pressed for an answer. "Tell me what you meant."

"That painting," Claudio sighed. "The Madonna of the Rocks...that is da Vinci's second version of that same painting."

"Okay...but it's just a coincidence that the angel looks like me," Alice declared impatiently. "Leonardo da Vinci died, like, five hundred years ago. He couldn't have painted me because I was born in 2012."

The poor guy is delusional.

"Right. In 2012, you were found by a nun in the chapel at the Convent of the Dominican Sisters near the Piazza del Carmine, here in Florence," Claudio recited. "You captured national attention and although an extensive search for your birth mother was conducted, she was never found."

"Well, that is pretty much common knowledge. Anyone with an iPhone could have found that out—"

"You were adopted by Reno and Barbara Ferro, who immigrated to the United States," he continued, ignoring her. "You have visited Italy only once before now and even then, you experienced anxiety and, at times, debilitating episodes of panic. They seem to have returned." He smirked, his voice bearing just a hint of self-assuredness at that last comment. "Do you ever wonder why you feel the way you do when you are here? Why you sense foreboding or feel fear in certain places and not in others?"

Alice massaged her temples. "I don't know why, but I suppose you're going to tell me."

"Your father is a physicist, correct? Has he ever talked to you about space? The laws of physics?"

"What?" she exclaimed, louder than intended. "What does that have to do with that painting? Or my panic attacks? And

Leonardo da Vinci for that matter?" She shook her head as she glared at Claudio.

"Fine, fine." Claudio scratched his head. "Some scientists believe that in space, when a star dies, it collapses into itself. This implosion, or inward collapse of energy, creates a gravitational field so intense that nothing can escape it, not even light itself. This is a black hole."

Alice gave him a blank stare. "Okay, I learned all that in grade eleven physics class, but I'll humor you...go on."

"Although this type of black hole would, theoretically, pull anything entering it apart, another type of black hole, theorized in 1963 by a New Zealand mathematician named Kerr, would allow safe travel between other times or even parallel universes." Claudio kept his voice calm as he took in Ali's skeptical expression. "You think I am crazy, I know...but try to keep an open mind."

Alice discreetly started rummaging in her satchel, looking for her phone to call her uncle.

"Alice, what are you doing?" he asked, watching her fumble in her bag.

"I think I want to go home," she said, her voice flat, her chin a stubborn line.

"Wait, just listen to me," he pleaded. "You have studied history, right?"

"Yeah, but—"

"Please...just let me finish. Put the phone away," he begged, his eyes honest. "When I am finished explaining, if you still think I am insane, I will pay your cab fare to the villa. You do not even have to come back with me. Agreed?"

Ali fell silent, deliberating. A muscle flicked nervously in her jaw, then, "Agreed." She hesitantly put down her phone. "I'm listening. You have two minutes."

"With every new discovery," he said, speaking quickly. "The world being round instead of flat, the earth circling the sun instead of the other way around, discovering bacteria and the fact that our humors do not dictate our health—people thought initially that all these monumental scientific advances were insane. Galileo had to recant his discoveries about our solar system until he was on his deathbed."

Ali listened, focusing her gaze on one bright glinting stone on the pathway...the pathway that led out of the garden, to the city, back to the villa and eventually out of Italy and to Boston, where she belonged with her mom and dad.

"Look." Her expression was one of pained tolerance. "I'm not going to tell you what you can or cannot believe, but I'm not going to agree with you that my face is in that painting because I time traveled back to da Vinci's time and then came back." She grimaced. "Do you see how I would have some difficulty believing this?"

"You traveled here," said Claudio matter-of-factly, "from Renaissance Florence...from the year 1512."

Alice found this strangely intriguing, which was weirdly unexpected. It compelled her to ask more, in spite of herself. "But I was born here. I was a baby, remember? So how could I have traveled into the future?" Her tone was heavy with sarcasm.

"Very well, Alice, I am going to be brutally honest with you. You were not found in the chapel at the convent. The truth is, in 1512 you were running for your life. In the midst of a battle, you ran to hide in a chamber that da Vinci created. No one knew exactly what it would do since we were still experimenting with it...but it transported you to 2012 in the form of an infant."

Ali burst into a humorless, loud laugh. "Right—a chamber that's a time portal." Her voice rang with disbelief. "There's no such thing as time travel."

Claudio ignored her and continued with his explanation about da Vinci and his experiment.

Alice didn't know what to say. Reason would have her laugh in his face. What were the odds that something like this was even possible? Then again, he seemed to really believe what he was saying. She had heard her father discuss theories with his colleagues, related to time and space and the possibility of manipulating the space-time continuum. But according to her father, to blend each one so seamlessly as to be able to travel through time using a space-based method was at least decades away.

She shakily took another sip of water. "Okay, I'll play along with this," she said, shifting her weight on the bench. "Even if it was possible against infinitesimal odds, to create the perfect conditions for a 'mini' black hole, why would it turn me into a baby?"

"We can only speculate why," Claudio answered. He leaned back against the bench. "Perhaps the neutrons did not have enough time to form a ring, or maybe the gravity was still too strong and pulled you through at an accelerated rate affecting your cell structure. To answer your question, as to why your aging process was reversed at such an alarming rate when you stepped through the portal, we can only guess. All we know is that when I stepped through to find you sometime later, I was unaffected."

"So...you're from the Renaissance, too?" She crossed her arms over her chest.

"I am."

"Right...and you keep saying, 'we.' Who is 'we'?"

"'We' are the people who are helping me. Who they are, is not important right now."

"Well, I think it is. There are other people who believe this?"

"When one sees, one believes...unless they are too arrogant to believe their own eyes, that is," he added, looking away from her.

"So why haven't I heard about this on the news? What's keeping you from sharing it with the world?"

"The balance and integrity of our history and our future depend on the natural timeline remaining as minimally tainted as possible. If anyone knew about this besides those whom I absolutely trust and need to tell, we would risk catastrophe on a global scale." Claudio's tone became grave. "Past and future events would be altered. Financial markets would collapse. It would change everything as we know it, especially if this knowledge were manipulated for the wrong reasons."

"Hmph! A time traveler with integrity." She chuckled, but there was no humor in it.

It may be a good time to get up and leave now.

"Look," Claudio said. "All I ask is that you at least consider that this may be possible. I know that your father has studied the feasibility of using certain deep-space phenomena as time portals. I have read some of his publications and I wager he would tell you that it could be achieved."

"Could be possible...maybe, but not in our lifetime." *He knows that much about my father?* "And why are you reading my father's publications?"

"I am a science student, Alice, in university, remember?"

"A time-traveling science student from the Renaissance... interesting. So, just out of curiosity, and I'm not saying I would, but if I wanted to see this 'time machine' of yours, where is it?"

"Where it has always been...at the monastery. Right up there." He pointed to an imposing complex on a hill above Florence.

"A time portal in a monastery." Her expression was dead pan. "You and I are both from the year 1512 and have traveled forward in time, in a time machine, which is in a monastery. And you would bring me there right now, if I wanted to go?"

"Of course, I would." He looked like she had asked to see his stamp collection.

"Okay," she declared. Every curve of her body spoke defiance. "I'll call your bluff. Take me to see this thing. But before we go, I have one condition."

"And that is?"

"I call my parents and my aunt and uncle, to tell them where I'm going. I call them when I get there, too. If no one ever hears from me again, they need to know where I was last...and with who. Oh, yes—by the way, I have a sub-dermal microchip, and only my parents have the code to de-activate the GPS locator."

"You do not trust me, do you?"

She paused and arched a brow. "Would you?"

He thought a moment and conceded. "Make the call."

She took out her device and spoke her mother's name. "Don't worry, I won't tell them what we're doing. They'll think I'm crazy."

Claudio didn't respond.

Surprisingly, hearing her mother's voice pulled at Ali's heartstrings, especially now that she was confused about whether Claudio was to be trusted or not. All this threw her into a state of massive confusion. Was he mentally unbalanced, or was this all an elaborate practical joke?

"Hi Mamma...yeah, everything's fine—I just wanted to hear your voice." She glanced at Claudio, then shyly looked away. "I miss you and love you too...today, I visited the Uffizi, and my next stop is a monastery for a-a tour...I will Mamma... don't worry. I'll call you as soon as I get there."

She spoke with her aunt and repeated the information about where she was going.

"Be careful on that Vespa, now...and promise you will call me back."

"Sounds like my aunt really doesn't trust your driving," Ali said, grinning as she minimized her device and tucked it in her satchel. He put his hand to his chest and made a face as if she had thrust a dagger in his heart.

"That really hurts," he declared. Ali rolled her eyes at his sarcasm.

They walked to the Vespa and hopped on to start for the monastery. Claudio turned on the ignition and spoke without turning around. "In seriousness, though, Ali...I love you, no matter what you may think of me."

Ali wished she was as certain.

Chapter Thirty-Seven

Certosa Monastery, Italy
2022

The Certosa Monastery had not changed much since the 1500s. A new door had replaced the heavy wooden one that Antonuccio had so much trouble opening. The entrance boasted towering polished-oak double doors with peepholes, updated brass hardware, and wheelchair accessibility for tourists and guests. The monastery was also a thriving bed and breakfast for families and young backpackers sightseeing in the Tuscan countryside.

"Ends have to meet in one way or another," the abbot was fond of saying. Father Enrico was a practical man—very devout and kind, but entirely pragmatic when it came to maintaining the abbey and ensuring its survival.

Abbot Enrico became very ill and was bedridden for quite some time before his death seven years before. He had called Brother Donato to his bedside one evening.

Knowing how ill Enrico was, Donato immediately rushed

to him, wondering what he could do to offer comfort in his last hours.

Abbot Enrico thanked Donato, his assistant and caregiver, expressing the need for privacy. When he was certain that they were alone, he pointed to his bedside table. "Must hurry...don't know how much time...Donato, open the drawer...put on the white gloves."

Donato did as he was told. Inside was a rosewood box adorned with no markings or decorations.

"Open it," the Abbot whispered, gasping in a breath. Nestled among old pieces of linen cloth, discolored with age, was an ordinary-looking key.

Brother Donato picked it up. "What is this for, Father Enrico?"

The old Abbot motioned beyond his bedside table to the inlayed crosses on the wall. "Push the crosses, left to right."

Donato did as he was told and with a series of clicks and whirrs, a portion of the wall below the crosses, beneath a small portrait, popped open, revealing a hidden space. Inside the space was a chest the size of a chocolate box, also fashioned out of rosewood. Placed carefully on top of that was a letter, sealed with a red wax dot and the letters EC—the current Abbot's initials.

Donato took the box and the letter in his hands and gave them to the Abbot, along with the key.

Carefully, Abbot Enrico unlocked the rosewood chest and offered the opened box to Brother Donato.

Dumbfounded, Donato asked, "You...you want me to inspect its contents?"

Enrico nodded and wheezed, his breathing laborious.

When Brother Donato took it, he saw that the box was filled with letters, dozens of them. Some were old and worn and written on parchment with wax stamps, while others were newer, written on modern monastery stationary. They all had one thing in common: they had once all been sealed with a dot of red wax embossed with a stamp, upon which were scribed various initials. The seals had been broken and the letters had obviously been read many times over.

Donato flipped a few of the letters open and glanced at the dates; they ranged from the 1500s to 2014.

The old abbot cleared his throat and spoke in a weak voice. "Brother, I asked you to come because I have recommended that you be appointed the next abbot of this monastery."

"You must not talk like that, Enrico," said Donato to his spiritual leader. "You will be well soon and back to your duties. God will hear our prayers. The entire abbey is—"

"There is not much time," Enrico interrupted in a voice not much more than a murmur. "This box has been in the abbey since the early 1500s. It was passed on to me from my predecessor, just as I will pass it on to you." He coughed and wheezed. "The newest letter is from me, the one with my initials. It will explain the others. You must read it carefully, along with the rest. They will explain what you need to know about the room in the far wing. I believe you are the one, Donato."

The kindly old Abbot closed his eyes and breathed noisily while Donato sat at his bedside and read Enrico's letter, his eyes widening with every line. When he was finished, he looked at the old man and wondered if he had lost his mind to the illness.

He read the next letter and then the next and the next, until he reached the oldest parchment at the bottom of the box. Each letter had been left by the previous abbot to his successor. Each letter verified the document left by the abbot before, one letter leading to the one before it until there were only two letters left. The second-last one held the initials F.G., from an Abbot Federico Girlando, dated 1512, and the very last one bore the initials L.V.

Once read, Donato understood. He was the one. He would be the abbot that would unseal the room in the far wing for the first time in seventeen years.

Chapter Thirty-Eight

Certosa Monastery, Italy
2029

Holding onto Claudio again felt natural. Having her arms around him on the back of the Vespa made the conversation they just had seem like it never happened. Still, she couldn't wait until the joke was over—she hoped it was a joke and that he wasn't delusional. He obviously had no intention of giving up the prank easily.

The Vespa roared up to the little Florentine suburb of Galluzzo, past the Tuscan villas and olive groves, to the imposing abbey. Ali expected it to look medieval, and she wasn't disappointed. The monastery was surrounded by walls, which made it look impregnable. From a distance, she could see the bell tower alongside what Claudio told her was the Church of Saint Lawrence.

As they rode up to the entrance, Alice was amazed that these walls once housed Florentine scholars.

"Oh, my gosh," said Alice, shading her eyes from the sun

and looking up at the impressive complex. "This place is huge."

"It is," agreed Claudio. "It once held thousands of monks. Some were also teachers, but there is only a fraction of that population living here right now. Many of the buildings have been converted to new uses. There is a book restoration wing where some of the living quarters used to be, and although it has been pillaged in countless invasions, there is still a decent art gallery."

"You certainly know a lot about it."

"You can say I have grown very fond of the place." He smiled. "Are you not going to call your parents...and aunt and uncle?"

"I think I'm okay for now," she said, nearly forgetting her suspicions.

Claudio opened the large double doors to the courtyard. The reception area was to the right, indicated by the sign, *Ufficio*, with an arrow under it. The arrow pointed to a glass door under one of the porticos. He took Alice's hand and guided her through. "Two, please, for the self-guided tour." Then he turned to Alice. "Will your relatives not be curious as to why you keep calling them?"

Ali pursed her lips at his comment. "Well...yeah. I'll just say I butt dialed them. So, they have public tours here?" she asked, surprised that they would allow just anyone in.

"Yes," Claudio responded. "They had to give up the Inquisition-type torture tactics when they opened up the bed and breakfast." He winked and paid their admission. After accepting the tour headphones from the cashier, Claudio entwined fingers with Alice and led her in.

"For the most part," he explained, "the brothers are self-supporting and maintain their old traditions. They keep to themselves as they are a cloistered order, distilling their own herb liqueurs and making small religious articles to sell at the gift shop. But to maintain this place, they have had to come up with some creative ways to raise money."

"That's very admirable...so where's the portal?" pressed Ali. There were signs placed at strategic locations directing tour participants in Italian, English, French, and German to various places of interest throughout the complex. Claudio and Ali strolled, listening to the information on the headphones, but when they reached the corner at the edge of the church, Claudio quickly ducked into a small room.

The headphones droned on about Gothic structures, cross vaults, and wooden inlays, but Alice saw only a fresco of the Crucifixion on the wall in front of her. Claudio pointed to a security camera in the corner and pressed a buzzer next to a door.

"May I help you?" asked a detached voice over the intercom.

"Yes, I am here to see the Abbot. Please inform him that Claudio Moro is here with a friend."

"One moment please," said the voice politely as the camera whirred and focused on the pair.

"The Abbot?" asked Ali, grimacing at Claudio.

"Abbot Donato is the spiritual leader of the abbey," Claudio whispered, turning his face away from the camera. "He is the one we need to see about the portal. Father Donato helped me when I came through about a year ago."

Alice's stomach jumped. Did she hear him correctly? Not bothering to reduce her voice to a whisper, she asked, "You came through a year—"

Claudio put a finger to her lips and nodded to the camera and intercom. Obviously, not everyone was in on this information.

The intercom crackled back to life and the door buzzed, signaling that the lock had been lifted. "You may come in. The entrance to the cloister will be unlocked, Signor Moro. Proceed directly to Father's office."

The two entered hand in hand, leaving the small room with the fresco and marble flooring. A pathway led them to the rear of the church and into the huge open area of the main Cloister. The cells in which the monks spent most of their lives in prayer, venturing out only for mass, chores and meals, lined the sides of the open area, elegantly divided by arches dating back to the early sixteenth century. It was white-washed and plain, but meticulously kept and deserted at this hour. They walked briskly under the archways to the end of the yard.

"So, what do I call the Abbot?" whispered Ali. It just felt right to whisper here. "Do I call him Father or Brother? I thought you called monks Brother? Or just Abbot—what was it—Donato?"

"You may call him Father or Abbot. It is up to you. Just be polite. He does not take well to sarcasm. And you have given more than your share today."

"I'd like to see how you would react if the tables were turned," she snapped, arching a brow.

The pathway led to a plain oak door simply marked Abbot.

"Are you ready?" Claudio asked.

"So, this abbot is going to bring us to the portal? The portal where I came from as a baby? From the Renaissance?" she asked, skepticism permeating her tone.

"He will."

She halted. "Okay...wait." Stuffing her hand in her satchel again, she pulled out her phone. "I'm going to keep this handy —just in case."

"Of course," said Claudio, raising his hand for her to proceed.

"Okay, now I'm ready."

∾

Claudio opened the door, walking in first, with Ali following close behind. There was no grand security system, not even a secretary, just a large Spartan-looking room. Directly opposite the door was an oversized desk, dark in finish, except where it revealed years of wearing at the edges. It was piled high with ledgers, files and very old leather-bound books. A plain, dark oak swivel chair, just as worn, stood behind the desk, minus its occupant. Bookshelves lined the wall behind the desk, holding a variety of hardcover volumes and paperbacks, old and new.

Two wooden chairs were arranged facing the desk. An old laptop was positioned on the left with a printer close by, on the right a phone, and on the wall above an image of the Pope and various saints and not too far from that was a very plain Crucifix.

"There's no one here," Ali snapped. "Now what?"

"Take a seat," Claudio said flatly, pushing a chair toward her. "Do not worry, he will be here soon."

Alice looked at Claudio, and he looked away. There was nothing he could do or say that would convince her that he was telling the truth. She had to see it for herself. If he were in her position, he would expect the same. A time portal in a monastery? At times, he still doubted his own sanity.

"Why don't you tell me what's really going on?" she yelled out, oblivious to the volume of her own voice. "This is totally ridiculous! What are you trying—"

"Shh! Keep your voice down, please," he said calmly, his eyes focused straight ahead on the pile of books stacked on the desk. "Remember you are in a monastery. Respect your surroundings."

She huffed out a breath, then reached for his hand on the armrest of his chair and squeezed it. "Can you talk to me, please? I feel like I don't even know you anymore."

"Look, Alice," he said, and finally turned to face her. "I cannot take you looking at me like I am a lunatic. No matter what I say, you will not believe me—though I cannot say that I blame you."

"Then just tell me the truth." She took his chin in her hand and locked onto his ebony eyes. "What are you hiding from me?"

Bringing her hand to his lips, he kissed it lovingly. "Alice, I swear I am not hiding anything. I am trying to explain."

The door beside the bookshelf squeaked open, and in the doorway stood a middle-aged man in a monk's habit. His hair was salt and pepper, and he had a neatly cropped beard. He wore glasses and was so tall that he had to bend his neck and tuck his head down to get through the door. Under his arm was a rosewood box. Both Claudio and Ali stood as he walked toward them.

"Buona sera, Claudio. Nice to see you again. How was your semester?" the monk asked. Smiling cordially, he extended his hand.

"Buona sera, Father. It went very well, thank you." They shook hands.

Alice stood by, forcing a polite smile.

"Anna and Dario keeping you busy?" the monk asked.

Claudio laughed softly. "Always." He gestured towards Ali. "Father, I would like you to meet my friend, Alice. She is the girl I told you about. Alice, this is the Abbot of the Cistercian Brothers, Father Donato. He oversees all matters at the monastery."

Alice shot a glance at Claudio and extended her hand to the abbot. "Nice to meet you, Father," she said, following Claudio's lead.

"Very good to meet you, Alice." After shaking her hand, he motioned to the chairs as he took his. "Please. My apologies for not being in the office when you came in, but I was retrieving something very important." He nodded to the rose-wood box and spoke directly to Claudio. "I trust you wanted me to have this when you..." he paused. "Have you told her yet?"

"I tried, Father, but as you may be able to guess, she is having difficulty believing me." Claudio turned his gaze from Father to Ali. "Not that I blame her—the entire story is quite incredible."

Ali rubbed her forehead.

Father Donato chuckled. "Indeed, I would be concerned if she had accepted your story as truthful right away." He glanced at Alice with kindly eyes. "You are probably very confused, yes?"

"Yes, Father, I am." Her gaze ricocheted from the Abbot to Claudio and back.

"Alice is extremely skeptical, Father," said Claudio. "Yet, she must understand everything. It is essential that she knows, so she can make her own decision. That was the purpose of leaving her here."

"Of course, but in the end, I'm certain she will understand why," the Abbot said with a half-smile. He turned his attention to Alice. "The decision to let you grow up here was not taken lightly. Under the circumstances, as I have understood them, it would have been dangerous in so many ways if you had been brought back right away."

"Perhaps she should read the letters first, Father," Claudio suggested.

"Can you please not talk about me like I'm not here?" Alice begged.

Claudio placed his hand over hers, noticing she was ashen gray. "Are you going to be sick?" he asked.

"Could I trouble you for some water, Father?" asked Ali, her voice a mere murmur.

"Certainly, one moment." He got up and walked swiftly out the door by the bookcase.

Claudio gazed at Ali compassionately. "Perhaps it would be

259

best if I brought you back to the villa. Just forget about everything."

"Now that we're here? No way. It's just a headache. And besides, I want to hear what Father has to say. I mean, out of everyone, I should be able to trust him to tell me the truth."

"Okay," Claudio agreed, "but if you feel light-headed, let me know."

"I will," she said, just as Father was coming through the door with a carafe and three glasses. He set the lot down and began pouring. Alice reached for a glass and gulped it down.

"Now," declared the Abbot, "I believe this is for me to give to you." He pushed the rosewood box across his desk and placed it in front of Claudio. "If I may say one thing to Alice before you explain the letters to her?" he asked, placing his hand over the box and turning to Ali. "Alice, I am merely a keeper of these letters, and I have no other stake in this but to carry on the tradition of maintaining their security within the walls of this monastery. However, if I may give you a bit of advice...coming from someone who knows a little bit about faith?"

"Of course, Father," Alice nodded.

"Often, we are called upon to believe things that go completely against what is widely accepted as the norm. Or perhaps against what we perceive is probable, or even possible." He paused and thought carefully. "Try to keep an open mind. Anything is possible." Donato removed his hand from the box, leaned back, and folded his hands on his desk.

"That seems to be a popular bit of advice today," Ali replied weakly.

"I suppose we should start then." Claudio drew a deep breath, took the box, opened it carefully and picked up the letters.

"Alice, remember when I told you that you come from a time long ago, as a baby through a time portal? And that the portal was contained in a chamber, created by Master da Vinci?"

Ali nodded but remained silent, her attention on Claudio's every word.

"These letters are a testament to that reality," Claudio continued. "They date back over five hundred years. The bottom two in the stack were written by two people who were actually at the monastery when it happened: Leonardo da Vinci and Abbot Federico, the Abbot here at the time."

Ali turned slowly from Claudio to Father Donato and asked quietly, "Is this true, Father?"

"Yes, Alice," he nodded reassuringly. "I'm certain the letters are genuine."

"But what about this 'chamber'? This time warp, or whatever it is. Do you know about that, too?"

"I do, Alice," he replied. "I have seen it. It was one of the first things I did when this box was bequeathed to me. This very same box has been passed down from abbot to abbot since 1512—since the ordeal which, through no one's fault, resulted in your arrival here, in 2012. That is how I know they are genuine—each preceding abbot has guaranteed the authenticity of the previous letter. You, Alice, were reborn to another time."

Beads of sweat formed on Alice's brow. "I feel like my head is going to burst," she said wearily, grabbing the armrests. "I don't feel—"

"Claudio, she's ill," Donato called out.

Claudio's hands, in split second reaction time, supported her under her arms as Alice's consciousness faded.

Chapter Thirty-Nine

Alice awoke to the sound of her ringtone—*bee de beep beep-bee de beep beep*—not even fully conscious yet, she felt around for her satchel.

Slowly, as her eyes opened to the light, she remembered where she was. There was a cool cloth on her forehead, and Claudio was cradling her in his arms. "That is your aunt, you know," he said. "You need to talk to her. The option is still on the table, if you want to go now, I will take you back." He flipped the cloth over to the cooler side and stroked her face. Father Donato was standing awkwardly nearby, a glass of water in hand.

"I'll call her back in a minute," she croaked out. "Hand me my purse, please, so I can take something for this headache."

She took deep breaths until she was strong enough to raise her head, then she swallowed down a pill with the glassful of water. After a quick phone call to her aunt, reassuring her that she was fine, she looked at Claudio and held out her hand. "So, now...give me the letters."

There were thirty-four letters in all. Alice started from the very bottom, which according to Claudio and Father Donato were the original two from 1512.

Donato handed her white cloth gloves and a small mirror from his desk. She looked at him quizzically as she held up the mirror. "I can understand the gloves, but the mirror?"

"You'll understand why in a moment," he said with a smile.

Ali carefully unfolded the first letter, as the parchment was very delicate and had begun to tear in places. This was where her parents' nagging to maintain their heritage and culture by studying their native language paid off, she thought to herself.

Her eyes widened as she saw the signature at the bottom—backwards: Leonardo.

"Oh my God." She held the mirror and positioned it, so she could read the words. "This note was written by Leonardo da Vinci?"

"The one and only," replied Claudio.

The words were in an old Florentine vernacular, but the gist was clear. She began to read.

Certosa Monastery, Galluzzo 1512

Esteemed Fathers,
This letter is written, in the presence of the Right
Reverend Abbot Federico, in the month of
September in the year 1512, in Florence, in the
hopes that what occurred here, not a fortnight ago,
will be remembered. As he was a witness to these
events, a letter written in Federico's own hand
shall accompany mine.

It is not a secret that I maintained a workshop here at
the monastery, and in the interest of the study of
Nature, conducted numerous experiments. One of
them, notably, attempted to capture the elusive

*power held in a bolt of lightning. I constructed a
secret chamber, within the walls of this abbey,
hoping to harness the flash of fire as it came down
from the sky. What I succeeded in doing, quite by
happenstance, was to create a doorway to other
places and times.*

*I, and my student, Count Claudio Moro, discerned
that it was impossible to study the oddity as it was
when the first lightning bolt was captured, due to
its instability. The adjustments improved the state
of the chamber so that it was safe to test—its many
currents to many times coalesced into one epoch
—yours.*

*However, during a critical point, when the lightning
was initially drawn into the chamber, a young lady
by the name of Elisa Beatrice de Povri, mistakenly
entered the portal, banishing her from her own
time as a young woman and causing her to emerge
on the other side, in the future, as an infant.*

*It is not known to me what forces were at work that
caused this terrible upheaval in the young lady's
life. I can only work to right the wrong. I write
this letter to advise the Abbot who will be responsible for the monastery on the very day the child
will begin to exist in your time.*

*I ask that provisions be made to find suitable
guardians for the baby girl when the time comes. I
also ask that when the young Count Moro comes
through the chamber after her, that he be sent back
at once. Should he object, I have penned a letter to*

convince him that it is in his best interest to return. It will not be his time to enter your world until much later.

Abbot Federico has given his word as an honorable man, and as a spiritual leader of the abbey, that the north wing on the far side of the abbey shall be restricted to only those whose presence there is necessary, in order to keep the existence of the chamber a secret. Upon my passing, I have left instructions that the chamber be left intact until Count Moro has crossed the passage into your time. He shall then take responsibility for the continued existence of the chamber, if he deems it appropriate that it should be allowed to exist at all. I have complete faith in my pupil. Please allow him every courtesy, see to his care, and assist him in any way you are able.

Your servant,
Leonardo

Alice felt like someone had knocked the last breath out of her. This was not possible. Not in any scope of logical thought. Everyone knew that Leonardo da Vinci liked the mysterious and unusual, that he was years ahead of his time intellectually, but she had never heard of anything like this.

And Claudio was his student? This boy sitting beside her? And...he was a count? It was all too bizarre.

"So, you're a count?" Her caustic tone concealed the mixed emotions swirling inside her.

Claudio nodded.

"I must be dreaming. Or hallucinating."

She read on. And on. Ali read the entire pile—all thirty-four letters, dating from 1512 to the last letter written by an Abbot Enrico in 2019, each letter verifying the authenticity of the one before. At the end of the last letter, she felt that everything inside her had been tied up to charging horses pulling in opposite directions. What was she to think? Who was she to believe? Everything she knew to be true about herself was wrong, in ways unimaginable, if she believed the contents of the wooden box.

She could just walk away. Claudio had said so. It would be easy to ignore it—easy to ignore everything that Claudio had confessed to her.

Yup, it would be easier to forget about it.

"Father," she said, lifting her eyes from the last letter. "Do you believe these letters are the real thing? That they're true?"

"Yes, I do," he said slowly. "I have no reason to doubt them. My predecessors have passed the messages to me, through centuries of war, political upheaval, plagues, and ideological change." He sighed and leaned back in his chair, removing his glasses. "Do I believe they are genuine? Yes— beyond a shadow of a doubt, I do. It is as if Abbot Federico had handed me the letter himself. The question is, do you believe?"

She swallowed hard, trying to manage a feeble answer. "I don't know," Ali responded flatly, weighing the whole structure of events.

"Can we get to the north wing today, Father?" asked Claudio.

"I suppose I could take you. Are you up to it, Alice?"

"To think about what's at stake...about what this would mean to me and how it will affect my life. But on the other hand, how could I live with myself not knowing the truth? And not seeing the chamber, if it really existed?"

I really have no option. "Yes, let's go," she said, slowly rising from her chair.

Father Donato led the way to the north wing. They retraced their way through the archways and back around the bell tower and chapel. There, a smaller courtyard opened before them and led to a staircase at the opposite end, heading to a lower level.

The Abbot scanned the area to ensure that no one saw them approaching the north wing. Since the monks were at vespers, they were pretty much alone.

There were windows situated in the stairwell wall looking out onto the olive groves and lowlands below the monastery. They stopped at the first landing in front of a planked wooden door. It was held fast by a series of locks, each different than the other, some with a keyhole, others requiring a combination. Father Donato pulled a ring of keys from under his scapula and went to work on them. Once unlocked, the door opened into a hallway, lined with barred up, open-air windows, presenting a steep drop to the valley below.

At the end of the hall were another door and more locks. Once in, Donato turned to his right. The windows were sealed with brick work. He reached for a battery-powered lantern and switched it on, lighting up the entire space. Alice saw candles on a shelf nearby as well as a lighter, probably in case the battery failed. But that was all.

When Donato flicked on the lantern, Ali saw an empty cavernous room, though it appeared it had not always been empty—on the walls were faded spots, nail holes, missing plaster and more sealed windows. Everything had been cleaned out of it a long time ago. The only other thing in the vast space was a table and a door adjacent to the inside wall on the other side of the room.

"What is this place?" she asked, her voice echoing.

"This," answered the Abbot, "is the ante-chamber, where da Vinci lived and worked."

Alice watched as Claudio brushed his hand against the wall of the room, as if to take hold of events that the walls had absorbed. He was deep in thought as he stared at the door, walking toward it with a transfixed look on his face. The same look that he had the moment that Alice first saw him.

The knots in Alice's stomach returned with a gnawing vengeance. As she followed Claudio through the room, she noticed there was something strange about the door. It was a different shape than all the others she'd seen in the monastery. The top came to a point like a teardrop, but it was straight across the bottom. And, even more odd, there was no door-knob or handle of any kind.

Claudio stopped in front of it, then lightly traced its molding with both hands. With closed eyes, he ran his fingers over it, starting at the top and working his way down, pressing invisible pressure points. Then, he thrust both palms of his hands against the molding and the door popped. It stood just barely elevated to the molding flanking it. With another nudge from his hand, it revolved open.

"I will go in first and set up the lantern," said Claudio. "This opens like a revolving door, locking again each time it goes around." Then he turned to the Abbot. "Will you open the door and let Alice in, Father?"

"I will," he assured.

Claudio spun the door and went through. It revolved shut again, and Ali heard the locks engage. "What is that, Father? I've never seen a door work like that."

Father Donato followed the same ritual to gain access for Ali. "Claudio designed and built it, mechanism and all," he replied, with almost fatherly pride.

Alice walked toward it, then stopped and looked back at the Abbot. "Father, this is just too strange to be true. If I walk through that door, and if what you and he are saying is true...I don't even know what to think."

Donato walked to her side, pensive, his hands folded in front of him over his chest. "Alice, I know what you're thinking, and I thought the same when this was presented to me seven years ago, but sometimes you have to take a leap of faith. Leave what you know behind and think outside of your own world."

Alice paused a moment.. "Thanks, Father." She nodded. "I'll try." *Keep an open mind, Ali, and just walk through the damn door.*

Chapter Forty

Alice mustered every bit of courage she had to proceed. She gave the door a nudge and strode through. Once she did, the teardrop door clicked back into locked mode behind her. In front of her, Claudio stood near a big metal box, waiting for her with lamp in hand.

The structure was big, but not imposing: a tarnished copper cube, the size of a small room with a height of about two meters. On top was a metal rod, which looked like it had been disconnected at the ceiling and had another metal piece soldered over to cover it. In the middle was a copper access, a basic rectangle, with the edges shaped to fit the door molding, forming a seal. The door handle was a drop-and-catch lever that would close and lock the chamber from the outside. If she had to guess, Ali would say that about three to four people could fit comfortably inside it.

"It's a box," acknowledged Alice. "A big copper box."

Father Donato had just come through into the interior room himself, and she heard him laugh quietly.

"Wait until you see what is inside the box," said Claudio, stepping toward the opening. He held on to the lever and turned it, then pulled up. The lock gave way with a loud metallic *clunk*, and then he opened it wide.

What Alice saw inside took her breath away.

Inside the cube, two copper plates about the height of a person stood across from each other. Between them was a single cone shaped black hole, with white strings revolving and undulating into themselves, swirling into infinity. The impossibility of the funnel to extend far beyond the limits of the metal structure defied any physical laws that were of this time and place. It was as if she was peering into another universe. She stood by transfixed and open-mouthed.

For an instant, she glanced at Claudio, but her eyes were pulled back to the phenomenon playing out in front of her. "The whole time you were telling the truth, weren't you?" she said, drawing closer to it. "This is the real thing. And everything about me...everything about me is true."

"I would not lie to you," Claudio affirmed, walking slowly next to her with his hands stuffed in his pockets. "This, Ali, is a rotating black hole. A worm hole passage to another time."

Alice could not tear her eyes from the chamber. A worm hole that led to another era, an anomaly on this planet that, she thought, could only be found in deep space. Yet, it had been here, on earth, in this room, for five hundred years. And for five centuries, the monks were able to keep it a secret. "I still can't believe it," she said quietly.

Donato stepped back toward the entrance to the ante-chamber. "Would you like some time to talk?" he asked Alice gently.

Her hand to her mouth, she turned to the Abbot and nodded. "Thank you, Father."

"I'll be in my office, if you need me." The door *whooshed* and closed behind him.

Alice reached for Claudio, grabbing a handful of his shirt and buried her face in his chest, eyes closed, her world crashing down around her. She began to tremble and once again she felt the light-headedness creeping up, trying to overtake her.

Enough. "No!" she called out and pulled herself away. Alice put her hands out in front of her. She knew he would try to support her, but she needed to do this on her own. Breathe in, breathe out...

Slowly, she felt the fuzziness in her ears and brain subside. Breathe in, breathe out...

She wiped the tears away with the back of her hand. Breathe in, breathe out...

Ali brought her gaze to the chamber and stared into it for a long time. When she felt her composure settling back into place, she turned to Claudio. "Oh, my God. I think I remember some of it," she uttered, her hands over her mouth. "Very disconnected, but...I remember a little."

"Tell me what you remember," asked Claudio, his voice hopeful.

"It's like remembering a dream—just shadows but," she cleared her throat and focused. "I remember being on a horse with you and laughing. I feel good when I think about us. We were happy...and then we...we were in a garden. We were in love. I know that now. So much in love." She smiled briefly, and then her face became troubled. "We were in Fiesole, too. At that door—that door the other day that was so familiar— the one with the old woman and the little boy. I was there before. We were there the night it all happened."

"Yes, Ali, that is right." Claudio urged. "Keep trying."

A suffocating sensation tightened her throat as she recalled that night. Claudio let her speak, listening as her thoughts fell like dominoes into place.

"There is a bad feeling about the palace. Someone there tried to hurt me."

Claudio clutched her hand. "That is Bruno. My God, Alice, you do remember. And all those other places—"

"Now I know why you took me to Fiesole. You took me there to try to shake my memories loose, hoping they were still inside me after all this time."

Claudio nodded. "In the hopes you would slowly come to know the truth. I hoped the memories I believed were embedded deep in your mind would flood out if I brought you to places that had strong connections for you." He paused, his dark eyes never leaving hers. "I am so sorry I was not gentler in divulging the truth about your past, but I was running out of time."

"Do my parents know about my past?" she asked somberly.

"No, they do not. You were brought to the Convent of St. Ursula in Florence by one of the brothers after you came through the chamber. They could not keep you here, and it was more believable that you should be found in a convent rather than in a monastery on a hill. Once the state took you in as a ward, you were put up for adoption. No one dreamed that you would be adopted by a couple who would eventually relocate to America. The brothers felt responsible for you—so they ensured they kept track of you."

"What about you? Did you come through the portal as a baby, too?"

"No. When I came through after you the first time, the portal had time to stabilize. We can only guess that it was because you entered immediately after the strike that you—"

"Oh, yes...my cells or something went into hyper-reverse mode...you told me." She held her arm out. "My God, I can feel my skin tingling," she said, stepping toward the chamber. Her eyes bore into in, spellbound.

Claudio covered her hand with his, leading her away from the chamber to a space near the wall. "Let us sit down. You need to get your bearings back." He placed the lamp on the cobblestones and sat, tapping his invitation for her to sit beside him on the barren floor.

"Wait!" Ali's hands held her head, as if to keep it from bursting. She gasped. "Wow. Oh. Oh, my gosh, wait!" Her eyes were huge zeroes, looking past Claudio. "My parents in the 1500s—they were murdered!" Her memories broke through like a breeched dam. "And I remember the Medici, you—a count, and me—a maid. But you wanted me anyway." How lowly she felt, shameful and angered at Bruno's taunting, the agony of growing up with no parents, and then her elation at finding love—a lifetime of feelings in the span of a few seconds.

She searched his eyes once more, beyond overwhelmed. "I remember...it was only for a short time, but...it was you and me. Like it was yesterday."

Claudio put an arm around her waist, pulled her against his chest and leaned in to her ear. "Our love transcended class and social boundaries just as it transcends time and space. I would have done anything to be with you, to protect you, just as I would now. You make me a better person." He pulled her closer and kissed her, and then kissed her again.

Alice felt at peace, with renewed tranquility in the fact that the Claudio she knew was back, not the stranger she had come to think he was this afternoon. All the love she felt for him five centuries ago, came back to her and melded with the love in her heart for him now.

She pressed her lips to his, caressing them more than kissing them, then pulled away, tracing his lips with her finger. "I'm sorry that I doubted you," she said softly. "I never will again."

Sitting back against the wall, her head comfortably on his shoulder, Ali broke the silence again. "I still don't understand something, though. How did you know when to come through again—when I was close to seventeen? You said you've been here a year or so?"

"Da Vinci made his calculations based on the first time we went through. We found that time itself, on the other side elapsed much faster, an approximate ratio of one minute our time to roughly sixty minutes here. We waited a little over three months and then I entered the passage again. The brothers knew I would be coming through, so they were ready for me. The notes, remember? As soon as I made the passage back, I began to research, to learn about this era. I had seen snippets of these times in the chamber, but I was not prepared for the technological advancements and the onslaught of information. It was overwhelming at first, and the monks had to help me to acclimatize. They taught me to drive a Vespa, speak the local vernacular, and they enrolled me in the university. I had time—we had to get you here." He smiled, took her hand, and kissed it lovingly. "It was quite a feat. My aunt and uncle at the villa, by now you have surmised that they are not actually my 'aunt and uncle', they are distant relatives. The monks reached out to Anna and Dario when I came through—they are also friends of your aunt and uncle. Put two and two together."

"So, they knew where I ended up," she continued. "Leda and Roberto probably invited my parents to visit, and through Anna and Dario's prodding, we all ended up at the villa."

"Right. It is only unfortunate that I could not have met your parents. I was looking forward to it, especially your father —I admire his work."

"Everything is a lot clearer, now." She breathed a sigh of relief and stared at the portal again. She knew deep down that she had to ask the question.

"So, you came back for me? Where do we go from here?"

Claudio looked like he was wrestling with the answer. "To be perfectly honest with you, after I saw you as a baby, wrapped up in your own clothes, held by that monk—I thought—just for a millisecond, that maybe I should just leave you be. Let you grow up and live your life here and grow old, not knowing the better." He brushed a few strands of hair from her eyes and let his finger trace the edge of her face to her chin. "But I could not. I had to come and find you. First, I love you too much to just leave you here without being certain you were all right. Second, I made a promise to you, never to leave you behind. Your last words to me were not to leave you, and I vowed that I would not. I could not have lived with myself if I had not come back. And..." He stopped.

"And?" Ali reached for his hand and wound her fingers around his.

He hesitated. "When I came through the portal, the monastery was still under siege by the Medici army. The guards failed in arresting me for treason and murder. After you left, I stayed at the monastery for safety. A few days later, a company of the Duke's guards arrived, poised to enter the monastery to arrest us and as many other people as they could, for interfering. This troubles me, as the brothers were only trying to protect us."

"The monastery is still under siege?" Ali grimaced. "Do you mean they are holding everyone inside hostage? Not letting anyone in or out? Because of what happened in Fiesole?"

"That is exactly what they are doing. They cannot enter Papal lands. It is forbidden. The brothers are self-sufficient and can wait it out for a time. I am concerned though, because when the guards tire of playing the waiting game, instead of a company of soldiers, they will send a regiment. And then there will be a true slaughter—because of me. Because the brothers are protecting you and me."

"Oh, no." Alice was horrified at the thought, a heavy feeling forming in her stomach. "No, they wouldn't."

"I think that the Duke can be reasoned with, if I can only

get to him face to face," Claudio said. "We tried repeatedly to get word to him, but our messengers were all intercepted and arrested. I could not take the chance of surrendering before I could get to you—in case it did not go well. But I believe I have a plan that will work."

The whole thing was still so unbelievable to Ali that she doubted her own senses. "Hey, I need you to know something." She brought her knees up to her chin and wrapped her arms around them. "I want to help you—I do, but...this is life-changing, to put it mildly. You're going to have to give me some time to let all this sink in."

"I wish we had that luxury, Alice, but it is not that simple." His voice held a heavy note of urgency. "Think for a moment... when you stepped through that thing, you altered the natural occurrence of life in ways we can only guess at. We do not know what the ramifications of any of this could be. The longer we wait, the more the events in 1512 could get out of hand. I need to get back. I have been gone for more than six days my time and..." He brushed his hair out of his eyes and forced himself to say the words, "I must go back tomorrow. There is no way to know how the natural timeline has already been altered...I cannot stay here. Whether or not you are with me, I must go."

With a roll of nausea, Ali realized what he was saying. She licked her lips and cast her eyes to the ground. "That didn't even occur to me. You *have* to go back, don't you?"

Claudio looked beyond Alice, to the chamber. "I am afraid so."

His words swirled around her head, echoing with a finality all too clear for Alice. She turned away, deliberating. The truth was clear, in all its wretched cruelty and ugliness. That was when her nausea quickly turned to acrid frustration and her eyes bore into him. "You made me fall in love with you and now you're going away?" she said, the words propelled by exasperation. "You couldn't just leave me here in blissful ignorance?"

"I am sorry if I made the wrong decision in coming back." Claudio straightened and looked away. "I made you a promise, Alice. I was not going to abandon you. You and only you can make your choice."

Her body went numb. "I need to think." She shook her head back and forth, helplessly. "Do you have to be so damned valiant all the time?"

Claudio remained silent as Alice felt wave after wave of contradictory emotions. Harsh anguish at discovering she was about to lose Claudio, frustration at her helplessness to do anything about it and anger at the cosmos for putting her here in the first place. Yet, she felt Elisa's need to take responsibility for the events creeping back, wrestling for a spot in her brain and in her heart: Bruno's lechery, Caterina's urging to remain 'invisible', Clarice's jealousy and, ultimately, Enzo's death. And now Claudio would have to go back to answer for it all.

There was only one way to satisfy the past and the present. "Okay, I'll do it," she said numbly. "I'll go back with you and make it right. All we need to do is tell the truth, right? I mean..." she shrugged, stoically, "you would do it for me."

A wide, bright grin exploded on Claudio's face—the expression broke Ali's heart. She knew that he was overjoyed, except now she had to let the other shoe drop.

"But I can't stay there." As much as she loved him, she couldn't bring herself to leave her parents, her life, and everything she knew.

His face sank as her words echoed in the empty room and then perished.

"Then do not do it," Claudio shook his head. "Ali, that makes no sense. You are risking your life coming back, and for what? For me? Do not do it for me. I cannot allow that."

Ali bristled. "Did you just say what I thought you said? You 'cannot allow' me? What century have you been living in for the past year?"

"Where I come from—and where you came from—that is the way it is," he warned. "Most of the time, men speak, and women listen."

"Well, maybe they'll let me speak for you," Ali insisted. "You're in trouble, and so is your family. I'll come back to help you. Let me help you."

He intertwined his fingers in hers. "I will think about it. Just the thought of you wanting to come to my rescue—for this, I am grateful."

"I'll just be telling the truth," she said softly.

He nodded, but his brows drew downward in a frown. "Yes, but you need to be aware of a few other things, too. You are thinking of twenty first century justice, where you are innocent until proven guilty and women are treated as equals to men. Remember, it is not like that where we come from. It is a brutal world of torture and double standards, of deception and injustice...where the rich and powerful overrule the poor and weak. And women are the poorest and weakest of all."

"If I could go back long enough to help you straighten things out, would they leave the abbey and the monks alone? Would your mother be safe?" she asked.

"Perhaps," he said gravely. "But the danger is very real." He paused. "With Leonardo's help, and if we could find the other guard and convince him to tell the truth about Enzo, we might have a chance. As far as the treason charge, I know in my heart that Bruno and Clarice are at the root of it. They will be forced to withdraw their accusations, I will swear to that."

"Don't worry, I can take care of myself. You'd be surprised."

Claudio chuckled softly, shifting his weight on the floor. "Are you certain?"

"As long as I can get permission to get away for...how long?"

"As little time as possible, I promise. I will not keep you there any longer than is absolutely necessary. The longer you stay in 1512, the greater the chances that your present, here in 2029, will change. And that is the last thing I want. You cannot stay long, anyway." He looked away. "You leave for Boston in a little over a week."

Alice nodded bravely, though she felt like her heart was in a vice.

"I will calculate it and then we can make the arrangements, agreed?" Claudio reached for her and pulled her close.

She realized there was another thing she didn't know. "Hey, I think I read it in Leonardo's letter, but," she nudged him, "what was my name?"

"Elisa," he answered, his mind far away. "Elisa Beatrice de Povri. You did not remember that?"

"I did...I just wanted to hear you say it." She smiled fleetingly. "I like that. Elisa Beatrice de Povri. That's beautiful."

"A beautiful name for a beautiful woman." He leaned his head back and gazed into her eyes with renewed optimism. "Not three hours ago you thought that I was certifiably insane. Now you are willing to travel back in time to save my life and probably my family's reputation. What an afternoon you have had."

"No one can say you're boring." She laughed heartily and then looked away. "I may have some ulterior motives of my own, though."

"Like what?"

"Like seeing Caterina again. That will be a good thing," she replied.

"You just reminded me again of why I fell in love with you." Claudio shifted. "You know... I really need to get up. Are you hungry?" He stood and offered her his hand.

"I guess all this deliberating and hand wringing has brought on a bit of an appetite," she grasped his hand and stood up, stretching.

He walked over to the metal cube and closed the door. "Maybe we can talk about how we are going to do this over dinner...I must figure out how long we have on the other side. We may have to come up with a reason why you are going to be missing for a few days. And your clothes...I hope the brothers still have them."

Claudio gave the impression that he was terribly busy and wrapped up in planning the details of their return, but Ali knew his heart was aching. And so was her own. To actually speak the fact that the next few hours together would probably be their last would be too painful.

Claudio was showing Ali how to trace the door with her palms when suddenly she stopped. Something didn't quite fit.

"Hey," she said. "You know, you never explained the portrait. How did I get my face in that painting?"

Claudio closed his hand over hers and directed her to the exit. "The Master was commissioned to paint it before all this happened. He had me working on this re-creation—this must be the end result. When I saw it hanging completed in the Uffizi, I knew it was a message to you, to Elisa—a tangible, real thing that is a testament to your existence in our time. I believe that he will finish painting it for you."

Chapter Forty-One

T hey started out before dawn the next morning, all contingency plans in place. Claudio's 'cousin' Luca and his girlfriend, Olivia, were their cover. The official story was that they were to spend the remainder of Alice's time in Italy at the seaside resort town of Viareggio with Olivia's family. In actuality, Luca alone was to stay in the chamber room just in case there was an emergency, while Claudio and Ali went through the portal. He, along with Father Donato, would hold vigil until Alice returned.

Claudio said *arrivederci* and thanked Anna and Dario the night before, letting them know that he and Alice were to go to the abbey the next morning. He had grown to care for them very much, and they had been so genuinely concerned when Alice first arrived. He knew that he would probably never see them again. Claudio asked them to back their story. The less people who knew about the time portal, the better. Luca, Anna, Dario and a few select monks were already too many.

Alternatively, Leda and Roberto had given everyone stern warnings about the horrible fate that awaited them all should they do something 'stupid.'

Everyone had given their word that nothing 'stupid' would transpire.

In the cobalt light of pre-dawn, Luca was waiting for Ali and Claudio behind the villa in his Fiat Uno. They threw their bags in the back, and before long they were speeding their way to Galluzzo. Time was of the essence—Claudio had determined that they would have no more than two and a half hours to set everything straight in 1512, with no time to spare.

Father Donato was waiting for them at the entrance and wished them a good morning. "Nice day to go back in time," he said with a half-smile.

Focused and somber, they strode through the familiar courtyard to the restricted north wing just as the sun peeked over the east wall.

They proceeded into the hall, on to the next door, and into the intense darkness of a windowless room. Father Donato reached for the lantern and switched it on, while Claudio walked past them to the tear-drop door. He lightly grazed the molding with his palms. Alice and Luca were waiting just inside the access outside the teardrop door, when Father Donato tapped Ali on the shoulder. He had a bundle in his hands, wrapped in plain linen and tied with cotton string.

"I believe you're going to need these." He held out the package.

Ali took it, untied the string, and flipped open the linen coverings. Inside was what looked like a well-worn period costume for a peasant boy. "Was this mine, Father?" Ali asked. "The one that I was found in?" She unfolded the breeches and tunic and let them drape down in front of her, amazed at the thought of where they had come from. They were a plain linen, brown and rough and obviously worn in spots, but still very much intact.

"The very ones, Alice," he replied, smiling. "Your clothing was kept safe. The brothers thought you may need it if you ever decided to make the journey back."

"Thank you, Father," said Ali, smiling up at the Abbot appreciatively.

"Oh," he said, fumbling under his sleeve. "Here." He handed Ali an old-style wristwatch. "Keep your eye on the minutes or they'll telescope into days on our end."

Alice took it and gazed at the face—a plain Timex watch, complete with a second hand. "That's perfect. You think of everything."

With a tip of his head, he turned and stepped outside so that she could change.

There was a swish and a breeze, and the door to the chamber room opened. Claudio stood framed in the threshold of the revolving mechanism. "I will wait for you inside, Alice. I will need to change as well."

This is it, thought Ali, as she dressed, neatly folding her street clothing and laying them on the table beside the lamp, then hid the wristwatch inside her belt loop under her tunic. *I can't believe I'm doing this. Stay calm, stay calm...you know what to do.* "Ready," she called to the waiting men in the other room.

One by one, they joined Claudio in the chamber room, each newly fascinated at the sight before them—the gateway to a world five centuries in the past.

Luca was mesmerized. "Unbelievable." His hushed voice hung like a billow of smoke in the still air.

"Believe it," said Claudio. He had changed into his peasant garb as well, looking every bit the 1512 commoner.

"Isn't that a little casual for a count?" Ali laughed nervously, her voice holding the rasp of excitement.

"I was in disguise, remember?" He reminded Ali with a wink. Then he turned to the men.

Father Donato and Luca listened carefully as Claudio went over the instructions once more. "Right now, I estimate that Alice will be on the other side no longer than seven days, your time. This will give us a little over two and a half hours in 1512, to do what we need to do and get her back. One of you will need to stay here at all times, in the event that something goes wrong. This portal has not changed one iota in five hundred years, so I do not expect it to begin fluctuating now."

"Two and a half hours? Isn't that cutting it a little close?" asked Luca.

"There will be no time to waste once we arrive. You will be here when she returns?" he asked Luca, looking for reassurance.

"Absolutely," Luca replied.

"Thank you, my friend. For everything." Claudio walked to Luca and hugged him. "You are like a brother."

"The honor was mine." Luca returned the hug and then backed away. "Be safe."

Claudio turned to Abbot Donato and held out his hand. "Father, I cannot thank you enough for all you have done for me and my family. We are forever indebted to you, to the Certosa brothers, and to the abbots who preceded you."

Donato shook his hand, and then made the sign of the cross over Claudio and Ali. "May God bless you and keep you safe on your journey."

"Thank you, Father," they replied.

Claudio turned to Alice, gently took hold of her shoulders and looked deeply into her sea green eyes. "Ali, if you are having second thoughts—you know that you can still go back to the villa."

"No," she declared, shaking her head. "I'm not backing out now. I promised I'd help you, and I will honor that. You did it for me. I'll do it for you." She held up a hand to his cheek. "I've got your back."

"And I shall always have yours." He smiled. There was inherent strength in his face, yet beads of sweat had already started forming on his forehead. His only worry was for Alice. "Now remember, on the other side only Leonardo, Francesco, and Abbot Federico know of the portal. And we need to keep it that way. Are you ready?"

Ali nodded.

"I will go first. I will be waiting for you on the other side."

Oddly opposite to Claudio, Alice felt harmony within her, a sense of peaceful purpose. She was fulfilling her destiny, and she was not afraid anymore.

Ali watched with wonder as Claudio stepped through the door of the chamber and into the spiraling wormhole. The blackness swallowed him, swallowing him up until he was no longer visible. She looked back at Donato and Luca.

"We will not leave you," reassured Father.

"You'd better not," she replied. She breathed deep, closed her eyes, and entered.

Once in, her skin tingled and quivered with a pulling sensation. Each cell in her body was drawn into the center without any effort on her part at all. She walked through a wall of thick honey, but it didn't offer resistance. Instead, she was pulled into the darkness as if she were falling backward into nothingness, her limbs drawn in by the ever powerful drag of the bolt.

There was a buzzing in her ears as she put one foot in front of the other, and then it was gone.

"Open your eyes, Ali," a voice said—it was Claudio's. She felt like she was coming out of one of her fainting episodes, that same foggy feeling and stuffiness in her ears. Maybe she had passed out and dreamed the whole thing. She would open her eyes and be in a piazza somewhere in Florence.

Ali slowly opened her eyes. She was standing, not in a piazza, but in the same room she had left. Though now, the space was entirely filled with strange-looking objects, strewn aside and abandoned. At one side of the room was a makeshift table, holding a half-eaten meal, and alongside it were several swords leaning against a wall. A stack of metal sheets lay on the opposite side, with a roughly constructed ladder placed over the top of them.

Her eyes trailed over the objects and then stopped on Claudio, standing in front of her, not three paces away. He reached for her, as if he needed to reassure himself that she was really there. "Do you feel all right?" he asked.

"Yeah...I'm good." Ali nodded, confident that she had passed her first hurdle.

As they hastily exchanged an embrace, her attention was drawn to the door on the far side of the room. It was opening. She braced herself.

"Ha-ha!" chortled a portly old man with long, white hair and a long beard. "I thought I heard familiar voices in here. Good gracious, Claudio—you found her." The old man, dressed in a sable brown velveteen jacket and breeches, headed straight for Ali, his arms outstretched. "You found our Elisa. Come here, child." With a sweeping motion he took Ali up in a huge fatherly hug. When he released her, he turned around to quickly brush a tear from his eye. It was Leonardo da Vinci!

"Claudio, my boy, good work," Leonardo declared, clapping his hand several times on Claudio's back.

"Master da Vinci," Claudio replied, "Elisa is now called Alice. Ali, this is—"

"Master da Vinci," she gushed and shook Leonardo's hand. "I can't tell you what an honor it is to meet you...uh, how good it is to see you again, sir. In my time, you've become something of a legend."

Leonardo puffed out his chest and grinned. "Why, she is even more charming now," he said to Claudio, who was peering into the outer room.

"Yes, she certainly is charming," responded Claudio. "Master da Vinci, we do not have much time. We must advance to the city straight away and seek an audience with the Duke." He grabbed a sheathed dagger, paused and then placed it back down. "Perhaps it is best if we go in unarmed."

"Straight to the Duke? Unarmed? Are you certain of that?" asked da Vinci. "How will we defend ourselves?"

"Hopefully we will not have to. Essentially, we are surrendering. Is Francesco here, Master?"

Leonardo became serious again. "He is. And since you have been on the other side, we have been fighting those devils almost daily. I tell you they are relentless. It is a fortunate thing that the brothers are skilled in warfare. Every so often they mount a skirmish in an effort to capture you, but..."

The sound of the outer door swinging open redirected everyone's attention. "Found your way back so soon, Count?" said a familiar voice. It was Francesco, leaning against the doorframe, a sly smile on his face.

"My friend! Just in time..." In a few steps Claudio was shaking his hand.

"Elisa is back, did you see?" said da Vinci, indicating Ali to Francesco.

"Master da Vinci, Francesco," interrupted Claudio. "Time is of the essence. Master, you told me once that when Niccolò Acciaiuoli built this abbey, he incorporated passageways and tunnels that led outside its walls. Do you know where they are, and do any remain accessible?"

"It is so, and I believe some do. One near the gate leads to a pasture below the abbey. Another leads from the vesting room in the chapel sacristy to the mausoleum of the Acciaiuoli family, just outside the abbey proper."

"The mausoleum in the village cemetery?"

"Yes, that is the one. What are you thinking of, Claudio?"

"Of the fastest way to Florence that does not involve fighting the Medici soldiers." Claudio turned his attention to Ali. "Alice, the chapel is our next objective. Francesco, please ask one of the brothers to alert the Abbot." Claudio turned and looked frantically through a variety of different size hourglasses on one of Leonardo's work tables. He chose the one he wanted and placed it on the center table. "Gather as many brothers as are willing to help us. They need to distract the guards at the front gate. It does not matter how. Keep your eye on the time-keeper. When the sands have run out, engage the soldiers. Ali and the Master are coming with me into Florence."

Da Vinci followed Claudio's lead and left the dagger in his belt behind. "You two go on to the chapel. I shall procure a lantern and catch up."

Ali and Claudio bolted, ever conscious of their time constraints. Although da Vinci was old and they had to slow their pace a bit, he met up with them shortly and kept up surprisingly well. They ran swiftly under the porticos, following the path around the expansive courtyard to the door of the chapel, and entered one of the few places in the monastery where they allowed opulence. The chapel frescoes depicting the life and passion of Christ were still new, their pigments vibrant and crisp. Ali marveled that she had just seen these same frescoes on the tour with Claudio yesterday...or, rather, five centuries from now.

As they raced in, they dipped their hands into the holy water and blessed themselves, then Leonardo darted into the sacristy, with the other two following. The sacristy was filled with sacred vessels and items used in the mass, such as the chalice and holy oils.

Putting a finger to his lips, the Master looked around and then pointed to one of the room's little alcoves. "It is this one," he whispered and walked into it. "This is the vesting room."

Leonardo went to work, searching the alcove for the opening to the tunnel. There were celebratory church vestments, neatly hung in an armoire directly across from the entry, and tidy piles of linens lining the shallow drawers of the credenza. A chasuble and a stole were laid out on top of the credenza ready, Ali supposed, for the next mass.

"Here, help me move this," da Vinci said, stepping to one side of the armoire. Claudio took the other side. "There." Leonardo pointed behind the armoire. The aged wooden door had faded to grey. Held together by iron strips, it was framed by stonework and boasted an iron ring handle. Claudio pulled it, and the simple latch slid away, allowing entry.

"I was not expecting it to be this easy," remarked Claudio, as Leonardo lit the lantern. The door opened to a flight of stone steps which lead down into the bowels of the monastery.

"Come on, let's go," chirped Ali. The men exchanged surprised glances.

It was complete darkness, save for the glow from the lantern. "Be careful, the steps are damp and slippery," warned the old man. Claudio slowed his pace, but precious time was slipping away. Every moment spent in the passageway was time taken away from the task ahead.

"Look," said Ali, pointing to the change in the stones. "I think we're finally going underground."

Down, down they stepped, the stone transitioning from the neat masonry of the monastery building to huge, eerie boulders. As abruptly as the steps began, they ended.

The tunnel ahead was built of imposing stones, arranged into an endless archway that stretched into the darkness. The ground was muddy, with puddles and big water droplets plopping into them from the tunnel ceiling.

"Watch your footing, Master," cautioned Claudio, as they walked warily into the dark passage around deep puddles. "The rainwater has created some additional obstacles for us." Even at a hurried pace, the short distance from the abbey to underneath the cemetery used up almost ten minutes of their valuable time.

Finally, another set of steps appeared. And they were steep. "These lead to the Acciaiuoli family crypt?" Claudio asked da Vinci.

"Apparently so," replied the old man, breathless.

"Are you unwell, Master?" asked Claudio. Da Vinci's face was showing fatigue.

"No, no. Do not worry yourself about me," he said, waving away Claudio's concerns. "On we go."

Climbing to the top of the steps was unnerving. The stones were greasy with dankness, however that did not compare to the unsettling feeling when Claudio drew aside the heavy slab of marble at the top, and they stepped into a crypt.

Ali peered around at the inside of the shadowy tomb as she climbed out of the tunnel and into a space about the same size as her bedroom. Its marble inlays were opalescent, cold and silent, like its occupants.

"Let's get out of here," Ali urged, trembling. She reached for the gate to open it, but it was locked. "This one won't be that easy...unless someone has the key," she said, her voice cracking.

"Stand aside, my lady," said Claudio. He braced himself against one of the walls of the mausoleum and easily kicked the old iron gate open. "Sorry, Niccolò," he remarked. They hastily departed the mausoleum, pulling the gate closed behind them.

In the near distance, they distinctly heard the sounds of

engagement. The shouts, although distorted by distance, were of a battle in the misty morning fog. Francesco and the novice brothers taunted the guards over the monastery walls. This was the diversion allowing the three to secure horses and make their hurried way down to Florence.

It was not long before they found a stable, complete with the transportation they were seeking. With no time for niceties, they helped themselves to two mares, one for Claudio and Ali and the other for Leonardo.

"How are you planning on entering the city without being detected?" asked the Master, as he mounted his horse. "The guards at the city gates will be watching for you."

"I am counting on that, sir," replied Claudio, snapping the reins.

Chapter Forty-Two

The horses were not of a fancy breed, but they were swift. Galloping down the hillside, the wind whipping through her hair and her arms wrapped around his waist reminded Ali of riding on Claudio's Vespa. The city itself was not far from the abbey, just a few kilometers away, with Florence, laid out before them like a tapestry comforter in the fine morning mist.

On the approach from Galluzzo on the hillside, the three riders had a clear view of the gates. There were indeed guards on the walls, overlooking the valley.

"Which gate, sir, the Porta Santa Maria or the Porta Rossa?" shouted the Count to his teacher over the thunderous sound of hooves.

"The Porta Rossa," da Vinci called back. "It is the closest to the Piazza della Signoria. They will take you to the Duke directly. Let us pray that they do."

Ali thought about Claudio's plan. He was willing to gamble that the guards would take them to the Duke the moment they were caught. They would not be able to resist showing off their prizes: a treacherous count, who had murdered one of the Duke's courtiers, with his scullery maid accomplice. The one unknown variable was the soldier who knew the truth about what really happened outside of the stable in Fiesole that night. Claudio had assured her that if he could find the guard, he knew he would easily convince him to tell the truth. Ali hoped so.

As they approached the Porta Rossa, Ali saw one of the sentries atop the turret wall signal down below. A few whistles alerted the gatekeepers on the interior of the walls, and two military men on horseback appeared from within with their swords drawn.

"Prepare yourself, Alice," Claudio warned her. "They may get a bit rough once they recognize me. Just stand your ground and be brave."

"I will stay as close to both of you as I am able," said Leonardo, as the horses slowed down to a trot. The gateway was not too far now. Alice felt a wave of light-headedness come over her. The fuzziness in her ears was back, and she felt like her head was underwater.

"Breathe," she murmured to herself, taking in a huge gulp of air. "Just breathe."

"What is this?" one of the guards hissed to his colleague as he recognized Claudio and his fellow fugitives. "These are the ones from the abbey! It is that rogue Count and his woman. And see here, that old buzzard da Vinci is with them."

They kicked their horses' sides and sprinted toward the three outlaws. "You, there! Halt! Stay where you are, all of you!"

His jaw tensed up considerably, but Claudio complied. He pulled tight on the reins and the horse snorted and whinnied as it stopped in a cloud of dust. Alice instinctively put her hands up in surrender.

"Gentlemen, if you please," said the old Master, calmly. He smiled at the sentries pleasantly, bowed his head, and held out his hands to show that he was unarmed. "I am Leonardo da Vinci. Duke Giuliano and Duchess Filiberta are my patrons."

Despite the Master's words, the two guards were on them in an instant. One of them charged at Claudio, seized him by the tunic, and threw him off his horse.

The other guard grabbed Ali and roughly pulled her off the mare. "What manner of woman dresses like a boy?" He laughed as he tied her hands in front of her.

"You there, be careful with the girl!" shouted Claudio, struggling.

"Silence!" shouted one of them. The sentinels wasted no time in calling for re-enforcements. They pushed Claudio to the ground, one with his boot on the young Count's back and the other with a sword to his neck. Claudio turned slightly to see who it was, and much to his satisfaction it was the very guard who had falsely implicated him of murder.

"You," Claudio growled at the soldier. "You are the one from Fiesole. You—"

Claudio did not finish his sentence. With ruthless precision, the heel of the guard's boot made contact with his jaw, jarring him to his very core.

"Stop it!" shouted Ali, as he fell into unconscious. "You're hurting him! Stop it!"

Insane with anguish, she struggled wildly to get to Claudio, as they kicked and tortured him. With uncanny precision, she managed to spin around and kick one of the guards in the groin. The guard let go of her ropes immediately, nursing his wounds.

A small crowd had gathered on the inside of the wall, watching the early morning spectacle. Some gasped at the audacity of a young woman attacking one of the Duke's guards, while a few of the men snickered.

Another guard grabbed the ropes around Ali's hands, turned her around, and slapped her hard across her face with the back of his hand. "You will learn respect," he snarled at her. Alice tried hard not to give him the satisfaction of falling over and passing out from the pain; he had slapped her so hard, blood pooled in her mouth. Defiantly, she spat out a mouthful of red at his feet.

Leonardo's voice came over the melee. "You dare to assault a Count of the House of Medici, here in public view, like a common criminal. How dare you! And a girl...how simple it is to attack a little girl!" His anger was apparent as he scowled fiercely huffing out his words.

Two of the soldiers tied Claudio's hands and dragged him roughly to his feet, holding him up under his arms. Another dragged his hand through the horse watering trough and splashed a handful of water at Claudio's face. He was slowly coming back to consciousness, sputtering and spitting out blood.

Though still groggy, he looked around madly for Alice and when he saw her face, he went wild.

"Filthy bastards!" he bellowed, thrashed himself loose and charging at one of the guards gripping her arm. With his head down like a furious bull cornered in the ring he rushed at them. "Get your hands off of her!" Claudio's face was a horrible grimace as he howled his anger at the soldiers.

His head made contact with one of them in the stomach and stunned him, making him cough and hold on to his belly and sputter for air. Another guard went for him, his sword drawn, but Claudio waited for him to get closer and then nailed him with a Taekwondo back kick to the jaw, knocking him out completely. The others stopped for a moment, and Ali realized that this was a maneuver they'd probably never seen in hand-to-hand combat—Claudio had brought this move back with him from 2029!

"Leonardo! Stop him!" shouted Alice to the Master. "They'll kill him!"

The old man, his arms out wide, jumped between Claudio and the guards, their swords drawn and ready to attack. "That is enough, gentlemen. This shall stop now. If they are to be arrested, then so shall it be. I, Leonardo da Vinci, am on my way to the palace." The soldiers got up slowly. Claudio's rage subsided, and he allowed them to regain the upper hand, though it was clear by the look on his face that he wanted them to pay for what they had done to Alice.

"I am aware of who you are, sir," interrupted the guard from Fiesole, grabbing Leonardo by the arm. "And I must take you to the Duke also, for collusion in treason. If you struggle, Master da Vinci, I will restrain you."

A deep voice, heavy with authority, thundered from the city gates: "Master da Vinci is correct, that will be enough!" It was the commander, with a young, breathless guard at his side. "You are not to render the traitors unable to speak to the Duke," he ordered. "Your purpose is to bring them to the palace so that they can be questioned. His Grace has been advised of their capture. Bring them." He turned on his horse and trotted into the city, not bothering to give them a second glance. The young guard, who had informed the commander of the skirmish outside of the city walls, stayed behind to assist the others.

"You heard the commander!" shouted one of them, roughly pushing Claudio through the Porta Rossa. "Walk!"

The crowds lined the street to watch the three outlaws being prodded forward by the swords of the men-at-arms. As they walked, the trio listened to the whispered speculations being bantered back and forth as to what punishment they would receive.

Oddly, though frightened by the experience of being

thrown into another time, Alice was equally intrigued. And as much as her mind bounced back to thinking it was all a dream, she had to accept this reality as true; the taut ropes around her wrists were beginning to hurt.

As they entered the Piazza della Signoria, more of Ali's memories surfaced. She felt she could fall back into the everyday routine of a scullery maid with ease. The fact that she was experiencing such a disconnected state of mind was more proof that she had lived a life here. She had memories here.

Leonardo walked next to her, and she tried not to stare as his eyes flitted from Claudio to her, to the guards, and to the palace in the distance. He was not tied up like Ali and Claudio and Ali reckoned that it was because of his close association with the Duke; the guards may be wary of treating him disrespectfully—until the charges were heard, at least.

"Elisa?" Leonardo looked straight ahead as he spoke softly to the worried young woman being paraded down the Via Lungarno with him. "Do not be afraid. The truth about Enzo shall prevail, and if I know the Duke, those who have falsely accused you and the Count shall pay for their lies."

"I hope so, sir," Ali responded, her voice trembling. "Because right now, it doesn't look good for us. I'm beginning to think we should have just stayed where we were."

"I know your fear, my child. But Claudio believes you have hidden strength that even you do not know about. Do not doubt the strength within you. Harness it. Use it to make things right. After all, these are only people, people with power, yes, but people."

She looked intently ahead of her at the palace, its turrets looming ominously in the distance. How could she and Claudio overcome the power of the Medici with mere words? "Sir," she whispered. "I think Claudio recognized the first guard on horseback as the one who saw what happened with

Spirit and Enzo the night that we were all in Fiesole." She winced as her hands chafed under the coarse ropes. "He must be lying for someone. Otherwise, how could he benefit from Claudio being convicted of such a crime? If we could get him to change his mind and give a factual account of what he saw, then maybe that would cast doubt on the other charges, too."

The guards led them to one of the side entrances of the Palazzo Vecchio, which was equipped with iron reenforced doors. The detachment commander pounded on it, prompting someone from the other side to open a peephole. Momentarily, bolts were drawn, and the door opened.

They entered a dusty courtyard, fortified with iron bars over the windows. A few of the guards rode their horses directly into a stable area adjacent to the gateway, while the remainder of the men-at-arms led the prisoners across the enclosure to the iron gate barring the entrance to the inside of the palace itself. One of the sentries on the interior immediately opened it for them.

"Wait here," ordered one of the soldiers. He dismounted and went inside. Claudio, Alice, and da Vinci stood waiting.

"My love, listen," Claudio whispered to Ali, "do not forget that you will be called Elisa. Master, they are preparing to bring us to Duke Giuliano. I am relying on the good sense of His Grace and the reason of the nobility on the panel. I am certain that my mother will be present, as will the Duchess, but we may also have to contend with Bruno and Clarice. I do not believe that, if Clarice has any influence with her uncle, she would allow the charges of treason to proceed...this is simply a warning to me to fall in line. As for Bruno, he will be livid that Enzo is no longer around to do his bidding, I am sure of it." He shifted his wrists within the ropes. "The Duke does not wish this for us, Master. He will make the decision, but he needs to have a reason to release us."

"You must take care not to insult those around the Duke, if

you understand my meaning, particularly Bruno and Clarice," Leonardo whispered. "Otherwise you run the risk of inflaming the situation even more. You must be delicate."

Claudio turned his attention to Ali. "You will be questioned regarding your part in this. They may be especially hostile toward you. You must be subtle and reverent to the extreme."

"Don't worry, I'll be on my best behavior," she said nervously. "I just wish they'd hurry up. What could be taking so long?" She discreetly glanced at the wristwatch she had looped around the inside of her belt. If it were discovered, it would be very difficult to explain.

"How long?" asked Claudio, looking up at the sky.

"An hour and forty minutes."

"Try not to worry, Ali," he said encouragingly. "These matters generally go quickly. We will have you out as soon as it is done, one way or another." One and forty, Claudio thought. Little more than sixty minutes left with her.

"Thanks... that's very reassuring—one way or the other," whispered Ali. Claudio offered his crooked smile. "I'm going to miss that," she murmured, looking away.

The old man cleared his throat. "I took the liberty of asking Francesco to join us as swiftly as he could. I believe he may prove to be quite helpful," said Leonardo. "And my dear," he said to Ali, "you must try to speak in our dialect—you do not wish to be tried for witchcraft as well."

Ali nodded and as she did, she observed through the closed gate that a fresh set of guards were coming their way.

Chapter Forty-Three

On a pedestal, seated on ornately carved chairs made with red tufted velvet and gilded in gold leaf, were Duke Giuliano de Medici, Duchess Filiberta of Savoy, and Cardinal Giovanni de Medici, Giuliano's brother. A most imposingly regal sight for anyone to behold.

All eyes were on the prisoners as they crossed the opulently appointed Audience Chamber, Claudio and Ali still bound in ropes. The slim-built, bearded Duke sat in the middle and watched them enter with narrowed eyes. The Duchess sat to his right, Cardinal Giovanni, in his red robes, sat to the Duke's left. Below them were the Duke's numerous advisors and counselors, ready with sound recommendations. Clarice and Bruno sat along the walls with many other members of the court and nobility. Claudio scanned the room for his mother. She was not there.

When Claudio, Ali, and da Vinci were properly in front of the Duke and Duchess, the men bowed deeply to the throne, waiting for a response before rising. Ali, trembling, followed their lead and dipped into a practiced curtsey.

The Duke's eyes scanned the three of them before he

spoke. "Good morning, gentlemen. You may rise." His voice had a cursory tone. "Count Moro, I shall begin with you. There have been rumors in the palace that you have been plotting to take over my throne. Is this true?"

Claudio had not expected such a direct question. "Your Grace, if he will permit me to say so, these rumors are lies. We have come here of our own accord, unarmed, to defend ourselves against these charges. We attempted to send messages to Your Grace, but the couriers were captured." His voice became laced with anger. "I no more desire Your Grace's throne than to raise his ire. However, I fear that I have done just that and for that and only that, I am guilty. In addition, I did not kill Enzo. He attacked my horse and was trampled, and for this I have a witness...one of your guards at the gate saw everything."

"You are a murderer and a liar!" Bruno thundered, moving forward.

"Silence, Bruno. Step back," snapped the Duke. He turned his attention back to Claudio. "Yes, Moro, in that respect you are quite correct. There is the matter of a member of my court...that little incident in Fiesole. We must address that, too, in good time. You have caused me a great deal of trouble, young man. Your capture and return to Florence became a bit of a challenge to my soldiers. And the abbey—ha!" The Duke was becoming agitated, laughing without humor and shifting his weight on the tufted velvet. "That entire situation was in every way unnecessary and caused a great deal of friction between the Duchy and the Church." His voice became progressively louder, which prompted the Duchess to lightly place her hand on his elbow as a reminder to stay calm.

The Cardinal's face was as red as his robes. "The Duke," he interjected, "in his wisdom, is saying that peace in Florence is in a very precarious state. The power, being newly restored to the Medici family, should be safeguarded and preserved at all costs. We do not wish Rome to feel ill-at-ease with us, Count. That is the only reason that we have been exceedingly patient with the battle of wills transpiring at the monastery. However, now that you have seen fit to surrender yourself up, we will call the army back and leave our kind brothers in the peace they deserve."

The Duke nodded his approval to the Cardinal, then began wagging a finger at Claudio. "You, young Claudio, have put me in a very delicate position by fleeing."

Then to Leonardo. "And you, Master Leonardo, you are a member of my court, yet you eluded your Duke and aided in hiding your pupil at a monastery. A monastery that has for almost four months, given you and your little band of outlaws here, sanctuary!" He spat out the last word. "What do you have to say for yourself?"

Master da Vinci calmly unfolded his hands, held them out in surrender, and nodded. "Yes, Your Grace, everything you say is quite true." There was a collective gasp from the court, peppered with whispers and raised eyebrows. "I concealed the Count because I am absolutely certain that he is innocent. Father Federico and I were concerned for his safety." His hands, palm up, remained outstretched before him. "However, he is also my pupil, and he was assisting me with a very important project, Your Grace."

"Master Leonardo," replied the Duke curtly, his head shaking in disbelief. "Young Claudio was wanted for questioning, and for questioning only. In charges of treason, whoever is suspect must be brought to me. You know there are no exceptions."

All Claudio could think was that his mother was not there. He took a huge risk of exasperating him even further. "Your Grace, if I may ask, where is my mother?" There was concern in his voice. "She is not here, is she not well?"

Filiberta replied in a gentle voice. "Your mother has been

asked to stay in her apartments until the accusations of treason have been heard. You will see her at the end of these proceedings."

Claudio understood the code, thinly veiled in the usual wording. The Countess had been confined—cast out as a noble until her son was cleared of any wrongdoing. "My mother has no fault in this, my lady!" he cried.

"If you are so concerned about your mother, a noblewoman who, undoubtedly, is faultless in this, and one who has had to bear your shame for these months, then you should have come forward sooner," snapped Ottavio, one of the Duke's counselors. "Answer the question, Count Moro. Did you, in fact, entertain thoughts of treason?"

Claudio looked at Alice, his eyes filled with guilt, and with a grimace replied, "Counselor Ottavio, we fled because I feared for Elisa's life and her honor." He turned to Giuliano. "I do not desire the throne, Your Grace, I desire only Elisa's safety."

Once again came gasps and whispers, especially from the women. Clarice was crimson with rage. "She is the traitor," she cried. "See how she tries to hide dressed as a boy? Scandalous! She forced him to turn his back on you, uncle. That...that scullery harlot tempted him." Clarice's face twisted into a grimace, as she held her hands tightly clenched by her sides. "She forced him to leave his mother and his lord—and everyone here at the palace who loves him!" Her shrill words reverberated through the quiet room.

"That is a lie as well, Your Grace," Claudio's quiet voice pierced Clarice's echo. "No person forces me to do that which is not right or not moral." Duchess Filiberta shot a look of daggers at Clarice, who stomped her foot and fell back into place with the rest of the court. The Duchess turned to Alice. "What is your name, girl?"

"If it pleases the Duchess, my name is Elisa Beatrice de

Povri." She bowed deeply, her voice even, but her eyes mirrored her fear. "I have worked in this noble house as a servant most of my life, first for the Borgia, and now for the honorable House of Medici."

"And why are you dressed as a boy?"

"I was forced to dress as a boy to escape from the guards, when the Count, my dear friend, and I ran from them."

"I knew it was her all along," snapped Clarice, pointing her finger at Alice. "She forced him to do it."

"There, you see, Your Grace?" howled Bruno. "She was helping him to escape. She is just as guilty as he is. And the old man, too."

"Your Grace, surely you do not believe—" began Leonardo.

"No, no," said Ali. "That is not what I meant! We ran because—"

"Silence, woman!" the advisor shouted. "Who is this maid? Who is she to dispute the word of a noble?" He finished off his sentence with a sardonic grimace and a humorless snicker.

Claudio thundered his response. "This maid is a woman, and she saved my life."

The crowd grumbled.

His voice calmer, Claudio continued. "Had it not been for her, I may as well have perished in the monastery at the hands of the men-at-arms. And that would have been very unfortunate, as the charges for which I stand here before you today, Your Grace, are entirely false. If she and Master Leonardo and the brothers at the abbey had not defended me, Bruno would have to answer for my murder, for I am innocent." Claudio took a breath and steadied his tone. "May I be permitted to ask a question in my defense, Your Grace?"

Giuliano nodded, now rubbing his temples. "In light of this, you may ask, young Claudio. And you..." He waved his finger at Bruno. "You...shall have your turn to speak in time."

Claudio shot a scowl at Bruno. "Who are my accusers, and

what actions of mine led them to believe that I desired Your Grace's throne?" The nobles gawped around the room and at each other, none of them desiring to point out the culprit, though Claudio was certain they all knew who it was.

Another advisor stepped to the Duke's side and said, "If I may say so, Your Grace, it really is none of the Count's business who it is that has made the accusation. He is responsible only for answering the questions, not for asking them."

Giuliano deliberated, then spoke, "I will allow you to confront your accuser." The Duke waved his nephew forward. "Bruno...come, come...tell him what you have told me. He should be granted the opportunity to defend himself. Advance and make your denunciation."

Bruno moved with a swagger through the members of the court, toward the center of the Hall of Justice, his hand resting on his sword and sporting a rather pompous look on his face.

"Your Grace, my lady, Your Eminence." Bruno's voice was confident. "It is no secret that at one time the Count and myself were fast friends. Claudio, Enzo, and I were companions since our boyhood, our families in exile, yet still faithful to the rightful ruler of Florence—my father, Piero. Until the throne was recently and rightfully restored to our family—to my uncle Giuliano—Moro was an ally, a friend to the Medici, but more and more he has become distant and involved in clandestine activities with the old man, da Vinci."

Bruno turned to the Master, speaking to the court, but keeping his eyes firmly on him as he continued. "Leonardo, who is commissioned by our family as an artist of the court, wastes more time in his so-called study of Nature than in fulfilling his duties to the Duke of Florence. His secretive activities grow more and more suspicious, so much so that the entire court speaks of him in whispers. But no one dares to accuse him. Except for me. Both he and the Count are not seen for days at a time as they work on who knows what, with unknown individuals. Even the Count's mother is concerned, having confided that fact to my sister."

"Your Grace," Claudio interrupted, "this is madness. It is all a fabrication, a fantasy created in his own mind, the mind of a vindictive, vengeful man who has nothing better to do with his own life than to destroy others—"

"Enough from you, Moro," interjected the Cardinal. "You will listen to your accuser until he is finished. You will be given the opportunity to defend yourself."

"Thank you, Your Excellency," said Bruno as he bowed to his uncle. He circled the room like a vulture going in for the kill, making eye contact with the members of the nobility, as he continued his denunciation. "I, myself, as well as other members of the household, have witnessed Moro in secret discussions in the servants' yard, while he pretends to draw water for this scullery maid. It is a ruse. He is plotting with the servants to poison the Duke's food. Why else would he frequent the likes of her?" He glowered at Alice and then turned away in disgust.

"Are you quite finished, Bruno?" asked the Duke.

"No, uncle, I am not." Bruno cleared his throat and prepared to continue.

The Duchess shifted in her seat and whispered into her husband's ear. Giuliano raised a hand to her and nodded to his nephew. Bruno resumed. "Moro and the maid were spotted, on several occasions, outside of the palace, in the gardens as well as in the valley near Fiesole, no doubt planning their escape route in case they were discovered." He turned a spiteful look at Claudio and Ali. "It did prove to be useful after all, did it not? As you ran to Fiesole when you realized you had been discovered." The more Bruno spun his lies, the redder Clarice's face became. Her elfin smile at the beginning of these proceedings had turned to a bitter scowl. It was apparent to Claudio that perhaps Bruno was not adhering to their plan.

"You are a lying snake, Bruno," Claudio hissed the words. "A lying—" But he did not finish. A guard slapped him so hard in the face that spittle and blood flew from his mouth. His teacher immediately reached out to steady him, and Ali screamed at the force of the blow.

"Mercy, my lord! Mercy for the Count," Ali begged, falling to her knees, her hands in a desperate plea to save Claudio from further harm.

"You will be silent," ordered the Duke calmly to Claudio, then he turned to the guard. "Hold your punishment, soldier. If Moro interrupts my nephew once again, bring him to the dungeon." Giuliano gestured for Bruno to continue.

Bruno renewed his arguments to the nobility, his pitch rising with every syllable. "But they did not stop there. Knowing they had been cornered in their attempted escape by His Grace's men-at-arms, the Count brutally killed one of our trusted courtiers and his friend, Enzo. In this crime spree, da Vinci became involved, running to the aid of his pupil. And they all hid behind the brethren at the monastery for nearly four months, giving rise to an almost irreparable rift between the Church and the Duchy of Florence. Not even the *ufficiali di notte* of our own parishes can recall such lawlessness within our fair city. For this, they should be punished severely, uncle. There is no doubt they were up to no good."

In a panic, Clarice slipped hurriedly past the other nobles and ran to Giuliano's side, clinging to his arm. "No! No Uncle. It was all her, not him!" She pointed at Ali.

Giuliano waved her away. "Go back to your place, my dear," he drawled in an impatient voice, then turned to Bruno. "Are you nearing a conclusion, nephew?"

Bruno sniffed and went on to complete his affirmation. "To conclude," he said calmly, while directing a disapproving glance at Clarice. "I declare that you, Count Claudio Moro, this servant, and Master Leonardo da Vinci, are involved in secret activities to overthrow the Duke and the murder of a courtier of the House of Medici." With a final dramatic appeal directly to the Duke, who appeared to be keenly awaiting the end of his nephew's denunciation, he bowed and shot a sneering glare at the three prisoners.

With a doubtful eye, the Duke glanced at Filiberta. In response, she pursed her lips with an air of impatience. "Nephew," Giuliano finally said. "I find it difficult to accept that a master painter such as da Vinci, with a reputation built up over many years, desires to take my throne...or even to become involved in a conspiracy to overthrow his lord." He rubbed his eyes and settled back into his position in the chair. "Is there anyone in this room who wishes to speak in support of these accusations?"

Bruno turned and walked haughtily back to his place among the nobility, taking a detour past Claudio and Alice. "I warned you," he muttered under his breath. "I warned you both to mind your places."

Claudio glared at him as Bruno moved very close to Ali. "You would have done well to indulge me, my sweet. I would have returned you quite unharmed to your precious Claudio in good time. Now you will both suffer needlessly in the dungeons. Pity—you have grown more beautiful in your absence."

It took everything Ali had inside her not to spit in his face. He strode back to take his place next to the other nobles, avoiding Clarice completely.

Claudio leaned in to Ali, his jaw tight. "One day he will answer for that."

Ali just shook her head for him not to react. She didn't want him losing his temper again.

"Uncle...uncle. May I speak?" asked Clarice, bustling her way into the middle of the hall. Without waiting for a response from her uncle, she said, "I declare that one of my

ladies-in-waiting did not witness the Count indulging in treasonous actions, but she saw him with that servant, multiple
times!" Her voice was absurdly screechy. So much so that some
nobles near her put their hands to their ears. "His mother was
concerned that he was being influenced by her, and not taking
his future seriously. I say that it is the scullery maid who is
responsible for his uncharacteristic behavior. She forced him
to turn his allegiance from the business of the Duke to his own
pursuit of study with that old painter. And I am certain that
the servant girl encouraged it. She—"

"Thank you, Clarice," interrupted the Duchess, clearing
her throat. "We will take your opinions into consideration." In
turn, Clarice huffed out noisily and pouted at being hushed.

Ali moved closer to Claudio. "Don't worry about what he
said to me," she whispered amidst the confusion, her cheeks
red with anger and humiliation. "When do I get to talk?"

"Are you certain you want to do this, Alice?" he said under
his breath. "Perhaps it is better if I address the Duke for the
both of us."

"No way, Claudio—I came here to help defend you. To tell
the truth. The more voices heard on your behalf, the better,
even if I am accused as well. Besides, if I read people correctly,
I think I have a sympathizer."

But, before she could speak, Leonardo raised his hand and
cleared his throat, prompting Giuliano to lean forward, his
interest in the hearing renewed, as he held the artist in very
high regard. "If the Duke will permit me to speak to the accusations," the old Master said, "I have information that will
shed some light on the reasons for my pupil's behavior. As an
apprentice under my guidance, he has been assisting me with
various projects, Your Grace, two of which will be brought
here shortly for your inspection."

"Of course, you may proceed, Master Leonardo," replied
the Duke. He bent down to speak to one of his advisors, "Fil-

ippo, go and fetch the Countess Maria." The man bustled off to fulfil his command, looking relieved.

Da Vinci bowed respectfully to Duke Giuliano and began. "The Count has been my pupil for some months now, and he has shown great promise in the Arts. Young Claudio has been assisting me and studying alongside my other pupil at my studios in the monastery." Da Vinci turned his gaze to Alice. "As to the girl, Your Grace, he was only protecting her from a horrible dishonor."

His words caused the room to buzz again. Bruno maintained his confident composure, despite the last revelation.

Claudio stepped forward. "Duke Giuliano, with your permission, may I please speak to that now?"

The Duke nodded, and the room fell to muted silence.

Chapter Forty-Four

Claudio, relieved at finally being able to defend himself, spoke so the whole room could hear. "Your Grace, I deny wholeheartedly and categorically, on my own behalf and on behalf of Elisa and Master da Vinci, the charges of treason and murder. The denunciations of your nephew are simply not true. They are invented, fictitious, and false in the fullest sense of the word." He could not get the words out fast enough.

"Elisa has been a faithful servant and does not have the resources or the desire to entertain the notion of turning against the house that clothes and feeds her. She wishes only to be left alone, free of the danger of being accosted by certain members of the court." He glared at Bruno. "Then there is Master da Vinci, who has been a vital part of the Medici court since before many of us here were born. And truthfully, I find it almost laughable that he is even under suspicion. He was given patronage by Your Grace's father, and all he wishes is to be allowed to serve his lord and to perfect his craft—"

At that moment, the advisor, Filippo, and Countess Maria entered the hall. Maria, breathless and almost at a run, immediately acknowledged her son and placed herself strategically near Duchess Filiberta. The Duchess sent a brief smile to the Countess.

Claudio knew that he had placed her in a position of horrible suffering and anguish for almost four months, not knowing if her son was dead or alive. He felt compelled to run to her, to comfort her, but the men-at-arms held him back. Though her eyes showed that her heart was breaking, a nod signaled that she was well.

Claudio regained his focus and continued with unmistakable sincerity. "And as for myself, Your Grace, I am loyal to you, as my father was loyal to your father. My father administered the Patronage Trust for the Arts on behalf of your father, Lorenzo de Medici. If my actions could be misconstrued in any way to suggest that my allegiance to the throne of Florence was questionable, I offer my heartfelt apologies. But I do have a stake in the welfare of the young lady. You see, I love her. Very much, in fact." Claudio looked at Alice with love in his eyes, unafraid to declare it, while the entire hall gasped. Clarice was on the verge of tears as Claudio continued. "If the woman you love was insulted and about to be dishonored by your peers, Your Grace, would you not step in to protect her?" He paused, his words hung in the silent room like acrid truths. "Your Grace, I can only surmise that these accusations brought forth by your nephew stem from envy and jealousy. The unfortunate young courtier who attacked my horse in Fiesole was a casualty of this envy. One of the men-at-arms who escorted us through the Porta Rossa today was present that very night in Fiesole. He would be able to uphold the events as I have reported them."

"In addition," Claudio continued, "as I have promised you...and my mother, I will take my place in the Medici empire, and I will work tirelessly in whatever capacity you see fit. All I ask is that you release Elisa and Master da Vinci and stop the siege at the monastery. The brothers have no part in this—they were only trying to protect us, at the request of Father Federico, who believes in our innocence. I thank Your Grace for his indulgence." Claudio bowed his head and stepped back.

There was a hush in the opulent room as the nobles digested all that Claudio had laid out for them. Bruno had quietly moved to the rear of the Great Hall, near the doors. The only sound that was audible was Clarice's sniffling. Countess Maria beamed with pride at her son.

Duke Giuliano waved the commander over and whispered to him, after which the commander left the room.

"May I ask a question, Your Grace?" The Duchess broke the silence.

"My dear, it is highly irregular, but for you, I shall make an exception," smiled the Duke indulgently.

"Your Grace is very kind." Duchess Filiberta directed her attention to Ali. "We have heard from everyone here except the girl. Elisa Beatrice, scullery maid in the House of Medici, speak in your defense."

Ali curtsied nervously and licked her lips. Claudio saw that her hands were shaking. "My lady is most merciful and gracious. Your Grace," Ali spoke directly to the Duke. "I am not a traitor. I am a faithful servant to the Duke and Duchess. The rumors about the Count and me as traitors are false."

"Of course, she will deny it," cackled Bruno. "What else would she do...confess to it?"

"But I have nothing to confess to," said Ali. "With respect, perhaps it is yourself, my lord Bruno, who should confess to repeated acts of aggression upon Count Claudio and me." There was an outburst of chatter from the ladies and laughter from the gentlemen.

"Hold your tongue, maid," sneered Bruno. "You are

addressing the nobility, and you shall speak accordingly...with reverence!"

"I agree," said the Duke. "Finish your defense, but remember your place."

"My apologies, Your Grace," Ali continued. "On the occasion of the first incident, if it were not for the Count, I am certain that my honor would have been taken from me by lords Bruno and Enzo." Her eyes darkened as she relived it in her mind, and her voice quivered. The court listened intently. "Claudio stepped forward and protected me for I could not have fought off an assault by two men."

Isolated gasps in the crowd punctuated her words.

"But how can you be so sure that it was not just words?" asked Filiberta.

"Because Bruno's hands were already on me, Duchess." Ali's eyes stung with tears, and her voice trembled. "He had his hands on me...and he was hurting me. He ripped off my bonnet and held onto me and pressed himself against me. I begged him not to, but he would not listen. He would have forced himself on me if Claudio had not been there."

There was a hush in the expansive room. All eyes darted from Alice to Claudio to Bruno and then to the Duke and Duchess. The Duke directed a rather disapproving grimace toward Bruno. Claudio moved closer to Ali to try to offer her some support, but his hands were still tied.

"But what does all this have to do with this hearing, Elisa?" asked Filiberta.

"Everything, Duchess," said Ali through tears. "Women who are of my social standing are at the mercy of men. There is no one protecting us. We who must work to eat and live. But because of one noble who thought differently—because of Count Moro's mercy, I am standing here before you with my honor intact."

Claudio noted that even Clarice was quiet, listening with the other women.

"You see, Duchess," said Ali, "Claudio and I fell in love, but there are some here in the court who envy the bond that we share. They envy it so much that it consumes them. They envy it so much that they cannot bear to see us happy. They would rather destroy us both than allow our love to abide in this world. Therefore, we stand before you today, Your Grace. Not because we are traitors, or murderers, but because we dared to love one another, and because we dared to speak out against a wrong. I saw what happened that night in Fiesole. The Count is innocent. Lord Enzo had ordered another man-at-arms to fetch his horses and the dogs. We burst out of the inn's stable on horseback to try to escape, afraid for our lives. I heard Claudio warn Enzo to step back away from Spirit and to mind his sword, but he would not listen. He bounded forward, sword high in hand toward Claudio—in the noise and confusion, Spirit only reacted out of instinct. Her forelegs kicked and stomped Enzo in the chest, thrusting him against a stone wall. He fell dead. That is how it happened, Your Grace."

Every person in the Hall of Justice was riveted by Alice's words—words that no one had dared to speak before this.

"Your Grace," Ali declared, "I stand here before you, speaking the truth. All that I ask—we ask—is that you please, believe us."

Filiberta sat stone still, processing the words spoken by the scullery maid. She looked at her husband and at his advisors. They appeared unmoved, but the women of the court were whispering.

"Thank you, Elisa," said Duchess Filiberta sincerely, her voice like silken oak. "Thank you for your courage, your eloquence and your honesty."

At that instant, the rhythm of boots could be heard rolling in from the hallway. There was a polite rap at the door and then it opened. The commander entered with three soldiers in tow.

"That is the one," said Claudio. "The middle one."

The commander ordered the man front and center. Duke Giuliano looked him up and down. "Do you know why you are here, soldier?"

"I do, Your Grace." He stood at attention, not making eye contact. "Your Grace wishes to question me regarding Lord Enzo's death at Fiesole."

The Duke nodded. The commander walked briskly to the guard until they stood almost nose to nose. "Now listen to me carefully, soldier. There is a young man facing a grave penalty if he is found guilty of murdering one of the Duke's courtiers. Do you understand me?"

"I do, sir."

"You reported that Enzo was killed purposely by the Count, that he set his horse upon him to trample him. Do you still believe that is what you saw?"

The guard's gaze focused on Bruno for a moment then faced the commander again. "The horse trampled Lord Enzo, sir," he said.

"But was it done purposely? Eyes straight ahead."

"I do not recall, sir. I believe that he may have been wielding a sword to try to force the Count off his horse," advised the soldier, licking his lips.

Claudio grimaced and cried out. "Do you think that may have had something to do with it, then?"

Silence pervaded as his words echoed in the Great Hall. The soldier did not respond.

"Answer! Did he warn Enzo to stay clear of the horse?" shouted the commander.

"He may have, sir." His gaze kept meandering over to Bruno again.

"Thank you!" snapped the commander.

The Cardinal took a deep breath and rolled his eyes. "I think the soldier's memory is failing him." He exhaled as he spoke, sounding exasperated. "Commander, I believe a fine is due from the guard—ten florins should do. Next time, soldier, if you are not sure of what you see, better to keep your mouth closed. Take him away," added the cardinal harshly. A guard led the soldier away.

"Commander, untie them," the Duke said. "I do not believe they are a threat." He looked at his counselors and to the Cardinal for any objections, but all were silent. There was a shadow of disappointment on their faces in not having an execution to look forward to, while a look of satisfaction crept across Filiberta's face.

"I have reached a decision," Giuliano said, his voice full of cool authority. "I declare that in the absence of clear evidence of any treasonous acts by the subjects before me, they are cleared of these accusations. I also declare that the death of Enzo da Carrara, was an unfortunate accident." Soldiers attended to Claudio and Alice's ropes, which were cut and taken off. They rubbed their chafed and welted wrists, an angry red in color.

Countess Maria rushed over to Claudio to embrace him. "My dear son," she gushed through tears. "I thought you lost forever."

"Mother," said Claudio, hugging her. "I have missed you so."

Alice smiled widely at Leonardo as mother and son were reunited. And then Claudio moved to Ali and kissed her cheek. His arms wrapped around her, holding her close to his heart. It was a glorious sight, and it drew applause from the other courtiers. Claudio looked up to see the crowd. Everyone was glad that he had prevailed—everyone except Clarice, who was clearly in the profoundest depths of misery over losing

Claudio, her head in her hands. Bruno stood glaring at Claudio from the corner of the Hall of Justice.

"That is it then, uncle? You are setting them free?" Bruno said to Giuliano with a twisted grimace. "But they will say anything to escape such charges. The guard was obviously coerced to 'forget' about what he saw."

"And by whom was he paid, boy?" The Duke craned his head to get a better look at his nephew. "And for what was he paid, hmm? It was obvious to all of whom he was afraid while he was speaking. He was more intimidated by you than by his own commander. If you have that effect on a man-at-arms, I cannot imagine how intimidating you would be to a young woman." He waved his finger at Ali.

Bruno laughed nervously through gritted teeth, as if he were amused by the entire ordeal, yet, it was apparent by his shifting eyes that he was rattled.

More sounds of bustling drifted in from the open door to the hallway—many footsteps and voices speaking in low tones. They drew nearer to the entrance.

"What now?" despaired the Duke in a wistful tone. "Have I not had enough comedy for one day?"

"Begging your pardon, sir," said the door guard to the commander, "but Abbot Federico is outside requesting an audience with Your Grace. And with him is a contingency from the Certosa Monastery, as well as...some other interested parties, with gifts for my lady Clarice and the Duke and Duchess."

The commander shifted his gaze from the guard to the Duke with raised eyebrows.

"Send them in," groaned Giuliano, sitting up. "What business could the Abbot possibly have found to come all the way into the city from the cloister?"

First through the door was the Abbot, nodding his acknowledgement to the three former prisoners as he walked past them to greet the Duke and Duchess with a bow. He acknowledged the cardinal with a kiss of his ring. Closely behind Abbot Federico were four burly novices carrying two freshly painted portraits: one of Clarice, beautifully portrayed, sitting in regal clothing and clutching a rose in her right hand, the other was of Duke Giuliano, handsome in his dark burgundy robes. At the sight, Clarice squealed her approval and clapped her hands together with delight.

Francesco followed, and of all people, Caterina was the last to enter the Hall. Caterina looked like she was having great difficulty keeping herself from flying to Ali's side.

"Your Eminence, Your Graces," began the Abbot. "My thanks for allowing us into your Hall of Justice. We would have been here sooner, but we were only just now allowed to leave the abbey." He turned to the commander, a slight hint of irritation on his face. "With God's will, your forces are withdrawing as we speak." And then to the Duke, "My infinite thanks, Your Grace. I hasten to express my sincere concern with this nasty business regarding the Count, who, incidentally, is a fine young man of good morals. I find it very difficult to believe that he has been denounced as a traitor. I would like to vouch for his—"

"Your encouraging words are much appreciated, Abbot Federico," interrupted the Duke, "however, the Count and his...his friend have been cleared of the charges." He looked back again at the portraits being held by the one-time French mercenaries, his expression easily conveying his thorough appreciation for da Vinci's exquisite work.

"I see that Your Grace approves of the portraits," said Leonardo proudly. "I will have the Duke know that I, and my students, Claudio and Francesco, spent a great deal of time and energy while the abbey was under siege completing these portraits in the hopes that one day we should be allowed to deliver them to Your Grace." He bowed deeply and directed a grin and a wink Claudio's way. There was a spontaneous outburst of applause from the entire hall, with the Duke following suit.

"Your work is highly complementary, Master Leonardo," declared Giuliano. "Quite extraordinary, indeed. Nevertheless, there is the small matter of the fine for keeping my army at bay for no reason. You and your assistants should have—"

Though the Duke technically had the floor, his voice was drowned out by comments from the courtiers in the Hall of Justice.

"...the Count was accused of treason and forced to hide in the abbey, yet he was working—assisting da Vinci with a portrait for the Duke."

"Poor young Claudio, and the poor girl. What a state they must have been in..." Some were shaking their heads in disapproval.

"... da Vinci, ever faithful to the throne."

"...indeed, such breathtaking work!"

Giuliano halted his speech as he listened to the comments around him. With a clearing of his throat and a twitch of his mouth, he reluctantly continued. "However, seeing that you have suffered unjustly under the erroneous assumptions of certain persons within the court, we are willing to forgive the fines and forgo their rightful collection."

Applause burst out, along with compliments as to the great generosity of the Duke. Maria and Filiberta were all smiles and appeared extremely content with the confusion.

The Duke glanced around the Hall, taking in the immense show of support for Claudio and his friends. Then he spotted Bruno, stunned face and all. "I will speak to you later," mouthed the Duke to his nephew, and with a wave of his hand dismissed him.

Duke Giuliano arose and with great pomp, departed, his

entourage following him with Clarice reluctantly in Filiberta's tow.

The Cardinal strolled over to the Abbot, and together they exited the Hall, but not before Father Federico looked back at Claudio and his friends, giving them an acknowledging nod. They bowed back to him, a gesture of thanks and respect.

Every concerned party in the room was reunited with their loved one. Countess Maria rushed once again to hug her son, accompanied by the Court Counsellor Filippo. Caterina darted to Alice, who genuinely hugged her old friend back with much affection. Francesco strode over to congratulate both Claudio and Ali. "Well done. I could not have said it better myself." Francesco beamed as he shook Claudio's hand. "And you, Elisa, very eloquent for a maid."

Ali bit her tongue.

"It is you who deserves congratulations," said Claudio. "The portraits are superb. You are proving yourself quite capable of holding a brush; they were nowhere near completion when I left. Certainly, you and the Master worked night and day to finish them."

Francesco chuckled. "Leonardo always says, 'There is nothing that will work better than stroking the ego of the court.'"

Caterina smiled wide with happiness. "Oh, my dear, how I have missed you," she hugged Ali so tight she thought she would burst. "I knew you would be worried about me, too," Caterina continued, "but you need not have been. I have been at service at Master Francesco's house. His family needed a servant and they were kind enough to take me in." She looked over at Francesco. "Francesco is very handsome, is he not?" she giggled.

Alice smiled. She knew Caterina deserved to be happy. "I wish you much joy, Caterina," she said. "I am so glad for you."

Caterina glanced over at Claudio and then whispered in

Ali's ear. "Keep him near to you and love him dearly. You will never need or want for anything with him by your side, Elisa."

When Ali heard this, her heart sank. She would not be near him for long. Caterina kissed her once more on the cheek. "Dear friend—come to see me at Master Francesco's home...I will miss seeing you every day," she added with a pout.

"I will have Claudio come to visit." But Ali did not have the heart to tell her that she would never see her again. "Goodbye, Caterina," said Ali hugging her tightly.

Countess Maria came to her son again and held onto his hands, seemingly afraid to let go. She looked at his plain clothing and shook her head. "Claudio, you know that I am happy to see that you are safe, but I am still very angry with you." She released his hands. "Then again, I can see what you find so fascinating in this young lady. She has a wisdom beyond her years, perhaps even beyond her time." She allowed Alice a fleeting smile.

"Mother, you do not know how right you are." He laughed, and scooped up Ali in his arms.

In turn, Alice wrapped her arms around his neck, inadvertently looking at her wrist. Wristwatch. Father's watch. Time! The time! She turned away and peeked under her belt to check Father Donato's watch. Her heart leapt into her throat when she saw how late she was.

"Oh my God, Claudio," she whispered in his ear. "I'm twenty minutes late. I have to get to the chamber—fast."

"Blast!" he pulled away and looked at Ali, his ebony eyes widening with alarm.

He turned to his mother. "I need to leave," Claudio said, taking Ali's hand.

"Wh-what?" sputtered Maria. "But why?"

"Well, Elisa needs to...to get back home." He stammered over his words. "She will not be resuming her position here...

because...she will be working...elsewhere." He shrugged at Alice, unsure of what else to say.

"Oh...well that is a pity," Maria said with a lilt. Ali didn't think she looked that upset at all. "Be well, my dear...Take care. And Claudio, be home straight away, please. You have been away much too long as it is."

"I promise," he said as he glanced at Counsellor Filippo and inclined his head. Then he leaned into his mother's ear, smiling impishly. "It appears you have acquired a new admirer in my absence, Mother."

"Never you mind that," she ordered, attempting to mask a smile of her own. Claudio turned to Alice, but she was halfway to where Leonardo was standing.

He was busy directing the novices as to where they should bring the portraits when she placed her hand on his arm. "Master da Vinci," she said softly, "I have come to say good-bye." She reached up to kiss his wrinkled cheek. "Thank you for everything. Please...please look after him for me."

The Master glanced over at Claudio. "Are you certain that you will not stay? He loves you so," said da Vinci as he cupped her chin in his hand.

Meanwhile, Claudio saw Francesco and dashed over to speak to him.

"I am certain, Master Leonardo...I must go back...my parents, my family, and friends. I cannot leave them." Ali wiped a tear from her eye.

"Of course, Elisa. You did very well today." He kissed her on the forehead. "You have the face of an angel and the heart of a lion—be well. I shall remember you." Then he turned and walked away, his hands clasped behind his back.

"How could one not remember the face of an angel?" she heard him murmur as he walked away.

Claudio worked his way back to Alice through the throng of nobles coming to congratulate him. He gently grasped Ali's arm and pulled her close. "Francesco rode Spirit here," he whispered. "He left her in the servants' courtyard. She will get us to the Certosa the quickest."

"Let's go," she whispered back.

And before anyone knew it, they had slipped away.

Chapter Forty-Five

S teady as an arrow, Spirit carried Claudio and Alice from the servants' courtyard, the place where they spoke their gentle words to each other, beyond the stables and toward Galluzzo.

With every step that Spirit took, with every gallop and jump, they were that much closer to the chamber and to saying goodbye. Alice held onto Claudio's waist, savoring every last moment together, her hands wrapped around his waist. She leaned her head against his back and closed her eyes, memorizing the moment and the way he felt against her skin. She fought hard to keep it together, swallowing the lump in her throat and biting back the tears. Never had she felt so confused, so torn and so loved.

The midday air was hot, and the sun was directly overhead, making the white masonry of the monastery glisten on the hilltop. To Alice, it was like a castle in a storybook, its bell tower like a turret. Everything was dreamlike. The time portal. The trial. Her leaving. But she had accomplished what she had traveled back in time to do. She had come to help someone who loved her unconditionally and who had risked his life and livelihood to protect her, only to honor a promise he had made to her. And now she was going home.

Ali thought how lucky she was to be alive in her era, to stand on the shoulders of all those who struggled for future generations of women, for equality, self-respect, and dignity of the person, struggles so often forgotten by her generation. Yet, there was still so far to go before true equality to men would be accomplished.

She marveled at how fortunate she was to be able to choose, to have the ability to enjoy all the benefits that other women had fought for, but she also thought of how things, in so many ways, were still the same.

Ali's thoughts returned to the present as Spirit's steady rhythm resounded on, kicking up dust and shrubbery in her wake, the sound of her hooves, making an even *clackety-clack* on the cobblestones up to the abbey.

Only a few soldiers remained in front, and they offered no resistance to Ali and the Count. Claudio dismounted and helped Alice off, holding her by her waist. She slid slowly between his hands until they were face to face. Any momentary reticence evaporated. They stood alone for the first time since morning, and all the effort that they had put into creating some friendly distance between each other was gone.

Claudio traced the shape of Alice's face with his fingers, then his mouth slowly descended to meet hers. When their last kiss was done, he lifted his head and Alice fixed her gaze on his eyes, their hands wrapped around each other and they held on, silently, for all too short a time.

When they let go, Claudio walked as if to his execution, to the intricately carved entrance of the abbey. "Please open," he yelled out with a shaky voice. "It is Claudio and Elisa."

"C-coming, sir," came a familiar voice. Brother Antonuccio,

a welcome face, struggled to open the door. "Abbot Federico will be back shortly. He instructed that I allow the young lady to be escorted to Master da Vinci's apartments."

"Thank you, brother," replied Claudio. "Please ask him to join us there when he returns." Antonuccio nodded his acknowledgement. Claudio took Ali by the hand and together they sprinted across the abbey grounds, heading to the north side.

∼

Ali was over forty minutes late, and that meant she was a day and a half late in 2029. She had no idea how she was going to explain it to her aunt and uncle.

The brothers were busy picking up after the maelstrom of activity over the past few months, all of them going about their business. No one seemed to understand that everything was about to change for the two young *innamorati*. No one seemed to care.

"Tell me about what you are going to do when you finish high school." Claudio's voice trembled as they hurried along the footpath adjacent to the courtyard. He held her hand tightly in his.

"What?" Alice asked, trailing after him. They were never going to see each other again, and he was asking about her plans for post-secondary studies?

"What do you want to be when you grow up?" He tried to laugh at his own humor, but it fell flat. "You know, university? College?"

"Now? But we're almost at the chamber. Why now?" They rounded the corner to the stairwell that led down to da Vinci's corridor.

"Just tell me what you are planning to do in the future so I can imagine you…you graduating…living your life." He stopped in front of the first door and faced her. "I cannot be there, but I can close my eyes and envision what you would be like."

He swallowed, grasped for the hidden keys above the brickwork, and looked down at the doorknob. He pushed the keys into the locks, opened the door, and led her in.

"I'm not sure…I guess I'll go to university." They hurried by the windows in the corridor. "Then a post graduate degree, maybe teach." Her eyes began to sting as the couple reached the outside door to the outer room. Claudio reached behind one of the limestone bricks on a windowsill for the key. He stuck it in the keyhole and turned. The door opened without difficulty.

Alice continued. "But on the weekends…" she paused, "I think I'll help my father on a project—a science project. To find a way to travel back and forth in time, without a rift in the velocity of its passage."

The more she spoke the more the tears wanted to come. Claudio took her hand and led her onward. "What would you name your children?" he questioned, guiding her to the door of the chamber room.

This was more than she could bear. "I don't know," she cried. "Stop it, please!"

"What would you have me say, Ali? Take care? Have a good life? Through loving you, I learned that the qualities I value most in people are honesty and integrity, fearless hope, and positivity. Everything that you are, I love, and now I am about to lose you." He saw the hourglass he had set there that morning, its top portion empty. He grabbed it, and furious with frustration, threw it against the wall, shattering it. "If I keep talking…I won't think about it." He stopped in front of the chamber.

She gasped and let out a weak chuckle.

"What is so funny?" he asked.

"You said 'won't'. You used a contraction. That's the first time I've heard you do that." But he didn't laugh with her; his eyes were downcast as he reached for her hands and held tight.

She bit her lip and choked back a sob. For the last time, she tilted her head, so he couldn't avoid her gaze, her eyes locking onto his. "Count Claudio Moro, you are the finest person I know. You're the best time I have ever had, and the best thing that ever happened to me. I have lived more in the short time we had together than I ever have, and I'll never forget you." Then she reached up and took his face in her hands. "Claudio, I love you." She kissed him with all the passion in her heart. "Don't ever forget that," she whispered, her voice trembling while her tears mingled with his.

They held each other tightly, her face in his chest, committing his aroma to her memory. Then Alice impulsively untied his handkerchief from around his neck and put it in her pocket.

"I love you more," he said, and he gazed into her soul with those deep, ebony eyes. Claudio grasped her hand one last time, kissing the palm. "Stay with me, Alice," he pleaded.

"I can't," she replied in a low tormented voice. "Come with me, Claudio."

"I cannot." He smiled a fleeting, beautiful smile, then became somber again. "You are exquisite." Distractedly, he tucked a lock of her hair behind her ear. "One day, Ali, one day perhaps we will walk together in the garden once again." He gently let go of her hand, opened the chamber door, and stepped aside.

In front of her, the portal spiraled and undulated silently with unsurpassed power. Ali looked back at him. Be strong and do the right thing, she said to herself. Slowly, she pulled herself away and stepped into the chamber.

"I will always remember you," she said, looking back as she crossed over the threshold and walked deeper into the portal.

"If there is a way...come to me."

As Ali was pulled deeper into the darkness, she saw him move toward the chamber. As his face disappeared before her eyes, he spoke, but she did not hear.

Chapter Forty-Six

"*inalmente*, Ali—what the hell have you been doing?" yelped Luca as he jumped to his feet. He looked like he just woke up. "You're late!"

Alice tried to speak between tears. "I...I'm...I'm s-s-sorry." Then she just sobbed. All of the heartache, worry, and tension from the last few hours escaped her.

"Okay...Okay," said Luca. He took a deep breath. "What the hell happened? Is Claudio all right? You don't know the lies I've had to spin to keep your aunt and uncle from calling the *carabinieri*!"

"Luca...please...just stop!" She hiccupped her response. "We actually did pretty good, I think. I mean, just a little over three hours and the Count's reputation and future is back on track."

"So, everything went well? He's been cleared?" Luca's eyes widened. "Hey, wait... is that blood on your shirt? And you've got rope burns on your wrists! What the—"

"Don't worry...everything's okay. This is nothing. Where's Father Donato?" she asked.

"Alice, it's four in the morning here—time's different,

remember? We have to go. You are meeting your aunt and uncle at the Pisa airport in just over two hours for your rescheduled flight." He began to gather his stuff together and started for the door, feeling around the edges for the sweet spots. It whirled open. Then he turned around.

"Ali?"

She was at the chamber, staring into the spiraling black wormhole, undulating into infinity. She felt it. It was pulling her in, the pins and needles on her skin a welcome sensation.

"Hey! Come on!" shouted Luca.

Snapping out of her trance, she looked over her shoulder at him. "Shouldn't you close this? I mean you can't leave it like this...wide open."

"Don't worry," he said. "Claudio left word with Father that once you come back through that he should destroy it. Something like this can't be left lying around for just anyone to use. It is too important and too dangerous."

"Right." So, this was it. It was final. "Then...let's go. You'll have to tell Father 'thank you' for me, Luca," she said, in a calm daze.

"Of course...are you certain you're okay?" he asked, peering at her.

"I will be," she answered.

He turned to the door, and she followed out after him.

The drive to the airport was a shadowy blur. Alice heard Luca talking to her in his car, but his voice sounded as if he was underwater. Her focus was non-existent.

She was almost two days late. Luca had told Ali's aunt that she and Claudio had gone on an excursion to Elba Island and had missed the ferry back. He had promised them that Olivia's parents would make certain that Ali would be at the airport in time for her flight.

Leda and Roberto would meet her there, along with the rest of her things from the Villa. She had changed into her regular clothes in the backseat while Luca raced like a maniac to Pisa. He had also given her his long-sleeved hoodie to cover the rope burns on her wrists.

Luca brought the car to an abrupt stop in front of the terminal doors and got out to help her. He led her into the terminal where her aunt and uncle were looking frantic.

"Alice!" Her aunt raced to hug her. "Oh, my goodness...you don't know how worried we were."

Her uncle looked at her puffy, red eyes. "Hey, what's wrong?" he asked, her chin in his hand.

"Nothing." She barely got the word out when her eyes started stinging again.

"Oh dear," her aunt said and wrapped her arms around her. "Something happened between you and that boy, didn't it?" Leda looked at her with concern.

"I knew that guy would break your heart," Roberto added, his mouth a thin white line.

"We broke up," Alice mourned. "Claudio and I. Yes, and... I'm upset because we broke up. He's decided to stay at Elba for a while...until...until school starts," Ali said, hoping she hadn't given away the fact that she was making it up as she went along.

Her aunt gently stroked Ali's honey-brown hair. "Oh, that's too bad. But it's just as well, my dear. Better that you have a clean break rather than dragging it out over a long distance." She kissed Ali's forehead.

Ali nodded, pretending to agree with her aunt. If she only knew the distance.

She followed Roberto as he grabbed her luggage and walked briskly into the airport. And then suddenly she remembered Luca. Luca, who had waited for her for days outside of the chamber. She jerked back and ran to him.

"Oh, my God, I'm so sorry," she whispered as he clumsily hugged her back. "I almost left without thanking you." Her voice was trembling again. She held him...her last connection to Claudio. Soon it would all be just a memory. "Luca...I..." The tears flowed.

"I know, Ali," he said, holding onto her tighter. "He was my friend, too."

She pulled away and brushed her tears dry with the back of her sleeve, smiling wanly as she mouthed another thank you.

Before she went through security, Leda and Roberto begged her to come back soon. She promised that she would. "Maybe next summer," she said, as she hugged them.

On the plane bound for London, where she would connect for Boston, she looked out the window. The clouds were white and fluffy, and the sun peeked over the eastern horizon, setting the wing tip ablaze with a vibrant streak of orange. She felt nothing looking at it and closed her eyes, reliving the pain of that final scene.

Ali swallowed the lump in her throat as the plane brought her closer and closer to the life she knew best. Her parents and friends would all be happy to have her back, but she knew one thing...she had to let Caleb go. It wasn't fair to him, to let him think there may be something between them.

For now, she just wanted time to heal. She hugged the little airline pillow tighter across her chest and wondered if it was possible to feel pain when you suffered a loss in love. Would she ever feel normal again? And if not, would it be better to just feel nothing?

Who was she kidding? Claudio had lived five hundred years in the past. He was dead and gone now. He had lived his life, probably fell in love, got married, and then, inevitably, died.

There were tears in her eyes again, but she brushed them

away defiantly, refusing to let herself be overcome with emotion.

"Coffee, signorina?" asked the attendant. The words startled her out of her reverie.

"No, thanks," she replied, faking a smile. Inside, she was cold and numb.

Ali focused on the sun getting bigger in the sky and dug into her satchel for her sunglasses. She had made the right decision...of course, she had, she knew it. But doing the logical, sensible thing didn't make it hurt any less.

Time would help, she assured herself. Time would heal. Time would always be there—her savior and her enemy.

She listened to the steady droning of the engines as she felt herself slowly approaching sleep. Maybe, when she got home, when she was ready, she would visit the university library. There would very likely be some information related to Count Claudio Moro, because of his close association with Leonardo.

There would be no harm in doing some research into how a young Count in early-sixteenth-century Florence made his mark in the world. Yes, maybe one day, she would do this... only to check on his contributions to the study of Nature, of course.

Slowly, she drifted off to sleep, dreaming vividly. She dreamed of the chamber. Of the undulating time portal, spiraling and inescapably pulling her back in.

~

Coming Summer 2023
The Alice Series Book 2
Angel of Time

Don't miss your next favorite book!
Join the Fire & Ice YA Books newsletter today!
www.fireandiceya.com/mail.html

~

THANK YOU FOR READING

~

Did you enjoy this book?

We invite you to leave a review at your favorite book site, such as Goodreads, Amazon, Barnes & Noble, etc.

DID YOU KNOW THAT LEAVING A REVIEW...

- Helps other readers find books they may enjoy.
- Gives you a chance to let your voice be heard.
- Gives authors recognition for their hard work.
- Doesn't have to be long. A sentence or two about why you liked the book will do.

~

Don't miss your next favorite book!
Join the Fire & Ice YA Books newsletter today!
www.fireandiceya.com/mail.html

About the Author

E. Graziani is the author of the YA novel, *Magenta* and *Everything That Was Us*. She is the author of *Breaking Faith*, a contemporary YA novel, listed on CBC Canada's Must-Read Books for Spring 2017, selected for the 'In the Margins' Book Award 2018 Recommended Fiction List and one of CCBC Best Books for Kids and Teens. Graziani is the author of the YA historical memoir, *War in My Town*, also one of CCBC's Best Books for Kids and Teens, and a finalist in the Hamilton Arts Council 2016 Literary Awards for Best Non-Fiction. Graziani has also written the YA time-travel Alice series, *Alice of the Rocks* & *Angel of Time*, and the novella, *Jess Under Pressure*. She resides in Canada with her husband and daughters.

Find Edy Online:

www.egraziani1.wixsite.com/egrazianiauthor
www.chch.com/tag/edy-graziani

 twitter.com/EGraziani1

 instagram.com/e.graziani

 goodreads.com/egrazianiauthor

Also by the Author

Alice Series

Alice of the Rocks

Angel of Time (Coming Soon!)

Novels

Magenta